Real readers love  :

On *The Last to Know*

'An **intelligent, surprising and enthralling** novel that had me awake till the wee hours.'

'Highly recommended, I've just bought all the others. A fast-paced, well written, **twisty** read with believable characters and an **enthralling** plot.'

On *All Because of You*

'**I'm hooked!!**'

On *Not What You Think*

'**Addictive.** That's the best word I can think of to describe this book . . . I really did not want it to end and Melissa Hill is now without doubt **one of my must-read authors.**'

On *Never Say Never*

'You won't want to miss this! Melissa Hill is **a great author** who just keeps getting better and better. I can't recommend her books highly enough.'

On *Wishful Thinking*

'**Heartstopping** . . . Melissa Hill does a fabulous job of making readers presume things and once again she tricked me all the way.'

melissa hill

before I forget

if you could hold on to
just *one* memory,
what would it be?

HODDER

First published in Great Britain in 2008 by Hodder & Stoughton
An Hachette UK company

First published in paperback in 2009

1

A CIP catalogue record for this title is available from the British Library

ISBN 978 1 444 71085 4

Typeset in Plantin Light by Palimpsest Book Production Limited,
Grangemouth, Stirlingshire

Printed and bound by Clays Ltd, St Ives pic

Hodder & Stoughton policy is to use papers that arc natural,
renewable and recyclable products and made from wood
grown in sustainable forests. The logging and manufacturing
processes are expected to conform to the environmental
regulations of the country of origin.

Hodder & Stoughton Ltd
338 Euston Road
London NW1 3BH

www.hodder.co.uk

Lots of love and thanks to my husband Kevin, Mam and Dad and all my friends for their continued support. To Amanda, who reads every first draft and gives me that all-important first reaction, and to Sharon who usually prefers to wait for the finished article! I couldn't ask for better sisters.

Heartfelt thanks to super-agent Sheila Crowley, who works unbelievably hard on my behalf – I owe you so much. Thanks too to everyone at Hodder especially Auriol, Breda and Lucy – all a joy to work with.

My thanks once again to the booksellers in Ireland, the UK and beyond who give my books such amazing support, it's very much appreciated.

To everyone who buys and reads my books, and who have sent me so many lovely messages through my website www.melissahill.info. *Before I Forget* is dedicated to you all and I really hope you enjoy it.

Dedicated to readers of my books everywhere.
Your support allows me to have the best job in the world.
Thank you.

Chapter 1

2.55 p.m. No doubt Kieran was already at the church, anxiously awaiting her arrival, and joking with best man Ger to disguise his nerves. Although, knowing Kieran, he wouldn't be the slightest bit nervous or worried about a no-show from the bride. His confidence was one of the things Abby loved about him. But she wondered if he would be at all anxious about the ceremony itself – unsure about his decision to commit himself to one woman for the rest of his life. Abby swallowed hard as she stared out of the car window. Her palms were clammy and she had to resist the urge to wipe them on her dress.

3.05 p.m. She felt her heart rate speed up. They were only minutes away from the church, and for a second she thought about telling the driver to turn the car round and go back – back home and away from all of this. She could lie low for a while, wait for the fuss to blow over. But Abby knew she couldn't do that – not now. Not when she'd come this far.

3.08 p.m. They reached the church, and as the car approached, she saw the wedding guests gathered in various groups outside the entrance, most of them chatting and smoking while waiting for the arrival of the wedding car. Among them she spotted Kieran's teenage sister, Katie, dressed in a rather revealing red dress and talking with a much older woman whom Abby didn't recognise. Abby raised an eyebrow, surprised that stuffy and conservative Margaret Redden had allowed her precious daughter to wear such a low-cut dress. Then again, maybe Kieran's mum had made allowances for the day, and there was no doubt that Katie did indeed look beautiful. Margaret must be inside already, dressed in her finery and doing her best to appear superior while waiting for the ceremony to begin. Abby suspected that the bride's late arrival would *not* go down well with her future mother-in-law. All of a sudden, there was a flurry of shuffling and stubbing out of cigarettes as the guests noticed the wedding car approach, and one after another they quickly piled into the church.

3.13 p.m. 'Here we are, then,' the driver announced, slowing the car.

Through her nervousness, Abby managed a smile. 'Thanks,' she said, running an apprehensive hand through her freshly styled blonde curls. Did she look all right? Was her make-up OK? Perhaps she should have worn her hair up, instead of down. With all the stress leading up to today, she'd dropped a few pounds, which at least made her dress fit that bit better . . . Nevertheless, it was especially important that she look her best today, of all days. She was almost tempted to ask the driver what he thought, but how idiotic would that sound?

Taking a deep breath, Abby reached for the door handle, but in the meantime the driver had got out and was already holding the door open for her.

'Thanks,' she said, stepping out gingerly. As soon as she left the relative security of the car, her mind began to spin and her heart raced even faster. What the hell was she *doing* here?

But there was no more time to think about it, as somewhere in the distance, Abby heard the organ start up, and the 'Bridal March' begin. Somehow her jelly-like legs managed to take her through the doorway and inside the church, where Kieran stood waiting to pledge his marriage vows. She saw the guests turn and smile in the dreamy way that people did at brides, and wondered how much longer she would be able to last.

Then Abby's gaze rested on Kieran, and little black spots danced before her eyes when she saw the expression on his face. The happy smile and look of pure adoration he gave as he watched his elegant bride approach was almost enough to shatter Abby's heart in two. And when the bride reached the top of the aisle and took her place alongside Kieran before the altar, Abby knew she couldn't take any more.

3.25 p.m. Tears streaming down her face, she quickly slipped through the side door of the church and outside to where her taxi was waiting.

'All right, love?' the driver asked when she was back in the car. 'You weren't long.' Then, noticing his passenger's obvious distress, he added in a kind voice, 'Ah, weddings can be very emotional sometimes, can't they?'

'Yes,' Abby replied, amazed that she could find her voice, before adding inwardly, *Especially when it's the wedding of the love of your life to somebody else.*

Sometime later the taxi driver deposited her at the front door of her Portobello flat, the one that she and Kieran used to share before—

But there was no point in thinking about that any more, Abby told herself, her eyes red-rimmed as she paid the driver. Kieran was married now, and no matter how much she'd hoped he might change his mind, no matter how often she'd wished that the wedding would be called off or hoped there would be some last-minute hitch, she'd seen today with her own eyes that there was no going back. No matter how much she'd loved him – how much she *still* loved him – Kieran was lost to her for ever.

And all she could do now was try and forget him.

Chapter 2

'You've forgotten, haven't you?'

'Forgotten what?' Abby replied absentmindedly. She cradled the telephone handset between her neck and shoulder, and sifted frantically through the pile of papers on her desk. Where on earth was that file?

'Mum's birthday dinner . . .'

The papers fell limply on to the desk, almost in tandem with Abby's insides. 'Oh, no!' she moaned.

'I knew you had,' her sister Caroline said, exasperation in her tone. 'That's why I thought I'd better phone now and give you a chance to get to the restaurant on time, rather than have us all waiting for you.'

'Thanks, sis,' Abby replied, meaning it. She checked her watch and saw that it was almost six. If she left in an hour, she would have just enough time to scoot back to the flat, get changed and make it to the restaurant by eight. The only problem was that there was still way too much to do here and—

'What are you doing at the office today, anyway? It's Saturday, Abby. Mum was right – you really *are* doing too much.'

'Oh, just trying to keep on top of things,' she replied airily, unwilling to admit to her sister that work was pretty much the only part of Abby's life right now over which she felt some semblance of control. Notwithstanding the fact that she *liked* working hard at Duffy Masterson, the accountancy practice.

It gave her a sense of purpose, kept her focused and helped keep her mind off . . . things.

Caroline harrumphed. 'It's really not good for a girl your age to be slaving away in an office at the weekend, you know. You should be out enjoying yourself.'

This was by now one of her sister's well-worn arguments. Caroline, by contrast, loved nothing more than going out and enjoying herself. But it was different for her: she had her lovely husband, Tom, and a fantastic life and not a care in the world. She'd never experienced anything close to the agony and heartbreak Abby was going through.

'Well, I'm going out with you guys tonight, aren't I?' she replied easily. Although whether or not this constituted 'enjoying' herself was debatable.

'Yes, but knowing you, you'll be fidgeting during the first course and making excuses to leave by the third.'

'That's not fair,' Abby retorted, stung.

'Well, it might not be fair but it's certainly true.' Then Caroline's tone softened. 'Look, we're just worried about you, OK? Lately you don't seem to have time for anything but work, and we've hardly seen you since . . .' She paused. 'Well, you know, since all . . . that.'

Since Kieran dumped me, Abby finished silently.

The break-up had happened seven months ago but her sister didn't know that Abby had gone to see her ex get married last week – no one did. As far as her friends and family were concerned, she hadn't seen or heard from Kieran in months. She couldn't admit to them that she'd been at the church on the day of his wedding, couldn't admit how pathetically stupid she'd been to think that he might change his mind.

Granted, in the run-up to the day, Abby had kept telling herself that the reason she was going to the church in the first place was to get that all-important 'closure', but the truth was that deep down she'd hoped – no, *prayed* – that the wedding wasn't actually going to take place, and that maybe Kieran, at the very last minute, would catch sight of her standing regally at the back of the church, their eyes would meet, and in that split second he would recall every instant of their five amazing years together, realise how much he still loved her, and wonder what the hell he was doing marrying someone else.

Then, having come to this realisation. Kieran would hurry down the aisle and into her arms, and he and Abby would race out of the church together, leaving everyone else behind them. But this was the stuff of Hollywood movies and TV soaps, and the reality, Abby recalled sadly, had been very, very different.

She didn't think she would ever forget the look on Kieran's face as he watched his bride walk up the aisle towards him. It was as if there was nobody else in the room but the two of them. At that moment, Abby would have been lucky if he remembered her name, he was so spellbound by his bride-to-be. How had that happened? How could Kieran have gone so quickly from planning a future with Abby to marrying someone who six months before she had never even *heard* of?

It was something that had plagued Abby every single day since the break-up that she just couldn't get over, despite her resolve on the day of Kieran's wedding to forget all about him.

Forget? That was a joke. He was the first thing she thought about every morning, the last thing at night, and – if she didn't occupy herself with something else – almost every second in between.

'Abby? Are you still there?' Caroline's voice broke into her thoughts.

'Yes, yes. Sorry – I was just . . .' she paused '. . . looking for a file.' No point in trying to talk to Caroline about this; her sister had little time for sentimentality and even less for Kieran.

'God, you really are a workaholic. Well, hurry up and get finished, and I'll see you at eight, OK? Oh, be sure to pick up a card for Mum on the way – I'll add your name to our present if you like, or did you remember to get something for her?'

Abby winced, feeling like an absolute heel. What kind of daughter was she to have forgotten something as important as that? 'No, it completely slipped my mind. Time's just flown by, and for some reason I thought her birthday was coming up *next* week and—'

'Not to worry – as I said, I'll add your name to ours. It's a couple of tickets to *Les Mis* at the West End.'

'Lovely. Thanks.' Caroline and her wealthy husband, Tom, rarely did things by halves.

'OK, so I'll see you later, then? Eight o'clock, remember?'

'Sure, thanks again for reminding me,' Abby said before hanging up.

She sat back down at her desk, and with a deep sigh automatically resumed her search for the missing file. She was disgusted with herself for forgetting her mum's birthday, and somewhat deflated by the fact that Caroline had brought up the subject of Kieran. Yes, it was always there, but lately Abby had been trying desperately to keep it to the back of her mind.

Why was it so hard to get over? she thought, bewildered. He was gone – long gone, married to somebody else now, for goodness' sake. He'd wounded her deeply, devastated her, and still Abby just couldn't seem to stop loving him. She couldn't forget the life they'd had together. Couldn't forget the way his skin always smelt slightly of coconut, the taste of his lips on hers, the dizzy warmth she felt when he smiled. Abby didn't think she would ever be able to forget Kieran.

And it was driving her crazy.

★   ★   ★

Thinking back on it, she should have realised that something wasn't right long before the split, but back then she'd been too blinkered, too blinded by her love for him. What had happened on her birthday, a few months before the break-up, should certainly have raised some alarm bells. But then again, hindsight was a wonderful thing, wasn't it?

She recalled how thrilled she'd been at the time, how surprised, to come home from work one day and find an unexpected message on their answer machine.

'Mr Redden, I'm calling from guest services at Dromoland Castle,' the friendly voice intoned. 'We'd just like to notify you of an upgrade to your Internet reservation for the weekend of the thirty-first. We're delighted to inform you that your booking also includes a complimentary treatment for two at our recently launched spa facility, and we look forward to being of assistance to you and your companion throughout your stay.'

Abby's eyes had widened with joy and she'd put a hand to her mouth, unable to believe her luck. Kieran had booked a weekend away for them at Dromoland Castle for her birthday? What an amazing and unbelievably *perfect* present! Never in her wildest dreams had she thought her boyfriend would spend so much money on somewhere like that, especially when they were busy saving for a house. But . . . wow! Abby was bowled over by this unexpected and (it had to be said) atypical show of extravagance. As a tax inspector, Kieran wasn't really one for wasting money on luxuries, so to think that he had booked a stay in one of the country's top and most *expensive* luxury hotels . . . If it were her *thirtieth* birthday, she might be able to understand it, but that wasn't till next year.

Abby hugged herself delightedly. Imagine her and Kieran spending the weekend in an amazing five-star hotel, exploring the castle grounds by day, then relaxing in the spa before having romantic dinners by night and— Oh, God, Abby thought, what on earth was she going to wear at those romantic dinners? Her current wardrobe surely wouldn't pass muster in an upmarket place like that, not when presidents and princesses and every manner of celebrity stayed there on a regular basis!

She wasn't sure if they'd be staying in the hotel for one night or two, but for one night she could use the dress she'd worn at her eldest sister Claire's wedding three years ago. If it still fit her, that was, she thought wryly. While she had never been a skinny malinks, she knew she'd put on quite a few pounds since then – so much so that Kieran had recently had to point it out to her.

'Maybe you should take it easy on that stuff,' he'd said, when one evening Abby arrived home from work and put a bar of Dairy Milk in the freezer, readying it to have in front of the telly later that night. It was her favourite treat; she loved the way the rock-hard chocolate melted away to nothing when dipped in a cup of hot tea, and Dairy Milk was one of her biggest comforts after a hard day's work. But Kieran was right: since she'd been promoted at the accountancy practice and work had got busier, she'd been eating more and more junk. Now the results were there for all to see. But she was *especially* glad that the phone message had given her some advance warning. Had Kieran sprung this surprise on her a day or so before they left, she wouldn't have had the chance to get herself organised with something new to wear. And while the thought of going shopping normally filled her with dread, for this Abby was prepared to face down the crowds (and the unforgiving changing-room mirrors) in the hope of finding clothes worthy of such sumptuous surroundings.

She might ask Erin to go along with her; as a buyer for a major Irish fashion chain, her best friend was *much* better at that kind of thing. In fact, Abby seemed to be the only woman around these days who didn't have a frenzied passion for shopping, something she knew Kieran really admired about her. 'A shower of peacocks, the lot of them,' he'd commented once, while they were watching some fashion programme on TV. Still a junior accountant at the time, Abby hadn't had much money to spend on clothes in any case, but she'd taken the comment on board and found herself reluctant to be classed as one of those self-same 'peacocks'.

So apart from her work suits for Duffy Masterson, she tended to wear just jeans and a casual top for day-to-day, and certainly nothing too fancy or expensive. But this time, Abby thought with a smile, Kieran would surely make an exception to her spending a few extra quid on a nice dress to help her look the part over their special weekend, wouldn't he?

The following Saturday morning, Abby had headed into town on her own, deciding in the end not to bring anyone else along on the shopping trip. Seeing as this weekend away was supposed to be a surprise, she couldn't run the risk of Kieran finding out that she already knew about it. Not that Erin would say anything; it wasn't as if Kieran had much to do with her friends.

Having scoured the rails of most of the high-street stores in Grafton Street for a suitable dress and come up blank, Abby decided to sneak a teeny peek in a few of the more upmarket boutiques in the surrounding area. As she walked along, she was waylaid by a pleasant-looking passer-by who surprised her by asking where she'd had her highlights done.

'Highlights?' She grinned, thrilled by this unexpected compliment from another woman. 'No, my hair is naturally fair – and the curls are natural too,' she added for good measure. Her hair was one of the very few things Abby liked about her appearance. Long, voluminous and honey-gold in colour, she tended to wear it down to frame her rather ordinary-looking face and draw attention away from her nose, which Abby felt was way too large and nothing like the cute little button with which her elder sisters had been blessed.

'Great!' the other woman gushed. 'Well, you might be interested in Hairwaves, a new salon that's just opened on South Anne Street! Today we're giving a discount of fifty per cent on all highlights and Easy meche treatments for new customers. Would you like to sign up for a six-course voucher?' she added, shoving a clipboard at Abby. 'I'll just need your credit-card details and—'

'No, it's OK, thanks,' Abby said, feeling like a right eejit. So much for the compliment! She should have known it was too good to be true. Why hadn't she copped the sales pitch, when anyone with half a brain would have? God, no wonder she was no good at this kind of thing, she thought, walking away, her good mood and confidence rapidly disappearing.

But she couldn't go home without something decent to wear, couldn't make a show of herself and Kieran in Dromoland Castle by relying on the same old out-of-date (and probably now ill-fitting) dress to wear on a romantic weekend away. Taking a deep breath, she tentatively entered a small, classy-looking boutique that she thought she'd heard Erin mention once or twice. Maybe they had a sale rail she could go through.

'Hello there,' the elegantly dressed lady behind the counter said.

Although she sounded friendly, Abby couldn't help but notice the woman give her a quick once-over. No, no, she was being paranoid; this was *not* a *Pretty Woman* Rodeo Drive moment: the woman was clearly just being welcoming.

'Is there anything in particular you're looking for?' the lady asked, as having failed to spot a sale rail, Abby had begun quickly flicking through the nearest one.

Blast it anyway! she thought, her heart fluttering in panic.

OK, so she had two options here: she could just thank the woman and walk out or she could accept her help and maybe be here for the day. Seeing as she couldn't afford even a *quarter* of some of the prices, the first option was clearly preferable, but at the same time Abby really didn't want to be rude.

She turned to the woman, and smiled shyly. 'Well, I was hoping to find a dress – something for a special occasion.'

She'd go through the motions, she decided then, maybe have a look at a couple of options before regretfully telling the woman that these clothes just weren't for her. It was only right that she did at least that, after wandering into her shop and wasting her time, wasn't it?

An hour later, Abby left the boutique, face scarlet, shopping bag in hand and credit card up to the limit. The whole thing had been excruciating, and worse, she'd ended up with a dress that she didn't even *like*, let alone fit into. But the shop assistant had *insisted* that she try on a variety of different dresses, all of which seemed to have been designed for malnourished teenagers. More embarrassing still, the sales woman had kept trying to get her to step out of the changing room and show off the dresses in front of a large mirror on the shop floor, seemingly not having the slightest clue that Abby hadn't a hope of fitting into any of the supposed size twelves and fourteens she was giving her!

'A second opinion can be so helpful', she had cooed, but Abby hadn't needed anyone to tell her that she looked like an *elephant* in that stuff.

Her self-confidence at rock bottom, Abby had eventually decided to put an end to the trauma by agreeing to buy one of the dresses, a hideous red chiffon and silk thing that accentuated every bulge, but at least she'd managed to zip it up. All that money wasted! Far from impressing Kieran on their weekend away, this outfit would surely make him want to run a mile. She bit her lip. And if he ever found out how much she'd spent on it . . .

Full of self-loathing and regret, Abby trundled to the bus-stop, too disheartened to walk home, although clearly she needed the exercise!

She wondered when Kieran would get round to telling her about the trip. She'd brought up the subject of her birthday a couple of times over the last few days, but amazingly he hadn't batted an eyelid. Maybe he wasn't planning on saying anything at all until they got to the hotel. It was strange, really, because Kieran wasn't the type for surprises.

Well, she'd know soon enough, Abby thought, smiling to herself and putting her worries about the dress to the back of her mind; this time next week she'd be ensconced in the most romantic Irish castle with the man she loved. What more could anyone ask?

By lunchtime the following Saturday, the day of her birthday, Abby was utterly perplexed. The hotel booking was for today, the thirty-first, and still Kieran had said nothing about them going away, or indeed anything at all about what they should do to celebrate. So what on earth was going on?

In the meantime, she'd dropped every hint under the sun, and had only just stopped short of asking him outright about it, something she knew wouldn't go down well at all, but . . .

When earlier in the week she'd asked what they'd do on the Saturday night, just to see what his reaction would be, he'd behaved very strangely, pretending almost as if he hadn't even realised her birthday was coming up. 'Well, what would you like to do?' he'd said.

'I don't know really. But I'd like to do something other than sit and watch TV. Go out for dinner maybe?' she added, grinning inwardly at his disquiet.

'OK, right. Well, if that's what you want.'

But now, her nerves in tatters, Abby finally decided to phone the hotel. She had to put herself out of her misery. This was really unlike Kieran. While he'd wished her a happy birthday first thing this morning, he'd since been quiet and unresponsive, which Abby had initially put down to his trying to keep the surprise under wraps.

But now she wasn't so sure.

She waited until he'd gone out to the shop to pick up the paper, then dialled the number.

'Dromoland Castle Guest Services,' a man's voice said.

'Um, hi there. I'm calling about a reservation for tonight in the name of Kieran Redden. I'm just enquiring as to what time your restaurant opens for dinner,' she added, thinking on her feet. 'I think we have reservations but I'm not sure . . .'

'Just one moment and I'll check. For tonight, you said?'

'Yes.'

'Hmm,' the man said, and Abby suddenly realised she was holding her breath. 'We *did* have a reservation in that name for this evening, but the stay appears to have been cancelled sometime last week.'

Her heart plummeted. 'Cancelled? The entire stay?' she gasped, disappointment flooding through her.

'Yes.'

'But why?' Abby couldn't help but ask, although she knew it was unlikely that the receptionist would be able to shed any light.

'I'm afraid there's no reason given, madam.'

'Oh, OK. Well, thanks anyway.'

Abby replaced the receiver and looked around the room, completely perplexed. What the hell was going on? Then she heard the front door open and Kieran return from the shop.

'Hey,' he said, catching sight of her rather dazed expression. 'What's up with you?'

'Nothing,' she murmured automatically, but her insides were churning with confusion.

Just ask him about it, she urged herself. Tell him you overheard the message and want to know what all this is about.

Why had he cancelled their weekend away, her lovely birthday surprise? Or *was* this her birthday surprise? Abby thought then, as a horrible, niggling suspicion struck her. Indeed, did it ever have *anything* to do with her?

But Abby wouldn't allow herself to go down that road; she couldn't go down that road, because she was absolutely terrified of what she might find at the end of it.

Chapter 3

Shortly after work, Abby arrived at the restaurant to find that the rest of the family – Caroline and Tom, her mum and her brother, Dermot – were already seated and awaiting her arrival.

'Happy birthday, Mum.' Abby put her arms round Teresa and gave her kiss on the cheek. She'd felt so guilty after Caroline's phone call that she'd picked up a bunch of flowers on the way, but now felt even worse as she realised how paltry her shop-bought bouquet looked compared to the oversized exotic arrangement already resting alongside her mother's chair.

'Hello, love.' Teresa stood up and returned her youngest daughter's hug. 'Thanks for coming.'

Thanks for coming? Now Abby felt even worse. Was she so unsociable these days that her mother actually had to *thank* her for turning up for her birthday? She knew she hadn't seen much of the family lately, but she'd been so busy with work and—

'It's just to be honest I wasn't really sure if the menu here would suit you . . .' her mother continued.

Abby quickly realised that Teresa was not, in fact, thanking her for coming along to the celebrations, but to this particular restaurant. But why? What kind of place was this, anyway? She took a seat and picked up the menu. Caroline had chosen it; that much was obvious, judging by the lovely plush surroundings and the leather-bound menus and . . . Oh, no!

'Mum, she'll be fine,' her sister said breezily, while Abby stared aghast at the menu.

Oh, God, it was Thai!

'There's plenty of choice there. Anyway, it's *your* birthday. Abby will be fine, won't you?' she repeated, giving her sister a warning glance.

'Grand,' Abby murmured, apprehensive. She'd really had no idea that her mother's birthday dinner was being held in a place where she wouldn't be able to touch a morsel. She knew she was pickier than most about her food – she was the very same as Kieran in that regard, which was one of the reasons they'd rarely eaten out. Her stomach began to turn as she read through the various dishes on offer. It was all really weird stuff in really weird sauces.

She just couldn't understand why nobody seemed to want to eat normal food like potatoes and vegetables any more, the kind of things they'd grown up with, instead of all this slithery stuff. But even her best friend, Erin, couldn't get over Abby's 'fussiness', as she called it.

'You really don't know what you're missing,' her friend had said one time she'd had Abby and Kieran over to dinner.

Sitting down at the table, Kieran had immediately reacted to the smell of an accompanying bowl of Parmesan and, after that, refused to let a single bite of anything 'abnormal' pass his lips. Abby had to agree that the Parmesan smelt absolutely awful, and from then on was rather hesitant about what was to come. In the end, she and Kieran had each had a jacket potato and grilled tomato instead of Erin's homemade pasta concoction – much to her friend's exasperation. As Kieran had so often argued, why would anyone pay out huge sums of money for this so-called 'food' when no one had a clue what went into it underneath all those smelly sauces? He'd once told Abby a story he'd heard somewhere about how Chinese restaurants regularly used stray dogs for meat.

Granted, she wasn't a big fan of dogs – was terrified of them, actually – but if it were true, she really wouldn't wish *that* on them!

Now, as she ran her gaze over the Thai menu, she gulped, sorry she'd reminded herself of that fact. Thai and Chinese food were the same kind of thing, weren't they?

'What do you think, love?' Her mother's voice broke into her thoughts. 'Is there anything there that might suit you?' Teresa sounded anxious as she looked doubtfully at her youngest daughter.

'Oh, no, it's fine, honestly,' Abby said, quickly forcing a smile. She wasn't quite sure *what* she was going to eat, but she wouldn't dream of ruining her mum's night.

'Tell you what, maybe we should go somewhere else . . .' Teresa began, biting her lip.

'No!' Caroline and Dermot cried in unison.

'Mum's wanted to try this place for ages,' Caroline informed Abby through gritted teeth, 'and we had to book it well in advance.'

Abby had forgotten that in recent years (and especially after their dad died) her mum had gone madly adventurous in trying all sorts of new things, especially food.

'Abby, surely there's something here you can eat,' her brother said, a touch impatiently. 'That chicken and mushroom thing should be mild enough for you, shouldn't it?'

Mildly disturbing! Abby thought to herself.

'Yes, I'll be fine with the chicken,' she insisted quickly, mortified that she'd created a fuss. 'Honestly.'

After that, it took a while for the tension to dissipate and Abby knew that Dermot and Caroline were annoyed with her. Once again, Abby felt deflated that these days she always seemed to be on a different wavelength to the rest of her family, a real fish out of water. They were all so happy-go-lucky and content with their lives, whereas she only ended up dragging everyone down. She'd tried to be upbeat since the break-up, she really had, but it was very difficult when inside she felt like some kind of walking zombie.

'Mum, have you heard from Claire?' Caroline asked, in an obvious attempt at changing the subject. Claire was their eldest sister and lived in New York.

Teresa smiled. 'Yes, she phoned shortly before I came out, and she and Zach sent me the loveliest card.'

'How is she?'

'She's on good form,' Teresa replied. 'They're hoping to try and get over for a visit soon, but it's just so hard for Zach to get the time off from work.'

Claire's husband, Zach, worked for the NYPD, something about which Teresa had been more than a little concerned when Claire first began seeing him. 'Be careful – they're all alcoholics,' their mum (who was a huge fan of American crime novels) had warned. But it turned out Zach worked in the traffic department, and they'd met when Claire tried to talk her way out of a parking ticket he was about to issue.

'Well, maybe we should all go over and see her,' Caroline said, winking at Abby. 'Any excuse for a bit of New York shopping. What do you think?'

Again, Abby felt tense and uncomfortable. For one thing, she was terrified of flying, and for another, since her exploits with *that* dress she was also terrified of shopping!

'Sure, we'll wait and see,' Teresa intervened quickly, and by her tone, Abby knew that her mother had sensed she wasn't particularly enamoured of this idea. She flashed her a grateful smile.

Still, shopping and flying aside, it would be nice to catch up with her eldest sister, whom Abby hadn't seen much of in recent years. Unlike the rest of the family, she'd never been out to New York to visit Claire, and she and Zach hadn't been home for too many visits since they got married. They were a fantastic couple and Abby thought they would make brilliant parents – she knew all her sister had ever wanted was to settle down and start a family. Claire had phoned often in the aftermath of Abby's break-up with Kieran, and Abby had been meaning to call her many times over the last while, but had just never got round to it. She bit her lip, hoping that Claire wasn't upset by the lack of contact on Abby's part, especially when they'd always been close.

'I must give her a call soon,' she said.

'Do – she'd love to hear from you.' Teresa smiled. 'So how have you been yourself, love?' she asked. 'How's work?'

'Oh, very busy.' Abby shifted with discomfort at having the conversation directed at her.

'Yes, Caroline tells me you've been working late in the office a lot,' her mother ventured softly. 'You shouldn't do too much, pet – work isn't everything, you know.'

But it's all I have now, Abby wanted to say, but didn't. None of them would understand that without work to concentrate on, she would have fallen apart a long time ago. 'I know that, Mum,' she said with a forced smile.

'Well, I might have just the thing to take your mind off work, Abs,' Caroline trilled. 'There's this fab new place in town called Rapture. It's a day spa, and they do all sorts of relaxing and de-stressing treatments. The three of us could go together for a pamper day sometime – my treat and—'

'Um, no, thanks,' Abby interjected quickly: the mention of the spa immediately triggered mortifying memories of the weekend away that never was. She'd been such an idiot, hadn't she? To foolishly think that Kieran was taking her to a fancy hotel and spa, when he'd intended no such thing . . .

In any case, Abby was self-conscious about the idea of some stranger putting their hands all over her body. Why people enjoyed that kind of thing was beyond her – as Kieran would say, wasn't it only another excuse to charge people an arm and a leg for something they really didn't need?

'It's just not my scene, to be honest,' she told her sister with a weak smile.

'Oh, OK, then.' Caroline seemed a little taken aback by this steadfast refusal of her generosity. 'Well . . . maybe you and I will try it sometime, anyway, Mum. What do you reckon?'

'We could certainly have a think about it,' Teresa said gently.

'Well, I think you need to chill out a bit, Abby,' Dermot said.

She turned to look at her brother, hurt. Why were they all ganging up on her like this and telling her she should slow down? Couldn't they understand that she desperately needed to stay busy in order to keep going?

'It's not that simple, Dermot,' she said, now trying to bite back tears. 'Being an accountant is different to being a mechanic.'

Her brother worked in a small auto-parts business, and at twenty-six, with few commitments and no mortgage to pay, he could be pretty carefree about everything.

'Of course it is, love: we all know that,' Teresa, ever the peacemaker, piped up quickly. 'We'd just prefer to see you taking it easy now and then. You seem to be doing a lot these days, and I suppose we're all a bit worried about you, that's all.'

'Well, there's no need to worry,' Abby reassured them for what seemed like the umpteenth time. 'Yes, work might be hectic, but at the same time I enjoy it.'

'Well, just don't make it your only focus. You know what they say about all work and no play . . .' Caroline said, topping up everyone's champagne glasses.

Earlier, her sister had ordered the most expensive bottle on the menu to toast their mother's birthday. Her sister's extravagance often made Abby feel inadequate by comparison and

Melissa Hill

she remembered how irritated Kieran used to get by the way Caroline used every opportunity to flaunt her wealth to the rest of the family. Or should she say *Tom*'s wealth? Caroline hadn't worked a day since they married – instead, she spent most of her time shopping for expensive clothes and eating in fancy restaurants like this. 'I don't know how your man puts up with it,' Kieran would say, referring to Tom. Although her brother-in-law was a man of few words ('hello' and 'goodbye' being about the extent of them), he was as easygoing as they came, and didn't seem to mind his wife's spending. In fact, Tom adored Caroline and worshipped the ground she walked on, something that Abby had always sorely envied – and even more so now.

Yes, her sister had it all: the fairy-tale life complete with adoring husband, plenty of money and, of course, stunning good looks. Whereas, she mused as the waiter put a plate of something strange and unappetising in front of her . . . well, she had none of those of things, had she?

Chapter 4

The following Monday morning, the phone rang, and coffee in hand, Abby went to answer it.

'Hello, stranger!' Erin said chirpily.

'How are you?' Immediately, Abby felt bad. She hadn't seen or spoken to her best friend in an age. Despite Erin's repeated attempts to get her to come out on nights on the town, she just couldn't bring herself to get dressed up and join in the fun. Her friend was so bubbly and carefree that Abby could barely keep up with her at the best of times, and again, she just didn't want her own circumstances to drag everyone down. But while she'd love a chat, she didn't have a whole lot of time now, not when it was eight fifteen and she was practically on the way out through the door . . .

Erin seemed to read her mind. 'I'm great, but listen, I know you're probably heading out to work soon, so I won't keep you.' She sounded excited. 'Myself, Miriam and Rebecca were out for a few drinks last night.'

Miriam and Rebecca were two more friends Abby hadn't spoken to in ages. It wasn't that she'd been avoiding them on purpose or anything; she just knew that nobody in their right mind wanted to be around her with the way she was at the moment. Chances were, the girls would be appalled by the fact that she hadn't managed to get over her broken relationship and move on with her life the way everyone else did. They were all strong, hugely independent girls who wouldn't *dream* of letting a man get them down like this.

But no matter how hard she'd tried, Abby couldn't get over Kieran, not when she continually felt like one of her arms had been hacked off. Who would want to be around a misery guts like that? No, much better to just keep to herself for a while, rather than trying to force herself to go on the tear with the girls and end up embarrassing herself and them by bawling into her drink at the end of the night.

Erin was still talking. 'So we came up with an idea for a long weekend away – girls only. What do you think about Dubai?'

'What do *I* think?' Abby knew little about the place, other than that it was supposed to be baking hot and was *very* far away.

'None of us has been there before, and it's supposed to be gorgeous – lovely warm sunshine, great shopping – and the four of us could have a good giggle. What do you reckon?'

'The four of us . . . You mean for me to go too?'

'Of course!' Erin said, as if this was the most obvious thing in the world. 'We were thinking maybe next month – around Halloween. We'd only have to take a couple of days off work.'

Abby panicked. They'd have to fly to a place like that, wouldn't they? And seeing as the very notion terrified her . . .

When she gave this excuse to Erin, her friend groaned.

'For God's sake, Abby, you got on a plane *once* – well, twice, I suppose, when you count the return journey.'

That was true, but as far as she was concerned, twice had been more than enough. She and Kieran had taken their first (and last) holiday abroad two years before. They'd gone to Spain for a week, and the flight over had been fraught from the moment they got on the plane.

'Most of these pilots haven't a clue what they're doing: they're only glorified bus drivers,' Kieran had gruffly informed Abby during take-off. 'And considering the prices they charge for these flights . . .'

Abby had thought the plane tickets were actually quite reasonable considering, but if Kieran was right about the pilot's lack of training, then she could understand why. Either way, it hadn't given her a whole lot of confidence in the journey, and when they'd hit some turbulence and things had got a little bumpy, his detailed knowledge of aeroplanes made things even worse.

'Tin cans is all these things are,' he'd told her, while Abby, her knuckles white, had tightly clutched the armrest and prayed it would soon be over. 'I don't know why they even bother with all that safety-procedure bullshit. Sure, if we take a dive, it's all over either way.'

After that, there hadn't been a hope in hell of her relaxing during the so-called 'holiday'; she had been so worried about the flight home. While there, the heat had made Kieran bad-tempered and irritable, so much so that on the very first day he'd got into a huge argument with a nice Spanish waiter about the ice in his drink.

'Full of bloody germs, ice is,' he'd insisted to Abby, before demanding the waiter get him a replacement Coke.

She'd spent the rest of the holiday drinking warm beer, and had been afraid to brush her teeth she was so anxious about being infected with some water-borne Spanish virus.

Although the food to her had looked perfectly normal, and to her surprise wasn't terribly Spanish at all – one place had even served Irish *stew* – Kieran hadn't touched a bite, protesting that the steak wasn't steak at all.

'How many cows did you see on the way in from the airport?' he had pointed out. 'God knows what kind of stuff these foreign chancers are feeding us.'

Abby, who actually thought the Spanish people she'd met had been lovely, and incredibly patient and accommodating (considering), didn't think they'd *dream* of trying to trick people, but unfortunately she hadn't been able to convince her boyfriend otherwise.

'And some of them would want to do a few night courses in English while they're at it. Your man there obviously hadn't a clue what I was saying when I told him to leave out the ice, although maybe he was just trying to spite me.'

The holiday had been a nightmare from start to finish.

No, Abby reflected, foreign climes just weren't for her – what with hot weather, dodgy flights and, if Kieran was to be believed, even dodgier food.

'I don't think so, Erin,' she said to her friend now, the thought of another trip to a faraway destination way down on her list of priorities. Notwithstanding everything else, there really was no way she could take time off from work at such short notice. The income-tax deadline was only a few weeks away, which meant Duffy Masterson would be snowed under. When she explained this, Erin didn't seem convinced.

'Ah, come on, Abby. You seem to be working every hour God sends these last few months; surely you're due some time off.'

'I really can't – things are just too busy.'

'OK. Well, maybe we could put it off for a while, find a time that suits everyone.'

Abby squirmed. 'Maybe,' she said non-committally.

'Abby, are you OK? Every time I talk to you lately you seem totally preoccupied with work, and this is the third time in as many weeks that you've turned me down.' Erin sounded hurt. 'Look, I'm sure you're still finding things hard but—'

'Erin, I'm sorry but can I give you a call back later?' Abby interrupted, completely unable to deal with this turn in conversation. 'I really have to go. I'm running late as it is.'

A brief silence. 'OK.'

'Look, you guys go ahead and book the trip and don't mind me,' she went on, trying to keep her voice light and upbeat. 'We'll try and meet up soon, I promise.'

'Fine.' Erin sounded a little put out.

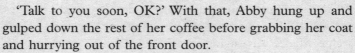

'Talk to you soon, OK?' With that, Abby hung up and gulped down the rest of her coffee before grabbing her coat and hurrying out of the front door.

She checked her watch. Eight thirty-five. Oh, no – she was *definitely* going to be late now! She rushed down the street towards town, and had to negotiate her way through a throng of people getting off at a nearby bus-stop. In her haste, she almost collided with a pedestrian coming in the other direction.

'I'm so sorry,' she said, ducking out of the woman's way at the very last second and swerving towards a ladder leaning against a building. OK, she thought, not bothering to go round it and get caught up among even *more* people; she wasn't a superstitious person anyway, so—

It was Abby's very last thought before there was a bright, blinding flash and suddenly everything went dark.

Chapter 5

When she woke up, a stranger's face was hovering above her.

'Hello, love, how are you feeling?'

'I'm fine, I think,' Abby managed groggily. She tried to sit up but the stranger, a middle-aged woman all dressed in white, gently resisted her attempts.

'No, pet, lie still there for a while until the doctor gets here; he should be over soon. Would you like anything? A glass of water, maybe? I'm Molly, by the way.'

'The doctor?' To her horror, Abby realised she was lying on a bed in what looked to be a hospital ward. And the woman in white with the kind face who was calling herself Molly had to be a nurse. What on earth was she doing in a hospital? she wondered, panicking.

'You had a little accident,' Molly said, as if reading her thoughts.

'Accident?'

'Yes.'

Abby realised that the nurse was trying her utmost to appear casual and impassive, but somehow her eyes gave her away. What was going on here? What accident?

'You don't remember?'

'No . . . I . . .' She blinked, her eyes heavy with sleep. 'How long have I been here? How did I get here?' Lifting her arm out from beneath the covers, she looked at her watch, as if this would somehow enlighten her as to everything that was going on. But there was no watch.

'Don't worry, all your things are safe and sound,' said the nurse, again second-guessing her. 'Your mother has them.'

'Mum? My mother's here?' Now Abby was seriously frightened. What was going on?

'Ah, you're awake,' said a male voice from the doorway, and a man whom Abby assumed was the doctor appeared at the end of the bed. He picked up her medical chart and gave it a quick once-over. 'How are you feeling?'

'I'm really not sure,' Abby said, regarding him worriedly.

'Any dizziness, nausea, anything like that?'

'No,' she replied automatically, but the truth was that she did feel dizzy – dizzy with panic and fear over what was happening.

The doctor nodded and scribbled something on the chart. 'Any pain or headaches?'

Well, yes she *did* feel some pressure on one side of her head, but . . .

'Look, will someone please tell me what's going on?' she asked, her voice trembling. 'How did I get here? What's wrong with me?'

The doctor looked up quickly from the medical chart. 'You don't remember?'

'Well, if I did remember, I wouldn't be asking!' Abby cried, biting back tears. 'What's going on?'

The doctor seemed determined to ignore her pleas and continued with his questions: 'Abby, do you know what day it is?'

Goodness, this was like an episode of *The Twilight Zone*! she thought, eyes widening. 'What do you mean "what day"? It's Monday of course.'

'And your telephone number?'

'My telephone number . . .' Abby shook her head at the absurdity of it all and, as she did, realised that it felt unusually heavy. She lifted up a hand to touch it and discovered that the top of her head seemed to be wrapped in some kind of . . . bandage. Oh, my God!

'OK, maybe we'll come back to that later,' the doctor said, noticing her distress. 'But, Abby, can I just ask what's the last thing you *do* remember?'

'I'm not sure . . .'

Confused, Abby tried to cast her mind back. Earlier that morning, she had been on her way to work, and was rushing because . . . because she'd been on the phone to Erin having a conversation about . . . about a holiday, that was it! It had been after eight thirty by the time she'd left the flat, and the streets had been packed with everyone racing here and there . . .

When she told the doctor this, he nodded sagely. 'You don't remember anything about a ladder?'

She blinked. 'What ladder?'

The doctor nodded again, as if she'd passed, or more likely *failed*, an important test.

One that Abby hadn't realised she was taking.

'Abby, you sustained a considerable head injury as a result of a roof tile falling from a building and hitting you on the side of the head,' he explained, his voice gentle. 'Initially, the force of the blow knocked you out, during which time we were unable to—'

'Dr Moroney.' Suddenly another stranger appeared at the end of Abby's bed, a woman with kind eyes who looked to be in her early forties. But unlike the others, this woman wasn't wearing standard hospital-type clothes; instead, she was dressed in a smart black pinstripe suit and bright-pink blouse.

'Oh, hello, Dr O'Neill. I'm sorry – I didn't realise you'd been called.' The male doctor stepped away from examining Abby to show her medical chart to the newcomer, and the two chatted among themselves in low voices for a few minutes, which made Abby feel even more uneasy.

Eventually, he returned to her side. 'Now, where were we?' He took a tiny flashlight out of his pocket and shined it directly in Abby's eyes, after which he made another notation on the medical chart. 'Ah, yes. Can you tell me your phone number?' he asked again, before adding jokily, 'Don't worry, I'm a happily married man.'

Abby was too full of anxiety to appreciate the joke, but she quickly rattled off the digits, all too eager to prove to him, if not to herself, that she was absolutely fine.

'And your home and work address?' he went on, picking up her right arm and taking her blood pressure.

Abby repeated both addresses with ease, her trepidation lifting by the minute, although she was still completely dazed by all this.

'OK, well, we'll get you down for an MRI soon to check out the damage,' the doctor said, finally putting the chart back, 'and I'll talk to you again after we've done the scans. In the meantime, just take it easy and don't move about too much, OK? You got quite a knock there, and were unconscious for a while, but Dr O'Neill will tell you all about that.' He and the woman exchanged looks before he eventually walked out of the room.

Tell me all about what? Abby wondered, barely able to take everything in. And how long had she been unconscious?

'Abby, hi. I'm Hannah O'Neill, but please call me Hannah,' the female doctor said kindly. 'I'm the consulting neuropsychologist here at St Vincent's and I'll be able to answer any questions you might have.'

Abby nodded gratefully, relieved that she might finally get some answers. 'How long was I unconscious?'

'Well, they brought you in this morning and it's now lunchtime, so no more than three or four hours.'

'Three or four hours? But what happened?'

'Well, as Dr Moroney was explaining when I arrived, you

were hit on the head by a falling roof tile,' she repeated pleasantly. 'That's why he needed to ask you those questions. Amnesia can be common after head trauma.'

Molly the nurse returned from tending to another patient. 'Are you sure you don't want a drink of water?' she asked again.

'Actually, I think I will.' All of a sudden Abby was parched – unsurprising if she'd been unconscious, she thought, still hardly able to believe it. A falling roof tile! She vaguely remembered veering across the pavement in order to avoid the person coming towards her, but couldn't specifically recall noticing the ladder. Not that it would have bothered her; she wasn't a particularly superstitious person, but clearly not walking under ladders had less to do with superstition and much more with safety . . .

'Was anybody else injured?' she asked, suddenly fearful that she might have been the cause of something more serious. Knowing her luck, it was a distinct possibility.

'Not that we're aware of,' Hannah said, allaying her worries on that score.

Soon after, the nurse came back with a glass of water, and helped Abby sit up against the pillows, while the psychologist filled in some more of the blanks.

'I'm not sure of the exact details, but it seems the roofer called an ambulance and stayed with you until it came,' she said. 'You had your office identity card on you when you came in, so admissions called your boss at the accountancy firm, who in turn called your family.' She tucked the sheets tightly around Abby and then handed her the glass of water. 'Your mother has been with you all morning but apparently just went down to the canteen to get some lunch. I've had one of the girls go down to tell her you're awake, so I'm sure she'll be back to see you very soon.'

Abby nodded, relieved that her mother was nearby. 'Any idea when I'll be out?' she asked.

But the psychologist wouldn't meet her gaze, which terrified Abby all over again – there must be something very wrong. 'Well, that'll depend on the results of the MRI, and we may have to do a CAT too,' she went on, her voice even. 'It all depends. Either way, you'll have to take things easy for a while.'

'Take things easy?' Abby cried, panicking. 'But I can't! I'm completely snowed under with work and Frank, my boss, will go ballistic!'

'Abby, you sustained a very serious head injury,' Hannah spoke gently as if addressing a young child. 'And until we know for sure how all of this will affect you, work and everything else will just have to take a back seat for a while.'

'How all of what will affect me? What does that mean?'

'Look, we'll talk about all of that when the scans come back, OK?' the woman soothed. 'For the moment, just relax here and try not to worry.'

But how could she *not* worry? Abby argued inwardly. This awful, scary thing had happened to her, a thing that might very well end up having greater repercussions than having to take time off work, which was bad enough . . .

'The last thing we want is to tire you out. You've had a big shock, so take it easy and rest a little,' Hannah told Abby kindly. 'The nurse will be back soon to take you down for your MRI, and I'll be checking in on you over the next couple of days to see how you're getting on.'

'Next couple of days . . .' Abby repeated, shocked. 'How long are you planning to keep me here? I really do feel fine, you know.'

But frustratingly, Hannah was having none of it and remained non-committal about the length of Abby's stay. 'We'll just have to wait and see,' was all she said, before promising to return the next day for another chat.

Flustered, Abby subconsciously lifted a hand to the back of

her neck, only to pull it away almost immediately. What on earth . . . ?

'What happened to my hair?' she gasped, disbelievingly.

Instead of her curly, long blonde hair, she was now sporting some choppy bob-type thing. She moved her hands all over her head, willing to find some of her precious hair – the only thing Abby liked about herself and what Kieran said was the very first thing he'd noticed about her . . .

Hannah was quick to reassure her. 'They had to cut most of it off, so they could examine the wound. But don't worry – it'll all grow back in time. Here, I'll have the nurse get you a mirror so you can see it properly.'

'They cut off my hair without asking?' Even as she said the words Abby knew how stupid they sounded, but she just couldn't believe it. All her lovely hair, gone! Despite herself, she burst into tears and stupidly, she knew – given the circumstances – her only concern was that now Kieran would *never* want her back.

Some fifteen minutes later, Abby's mother arrived at her bedside looking suitably worried, but at the same time hugely relieved that her daughter was now awake and talking.

'How are you feeling, love?' Teresa asked, giving her a kiss on the forehead. 'I'm sorry I wasn't here when you woke up, but Molly made me go down to the canteen for a bite.'

Molly? Abby had to smile. She had only been here a few hours and already her mum was on first-name terms with the staff.

'That's OK,' Abby reassured her, greatly relieved to have someone she knew by her side, 'and I'm OK too, I think, but it seems I'm stuck here for a while longer,' she added, explaining to her mother what Hannah had said. 'It's odd because I really do feel absolutely fine.'

'Well, I suppose the doctors know best all the same.' Teresa patted her on the arm sympathetically. 'So do you remember what happened? Before you blacked out, I mean.'

Again Abby outlined how she remembered every single thing that had happened that morning except actually walking under the ladder. 'I was late for work, and in a bit of rush, and the last thing I remember is making my way through the crowds. Next thing I know I wake up in here.' When her mother looked troubled, Abby was quick to reassure her. 'Don't worry, Mum, I'm absolutely fine. I can only imagine how worried you were when you got the phone call, though.'

'Well, of course I was,' Teresa said. 'We all were – Caroline, Dermot and Claire.'

'Claire?' Abby's eyes widened. 'Mum, it's only a tiny bump on the head; why would you bother her with something like that?' Clearly her mother thought this was a much bigger deal than it really was, she realised, her heart racing once more.

But why? Had the doctors told her mum more than they'd told her? While her mum was a bit of a worrier by nature, there was no denying that she now seemed troubled by something, something more than just a bump on the head.

'Mum? What is it?' she asked fearfully. 'Is there something else going on here? Something I don't know about?'

'Of course not,' Teresa reassured her. 'And I wouldn't have said anything at all to Claire, only she phoned while I was leaving for the hospital, so naturally enough I told her.'

'Oh, OK.' Abby's relief was palpable. God, all this stuff was making her neurotic!

'So how's the patient?' came a voice from what looked like a colossal walking bunch of flowers, before Caroline's smiling face peeped out from behind it.

'I'm grand,' Abby replied, unsettled by all this fuss. 'What are *you* doing here?'

'Well, that's a nice way to greet your favourite sister.' Caroline grinned, reaching across to give her a peck on the cheek.

35

'I'm here to see you, and of course to give you these.' She set down the humongous bunch of flowers that by Abby's reckoning looked to be about five foot high.

'Thanks, they're gorgeous, but there's really no need.'

'I know, but while you're here we might as well make the place a little less dreary. Oh, and I brought some smellies too,' she added, taking out a couple of travel-sized Clarins bottles from her bag, along with a bottle of Chanel No. 5. Abby shook her head as her sister duly set about spraying the bed linen. She truly *did* live on a different planet to everyone else!

'So,' Caroline said then, once Abby had convinced yet another person that she was feeling fine, 'Mum was just about to tell you about Claire, weren't you?' she said, glancing at their mother.

Teresa wrung her hands. 'Well, I'm not sure if now is the right time to say it, what with you being in hospital and all.'

'What about her?' Abby asked.

'Well, as I said, I was talking to her on the phone earlier and . . . well, she had some good news.'

'Really? What?'

'Well, it turns out she's pregnant,' Teresa finished awkwardly, and Abby knew immediately that her mother felt guilty about the timing and even more guilty for being so happy about one daughter's fortune while another was experiencing definite *mis*fortune. But there was little need for her to worry.

'That's amazing news!' she gasped, thrilled for her eldest sister.

'Isn't it just?' Caroline agreed, smiling.

'So, how far along is she?'

'Six months, believe it or not,' her sister informed her before Teresa could reply.

Now Abby was even more shocked. '*Six* months? And she's

only telling us now?' Maybe her sister was nervous about broadcasting her happy news before she knew for sure that everything was OK – people sometimes did that. Still, six months seemed excessive for—

Then Abby thought of something. 'But how come she never said anything the other day,' she wondered out loud, 'when she phoned to wish Mum a happy birthday?'

The others exchanged a look. 'Well, she probably didn't want to take away from or overshadow Mum's celebrations,' Caroline suggested. 'You know what Claire's like.'

Abby did, although she really couldn't understand how her sister could have withheld such amazing news for so long. She was ecstatic for her, though, and she'd definitely have to give her a call now. Or at least, whenever she got out of this place . . .

'Anyway, are you sure you're OK?' Caroline asked her again. 'Although, I have to admit you look pretty good to me.'

'I'm absolutely fine,' Abby reiterated for the umpteenth time that day. 'I think they're making a huge fuss over nothing keeping me in here – not to mention wasting a bed on someone who *clearly* has nothing wrong with her.'

The shadow that crossed Teresa's face when Abby said this suggested that her mother didn't share her optimism.

Chapter 6

'I'm afraid there is indeed evidence of damage,' Dr Moroney, the neurologist, said, his tone sombre.

It was two days later and Abby and her mother had been called to his office for the results of her MRI and CAT scans. As the nurse had wheeled her inside on the hospital wheel-chair, she had noticed various skull-shaped images displayed on a light-box behind him.

'What kind of damage?' she asked croakily. 'Where?' A stupid question, seeing as they were here to discuss the results of a CAT scan on her *brain*. But perhaps stupid questions were a symptom of the problem.

'The blow was a severe one, and it caused injury to your left temporal lobe – there, under your temple, exactly where you were hit,' he said, pointing to the relevant location on the scan of Abby's brain.

She couldn't really see anything out of the ordinary, but then again, why would she? Like most people, she wasn't exactly familiar with the inside of her own brain. Still she nodded wordlessly, and waited for him to continue.

'Well, I'll try not to get too technical, but just to give you an idea of what we're dealing with, the temporal lobe houses the hippocampus, which makes up part of the region of your brain responsible for emotion and motivation.'

He spoke in a monotone voice that reminded Abby of the bored way the air hostesses had gone through the safety infor-mation on that first plane trip she'd taken. Fair enough if he had to repeat the information time and time again to different people, but this was her first time hearing it, so couldn't he at least try and *sound* some way interested?

'But what does this mean?' she asked, glancing at Teresa for her reaction. But strangely, the calm way in which her mother was taking the news suggested to Abby that she had already suspected there would be some repercussions. 'How will this damage to the hippocampus, or whatever it's called, affect me?'

'Take it easy, love,' Teresa said, reacting to the panic in her voice. 'Best to just wait and let the doctor explain everything.'

Dr Moroney breathed out deeply, and sat on the edge of his desk. 'Abby, when people develop Alzheimer's, the hippocampus is usually the first region of the brain to suffer damage.'

An intense range of emotions attacked her all at once. 'Alzheimer's?' she gasped. 'You're telling me I have Alzheimer's?'

The doctor shook his head quickly. 'No, no, I'm not saying that at all. All we know is that there's damage to the hippocampus, and that this will have an effect on you long term.' There was no mistaking the consultant's grave demeanour. 'Abby, when we got these scans back, we weren't entirely sure what to make of them, so we forwarded the file to an expert in the US, a Dr Franklin. He's one of the highest-ranking neurologists in his field, particularly in the area of hippocampus injury.'

Abby's hands grasped the edge of the chair, and again she wished the doctor would just say what he had to say.

'Anyway, I'm glad we did send the scans, because as it turns out, he noticed something that we hadn't – something curious.'

'Like what?' Abby's gaze was drawn once again to the light-box displaying the scans.

'See here?' The doctor indicated a tiny blur just to the left of the injury he'd shown her before. 'It indicates some addi-tional trauma – older trauma. Now, we've checked your medical records, and there's no sign of you presenting or being treated here for any such head wound in recent years. Any idea what it is, or when it might have occurred?'

'No idea at all,' Abby replied, unable to recall such a thing. She glanced at her mother, who seemed just as clueless.

'You're sure?'

'Absolutely.'

The doctor seemed to be watching her closely, almost as if he expected her to come up with an explanation.

'Well, our concerns are – or rather, Dr Franklin's concerns are – that this older trauma, which occurred in the same vicinity as the new one, could very well have a bearing on how this newer injury manifests itself.'

'What does that mean?' Teresa asked.

The doctor looked directly at Abby. 'Well, the only thing we can be sure of is that your long-term memory will suffer.'

She felt her heart rate speed up. 'Suffer in what way?'

'Well, as I said, it's difficult to explain, but to try and make you understand how the hippocampus works, let me use an analogy. Think of the hippocampus as a bridge. On one side you have all your long-term memories, and on the other your short-term memories. Now, when your brain creates a new memory – a short-term one – it needs to pass over the bridge into your long-term memory in order for you to retain it and recall it whenever you need to. Are you with me so far?'

Abby nodded.

'But this more recent trauma has damaged the bridge, put a crack in it as such. So when new memories want to cross to the long-term side, they need to get across the crack. Some of them, however, may fall in.'

Her eyes widened. 'Fall in? Fall in where?'

'As I said, this is purely for explanatory purposes – it isn't intended as scientific fact,' the doctor said, a little impatiently. 'What I'm trying to illustrate is that some of your memories may not end up on the other side, or if they do, you might have trouble getting them back. This means that while you can easily form new memories and send them across the bridge, we have no way of knowing what you'll be able to get back.'

Abby stared at the scans, unable to take this in. She had a mental picture of an old stone bridge with a huge crack in it and all her memories falling through.

'But what has the older injury got to do with this?' Teresa asked. 'Will it make things worse or . . . ?'

'No, the newer injury is really the root of the problem, but the older one may yet have a part to play. We're just not sure at the moment. Again, there are no certainties when it comes to the human brain. I really wish there were.' The doctor opened a drawer. 'I'm discharging you tomorrow, but from here on in what I need is for you to monitor yourself over the next couple of days and weeks. Let us know if you notice anything out of the ordinary, any temporary blackouts or things like that.'

A rod of panic travelled through Abby. 'What?' she cried, terrified. 'I could have Alzheimer's and you want to just send me home!'

Not that she had much of a clue about the condition other than what she'd learnt from TV and books, but right then Abby couldn't help but picture herself standing in the local shop dressed in her nightclothes, confused and wondering how she got there. And seeing as she lived alone, there would be no one around to keep an eye on her, no one to prevent her doing things like that, no one to help her . . .

The doctor quickly moved to allay her fears. 'Abby, as I said, that really isn't the case. Yes, you will almost certainly suffer some form of memory . . . displacement . . . but nothing as serious as Alzheimer's. While we can see the damage to the hippocampus on the scans, we can't really tell how severe that damage is, or if it's progressive. That's the thing about the brain, Abby – it's the most complex part of the body and still the part that we know the least about.'

He handed her a card. 'You remember Dr O'Neill? She may have already told you that she's a neuropsychologist, specialising in TBI – traumatic brain injury. She'll help you make sense of the day-to-day impact of all of this in a way we can't, and also she'll be able to monitor any changes that may occur from now on. You haven't noticed anything different yet?'

'Definitely not. I'm tired and I've been getting some headaches but . . .'

'Very common following TBI,' Dr Moroney said, nodding sagely. 'Just keep a close eye on yourself for the next while, until I talk to you again, OK?'

Abby looked at the card he had given her. She didn't like the idea of having to go and consult with yet another person, another doctor who would have an opinion on what might happen next and how she should deal with it.

She just couldn't believe this; as far as she was concerned, she felt fine! Yes, there was a little bit of pressure in her head, and she was anxious about having to miss work at such a busy time, but other than that she felt perfectly normal.

And hadn't the doctor already admitted that he and that so-called American 'expert' were only second-guessing what might or might not happen? Chances were, they were over-analysing the extent of this injury and she could very well turn out to be fine.

'But at the same time, there might be nothing at all wrong with me?' she asked, pleading with him to give her at least a semblance of hope. 'I mean, none of this might happen, right?'

'Perhaps so, but it's unlikely . . .' the doctor fudged, and Abby didn't like the grim set of his jaw, or the very obvious doubt in his eyes.

Chapter 7

Finn Maguire was in a hurry and Lucy wasn't helping. The ceremony was due to start at two thirty and there she was, still lingering over lunch, not a care in the world. 'Luce, hurry up and finish that, will you? We'll be late.'

Lucy looked up and, with a barely perceptible sigh, sulkily walked out of the room.

'Oh, come on – there's no need to be like that, is there?' he called after her. 'You know what the traffic's like: it could take us an hour to get there.'

He grabbed a jacket and stole a quick look at his reflection in the hallway mirror on the way out, realising then that he'd forgotten to run a brush through his hair and it was now sticking up in thick, dark clumps all over his head. Blast it anyway, Finn thought, trying to smooth it down. Lucy waited patiently while he did his best with his unruly hair, then led the way outside to the Jeep.

Finn's heart melted at her downcast expression, and for the first time that day he reminded himself that even though this thing was a celebration, at the same time it might not be easy for her. Maternal instinct and all that.

'Hey, I'm sorry for shouting at you, OK?' he said, unlocking the car and holding the passenger door open for her. 'I was in a hurry and it's getting late, and you know how I much I hate being late, don't you?'

Refusing to meet his eye, Lucy settled herself on the front seat.

OK, so he wasn't getting away with it *that* easily today, Finn thought with a sigh. He started the engine, deciding he was probably better off just staying quiet and letting her sulk away to herself for a while. She'd snap out of it . . . eventually.

They were halfway to the school before he spoke again. 'I know these things can be hard for you, Luce. Hell, they're hard for me too in a way, but it'll be a great day, and you should be very proud. This is – what? – the fourth of these things we've been to and not one of our lot have ever failed to make the grade, have they?'

He glanced sideways at her to see if his words were having any effect, but Lucy continued staring straight ahead, her gaze fixed on the road in front. 'I know you'll miss them. I'll miss them too, but they're at the age now where they need to make their own way in the world. And they'll be fine; you and I have made sure of that, haven't we?'

But it seemed there was no consoling poor Lucy today. Fully grown adults or not, at the moment she was still missing her babies. There was nothing more he could do or say now, Finn thought, pulling into the school gates. They were here, and judging from the number of people hurrying into the main hall, the ceremony was just about to begin.

'Finn – up here! I've saved a seat for you!'

As he and Lucy entered the hall, Finn looked up to see his colleague Angela waving at them from the front row. Ignoring a deep sigh from Lucy, he made his way through the crowds to where she sat.

'Hey,' he said, taking the chair alongside her. 'Thanks for that. Busy here today, isn't it?'

'It sure is. Did you two get a chance to see the guys before-hand? Are they all really excited?'

Finn gave her a look and muttered out of the corner of

his mouth, 'No. I always think it's better for all concerned that we don't.'

'Oh, of course, silly me.' She looked apologetically at Lucy, who again steadfastly ignored her. 'And I suppose we don't want them getting too excited either, do we?'

'No.'

Angela sensibly decided to change the subject. 'But don't you scrub up well!' she said, flashing Finn a flirtatious grin. 'Great suit.'

'Thanks.' Finn self-consciously loosened his tie. 'Erm . . . so do you.'

Angela did indeed look well in a clinging black dress with a disconcertingly low neckline that Finn wasn't entirely sure was suitable for the occasion. Still, what did he know? His fashion knowledge extended to his work attire of mostly jeans and T-shirts.

'Thanks – and I'm so glad I remembered at the last minute to wear waterproof mascara.'

'Waterproof mascara?'

She opened her handbag and took out a small packet of tissues. 'For the ceremony of course. I always end up bawling at these things, don't you?'

But Finn had no time to reply, as just then a voice he recognised spoke softly through the microphone. He looked up to see Brendan O'Sullian addressing the audience.

'Ladies and gentlemen, I'd like to welcome you to what is always a hugely important event in our calendar. Today's graduates have studied hard to get where they are, and are now ready to tackle any challenges the world throws their way. We're gathered here now to celebrate their achievements, and to set them on the road to even greater things.' He paused and looked to his right, before smiling. 'I'm going to introduce them to you now, but for the benefit of those members of our audience in attendance for the first time, can I remind you not to applaud for fear of upsetting or unsettling them.'

Finn nodded approvingly at this. Brendan had forgotten to make this announcement last time, and the applause had really distracted some.

'So, without further ado, I'd like to introduce to you, in alphabetical order'– As Brendan began calling out the names, Finn stole a sideways glance at Lucy – 'Maisie, Marie, Martin, Michael, Michelle, Molly and Morris!'

When the first one appeared, there was a brief clap from someone who'd obviously forgotten Brendan's earlier warning, or who'd got so carried away by the sight of the graduates that they couldn't help themselves. Lucy gave a brief whimper as she recognised her 'babies', and as each walked on she moved her tail every so slightly, until eventually, when all three had emerged, she stood up and wagged effusively. Lucy and Finn watched proudly as Marie, Michelle and Morris one by one turned and quietly stood to attention alongside their fellow graduates.

'Ladies and gentlemen,' Brendan continued with a flourish, 'I'm delighted to present to you the Leinster Guide Dog Centre's trainee class of 2008, now fully qualified and today to be officially presented to their new partners, for what all of us here at the training centre hope will be a long and mutually fulfilling companionship!'

'Well, that wasn't so bad, now was it?'

Once the official graduation ceremony was over, Finn picked up Lucy's lead and went outside to where the newly inaugurated guide dogs were chasing and wrestling with one another on the grass, their ex-trainers and their proud new companions grouped around the sidelines. Now off duty, the younger dogs were making the most of what would probably be their last few hours together as a group, before each in turn went home with their visually impaired partners.

It was a wonderful day and a true validation of the work that Finn and his fellow trainers at the Leinster Guide Dog Centre carried out from year to year. There was nothing more satisfying than taking a seemingly mischievous puppy and grooming it to become a worthwhile and essential aid to the visually impaired. But while Finn, like most of his colleagues at the centre, had a huge affection for each and every dog he trained, he also had an additional attachment to some, Lucy's offspring in particular. Now a retired assistance dog, Lucy's even temperament and incredible intelligence made her an ideal candidate for the centre's breeding programme, and she'd so far produced three different litters who had gone on to become model trainees.

Her earlier sombre mood now greatly improved, Finn released Lucy from her lead and she raced off to join her offspring, while he went to speak to the companions.

'Hi, everyone. Enjoying the day?'

'It's fabulous,' replied Susan, a partially sighted woman in her mid-thirties who had been partnered with Michelle, one of Lucy's pups. 'They seem to be enjoying it too.' She smiled in the direction of the dogs.

Now Lucy was lying on her back with all four paws in the air, happily letting the other dogs climb over her. As Lucy only attended the centre throughout the breeding programme and for a brief period after giving birth, she didn't have much contact with the centre, except on days like today. Normally, she stayed at home with Finn, who as well as being a qualified guide-dog trainer also acted as a puppy raiser for some of the potential trainees – usually Lucy's. When the pups were about nine weeks old, he brought them home with him to help socialise them, teach them good behaviour and manners, and get them accustomed to living indoors.

Finn laughed as Lucy nipped one of her charges for being

too overzealous in his energy. 'Lucy knows how to put the younger dogs in their place!' he explained to Susan.

'Brendan told me she was a working dog herself once, but she seems very young to be retired.'

Finn sighed. 'She's six, but was only three when we had to retire her. Halloween fireworks,' he added in a flat voice when Susan gave him a questioning look. 'The noise frightened her so much it rendered all of her specialised training useless. She was only on the job for a few months.'

'Oh, no, what a shame.'

Finn nodded. It was a crying shame, and was happening more and more as time went on. He sorely wished that the parents who were stupid enough to buy illegal fireworks for their little darlings could be around to see the damage they caused. If they could only experience what he had – the sight of a terrified dog shaking and cowering in a corner and refusing to eat for days – it would be more than enough to make them change their minds. Or would it? Finn didn't know. He didn't have a whole lot of faith in human decency any more, which is why he spent all his time working with animals.

Finn had been Lucy's original trainer, and the two had shared a special bond right from when he'd first brought her home to raise as a puppy to when he'd eventually handed her over to her new partner at a graduation ceremony just like this one. Then, when the incident with the fireworks had occurred and Lucy's partner had applied for a replacement dog, Finn had decided to take her in. And though her fear had been so extreme there was no way she could be re-trained as a working dog, in time he managed to coax the frightened Labrador out of her anxieties and bring her back to the intelligent, loving companion she was.

Now, watching Lucy play happily with her equally clever and talented offspring, Finn was reminded of a comment

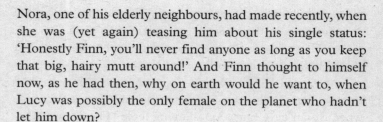

Nora, one of his elderly neighbours, had made recently, when she was (yet again) teasing him about his single status: 'Honestly Finn, you'll never find anyone as long as you keep that big, hairy mutt around!' And Finn thought to himself now, as he had then, why on earth would he want to, when Lucy was possibly the only female on the planet who hadn't let him down?

49

Chapter 8

The following Sunday afternoon, Finn opened his front door to find his father standing on the doorstep.

'Hey, Dad, how's things?' he said, stepping back and beckoning him inside. As he did so, Lucy – who adored Pat – bounded down the hallway to greet him, her tail wagging furiously.

The feeling was mutual.

'Ah there you are, my darlin'.' Pat bent down and ruffled Lucy behind the ears. 'How was she at the ceremony?' he asked. Pat, like Finn, knew how lonely Lucy got when her pups went out into the big bad world.

Finn shrugged. 'Not too bad. A bit moody in the morning, but much better when it was all over.'

Pat followed Finn through to the kitchen. 'Isn't it gas the way they know what's happening all the same?' Pat said, shaking his head. 'Imagine pining over her young ones like that. Aren't they nearly human sometimes?'

'Better than some humans in that way.' Finn's expression tightened and he moved to the sink. 'At least she actually gives some thought to her offspring. Cup of tea, Dad?'

'That would be grand, thanks.' Pat took a seat at the kitchen table and looked at his son. 'Lookit, there's no need for that kind of smart talk, is there?'

Immediately Finn felt guilty. There *was* no need, and it wasn't fair to his father – especially after all this time. But sometimes he just couldn't help but revert to behaving like some sulky teenager instead of the grown man of thirty-five he was.

'Sorry, it's been a busy week and I'm a bit stressed out.' Finn stood by the counter as he waited for the kettle to boil.

'Stress, stress, stress – everyone in this country is stressed these days. Whatever happened to just taking things easy?'

Finn smiled. 'Look who's talking! When was the last time *you* took things easy, Dad? Sixty-eight years of age and you're *still* going up and down ladders like a madman.'

Pat was a cabinet-maker by trade, but for as long as Finn could remember he'd been working as a painter/decorator and odd-job man in the Balbriggan area. His father could turn his hand to anything: plumbing, carpentry, electrics.

'Well, I might have to give up those ladders for a while soon,' Pat said, and hearing a slight catch in his voice, Finn looked up.

Suddenly realising that this was no casual visit, he stared at his father. 'What does that mean?' When Pat didn't answer immediately, Finn frowned. 'Dad, what's going on?'

'Finish making that pot of tea and I'll tell you,' his father replied, leaving Finn wondering what on earth was coming.

Finn waited anxiously while Pat poured the milk.

'My health's not the best at the moment, son,' Pat announced at last.

He said nothing; he simply waited for his father to elaborate.

'I've been a bit weak in myself these last few months, which isn't like me.'

No, it's certainly not, Finn thought. His father was one of the fittest, most active people he knew. Up at dawn every day without fail, Pat would go for a good long walk in the morning before putting in a solid day's work, and then coming home to tend to the household. He'd always been scrupulous about looking after himself, and because of this tended to be fitter than even his thirty-five-year-old son. At least, that was what Finn had always believed.

'So I called down to Dr Murphy, who said that I was probably just low on iron and put me on some tablets. But nothing changed.'

'Well, I can't see why he thought that,' Finn muttered. 'You're a demon for red meat – he should know that.'

'That's what I thought, but sure you know yourself what doctors can be like sometimes.'

I sure do, Finn thought irately. Don't bother checking anything out in detail or asking any questions; just think of the first reasonable explanation and then stick the hand out for your fifty quid, thanks very much.

'Anyway, they did a few blood tests, and to cut a long story short, it seems they have to keep an eye on me from now on, just in case.'

'In case of what?' Finn demanded, while trying his best to keep his thoughts in check.

Pat looked almost embarrassed. 'Prostate trouble – the numbers they use to measure these things – PSAs, they call them – are high, apparently. Lookit, don't you be worrying about me now,' he said, sitting forward in his chair. 'That's not why I'm telling you. The last thing you need is to be worrying about me.'

'How could I *not* worry about you? You're my father, for Christ's sake!'

Not to mention the only family I have, he added silently, his thoughts frantic. The doctors must have made some kind of mistake. But for his dad's sake, Finn knew he couldn't panic: he had to get a hold of himself.

'The only reason I'm telling you now is that I have to go for some more tests soon – next month in St Vincent's.'

'Next month . . .'

'Yes. So I might need you to give me a lift in there now and again if you don't mind.'

'Well, of course I don't mind.' Finn would do anything for his father, in the same way that Pat had done everything for him throughout his life. He felt stunned . . . numb at the thought that this was happening now, that some form of illness had raised its ugly head. 'So these tests . . . what'll they achieve?'

'God only knows, but, Finn, these things happen to men my age.' Pat was being remarkably practical. 'Who knows how it'll go? What will be will be.'

Not for the first time, Finn wished he'd inherited some of his father's strength of character, his extraordinary ability to face head on any challenges life threw his way. Instead Finn simply felt weak, spineless and afraid – pointless traits he knew he'd inherited from his mother.

Chapter 9

Abby arrived at Dr O'Neill's office in Leeson Street for her first appointment. It was three days since she'd been discharged from the hospital, and despite her initial reluctance to share her feelings about the prognosis with someone who was by all accounts a stranger, her thoughts were so all over the place that she was starting to welcome the opportunity.

Hopefully the neuropsychologist would be able to shed some more light on her condition and tell her what to expect. She still hadn't noticed anything out of the ordinary, and as far as she was concerned, her memory was in perfect working order. Unfortunately, the same thing couldn't be said for her state of mind.

'Hello there – good to see you again.' Hannah got up from her desk to shake Abby's hand when she entered the office.

'It's nice to see you too,' Abby replied.

Despite her reluctance, Hannah had made a good impression on Abby back at the hospital, simply because she was the only one there who had been willing to give her a straight answer. The nurses and Dr Moroney had tended to hide behind platitudes and a 'try not to worry' attitude, whereas Hannah had been direct and approachable.

The doctor smiled. 'So, I suppose we might as well get started, then. Have a seat. Anywhere you like,' she added, when Abby looked unsure which to choose from – the two purple velvet armchairs in the centre of the room or the scarlet chaise longue by the wall. This place was nothing like she'd expected from a psychologist's office, and instead of being clinical and austere, the room was warm and cosy, with its cerise ostrich-feather lampshade on the desk and fluffy cushions on comfortable-looking furniture. A large wooden Balinese-style wall-hanging was suspended beside some funky shelves containing a wide range of books (Abby spotted some of her own favourite authors) as well as various pretty knick-knacks that looked to be travel souvenirs, and there was a large Oriental rug on the floor. Looking around, she felt a really odd sense of . . . almost déjà vu. Unwilling to give in to this feeling, or admit that it might have anything to do with her injury, she quickly erased the thought from her mind.

'I know,' the psychologist said, reading Abby's reaction. 'Some of my other patients have compared this place to their teenage daughters' bedrooms! But I love lots of colour and warmth at home, so why should my workplace look like it's been dropped in a tin of mushroom soup?'

Abby sat down on one of the velvet armchairs, and Hannah took the one directly opposite.

'It's great,' she said, warming more and more to the idea of being here. If Dr O'Neill was anything like her office, then these visits might not be so difficult after all.

'I'm glad you think so, because we'll be spending quite a bit of time together here over the next while – at least, I hope we will,' the psychologist added, eyeing her new patient speculatively. 'Would you like a glass of water, or maybe a coffee?'

'No, thanks.' Abby shook her head. 'Look, to be honest, I'm not entirely sure why I'm here,' she told the other woman in a small voice, deciding it was better to be frank from the outset. 'I mean, I know it's because I have this injury,' she said with a tight smile, 'but as far as I'm concerned, there's nothing wrong with me.'

'Well, that's good to know, and let's hope that's the way things will stay,' Hannah replied, her tone bright. 'But – and I'm sorry there has to be a but,' she added with a smile, which Abby returned weakly, 'as we explained to you at the hospital, the damage sustained to that particular part of your brain will almost certainly impact on your memory function. You got one hell of a whack on the head, Abby. Because of this, it's important we keep a close eye on you to see how things will go.' To Abby's surprise, she kicked off her shoes, tucking her long legs beneath her. 'I take it Dr Moroney outlined in detail how the damage to your hippocampus will have an effect on how your memory works?'

Abby shrugged. 'He tried, but to tell the truth, it all sounded so technical that I couldn't really follow.' At the time, she'd been so terrified at the mention of Alzheimer's that she hadn't been able to concentrate on anything else.

'OK, well, let me try and explain as best I can. Let's start with memory – normal, undamaged memory,' the psychologist said, speaking softly. 'There are three main stages in the formation and retrieval of memory. The first is encoding – by which I mean creating the initial memory; then storage, whereby our brains create a permanent record of the information, and finally retrieval, which, I suppose, is self-explanatory.'

Abby nodded studiously.

'Now, there are within this process – as I'm sure you know – two distinct types of memory: short term and long term. For example, if I show you a random seven-digit number, you might remember it for only a few seconds and then forget it altogether, which means it was only stored in your short-term memory. On the other hand, people remember telephone numbers for years through repetition, and these long-lasting pieces of information are said to be stored in our long-term memory. Are you with me so far?'

Abby nodded once more, determined to understand. 'Yes.'

'To use a common analogy, the hippocampus – the part of your brain that's damaged – acts as the bridge between your short-term and long-term memory,' Hannah went on. 'Short-term memories, after the initial learning, travel across this bridge to the long-term "department", shall we say,' she said, smiling. 'From here, they can usually be recalled whenever required. Does that make sense to you?'

'I think so,' Abby said. 'The doctor said that in my case that bridge may have a crack in it and that some memories may fall through.'

'Well, yes, he's right in some respects but unfortunately it's also a little more complex,' she said, with an apologetic smile. 'So let's break it down a little further. Long-term memory can be further subdivided into two more categories: semantic memory and episodic memory.' Seeing Abby's dubious expression, the neuropsychologist paused. 'OK, I can see I'm in danger of losing you now, but it's important for you to try and understand how the entire process works, or at least as much as we know about how it works.'

'OK, so semantic and episodic memory,' Abby repeated, trying her best to keep up, although all this technical stuff was *already* frying her brain!

'Well, semantic memory is concerned with the retrieval of abstract knowledge about the world, things like, say, Dublin is the capital of Ireland. Episodic memory, on the other hand, is used for more personal memories, such as the personal experiences and emotions associated with a particular time or place. OK?'

'OK. So are you saying that because of the damage, I might not be able to make new memories?'

'No, the concern is that you may not be able to *recall* new memories. Your short-term memory will continue to act as normal, in that it'll file away day-to-day events and, based on your reaction to them, will send them accordingly to your long-term memory. But depending on the strength of these reactions – and most importantly whether or not they are semantic or episodic – some of these memories may fade or become lost along the way.'

'Semantic and episodic . . .' Abby repeated, her mind whirling. 'I still don't understand.'

Hannah sat forward.

'I'm trying to emphasise the importance of emotion when it comes to memory retention. Semantic memories are *learned* memories, whereas I suppose episodic memories are *experienced*, and often emotionally charged. They're felt,' she clarified, pointing to her heart.

'I think I understand.' But Abby was still unsure what it all meant in relation to her injury.

The psychologist seemed to read her thoughts. 'Abby, because of the complex nature of the brain, and the many millions of neural pathways inside, we still have no *absolute* way of knowing how this injury will affect you long term. The only thing we can be sure of is that it will – almost without doubt – affect your ability to recall episodic memories.'

Abby's stomach dropped. 'But what about my existing memories?' she asked. 'They won't be affected, will they?'

Hannah sighed. 'It's possible, but at the same time unlikely. I know that must seem very frustrating to you, but unfortunately that's as much as we can tell at the moment. And of course there's the issue of the older injury that Dr Franklin found on your scan. This makes things even more complicated because we could be talking about some dual effect we can't anticipate.'

'I already told them I don't know anything about an old injury,' Abby insisted, frustrated that the only thing any of these medical people were certain about was that they couldn't be certain of anything! What good was that to her?

'Abby, I know how difficult this must be for you – especially when you haven't yet spotted any noticeable difference in brain function. But this sort of thing can take time to manifest, which is why we need to keep a close eye on your progress for the next while to see if anything . . . unusual happens. After an injury like this, incidental memory blips or even blackouts are common, so I need you to keep a very close eye on yourself too.'

'But when will this happen?' Abby cried, distressed at how inevitable all of this seemed. 'When will my memory problems start? Will it be now, next week, next year, when?'

Hannah shook her head slowly. 'As I said, as of yet we really don't know for sure. For the moment, Abby, we just have to wait and see.'

Chapter 10

'How are you feeling, love?' Teresa asked, putting a cup of tea and some chocolate biscuits on the table in front of Abby.

It was a weekday afternoon, some three weeks after her release from the hospital, and seeing as she was on medical leave from work and had plenty of time on her hands, Abby had called over to her mum's house for a chat.

'OK,' she said, with a grateful smile. Although, of course, this was the furthest thing from the truth. In reality, she didn't know how she was. Since discovering the nature of her injury and what it might mean, her emotions had swung between anger, distress, fear and absolute denial. But for today at least, she supposed she felt OK. The worst part was not knowing. Not knowing when her brain would decide to start 'losing' memories and, worse, not knowing which memories they would be.

'Most of the time, I don't know what to do with myself,' she confessed to her mother. 'I'm so used to having a million and one things to do at work, whereas now I have all this time on my hands.'

'Well, if you don't mind my saying so, there's probably no harm in that. You were working way too hard before all of this happened, rushing here and there and everywhere – you needed to slow down sometime.'

'I know.' Abby bit her lip. 'It was because I was rushing around that this happened in the first place.'

Her mother was silent, obviously unwilling to agree that

Abby was responsible for her own misfortune. 'Well, it could have been much worse, couldn't it?' Teresa said. 'That falling slate could have killed you. And speaking of which, I was talking to the solicitor yesterday about the insurance.'

Following the accident, the hugely apologetic roofing contractor had been in contact with Abby's family in relation to a claim. Because the accident had happened on a public road, Right-On Roofing was obliged to pay Abby a considerable amount of compensation for her accident. Teresa, who'd offered to deal with all the paperwork on Abby's behalf, had learnt that the contractor's insurance company were currently processing the claim and, to the family's great relief, were also liaising with the hospital to cover her medical costs. As there was no issue over liability, she would also be entitled to a one-off lump sum, which Right-On Roofing's company director informed her would be paid as soon as the claim was settled.

'The solicitor reckons it should be sorted fairly soon,' Teresa said.

'Really?' Abby was taken aback that it was all going so smoothly. Then again, the roofing company was probably anxious to get the whole thing dealt with as soon as possible – just in case the doctors discovered more serious damage in the meantime. Still, she wasn't going to complain, if the lump sum did come through relatively quickly, then at least she wouldn't need to worry about money. Her company were still paying her salary, but how long would that last? Thankfully, she also had her savings to rely on – the nest egg that was supposed to go towards the purchase of her and Kieran's first home. But seeing as that wasn't going to happen now . . .

Her mother seemed hesitant. 'Love, I don't mean to sound negative and I don't want to upset you or anything, but what if . . . Well, what will you do when what the doctors say will happen *does* happen?'

'I don't know,' Abby answered, swallowing hard. 'Dr Moroney tells me that I should be OK, and that my normal day-to-day life shouldn't be affected all that much other than the odd memory blip here and there, but to be honest, there are too many "should"s for my liking. All I know is that I seem absolutely fine so far, and apart from the occasional headache and a bit of tiredness, I haven't noticed anything different. To be frank, I'm wondering if they're blowing the whole thing out of proportion.'

'Wouldn't you think they'd be able to tell you something more concrete at this stage!' her mother harrumphed. 'All this "wait and see" stuff is just not fair to anyone. Either they know or they don't know!' Teresa took a sip of coffee, and Abby noticed that her hands were shaking with anger, or was it fear? It couldn't be easy to think that her youngest daughter could end up forgetting everything.

This was something that Abby feared too. After all, it happened to Alzheimer's patients, didn't it? But the doctors had reassured her she didn't have anything like Alzheimer's, and that it was this so-called episodic memory rather than normal day-to-day working memory that would be affected. But how well did they really know that?

Abby sighed. What really terrified her was that there was no guarantee that she wouldn't end up forgetting all the people dearest to her. And to think, she recalled sadly, that she had spent the last year trying her utmost to forget about Kieran. Be careful what you wish for and all that . . .

'What about that other injury, the older one Dr Moroney told us about?' her mother asked then. 'Do you have any idea at all what that might be?'

Abby shook her head. 'None at all. I've been trying to recall some previous circumstance where I might have hit my head or fallen over, but I just can't think of anything.' She smiled inwardly, thinking about Erin's take on this.

'It must be drink-related,' her best friend had insisted, while visiting Abby at the hospital. 'Drink- and stiletto-related.'

It had been quite a while since Abby had been drunk enough to fall over, let alone go out on the town in stilettos! Still, as she couldn't think of any ready explanation, she supposed it was something to consider . . .

'That's a very strange one altogether,' Teresa went on. 'Especially as they seem to think it could affect this later one in some way.'

'I know, but there's not a whole lot I can do about any of it unfortunately. I think I just need to try and get on with my life as normal, otherwise I'll go out of my mind.' Abby grinned then, realising what she'd just said. 'Although I suppose that's part of the problem in a way.' She took a sip from her coffee mug. 'Well, whatever happens, I'll just have to deal with it,' she finished, hoping to allay her mother's worries.

'I really don't know how you can be so calm about it all, though.'

Because I don't want to worry you, Abby said silently. As it was, she was being particularly careful about putting her mind under any strain at all and of course the medication that the doctor had prescribed her also went some way towards maintaining her Zen-like attitude. But instead of confessing her fears, and worrying her mother even more, she now feigned a carefree shrug – something she'd perfected over the months following the break-up.

Just then the telephone rang, and Teresa picked up the portable handset lying on the kitchen table.

'Hello? Yes, that's right. You're there now? OK, just give me one minute and I'll be over. OK. Thanks.' Hanging up the phone, she turned to Abby. 'I told Mary Collins I'd take in a delivery for her and that's them now. Will you be all right here if I pop over and let them in?'

Mary Collins was a good friend and nearby neighbour of

Teresa's and each woman held spare keys to the other's house.

'Of course. You go on. Unless you want me to go with you – do you need a hand taking it in?'

'No, no, it's only a parcel. You stay here and relax, and I'll be back in a jiffy,' she said, putting on a jacket. 'Make a fresh cuppa and go on into the sitting room. *The Afternoon Show* will be on soon.'

Switching on the kettle again, Abby did as she was bid and carried the plate of biscuits into the living room. As she had nothing better to do while waiting for her mother to return, she turned on the television. Nothing but ads, ads and more ads, she thought, looking around for the remote control, which she eventually spied sitting on top of the piano at the far end of the room.

Abby approached the piano, but instead of reaching for the remote control like she intended, she impulsively lifted the lid and pulled out the small stool tucked beneath. Then she sat down and began idly running her fingers along the keys.

Some ten minutes later, Teresa returned from her neighbour's to a house filled with music, and her youngest daughter in front of the piano in the throes of Beethoven's *Ode to Joy*.

'God, it's years since I heard that,' Abby's mother said fondly. 'Actually, it's years since I heard you play at all – we really should get you in front of that piano more often.' Then she turned and went back into the kitchen to make a fresh pot of tea.

Slightly shell-shocked, Abby stayed sitting in front of the piano, her fingers tingling, and not just from striking the keys.

Because as far as she knew, she had never played the piano in her entire life.

'No need to worry, that sounds perfectly reasonable,' Hannah informed her the following afternoon, after Abby had frantically phoned her office for an immediate appointment. She'd been completely upended by the incident at her mum's house, not just by her surprising ability but moreover by the fact that her mother seemed to think that it was nothing out of the ordinary.

'*Reasonable?* How could it be reasonable?' Abby cried, slumping miserably into Hannah's purple armchair. 'I don't remember ever playing the piano in my life!' She shook her head. 'As far as I'm concerned, I don't know how.'

'As far as your *episodic memory* is concerned, you don't know how,' Hannah clarified smoothly, 'because you can't specifically remember learning. Your everyday working memory, on the other hand, isn't concerned with when or how you learnt this particular skill, as it's only responsible for retaining it.'

'I don't understand . . .'

'Forget the head injury for a moment. Let's look at a completely different example. I'm willing to bet that you can't actually remember learning to walk, can you? You can't remember going from crawling on all fours to balancing upright and taking those first steps?'

'Well, no.'

'But yet you still know how to walk, don't you?'

'So far, yes,' Abby muttered wryly.

Hannah folded her arms. 'That's because when it comes to learning a skill, such as walking or playing the piano, episodic memory is responsible for the recollection of "where and when" you learnt it, whereas day-to-day working memory is responsible for the skill itself. The brain remembers the skill but not how you learnt it. Am I making any sense?'

Abby nodded thoughtfully. 'I think so.' Although it was still very scary, at least she was beginning to understand the reasons behind it.

Hannah looked pleased that her patient was following her. 'Working memory is extremely durable, episodic not so much, which is why most of us can't recall learning how to walk or specific memories from early childhood. But in your case, because of the damage to the hippocampus, its durability is even worse.'

'It was so weird,' Abby said, shaking her head at the peculiarity of it all. 'It really was as if I'd been playing the piano all my life. I just sat down in front of it and my fingers seemed to know exactly what to do.'

'That's because they did know, Abby. In a way I'm glad something like this has happened.' When Abby looked at her wide-eyed, Hannah held up her hands in a gesture of apology. 'Forgive me, but what I mean is that it's a useful way to help you understand the nature and extent of your injury.'

Abby didn't know what to think. This was supposed to be a *good* thing? 'Well, I'm sorry, but I just don't share your enthusiasm,' she said flatly. It was really happening, wasn't it? No matter how much she tried to tell herself that the damage might not be so bad, and that she might be OK, there was now no denying that there really *was* something wrong.

'Abby, little things like this will be par for the course from now on,' Hannah said gently. 'Some things you'll notice, others maybe not, but either way you'll need to come to terms with the fact that because of the damage, much of your memory will no longer function the way it used to.'

After a brief pause, Abby sighed. 'Well, as you say, as long as I can live a normal life, I suppose I could put up with forgetting a few small things here and there.' When Hannah didn't reply immediately, Abby's eyes narrowed. 'What?' she asked fearfully. 'What am I missing?'

'Abby, any changes, however small, in the way your memory works merely confirms the damage to your hippocampus.' She paused before continuing. 'I'm sorry, but what happened yesterday is just the beginning.'

Chapter 11

Abby realised that over the last few years she barely had a memory – good *or* bad – that didn't include Kieran. He'd been there for her graduation, smiling proudly along with her parents as she stood on the podium to accept her accountancy qualifications. They'd had their first foreign holiday together, he'd been at her side for Claire's wedding, and also when her dad had suffered a heart attack and died a few years back.

Now, all those wonderful memories were tainted. In fact, *all* of Abby's memories were tainted, so really, what did it matter if she ended up losing them?

'That's such a depressing attitude,' Caroline chided, one evening not long after the incident at her mum's house.

Since the accident, Abby's sister had been unbelievably attentive, to the point that when Abby came out of hospital she'd offered to stay over for a few days to 'look after her'. As having hyperactive Caroline around at the best of times was enough to drive most people insane, Abby had declined.

'To be frank, I think you need to stop moping around and letting this whole thing get you down,' her sister scolded now. 'For goodness' sake, Abby, when's the last time you went out and enjoyed yourself – really enjoyed yourself? It's no surprise you can't find any good memories, because lately you haven't bothered creating any!'

Abby stared, stung by the vehemence in her tone. 'Was I that bad?' she asked croakily.

'Yes!' Caroline exclaimed. 'And I'm sorry, I don't mean to upset you, but I'm your sister and I really think you need to hear this, have needed to hear it for a while, and God knows I've held my tongue long enough.' She looked away, and her voice softened. 'Look, I wasn't going to say anything before, but I really think I have to now. Abs, there's no going back. You need to forget all about Kieran and start getting on with your own life.'

'You think I haven't tried?' Abby cried, wounded. 'You think I've *enjoyed* spending every waking minute of the day thinking about him, and most nights crying over him?' Then she stopped short, realising that she'd just admitted this out loud. God, now Caroline would think she was pathetic, a complete idiot . . .

'Hey, it's OK.' Now Caroline's tone was soothing. 'I can only imagine how hard it's all been for you. But, Abby, the truth is that you haven't really tried to move on. And you refuse to let any of us help you. Erin tells me you're always crying off on nights out, or even small things like a couple of drinks after work. Before this accident, you seemed to spend every waking minute working late in the office, and you hardly saw or spent time with any of us until Mum's birthday. For goodness' sake, Abby, the doctors say you can't go back to work for months yet, and you'll need their approval before you do. You can't spend all that time moping around.' She reached across to hug her, her expression remorseful. 'Abby, I'm sorry and I know you're still hurting, but you have to realise that Kieran isn't coming back.'

'I know,' Abby replied, her heart breaking all over again at having to hear someone say it out loud. 'I know that.'

Releasing her, Caroline sat up straight. 'OK, so here's what I think. And you might think I'm crazy' – she gave her a sideways glance – 'but I reckon that blow to the head might have been a wake-up call, something to remind you how much you're missing out on life. You said yourself that everything in the run-up to the accident isn't worth remembering anyway,' she added lightly. 'So now's the time to do something about that. Let's go out on the town this weekend – just the two of us. We can go out for a nice meal somewhere and have a good old gossip and a bit of craic.'

Abby bit her lip, an all-too-familiar thought intruding. 'Oh, I don't know, Caroline, you know what I'm like with restaurants and everything . . .'

Her sister rolled her eyes. 'Why let a tiny thing like that hold you back? Look, we don't have to go anywhere "weird", just to a normal burger place like Captain America's or something. See, this is a perfect example of what I'm talking about. I don't think this "thing" of yours has anything at all to do with food; I think that you've been falling back on any excuse to prevent you from getting on with life without Kieran.'

'That's simply not true!'

'Are you sure?' her sister said, eyeing her. 'When's the last time you went out somewhere without him? To a movie or a concert, or even as far as a bloody shopping centre! You were so used to being part of a couple it's almost as if you've stopped remembering how to function on your own – and that has nothing to do with your head injury by the way.'

'That's not fair!' Abby exclaimed, hurt.

But of course it was. Caroline's assessment might have been blunt, but deep down Abby knew it was correct. She *had* forgotten what it was like not to be part of a couple. She and Kieran had been with each other so long and done so much together that since the split she'd almost felt as though part of her was missing.

Caroline was right; these days she didn't even go to the supermarket, preferring to order her weekly shop online. And a movie or a concert? Abby wouldn't have the confidence to go somewhere like that on her own, let alone get ready for a night out on the town with anyone other than Kieran. Instead, she'd retreated into herself, stopped enjoying her life, and had put it on hold. And for what? As Caroline had so painfully pointed out, Kieran wasn't coming back. She'd seen that for herself at the wedding.

'You're right,' she said resolutely. 'I'm not going to sit around any longer and let life pass me by. I'm going to go out there and start enjoying it – while I still can,' she couldn't help adding.

'That's what I like to hear!' Caroline grinned. 'To be truthful, I've wanted to say all this to you for a while, wanted to try and buck you up somehow. But at the same time,' she continued gently, 'I know it's been hard.'

Abby gave a watery smile. 'It has, but you're right. I can't keep going on like this. Thanks for being so honest.'

'I'm sorry I had to be. But I couldn't sit by and watch you waste away.'

Well, no more, Abby decided determinedly.

From now on everyone was going to see a *very* different girl to the one who had locked herself away from the world, terrified to experience all it had to offer. From now on Abby was going to forget all about Kieran and her old ways, and instead get out there and grab life with both hands.

A few days later she arranged to meet up with Erin. Her friend had only recently returned from her girlie weekend in Dubai, and as Abby made her way towards their arranged meeting spot – a cosy pub just off Grafton Street – she thought again about how long it had been since they had enjoyed a night out together.

Erin had been trying to arrange something like this for months before the accident, but as usual Abby had come up with a barrage of excuses not to go. Caroline had been right; she was lucky to have any friends left at all with the way she'd behaved over the last while. Since her sister's pep talk Abby had thought a lot about her life and her actions in the run-up to the accident, and she'd realised that even though she'd done her utmost to keep people at bay and out of her life recently, they'd still rallied round in the aftermath of her diagnosis. And she was grateful for that.

So no more hiding away: from now on Abby was going to ensure she saw as much of other people as possible, starting tonight.

She reached the pub, a popular place that also served good (normal!) food and, once inside, saw that Erin had already arrived.

'Hi there,' she said, standing up and giving Abby an effusive hug. 'You look great!'

Abby raised a self-conscious hand to her head, and through her horrible shorter hair. 'I don't think so,' she said softly. Although it had started to grow back, it would likely be years before she could be happy with it again.

'Well, I think it's very trendy,' Erin insisted, evidently trying to make her feel better. 'What'll you have to drink?'

'Just a Coke, thanks,' Abby said, smiling at the lounge girl. 'Doctor's orders, I'm afraid,' she explained ruefully, when Erin looked crestfallen.

'You can't even have one glass of wine or anything?'

'Not for the moment, no.' The doctors had put her on medication for the intermittent headaches she'd been experiencing since the accident, but even so Abby was reluctant to do anything that might adversely affect her senses – particularly after the piano incident. If anything else like that happened, she wanted to be sure she noticed the changes as soon as they occurred.

'Oh, well, you don't mind if I get something stronger?'

'Not at all, go right ahead.'

'OK, I'll have a glass of white wine, then,' Erin said to the lounge girl. 'So how have you been since you got out?' she asked Abby, when the girl had taken their food order. 'Are you feeling OK?'

'I'm OK,' Abby said, not yet ready to confide in Erin about the piano incident. Seeing as her mum had hardly let Abby out of her sight since, she really didn't want someone else worrying and fussing over her. 'I feel perfectly normal.'

Erin looked down and bit her lip. 'Well, I still feel really guilty.'

'Oh, no, please don't.' When visiting her at the hospital, poor Erin had been hugely apologetic, convinced that she was the one who was to blame for Abby's accident.

'But it *was* my fault you were late for work in the first place, wasn't it?' she insisted. 'If I hadn't kept you on the phone, banging on about Dubai . . .'

'Don't be silly. I keep telling you it's not your fault. It's just one of those things, that's all.'

'Yes, but it was my fault you were rushing and—'

'Erin, please don't do that to yourself. It was an accident, nobody's fault. If anything, *I* should have known better than to walk under that ladder. OK, so it might be superstitious but there's also a very good reason for it,' she said with a grin. 'It's just not safe.'

'So how is . . . everything now?' Eric glanced surreptitiously at Abby's head.

'Truthfully? I'm OK.' Abby didn't want to admit that she spent practically every waking moment worrying about it, and every night lying awake and thinking about what else could happen. 'The doctors want me to keep a close eye on my activities from day to day – see if I notice any changes. I don't know what to expect, really.' She tried to sound offhand, unwilling to confess to her friend that she was absolutely terrified of what might happen.

'But you're feeling all right?' Erin probed again.

'Well, I get the odd headache now and again, but other than that I feel right as rain. Anyway, forget about me,' she said, brightening. 'How are things with you? Was Dubai fabulous?' Then she frowned. 'I'm sorry but I have to say you don't look very brown, which isn't like you.' A fervent sun-worshipper, Erin usually turned a deep shade of mahogany following any exposure to the sun.

'Oh, the weather wasn't great, actually,' Erin said dismissively.

'Really? I thought it was always hot and sunny there.'

'So did we,' her friend groaned, before launching into a full-scale report of the girls' recent trip. 'But the shopping was amazing and we spent an absolute *fortune* on clothes and jewellery! We missed you – you would've loved it.'

The two girls chatted easily over the next while, and by the time their food arrived Abby had really begun to relax and enjoy herself. It had been yonks since she and Erin had got together for a natter – why on earth had they left it for so long?

But Abby knew there was only one answer to that. *She* hadn't wanted to face the world, hadn't really wanted to move on with her life. Instead, she'd retreated from everything, and like some weird recluse had refused to confide in anyone just how much she was hurting. But a bump on the head was a pretty good way of waking a person up and reminding them what they were missing, wasn't it?

'Penne all'arrabbiata,' the waitress announced, placing a steaming bowl of pasta on the table in front of Erin, and then a slice of lasagne before Abby.

'Thank you very much,' Abby replied, her mouth watering at the sight of it.

'Parmesan?' the waitress enquired.

'Not for me, thanks,' Erin replied immediately.

'Madam?' She looked at Abby, waiting for an answer.

'I'm sorry – what?' Abby hadn't the faintest idea what the woman was talking about and was vaguely impressed that Erin seemed to.

'Would you like some Parmesan?'

She looked across at Erin, hoping her friend might enlighten her as to what the waitress was saying. What on earth was Parmesan?

'I'm sorry . . . I'm not sure I understand . . .'

Erin glanced across at her. 'Do you want Parmesan on your lasagne?'

She looked down at her plate, feeling very gauche indeed. Evidently Parmesan was some trendy new Italian herb. The last time Abby had been out for a proper Italian meal, sun-dried tomatoes were all the rage, but according to Caroline, were now '*soo* nineties'. Being the furthest thing in the world from a 'foodie', Abby had never been any good at keeping up with that kind of thing. But what the hell, the stuff looked innocuous enough.

'Yes, please,' she said, smiling up at the waitress, who duly sprinkled some of it on top of her lasagne.

Erin seemed surprised. 'Well, *that's* certainly a turn-up for the books,' she said once they were alone again. 'Didn't you say before you thought it smelt like mouldy socks?'

'Did I?' Abby reckoned Erin had to be confusing her with someone else, as up until now, she hadn't a clue that this stuff existed, let alone be able to pass comment on what it smelt like!

'So what else did you get up to in Dubai?' she asked then. Judging by what her friend had told her so far, it seemed she'd missed all the fun.

Chapter 12

Finn was about to begin training a new batch of recruits: his favourite part of the job. The young dog he was working with today, Jack, had a lovely, gentle manner, and was so far responding extremely well to his obedience training. He learnt very quickly, reacted brilliantly to all of Finn's cues and, unlike some other dogs, hadn't batted an eyelid at wearing the harness. That morning alone, Finn had taught him how to walk in a perfectly straight line from A to B, and without any major prompting, Jack had also walked Finn safely around the obstacles placed in his path. It was remarkable progress, and from what he'd seen so far, Finn was hugely confident that Jack would sail through the rest of his training and eventually qualify as a working guide dog.

But shortly after lunch, Finn discovered Jack's Achilles heel. Exposure to distraction was a major part of the process and for this purpose, while the young guide dogs were in training, other breeds were allowed to run freely in the area – dogs who were hugely inquisitive, sometimes aggressive and who loved nothing better than getting close up and confrontational with larger ones. Jack Russell terriers were notorious for this 'in your face' behaviour, and the centre manager's own pet terrier was a perfect example. Small and annoyingly yappy, Rasher loved nothing better than to run up and bark at the training dogs, and do his best to try and distract them. It was the ultimate test of patience for any dog – trainee or not – and the majority, including Jack, passed it with flying colours and, much to Rasher's chagrin, ignored him completely.

For the next challenge, the trainees were introduced to an entirely different animal, one they'd been waging war with since the beginning of time, a relentless battle that over the years had spawned a multitude of cartoons, books and films. Not to mention one that found the prospect of trying to distract the trainees even more of a pleasure than Rasher did.

Let's see how you fare this time, Finn thought to himself, as he once again attached the harness, and he and Jack set out on a supposedly casual walk around the paddock. They'd walked only a couple of yards before the harness went rigid and Jack stopped short quickly, his hackles raised. Then he pulled so furiously on the harness that Finn lost his grip of the lead and Jack bounded off. He didn't stop until he reached the boundary wall, where a black cat was washing herself lazily in the sun. The young dog began barking wildly at the cat, who determinedly ignored him and continued washing herself.

'Jack, meet Sooty,' Finn muttered, his tone filled with disappointment at the dog's reaction.

Despite his earlier promise, Jack would *not* be graduating as a working guide dog. After this, Finn thought sadly, he'd be lucky to get a job at all.

That evening, he relayed the story in full to his dinner companion. 'It's a shame – he is a great dog, and has so much promise too.'

'Really.' Finn's date, Karina, was playing with the stem of her wine glass and, he realised, seemed to be only half listening. OK, so he had probably banged on a little too much about his job, but what did you talk about when you barely knew the person sitting opposite you?

They'd bumped into one another a few times at parties and social gatherings held by Finn's best mate, Chris, so tonight couldn't exactly be described as a blind date, but it might as well have been. Finn didn't know a whole lot about Karina Dowling other than she was single, nice-looking and evidently wasn't all that interested in the ins and outs of guide-dog training.

Then again, why would she be? If Karina had spent the entire date so far going on about her beautician's job, Finn's eyes would probably have glazed over too.

They were in a restaurant in the centre of Dublin called Pepe that Chris had recommended. Finn had asked his mate for advice because for the life of him he didn't know where to go in town these days.

After a stint of travelling and working abroad – mostly in the US – a few years back Finn had decided to come home to Dublin and settle down: at least, that had been the plan. He'd bought his current place shortly after taking up work in the training centre, deciding that a run-down, crumbling old farmhouse in the rural and more peaceful North County Dublin would suit him a lot better than the hustle and bustle of the city centre.

Even though Balbriggan was only a few miles from the city, it might as well have been a completely different country in terms of facilities, and as Finn didn't venture into town all that much to socialise, he found it difficult to keep up with what was and wasn't the city's latest hotspot.

Most of his old mates still lived and worked in the city, and the cosmopolitan lives they led were a million miles away from the quieter, rural pace he preferred. As the only still-remaining unattached male of the group, his friends seemed to think it was their duty to fix him up with various available women, and just didn't believe Finn when he tried to tell them that he was happy enough on his own and, since Danielle, had little interest in a serious relationship.

The place Finn and his latest companion were in now was

supposed to be one of the 'in' places in the city, but Finn had so far found it cold and pretentious. The staff were stiff and condescending, and upon his arrival had looked down their noses at Finn's casual attire of jeans and black short-sleeved shirt. And although he couldn't be absolutely sure, he could have sworn he heard them poking fun behind his back at his wine-tasting. Finn wasn't into all that sniffing and swirling it round in the glass bullshit – in fairness, he wasn't that much into wine at *all*, but Karina seemed to like it, so that was OK with him. In any case, he couldn't imagine a bottle of beer being allowed within ten feet of a place like this, so concerned they'd be that such a populist drink might affect their precious credibility.

'Anyway, how's your starter?' he asked now, deciding to change the subject from dog training.

'It's just delicious,' said Karina. 'The scallops are perfectly cooked, with just the right amount of seasoning, and I'm getting a faint hint of something in the sauce that I think might be cinnamon. Yours?'

Finn gulped and looked down at his fairly ordinary-looking fishcakes. 'They're, um . . . grand,' he said, but Karina was still looking at him, evidently waiting for him to elaborate as if he was some kind of expert. 'They taste . . . very nice.'

'Right. Well, that's good. It'll be interesting to see what the chef does with my main. The last time I had pork in a restaurant like this, it looked and tasted like something you'd get in a pub.' She rolled her eyes. 'Soooo disappointing.'

Finn was wondering why food from a pub was such a terrible thing when in fact pubs usually dished out tasty grub in nice big portions, not like the microscopic servings he saw them putting out on tables here – plates of food so small they wouldn't fill a sparrow, and consisting primarily of scraps of barely cooked meat smothered in blades of green grass. And why did she have to make a song and dance about what the chef 'did' with things? As far as he was concerned, it was just food, not a bloody performance! Sometimes Finn didn't recognise the country he'd returned to while the nation now seemed to have a lot more money, he wasn't entirely sure it was the better for it.

But whatever Karina's choice for the main course, at least he'd played it safe and gone for a nice, juicy sirloin. He'd need one, what with the size of these fishcakes. Each no bigger than a fifty-cent piece, Finn had consumed them in double time, and was looking forward to filling up on meat and veg.

'I just think Dublin restaurants have a really long way to go before they can compete with those in London, don't you?' Karina was saying, and Finn realised that this was the third time in the last half-hour that she'd picked up her bag and started rummaging inside it. The strange thing was that she never seemed to take anything out or put something in.

'What's the matter?' he asked, indicating the bag. 'Have you forgotten something? Do you need a tissue or anything?'

Karina smiled. 'Sorry – I just can't help it. It's Chloé, and it's just sooo soft.'

What? Chris hadn't said anything about her having a daughter. Not that Finn minded or anything, but . . . 'Chloé?'

'Yes. It's the new one. Cost me nearly two grand, but it's worth every penny. Especially,' she continued, her eyes lighting up as she surveyed the room, 'as every woman in this room is going green over it!'

OK, now Finn was *seriously* lost.

'There was a six-month waiting list in BT's. I think Victoria Smurfit got it a day or two ahead of me, whereas Andrea Corr was *miles* after.' She smiled gleefully.

Waiting list? Brown Thomas? What the hell was this woman going on about?

Karina must have realised that the tables had been turned

and it was now Finn whose eyes were glazing over, because she quickly put him out of his misery. 'You know, the new Chloé handbag, *designer* handbag? I can't believe you don't know. I thought *everyone* knew about these; they were on the news and everything.'

Finn couldn't help thinking that he'd probably got side-tracked by some unimportant stuff like the country's growing crime rate or the state of the economy. Bags called Chloé . . . how on earth could he have missed it?

As he watched Karina's self-satisfied expression, he suddenly wanted to bolt from this shallow, over-hyped, pretentious excuse for a restaurant, and run a million miles from his equally shallow and pretentious excuse for a date. What the hell was he doing here, trying to have a conversation with a woman who seemed to value nothing but appearances, and by all accounts seemed to think she was in an episode of some American soap opera?

'Of course I know it's a Chloé bag,' he said, and picked up his wine glass before adding mischievously, 'A good friend of mine got the latest one for her birthday last week.'

Karina's eyes widened. 'You mean the *very* latest one?' This was said with such reverence that Finn nearly choked on his wine, and because he and Karina could just as easily have been talking about alien life forms, he nodded in reply. 'But how? It won't be released here until January!'

Yikes! Finn thought quickly. 'Well, I think her husband picked one up in New York; he goes there on business quite a bit.'

'Lucky cow,' Karina said dreamily, and there was such naked envy in her eyes that Finn felt almost guilty.

'Well, I don't know – maybe it wasn't the new one after all; maybe it's the same one you have. I'm really not sure.'

'No, I don't suppose you would know. Honestly, I really would be very surprised if she's got her hands on the newest design.' She lowered her voice. 'If she has, she really wants to make sure it isn't a fake. You have to be careful with these things, you know.'

Don't I just, Finn thought wryly. By now he was beginning to feel sorry for Karina. What kind of life was this, spending a fortune trying to keep up with the latest fashion must-haves, only to find that there will always be someone who is one step ahead of you, so you'll be forever chasing your tail? Were all women like that these days? Looking about the room, you'd certainly think so. Each and every one of them seemed to be glancing around and had their eye on everything and everyone but their dinner partners.

Finn sighed inwardly. He just wasn't into this any more, and he sorely wished he could go home to the one female who didn't care anything about designer handbags or fancy food and was perfectly happy with a tin of Pedigree Chum! Good old Lucy rarely troubled him, even when he abandoned her to go abroad on training conventions and had to leave her in the care of his dad. And speaking of which, Pat had a consulation with the specialist early the following morning, which was as good excuse as any for Finn to go home early.

Still, seeing as the food in this place cost a small fortune and he was now absolutely starving, it would be almost criminal *not* to stay on and enjoy it, wouldn't it? Just then the waiter arrived with Finn and Karina's main courses. And when he saw that on his plate was a piece of sirloin steak that was no bigger than a golf ball – and covered in that blasted grass – Finn knew for certain that this was turning into the date from hell.

Chapter 13

'You're an auntie!' Caroline cried down the phone.

'What? Claire had the baby?' Abby sat up in bed and checked the time on her bedside alarm clock. It was 6 a.m. but Caroline sounded as though she'd been awake for some time. 'But she's not due for another four weeks!'

'I know, but she went early. Zach just phoned Mum and he's over the moon. It's a girl, and I think they're calling her Caitlyn. And Claire's fine – not a bother on her, apparently. But then again, Zach *would* say that, wouldn't he? He's a man!'

'Caitlyn,' Abby repeated softly. 'That's a really beautiful name. I can't wait to see her.'

'Well, you won't have to wait too long,' Caroline trilled. 'Better get packing 'cos we're leaving on the nineteenth!'

'What?' Abby blinked, unsure if she'd heard right.

'You and Mum are coming with Tom and me to New York to see the newest member of the Ryan family!' When there was no immediate reply, her sister's tone changed. 'What, you don't want to see your one and only niece? And don't you *dare* say a word to me about this "afraid of flying" nonsense – I told you before, it's all in your head.'

Abby gulped. The thought of getting on a plane again was terrifying, particularly when it was such a long flight, but on the other hand, she'd absolutely *love* to see Claire and the new baby. And to think, New York of all places . . .

'I promise you you'll love it,' Caroline insisted. 'Especially this time of year.'

Then it hit Abby what time of year it actually was. 'But
. . . but that'll be Christmas week!' she blurted. 'Even if I
did decide to go, it'll be so busy – there's no *way* we'd get
flights and—'

'Already taken care of,' her sister said blithely. 'Consider
it your Christmas present.'

'What? But I couldn't . . .'

'Of course you could. And quite frankly, Abby, I think after
everything that's happened lately, you could do with a little
break. It's just a shame Dermot's already made plans to go
away with his friends. Anyway, Claire will be over the *moon*
to see us – and you in particular, seeing as you've never been
to her and Zach's.'

'Well, it would be brilliant, but are you sure Claire will
want to see us so soon?' Abby was sure the new parents
would want some quiet time alone with their baby daughter,
and the last thing they'd need was a load of relations arriving
on top of them in their New York home.

'I've already OK-ed it with Zach and he thinks it's a brilliant idea, especially having Mum around to give Claire a
hand.' She sniffed. 'He obviously doesn't think I'd be much
help.' At this, Abby raised a smile. 'But imagine, all us girls
together for Christmas in New York. Abby, it'll be fantastic!'

Her sister's enthusiasm was certainly infectious. Abby
couldn't wait to see her baby niece, and what else would she
be doing except moping around the apartment, worrying and
obsessing about things? The change of scenery might do her
some good, mightn't it?

'I'll pay you back for the tickets—' she began.

'Don't be silly. I told you – it's your Christmas present.
Anyway, I put them on Tom's Visa, so he's paying for them
really.'

Whether he likes it or not, Abby thought, smiling. 'Well, I
owe you both one, anyway.'

'Honey, you owe me nothing. So, I wonder what Caitlyn's like,' her sister went on, chattering a mile a minute. 'I do hope she hasn't inherited the Ryan temperament. Otherwise our poor sis will seriously have her work cut out for her!'

'Christmas in New York, how lovely!' Hannah enthused.

Abby hadn't been sure if the psychologist would have reservations about her travelling so far (and in truth she had half-hoped Hannah would – it would certainly get her off the hook in terms of flying at least!), but it seemed not. 'Yes,' she replied with a watery smile.

'You don't sound too enthusiastic about it,' the other woman said, a question in her voice.

'Well, it's really the flying part I'm not enthusiastic about.' Abby went on to explain all about her previous flying experience. 'Kieran really hated it.' She shrugged in conclusion.

Hannah was silent for a moment. 'Kieran is your ex-boyfriend?'

Abby squirmed, annoyed with herself for being stupid enough to even raise the subject. 'Yes, we broke up about a year ago.'

'That's a shame.' It was obvious from Hannah's sympathetic expression that she could tell Abby wasn't the one who had initiated the split. 'Were you two together long?'

'Almost five years, but it's fine – I mean, I'm fine.'

'I see.' But again she could sense that Hannah knew well she was the furthest thing from fine, but in fairness she didn't push it. 'So what do you think he would make of all this – your injury, I mean?'

Abby brow furrowed. She wasn't entirely sure what Kieran would think about it all. For one thing, he *hated* hospitals and had always been hugely uncomfortable around illness in general. Even if Abby was sick with a heavy flu or a tummy bug and had to spend a few days in bed, she always got the feeling she was letting him down somehow, that all this lying around was in his eyes overdramatic and unneccessary. But then of course if *he* happened to get sick . . . well, that was a different story altogether!

No, Kieran probably wouldn't be the best person to have around just now, Abby admitted. It wasn't that he was unsympathetic or anything: he just found these things difficult to handle. But of course she wasn't going to admit this to Hannah. And wasn't it a pointless question in any case?

'Well, not that it matters, but I think he'd be a great support,' she lied. In truth, if Kieran was still in her life now, she thought sadly, her injury would probably have been the straw that broke the camel's back.

'Yes, from what you've told me about your holiday, it seems he had quite a . . . strong personality.'

Despite herself, Abby chuckled. That was an understatement! 'Yes, I suppose you could say that.'

Hannah looked to be on the verge of saying something else, but apparently decided against it. Abby suspected that the psychologist couldn't help but want to dig deeper into her state of mind after the break-up, but had to remind herself that this wasn't the reason she was here. Abby was relieved: the last thing she wanted was an interrogation about Kieran, particularly when she was trying her utmost to put all of that behind her.

'So, the Big Apple, then,' Hannah said, evidently deciding to move on. 'I'm quite jealous, actually. But, no, I'd have no problem at all with you travelling. In fact, I think it might do you the world of good.'

To Abby's huge relief, and despite her nerves, the flight to New York wasn't that bad at all, which might have something to do with the fact that (unlike the last time) her companions didn't seem the slightest bit stressed or worried about it.

In fact, there was a bit of a celebratory aspect about the journey, helped no end by Caroline's insistence on ordering a bottle of champagne for everyone once the plane was airborne. Abby had read somewhere that you shouldn't drink alcohol while on a flight (or was it Kieran who'd told her?) so at first she was a little unsure about accepting, but she didn't want to appear the party pooper, particularly when the rest of the family – even Teresa – were happily swigging it back. The doctors had finally lifted their alcohol ban, and Abby had to admit that the few sips she'd taken had really relaxed her.

So by the time they landed at JFK, she couldn't quite understand why she'd been so nervous about it all before, when – as Caroline had insisted repeatedly on the way to the airport – there really was nothing to it. But perhaps the pilots on the long-distance flights were better qualified, and the bigger planes safer. Either way, Abby was glad they'd made it to New York in one piece!

Now on solid ground, she stared out of the car window, trying to take it all in. The city was incredible – like something from a dream, completely out of this world. Zach had met them all at the airport, and as he drove them from JFK, she couldn't help thinking how everything looked like it was straight out of a movie set.

If *this* was anything to go by, Abby was unlikely to forget her first experience of New York in a hurry. The place was magnificent, awe-inspring and totally *un*forgettable. But, boy, was the weather cold! Caroline, who was a veteran of New York winters, thanks to her regular shopping trips, had warned Abby and Teresa to bring warm clothes, but in truth Abby had been expecting temperatures similar to those back home. But this was something else! As their car navigated the city streets, she could see steam rising from the subway air vents on the pavement and then almost immediately fall to the ground as ice crystals. She shivered.

'I told you it would be cold,' a fur-encased Caroline grinned beside her.

Back at Dublin Airport, Abby had had to laugh at the sight of her sister and Tom, who she thought looked like a couple of grizzly bears, what with Caroline's full-length faux fur and Tom's heavy fleece-lined jacket. Now who was laughing?

'I hope to God you have the heating on full blast at home, Zach,' Teresa said through chattering teeth. 'This place is like Siberia!'

But despite the cold, Manhattan looked like something out of a fairy tale – its streets were ablaze with sparkling trees and fairy lights, and as they made their way along in the car, Abby marvelled at the way the white lights glittered in the darkness and cast a magical glow on to the pavements below.

Their route towards Claire and Zach's apartment took them past the giant snowflake decoration at the corner of Fifty-Seventh and Fifth Avenue, which Abby had seen a million times on TV and in magazines, but in reality she couldn't get over its immense size. And as she craned her neck upwards for her first proper look at the Empire State Building, and saw its lights change from green to red, she realised that the famous landmark – like the rest of the city – was all dressed up and ready for the holiday season. She'd never seen anything like it.

'Wow, it's absolutely breathtaking, isn't it?' she gasped, completely overwhelmed by the beauty of it all.

'You think this is something – wait till you see the Rock-efeller tree,' Zach commented from the front seat. 'And Park Avenue looks kinda hot this time of year too. Maybe we should swing by there on the way . . .'

Teresa looked at her son-in-law in horror. 'Zach, to be honest, the only "hot" I'm interested in at the moment is a nice cup of tea,' she said, her tone brooking no nonsense.

'So forget about showing us the bloody Christmas lights and get on with showing me my only grandchild!'

Some thirty minutes later, they reached the apartment on the Upper East Side, where a beaming Claire greeted their arrival, a sleeping baby in her arms. Little Caitlyn was beautiful, as indeed, Abby thought, was Claire. Her sister, although obviously tired, glowed with health, and her eyes shone with pride as she presented her baby daughter to her family.

'She's so like you,' Abby whispered, gently stroking the baby's soft skin, 'and there's a bit of Dad in her too, I think.'

'I thought so too!' Claire was pleased. 'What do you think, Mum?'

'She's a little stunner, that's what she is,' said the proud grandmother, her eyes glistening with delighted tears. 'And, yes, she has your father's stubborn-looking chin, I suppose.'

The girls laughed.

'I just can't believe how quickly all of this has happened,' Abby gasped when they'd removed their coats and were settled inside Claire's warm and cosy living room. 'It seems no time at all since we first found out you were pregnant and then all of a sudden she's here!'

Claire reddened. 'Well, I didn't want to jinx anything, you know.'

'I do.' Clearly she'd embarrassed her sister, so Abby tried to make up for it by praising the apartment. 'Wow, this place is great – so huge!'

'Well, we'll have to start looking for something bigger soon, or think about a move out to the suburbs, won't we, Zach?' Claire teased. Her husband, a born-and-bred Manhattanite, didn't seem too enamoured of the idea.

'Not on my watch,' he muttered darkly, and again everyone laughed.

'So how was "it"?' Caroline asked later, when they were

all settled and little Caitlyn was back sleeping in her cot. She squirmed. 'Never again, I suppose?'

But instead of agreeing enthusiastically, Claire simply smiled and shook her head. 'It was the most unforgettable experience of my life.'

'Well, I know *that*.' Caroline rolled her eyes. 'No woman forgets *that* – unless they get whacked on the head by something,' she added jokingly, but almost immediately her face went white. 'Oh, God, sorry, Abby,' she gasped, realising she'd put her foot right in it.

'It's fine.' Abby was completely unperturbed.

'Oh, yes, of course!' Claire cried, turning to her youngest sister, suddenly remembering too. 'How are you? You look so well I'd almost forgotten ... Oh, bloody hell ... I mean ...'

'It's OK.' Abby couldn't help but smile at both her sisters' unfortunate choice of words. 'And I'm good ... I think.'

Out of the corner of her eye, she saw her mother watching her closely. Teresa had been treating her with kid gloves over the last few weeks, especially since the piano incident.

'I'm grand, honestly,' she insisted to Claire, feeling uncomfortable that she'd suddenly become the topic of conversation and had dragged down the celebratory mood. 'It was a bit of a shock to the system and I think we can safely say the hospital won't win any prizes for hairstyling, but, hey ...' She tried to feign an indifferent smile. 'Anyway, enough about me; tell us more about how you're getting on with Caitlyn.'

As Claire evidently knew better than to push the topic, and Abby was determined not to dampen the mood, they left it at that. Instead, she sat back and listened to her sister discuss in long and loving detail what she considered the most unforgettable experience of her life.

Chapter 14

'So, tell me really, how have you been?' Claire asked Abby the following morning. Jet lag had woken Abby in time for Caitlyn's early-morning feed, and she and Claire were having coffee in the kitchen.

'I'm grand, honestly,' Abby replied, and had to laugh when Claire raised an unconvinced eyebrow. She always could read her like a book. 'OK,' she admitted bashfully, 'I'm finding a couple of things hard – not so much the injury, but more the uncertainty of it all.' She went on to tell Claire all about her surprising piano-playing abilities. 'I had absolutely no recollection of ever learning,' she said, shaking her head in bewilderment, before filling her sister in on Hannah's explanation for it. 'But worst of all, because it happened right in front of Mum, she can hardly let me out of her sight now.'

'I'd noticed that, actually,' Claire said wryly. 'Ever since you guys got here, she's been watching your every move. It's understandable, though – while we're all concerned about you, for Mum it's got to be ten times harder.' She smiled softly. 'I'm only getting an inkling of what it must be like myself now. If anything happened to Caitlyn, I'd go out of my mind with worry.'

'I understand that, and I don't blame her, but all this over-protectiveness is really starting to stifle me a bit. Honestly, Claire, she's been by my side every waking moment over the last few weeks, and she's trying to persuade me to move in with her so she can keep a closer eye on me. Don't get me wrong, she's been a brilliant help, but by treating me with kid gloves it's like she's making a much bigger deal out of it all, whereas I just want things to be as normal as possible.'

'Well, it certainly must be difficult for you to try and take your mind off the whole thing if Mum is watching your every move, waiting for something else to go wrong.'

'Exactly.' Abby was glad her sister understood, and was relieved that she didn't think she was being unreasonable or, worse, ungrateful. 'I suppose now I just want to move on, and if anything else happens, well, I'll just have to deal with it then.'

At this Claire gave a watery smile, and Abby suspected that her sister was probably wondering the very same thing as herself: what exactly *would* happen to her in the future, and more importantly, was she really sure she would be able to deal with it?

Over the next few days, Abby and her mother spent lots of time with Claire and the baby, while Caroline spent her days shopping, often leaving poor Tom alone at the hotel to entertain himself.

On the fourth evening of their visit, Claire urged Abby and Teresa to follow Caroline's example. 'You're in New York and it's Christmas! Don't feel as though you have to hang around here with me all day tomorrow too. The two of you should go out and do some shopping, or go see the sights.'

'You must be joking!' Teresa scoffed. 'There's no way I'm traipsing around in that kind of cold. Anyway, to be truthful, I really can't be bothered. It could be some time until I see my only granddaughter again and I want to spend as much time with her as possible.' She looked at Abby. 'You should, though. Caroline told me she's heading out to Woodbury Common tomorrow. Why don't you join her?'

'Do!' Claire insisted. 'I'm sure Caroline would love some company.'

The thought of trekking an hour or so upstate to visit a designer-outlet mall didn't appeal to Abby in the slightest. Why travel all this way to end up in the same old places selling the same old things? It seemed such an awful waste when there was so much else to see and do. OK, so the department stores such as Macy's and Saks were New York destinations in themselves, and Abby wouldn't mind taking a look at their Christmas window displays, but unlike her spendthrift sister, she just had no interest in the stores' actual contents. And as tomorrow was Christmas Eve, Abby had to admit she would like to do something a little more interesting.

'Well, I think I'd like to do a bit of exploring around the city, actually,' she told them. 'Don't worry – I won't go far,' she added quickly, seeing her mum's alarmed expression.

'I just don't like the idea of you wandering around a strange place on your own, Abby. What if something happens . . . ?'

'Mum, she'll be fine,' Claire said firmly, and Abby gave her a grateful smile. Clearly her sister had taken on board her concerns about Teresa's overprotectiveness and agreed that this would be a perfect opportunity for her to get some much-needed time on her own, away from her mother's worried gaze. Seeing as she'd never been in New York before and might not get the opportunity again, a few hours by herself in the city that never sleeps sounded like absolute heaven!

'So that's settled, then,' Claire continued. 'We'll all do our own thing tomorrow and then meet up back here in the evening for a nice family dinner before heading on to St Pat's Cathedral for midnight mass. How does that sound?'

'Absolutely perfect,' Abby replied with a grin.

On Christmas Eve morning, Abby woke up early, eager to get going. It was a bright, crisp but, again, startlingly cold day so she made sure to wrap up well. Having borrowed a beautiful and wonderfully warm cream-coloured duffel from Claire, and teamed it with her own red woolly hat and matching scarf and gloves, she felt and looked suitably Christmassy as she let herself out of the apartment and headed south towards Midtown.

Although it was desperately cold, there really was a magical feel about the place at this time of year, and the neighbourhood was festooned with Christmas finery. Wreaths hung above brownstone doorways, and pine boughs wound luxuriously round wrought-iron fences. As Abby neared the shopping district, she spotted Santas on almost every corner and heard Christmas music ringing out from all directions, while shoppers bustled in and out of nearby stores and markets.

This was what New York was really about and, despite the cold, was much preferable to being cooped up in a centrally heated department store, aimlessly seeking out bargains that would probably never even be worn! No, this was pretty special, she thought, darting out of the way of a deliveryman carrying a consignment of what looked like freshly baked bagels into a nearby café. Abby's stomach rumbled, reminding her that she hadn't yet had breakfast, and seeing as the café looked nice and warm . . .

A minute later she was sitting at a table trying to choose from the café's mouth-watering menu – raspberry or pumpkin waffles, cranberry and pear bread pudding, omelettes, bagels and a whole rainbow of different-flavoured muffins. While normally she'd baulk at such an unusual selection of food, today she was fully determined to throw herself into the New York experience. To hell with it, for once she was going to order something more interesting and exciting than just plain old bread rolls and coffee!

Eventually, choosing French toast covered with chocolate, pistachios and strawberries, Abby spent a pleasant half-hour eating, drinking coffee and watching the world go by from her window seat. It was absolute bliss, and she couldn't remember the last time she'd enjoyed herself this much.

It struck her again how much she'd withdrawn from life in the aftermath of the break-up, and how much she'd closed herself off from everything. When was the last time she'd spent a morning in Dublin like this, sauntering along Grafton Street, or O'Connell Street without a care in the world?

Tearing herself away from the warmth of the café, Abby decided to head along Fifth Avenue, hoping to soak up the festive atmosphere and take a look at some of the department stores' world-famous window displays. She marvelled at how creative and wonderfully magical the exhibits were, especially the Christmas angels at Bergdorf Goodman, but all too soon the incessant crowds became difficult to handle, so instead Abby decided to head for quieter surrounds. She left the busy shopping area and continued walking along the avenue for a while before eventually reaching Central Park South.

The tourist carriages were lined up outside the entrance, the horses dutifully waiting for their next passengers, and while the notion was tempting, particularly after all the walking she'd done that morning, Abby decided against taking a trip on one. There was just something a little depressing about doing something like that on her own, wasn't there? Horse and carriage rides around Central Park were the preserve of couples on a romantic Christmas break here, not for sad singletons like her. Not that she felt sad at the moment – this had been one of the nicest days she'd experienced in ages, and rather than let such thoughts get her down, they made her doubly determined to enjoy it even more.

But first, she thought she'd find some lunch to take into the park, sit on a bench and just take it easy for a while, maybe do some people-watching while she was at it. Buying a sandwich from one of the coffee stands near the entrance, Abby went inside the park and found an unoccupied bench near the lake. She sat back, sipped her coffee, and allowed herself to simply relax and take it all in. This place really was a haven from the hustle and bustle of the city streets, and although the park was a hive of activity, with joggers, walkers and tourists out enjoying the open space, the lake and woodland areas were a peaceful contrast to the frantic commercial activity outside.

She could see why New Yorkers loved the park and why it was so important to them, but at the same time, she hadn't anticipated its sheer size, or the strangeness of having such a huge green area amid all these soaring skyscrapers. As Abby struggled to open the packaging of her sandwich through her heavy woollen gloves, she realised she'd attracted the attention of a couple of nearby grey squirrels, who, evidently sensing the promise of food, were now gathered cheekily at her feet. One squirrel in particular seemed especially interested in her lunch, as he sat on his hind legs and focused his shiny eyes on her, his bushy tail twitching from side to side.

'Go and get your own,' she scolded him, tickled by his bravery. 'Or even better, go and find some nuts for yourself!' She looked to the side and reddened, realising that while she was wrestling with her sandwich wrapper, someone else had sat down on the same bench. And here she was yabbering away to the squirrel like an eejit!

'Yeah, Phil here,' she heard the man say into his mobile phone. She breathed a slight sigh of relief when she realised his attentions were obviously elsewhere. 'No, I'm still here. Bloody flight got cancelled . . . Yeah, I'm booked on a late one, much later tonight, though. Sorry, I hate to do this to you – especially today. No, it's not fine, but what can you do?'

Abby tried not to listen in, but she couldn't help it. He seemed pretty annoyed and she supposed she couldn't blame him. Having your flight cancelled on Christmas Eve sounded like an absolute nightmare. She'd become so focused on what the guy was saying that her concentration had strayed completely. The squirrel at her feet saw his chance, and before she realised what was happening, he'd hopped up on to the bench and snatched away her sandwich.

Abby's eyes widened. 'You divil!' she cried, amazed at the departing squirrel's brazenness.

'Cheeky little fellows, aren't they?' the man beside her said, putting his phone into his pocket.

Abby turned to look at him, completely bemused. 'You saw that?'

'Yep,' he said, his eyes shining with amusement.

'I can't believe they could be so brazen! I didn't even know they could *do* that.'

He shrugged in the manner of someone who was well used to the squirrels' antics. 'They've been known to – especially around here.'

He's probably a local, Abby thought, although it was difficult to tell from his accent.

'I suppose they're so used to being fed by tourists that they start to expect it, and if they don't get it, they help themselves.' Then he smiled. 'Something similar happened to me one time in Thailand, except this time it was monkeys doing the stealing.'

'Really? What did they take?'

He chuckled again. 'Well, it was my own stupidity, really. I was in a touristy spot, and I decided to go to a shop nearby and buy them some bananas. While I was there, I bought myself a couple of snacks – crisps, chocolate, that kind of thing.' He smiled at the memory. 'So I came out of the shop and held out the banana to a little monkey standing watching me, but this guy had *no* interest in bananas. Nope, he was much more into my bag of snacks, and before I knew it, he'd reached up and grabbed the lot!' He chuckled in admiration. 'Leaving me standing there open-mouthed with the banana.'

Abby laughed too. 'Good to know that these kind of things don't just happen to me, then,' she said with a groan.

He's nice, she thought, childishly pleased at the unexpected encounter. Not to mention *very* cute, in that clean-shaven American kind of way. He looked to be about the same age as she was, possibly a bit older, and had dark but rather unkempt-looking hair, a strong jaw-line and striking deep mahogany eyes. Woven into all of this was a gentleness that put Abby at ease. She liked the way he'd just started chatting out of the blue like that too – it wasn't something she'd expected in such a huge city, but perhaps it was so huge that people found it easier to talk to strangers, safe in the knowledge that they'd probably never see the other person again. But she had to smile at the mention of Thailand, considering that not too long ago she'd been bemoaning the country's food.

'Is Thailand nice?' she asked.

'Amazing,' he replied with a shake of his head. 'I keep promising myself I'll go back, but I just haven't got round to it.'

Abby understood. There were lots of things she too wanted to do, and funnily enough, since she got here she'd been thinking about them more and more. This was the first time she'd been outside Ireland since that disastrous holiday to Spain, and it was wonderful. Why didn't she do more things like this?

'Vietnam was great too – really friendly people,' he continued. 'Actually, most of Asia was great.'

'You've obviously travelled a lot,' Abby said, surprised to find herself feeling a little jealous.

'I used to – back in my younger days,' the man replied with a wistful sigh. 'Let me see, I've been to Australia, Asia, most of America, Canada, all over Europe . . .' He counted off each place on his fingers.

Abby was impressed. 'Wow, you really *have* travelled!' she said, again feeling very unadventurous and provincial by comparison.

'Not lately, unfortunately,' he added, grimacing. 'These days duty calls, I'm afraid. Family, work – you know the story.'

She nodded. 'I know.' But the truth was, she *didn't* know. For some reason, she'd never been bitten by the travel bug – well, actually she did know the reason, and it was mostly because Kieran never liked going outside of Ireland. And of course the one time they *did* try had ended in disaster, so who could blame him?

Then the man sat forward and looked at his watch. 'Speaking of duty . . . I'd better get going.' He stood up and put his hands in his pockets. 'It was nice meeting you.'

Abby smiled. 'You too.'

'Hope you enjoy the rest of your day, and don't let any more of those squirrels get the better of you,' he said with a wink.

She grinned. 'They certainly will not – I have their number now! Although I suppose I'd better go and get myself another sandwich,' she groaned, realising that she was still hungry.

'You should try the Boathouse over there,' he said, pointing to a building in sight of the lake. 'I'm meeting a friend for lunch there now. It's warm, they do great coffee, and even better, there are no squirrels.'

'Sounds good. Thanks for the tip.'

'Well, enjoy your day. Oh, and I almost forgot,' he added with a grin, 'merry Christmas.'

'Same to you,' she replied, giving him a friendly wave as he walked away further into the park.

Chapter 15

Abby remained sitting on the bench for a little while longer after the man had left, smiling to herself with pleasure at this unexpected encounter. But it was starting to get pretty cold and she really did need to think about finding something else to eat. Abby considered his recommendation of that Boat-house place. The thought of somewhere cosy and warm appealed enormously.

She got up and headed in the direction the man had taken a few minutes before. Just ahead on the lakeside, she spied the place he had been talking about. It must be really beautiful in the warmer months, she thought, approaching the restaurant. With its picturesque lakeside location, formal gardens and fountains, all framed by towering trees and skyscrapers, the place was a welcoming sight. Some hardy diners were sitting outside on the terrace watching the rowing boats, gondolas and the occasional duck or swan drift by on the lake, but Abby was starting to shiver now and hurried inside.

The café area was busy, and to her utter dismay, there were no tables free. So much for a cosy corner . . . But then, just as she was about to leave, out of the corner of her eye she saw someone waving in her direction. As she turned to look, she realised it was the guy from the bench.

'Hello there,' he said, when Abby approached him. 'Took my advice, then?'

'I had no choice – I had to get out of this cold,' she said, teeth chattering.

'Well, feel free to sit here. There's plenty of room, and to be honest, I'd enjoy the company. My friend just cancelled lunch. Some work thing, apparently.'

Abby started to say no, but then decided against it. What harm could it do? He was a nice guy, there were no other seats, and it really *was* freezing outside. 'You're sure you don't mind?'

'Not at all. What can I get you?' He signalled to the waitress.

'Oh!' Again Abby was taken aback at his friendliness. 'A coffee would be great, thanks.'

'I'm having a tuna sandwich too. Do you want one, seeing as the little guys did a job on your old one?'

'Um . . . yes, that would be great,' she said, removing her things and hanging them on the back of the chair.

They chatted easily for a few minutes while waiting for the food, Abby marvelling at how easygoing he was, and wondering what kind of strange liberating effect New York was having on her that she'd ended up chatting and having coffee with a total stranger! While a small part of her worried that he could very well be some weird psycho, she really didn't believe this to be the case. He seemed so friendly and normal that Abby soon found herself relaxed and enjoying his company. In any case, at least they were in a public place.

'This is nice,' she commented, looking around the restaurant.

'It's great – especially in summer – and you should really try eating out on the deck sometime.'

Definitely a local, she thought, but didn't want to ask for fear of appearing rude.

Introductions were soon made, although Abby didn't like to admit that she already knew his name was Phil from earwigging on his telephone conversation earlier. Then their drinks arrived and Abby cupped her hands round her coffee in the hope of warming them up.

'So you said it's your first visit here?' he said, and she nodded, explaining about Claire and the new baby.

'Are you here long?'

'Just a few more days unfortunately. We go back on St Stephen's Day – the day after tomorrow.'

Phil bit into his sandwich. 'Short stay, then.'

'More's the pity,' she groaned. 'I had no idea there was so much to this place, so much to do. I don't think you could see it all in one lifetime, let alone a single visit.'

'I know what you mean. Every time I come back I find something I haven't seen before.'

'What?' Abby's head snapped up. 'I assumed you were from here.'

'You mean you don't recognise the accent?' he chuckled. 'Well, OK, maybe there is a bit of a twang from when I lived here before, but I'm Irish – same as yourself.'

'Oh!' Abby laughed at herself, and was amazed to discover that not only was he from Ireland but also from Dublin, and was over on business.

'I was due to fly out this morning, only the bloody flight got cancelled. Luckily enough, I got another one going out tonight, but I figured there was no point in sitting around the airport all day; I might as well come back and kill a few hours here – seeing as it's Christmas Eve and all that.'

'It's an incredible city,' Abby said, shaking her head in wonder. 'I really don't want to go home now, not when there are so many things I want to see and do – especially this time of year.'

'Like what?' he said, drinking from his coffee.

'Well, you know, see all the Christmassy things, like the Rockefeller Christmas tree, Macy's window . . . What?' she asked, seeing him grimace.

'Ah, those are all nice enough, I suppose.' He took a bite out of his sandwich. 'But if you really want to fall in love with the place, you need to see some of the stuff that most tourists don't even know about – *real* New York things.' Then he looked at his watch. 'Tell you what, seeing as you haven't been here before and you won't be for much longer, why don't I take you on a sort of whistle-stop tour – if you're free this afternoon, that is.'

Common sense would normally have told her there was no way she should even *think* about wandering around New York with some stranger, but today was all about getting out and exploring new things, so Abby decided why the hell not? It sounded like fun – something she was sorely in need of these days.

'I am free as it happens,' she told him, 'but I'm due back around seven for a family dinner. What about you, though? I don't want to put you out or take up too much of your time.'

'Believe me, I'm only trying to fill time. And seeing as my mate cancelled lunch . . .' He rolled his eyes and took another sip of coffee. 'Putting it mildly, today hasn't worked out well for me so far, so I'd be only too happy to wander around the sights with you, if you don't mind the company.'

'I'd be delighted,' Abby said, meaning it.

Finishing lunch, they left the park via Park Avenue and headed south for a while, Phil leading the way and keeping up a seemingly endless stream of chatter and pointing out various sights and interesting bits and pieces of Manhattan-related trivia as they did so.

'Did you know that it took seven *million* man hours to built that?' he said, pointing to the Empire State Building, which was easily visible above the other skyscrapers. 'And fifty-seven thousand tonnes of steel.'

'Cool.' While the facts were amazing, it was the thought

of all those men balancing so high above the streets on nothing but girders that really took Abby's breath away.

Seemingly determined to slot into his tour guide role, Phil followed this up with an equally detailed analysis of the construction of the Chrysler Building, before eventually they ended up outside a large ornate building, which at first Abby didn't recognise.

'What's this?' she asked.

'You don't know?'

Abby looked up at the clock surrounded by statues and sculptures, and at last the penny dropped. 'Grand Central Station?' she gasped excitedly, again having seen this building a million times on TV, but still it was no substitute for the reality.

Phil smiled. 'Grand Central *Terminal,* to give it its proper name, but, yeah, you're right. Will we go in?'

Abby briefly wondered if he was planning on taking her somewhere on a train, but he quickly allayed her concerns: 'There's something here I think you'll like.'

Going inside, they passed through the building's main concourse, which was packed with people dashing to and fro and up and down the escalators, and navigating the building at record speed. Enthralled, Abby gazed open-mouthed at the stunning marble staircase, huge chandeliers and immense arched windows. In the centre of the building stood the marble and brass information booth and its famous four-faced clock – another instantly recognisable New York icon.

She followed Phil's lead out of the way of the frantic commuters and stood alongside him against a nearby wall.

'Let's just wait here for a minute,' he said, glancing at his watch.

'OK.' Abby was silent, wondering what on earth they were waiting for. A few seconds later, she found out. Seemingly out of nowhere, there came a blast of classical music, and seeing

Phil look upwards, she followed his gaze and for the first time noticed a magnificent blue and gold mural of constellations spread out over the ceiling.

'Wow, look at that!' she gasped, realising that some kind of laser light display had just begun; its multicoloured lights and different shapes moving across the ceiling in tandem to the music. A delighted thrill ran up her spine. She and Phil stood watching the fantastic show, while all around them seasoned New York commuters continued to hurry to and fro.

'That's incredible,' she enthused, when the display finished and the music stopped. 'How did you know?'

He grinned. 'I thought you might enjoy that. They do it here every half-hour at Christmas to different pieces of music.'

'Wow, it's amazing.'

'It is, but it isn't what I brought you to see. Still, while we're here, do you notice anything strange?' he asked, looking upwards again. 'Strange about that mural?'

Abby's brow furrowed as she peered up at the blue and gold ceiling. 'No – what?'

'Well, you know it's the zodiac?'

Abby hadn't actually, but she wasn't going to admit it. 'Yes, but what's strange about that?'

'Well, the fact that it's back to front for one.'

She looked again. 'Back to front?'

'Yep. Most people reckon it was a mistake by the artist, but the real reason is that he was inspired by a medieval manuscript that showed the heavens as they would have been seen from *outside* the celestial sphere.' He looked at Abby and grinned. 'A present-day Michelangelo, eh?'

Well, that was a mouthful! 'Wow,' she said, unable to think of any other reply. Phil's excited enthusiasm for all these little facts was infectious – and it seemed the supply was endless.

'Notice anything else out of the ordinary up there?' he asked then.

She screwed up her eyes for a better look. 'Other than the back-to-front zodiac and the lasers, I don't think so.'

'How about that little dark-blue patch over there?' He pointed to an irregular-coloured section of the mural on the right-hand side, and as soon as she spotted it Abby couldn't believe she hadn't noticed it before.

'I do see it! And what does that signify?' she asked, knowing that no doubt a ready explanation would be forthcoming.

'Well, when they did the renovation work on it back in the early nineties, they left a tiny patch of the old colour unpainted, as a reminder of how much work was actually done. It's something like eighty thousand square feet in here, so that must have been a hell of a lot of painting.'

'I can imagine.' Abby shook her head in awe. 'But I never would have noticed that if you hadn't pointed it out. Not that I'd have noticed the zodiac being backwards either; I'm no expert on that kind of thing.'

'Well, neither am I – someone else showed it to me – but I have to say I love little bits of trivia like that. It really gives a place character, doesn't it?'

Next, he led Abby downstairs to the dining concourse, and for a moment she thought he was taking her somewhere else to eat. But instead they moved past the various eateries and walked until they reached an area filled with low ceramic arches.

'Right, you stand there for a second,' he said, positioning Abby in a spot alongside one of the arches.

'O-K.' She smiled nervously, unsure quite where this was going, but certainly interested in finding out.

Phil then pointed to another position in the opposite corner of the room. 'Now, I'll stand over there, and when I give you the signal, I want you to whisper something into the corner.'

'Whisper?' Abby giggled at the mysteriousness of it all. 'What will I say?'

'I don't know. Anything you want. Just don't make it

anything *too* private,' he added with a playful smile, leaving her wondering what on earth was going to happen. With that, he hurried off and, a few seconds later, gave her the signal.

Intrigued but unsure what she was supposed to say, Abby took a deep breath and whispered the very first thing that came into her mind. 'Hot chocolate.'

Across the way, she saw Phil smile, lean forward and whisper something into his own corner. And when she heard him reply, 'Hot chocolate? Great idea – let's go get some,' in a voice that was as clear and loud as if he were standing right next to her, she drew back in delighted surprise.

'How on earth . . . ?' Her eyes grew wide, and her smile broadened when he returned to her side.

'Cool, isn't it?' Phil sounded mightily pleased with himself.

'It's incredible!' she said, laughing. 'How do you *know* these things?'

He shrugged nonchalantly, but Abby could tell that he was secretly chuffed by her reaction. 'I just do. Anyway, about that hot chocolate,' he added, giving her a mischievous wink. 'You must have read my mind.'

The evening was just beginning to darken when they left Grand Central Station, but to Abby, this was something that only served to highlight the sheer magic of their next destination.

'So what do you reckon?' Phil said, as he and Abby sipped their takeaway hot chocolates and stared up at the biggest, brightest and most famous Christmas tree of them all.

It was, quite simply, breathtaking. Ice-skaters swirled round the rink beneath it, while shoppers and sightseers stopped to stare and admire. Carol singers serenaded beneath its branches, their voices climbing as high as the shining star on top, and children and adults alike were held rapt by the thousands of fairy lights that blanketed its limbs, glistening like fresh snow in the moonlight.

'It's amazing,' Abby gasped, trying to take in the sheer size of the Rockefeller Center Christmas tree.

While she'd known it would be something special, she hadn't expected a simple tree to provoke such an emotional reaction. Not that there was anything simple about an eighty-foot-high spruce, lit up by tens of thousands of coloured lights.

'What's that statue?' she asked, pointing to a dramatic gilded statue, which overlooked the crowded ice rink. No doubt he would know, Abby thought. When it came to New York, there seemed very little he *didn't* know.

'It's the Greek god Prometheus,' he said easily, before giving her a sideways look. 'I studied a little Greek mythology in college, just in case you're beginning to think I'm some kind of anorak.'

Abby smiled guiltily as she had been thinking just that. 'Well, there's certainly no denying you know your stuff, and I'm really glad I have you as my tour guide.'

Now Phil looked at his watch. 'You said you needed to be back at your sister's place by seven?'

'Yes.' Abby checked the time, and to her surprise, realised that it was now five thirty. With all the walking around they'd done, the afternoon had simply flown by.

'I'll have to head back to JFK myself soon,' he said, 'so let's just do one more thing before we go.'

Abby nodded, happy to let him lead her once again.

Some twenty minutes and a seventy-storey elevator ride later, she was glad she had. The view from the top of the Rockefeller Center was astonishing. Seventy floors up and unobstructed for three hundred and sixty degrees, the breathtaking New York skyline stretched for miles in every direction. There was a panoramic view of Central Park and the northern half of Manhattan, as well as the city's other famous landmarks, including the Chrysler Building, Times Square, the Brooklyn Bridge and the Statue of Liberty. It was the most spectacular and magical view Abby had ever seen, and standing on the observation deck so high above the bustling city, she felt an incredible sense of peace.

The air seemed to tingle with anticipation, and Abby experienced a sense of wonder she hadn't felt since she was a young child waiting for Santa. There was something about this place that did that to you, something about Manhattan that took you back to those enchanting days of a childhood Christmas. Tears came to her eyes as she and Phil stood silently taking in the view, and Abby thought to herself that whatever might be going on in her brain at the moment, and whatever happened in the future, she would surely never, ever forget this.

Eventually Phil spoke. 'Pretty cool, isn't it?' he said softly.

Abby nodded, almost sorry that the spell had been broken. 'It's amazing,' she whispered, turning to look at him. 'Thank you for bringing me here.'

'Are you OK?' he asked, concern in his eyes, which in the dim light appeared almost black.

'I'm fine,' she said, before adding quickly, 'Well, at least I think I am.' Then just as quickly, she shook her head and smiled, unwilling to let thoughts of the future get her down. Especially not now. 'Let's just say that things have been a bit . . . weird for me lately and I really needed this.'

Phil seemed to know not to push the topic further. 'Well, I'm glad you enjoyed yourself,' he said, before turning again towards the vista of the city. 'It's a pretty special place, New York. I've been here many times, yet every time I come back I go away with another great memory.'

Abby smiled wistfully at his choice of words.

'But that's what it's all about, isn't it?' he went on. 'Enjoying life and gathering great memories.'

He was right, she realised suddenly, that expression 'gathering great memories' instantly capturing her imagination.

But gathering memories – at least not any *great* ones – was something Abby hadn't done in a very long time.

She thought back to the way her life had been just before the accident, and how she'd had little to show for it other than heartbreak and misery. Where was all the fun and excitement – where were *her* great memories? But worse, now that she'd realised this, she didn't know if it was too late to get out there and start looking for some. If she did seek out more experiences like this, she might not be able to hold on to them anyway.

Just then, Abby drank in the view from the observation deck as if she might never see it again, the pulsating, glittering city beneath a Christmas Eve sky, unable to imagine how something so wonderful could be forgotten.

No, Abby thought, the realisation hitting her like a bolt from the blue, she was going to beat this memory thing; she *had* to beat it. Because, as Phil had pointed out earlier, what good was life without moments like this?

Shortly afterwards, she and Phil reluctantly returned to ground level, Abby sorry that their enjoyable jaunt around the city had to come to an end.

'I think I'll walk back, actually,' she said, when Phil went to hail her a cab. While she was here she wanted to take in as much of the atmosphere as she could, and even sitting in the back of a classic yellow taxi wouldn't achieve that.

'You will not!' Phil scolded. 'It's not safe to be wandering the streets at night on your own, Christmas Eve or not. But if you insist,' he said, capitulating somewhat, 'then at least let me walk you.'

'But you've got to get back too,' she protested, but he quickly waved her objections away.

'There's loads of time left, and I can easily get a cab afterwards.'

'You're sure?' Despite herself, Abby's heart leapt at the notion of Phil walking her home.

'Honestly, there's loads of time. And it's Christmas Eve for me too, remember, so any excuse at all to stay away from the madhouse that is JFK!'

'Well, OK, then.'

On the way back, and to Abby's utter delight, the two of them came across a street-seller roasting chestnuts. God, this place really was Christmas personified, she thought, while Phil paid the man for a small tub for them to share.

Munching on warm chestnuts, the two of them made their way back along the streets, chatting easily about this and that. Phil was so funny, not to mention *very* attractive, and as she walked alongside him, Abby revelled again in how relaxed and at ease she felt in his company. It was something she hadn't experienced in a very long time, and she was glad that fate – or whatever it was – had arranged their meeting to remind her that despite her recent worries, there was still plenty about life to be enjoyed.

Finally, they stopped outside Claire's building. 'Well, here we are,' Abby said, suddenly feeling a little awkward. 'Thanks for a really brilliant day.'

'I enjoyed it too,' he said, smiling, 'and it was a pleasure showing you around.'

Their gazes met, and as she looked into those incredible, fathomless dark eyes, she realised she was having difficulty catching her breath.

'So, would you like to come in for a while, or . . . ?' she murmured. She knew he wouldn't have the time, but she couldn't think of anything else to say. Let alone the fact that her family would probably go apoplectic at the notion of her bringing home some stranger she'd met in Central Park!

Phil shook his head regretfully. 'Thanks, but I'd really better get going,' he said, his eyes never leaving hers. 'Enjoy the rest of the night – especially St Patrick's. I've been to midnight mass there a couple of times and it really is something special. Oh, and while you're tucking into your turkey, don't forget to spare a thought for me and a hundred others cooped up in some tin can flying somewhere over the Atlantic!'

'I will.' Abby grinned. She figured she'd be sparing more than just one thought for him after this. 'Well,' she said, strangely reluctant to see him leave, 'have a lovely Christmas when you get back home, Phil, and thanks again for showing me around.'

'It was a pleasure. Merry Christmas, Abby.' Then, quite unexpectedly, he reached forward and gave Abby the softest, gentlest kiss on the forehead. The pure tenderness of the gesture touched her more than a kiss on the lips could ever have, and when Phil stepped back, she looked again into those amazing dark eyes and smiled.

'Merry Christmas,' she croaked in reply.

'Oh, and by the way,' he called back, a smile in his voice, before finally retreating into the darkness, 'my name is Finn.'

Chapter 16

'For goodness' sake, where have you been?' Teresa's worried tones assaulted Abby almost as soon as she was in the door of Claire's apartment.

She took off her coat, gloves and scarf, her cheeks flushed and forehead still tingling with the imprint of his kiss, *Finn*'s kiss. Not Phil's, like she'd thought. Abby couldn't believe she'd been calling him the wrong name all day! God, he must have thought she was a right eejit!

'I was out and about,' she replied mildly, although inside she was walking on air.

'You mean you were wandering around the place all day?' Her mother continued her questioning, baby Caitlyn in her arms.

'Yep.' Abby went to say hello to the baby before stepping past her mother and through to Claire's front room, which, like the rest of New York, was looking beautifully sparkly and festive. The dining table was set and decked out in a crisp white cotton tablecloth, upon which sat a gorgeous centre-piece of fresh holly and berries round an elegant gold cande-labra. A selection of black and gold La Maison du Chocolat crackers lay elegantly alongside each table setting.

'Wow, this looks incredible, Claire,' Abby said to her sister, who was bustling in and out of the kitchen getting things ready. 'Can I help with anything?'

'No, it's all pretty much done now,' Claire replied pleas-antly, pausing for a second to look at her. 'Did you enjoy

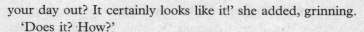

your day out? It certainly looks like it!' she added, grinning.

'Does it? How?'

'Well, your eyes are sparkling and your cheeks are really flushed, although I suppose that could be the cold. Either way, you must have enjoyed it – you were out long enough. So, what did you get up to?' Claire asked, polishing crystal champagne flutes and putting them on the table. 'Actually, no, don't tell me. Everything's pretty much ready to go here, so why don't we wait until dinner to catch up.' She glanced at her watch. 'I hope Caroline and Tom make it back from Woodbury on time – I did tell everyone seven thirty, didn't I?'

Almost as if on cue, there came a high-pitched voice from the hallway. 'Hi, everyone. Santa's arrived!' Up to her armpits with shopping bags of every designer brand imaginable, Caroline bustled into the living room, a beleaguered-looking Tom in tow. 'Guys, we've had the most *amazing* day, and, Claire, you'll just *die* when I show you the baby bling I picked up for Caitlyn. *Fabulous* gold Dior bootees that will look so cute on, and a gorgeous Marc Jacobs babygro . . .'

Abby and Claire exchanged a glance. *Baby bling?*

Abby laughed, thinking that while she'd thought she'd had an interesting day, the evening seemed destined to turn out just as lively!

Dinner was great fun, everyone was on fine form, and the jokes were flying. Abby told the family bits and pieces about her day's adventures, although she decided not to mention anything about meeting Finn. On the one hand, she was afraid that her mother would lecture her about the stupidity of wandering around the city with a stranger ('especially in your condition'), but there was also something so surreal and magical about it that there was a side of her that wanted to keep the majority of it private – especially that kiss.

Caroline was regaling the family with tales of her shopping exploits in Woodbury Common. 'So while I wouldn't normally *dream* of doing such a thing, in this case I think it was worth it.' She went on to explain how she and another shopper had almost wrestled each other to the ground over a handbag they both wanted. Much to her own satisfaction, Caroline had eventually emerged the victor.

Zach shook his head and grinned. 'I really wish I'd been there to see that.'

'I don't know where we got you from,' Teresa tut-tutted, taking another slice of turkey. 'Your father and I certainly didn't raise you to carry on like that.'

'But it was Miu Miu!' Caroline gasped, as if this explained everything.

Abby couldn't help thinking that if her mother was horrified by Caroline's antics, she couldn't even *begin* to imagine what Kieran would think if he'd been here! She was instantly sorry her thoughts had strayed to her ex, particularly when she was enjoying herself so much. And for the first time ever, Abby realised she was actually *glad* Kieran wasn't here.

It was strange, but she hadn't felt so comfortable and easy around her family in ages, and wondered why she'd always shied away from family gatherings. Was it partly because Kieran usually hated those kind of things, so by default Abby had grown to dislike them too? His family were notorious for having arguments that could carry on for ages – sometimes with certain family members refusing to speak to others for years! There'd always been a tension in the Redden household that made visits there uncomfortable, something that Abby realised now had never been the case in her family home. Her dad and Teresa were the most easygoing and welcoming parents around, and always went out of their way to open their home to their children's friends and make any visitor feel at ease. Yet somehow, over the years she and Kieran had rarely accepted Teresa's many Sunday-lunch invitations, as he had mainly preferred that they did their own thing. And since Margaret Redden had never been particularly welcoming towards Abby, they weren't exactly regular visitors at his mum's either.

'It's true what they say about not being able to choose your family,' he used to grunt, and while back then Abby had agreed, now she wondered why she'd ever gone along with this notion. Despite what Kieran had thought, her family were far from being nosy and interfering, and in truth were actually quite good fun.

That evening, just before midnight, they all wrapped up well and made their way downtown to St Patrick's Cathedral. As they entered the magnificent edifice, the first thing that struck Abby was how diverse the congregation seemed to be. Be-suited businessmen and distinguished senator types intermingled with awkward teenage goths, while designer-clad ladies in mink took their seats next to hippies in torn jeans.

It didn't seem to matter who you were or where you were from, and Abby got the sense that even if some of these people weren't regular church devotees, they all intuited that there was something special, something magical about tonight. And as the choir began to sing 'O Holy Night', Abby stole a glance at her family, all kneeling silently together in the pew, and felt a closeness and appreciation for them that she hadn't experienced in a long time.

On Christmas morning, the family were awakened bright and early by little Caitlyn's ear-splitting cries, and when Abby woke up, it took her a few seconds to figure out where she was. When she realised she was in New York with her new niece, it felt like the best present. After breakfast, during which Zach served bucks fizz and Caroline insisted to Claire that the baby should have some too – 'But it's her first Christmas!' – they all got together around the beautifully decorated Christmas tree to exchange gifts.

Seeing as her flight tickets were supposed to have been her sister's Christmas present to her, Abby was taken aback when Caroline handed her a tiny robin's-egg-blue box wrapped in white satin ribbon.

'What's this?' she asked, looking up in surprise.

'What do you think it is?' Caroline replied archly. 'It's your Christmas present of course.'

Abby tentatively opened the package, thinking that her sister had already forgotten about paying for the flights and . . . Then her eyes widened.

'Oh . . .' she cried. Inside the box was a stunning silver link bracelet. Attached to this was a single heart-shaped charm that had some kind of inscription on it. And when upon close inspection Abby read the words on the charm, her hand flew to her mouth: 'Tiffany & Co., New York.' 'Oh, my God . . .' she gasped, hardly able to speak. Only yesterday she had stopped to stare in the window of the world-famous jewellery store, wondering if she'd ever be lucky enough to own something from it. 'This is incredible – truly incredible,' she said, tears forming in her eyes as she reached across to hug her way-too-generous sister.

'You're so welcome,' Caroline said. 'I thought it might be a nice memento for your first trip here. After enjoying yourself so much yesterday, I doubt it'll be the last.'

'God, I feel awful now. I didn't know what to get you.' Abby was horrified, and was now kicking herself for being so unimaginative. As usual, she'd bought each member of her family the obligatory, boring-as-hell gift voucher.

'It's OK,' Caroline waved her Brown Thomas gift voucher in the air delightedly. 'We all know how much you hate shopping, and seeing as I *love* it . . . this is perfect!'

Abby winced, and ran her gorgeous new gift across her fingers. A miserable old gift voucher versus a sterling-silver Tiffany charm bracelet. What kind of sister *was* she?

Soon it was Teresa's turn to gasp as she too opened Caroline's present; this one placed in a Christmas card. 'My goodness, Caroline, Tom,' she said, turning to her bashful-looking son-in-law, who, typically, said nothing, 'this is miles too much.'

'Oh, don't be silly. You deserve it, Mum. But more importantly, what do you think? Do you like it?'

'It's . . .' It seemed that Caroline had once again rendered a member of the family speechless.

'What is it, Mum?' Claire urged. 'What's in the card?'

'Tickets,' Teresa said. 'Tickets to Verona to see a live performance of *Aïda*.'

'Wow, Tiffany bracelets, Italian operas and Baby Dior bootees, you really do have this gift-giving business off to a tee, don't you?' Claire was laughing. 'Fabulous stuff, Car, although it'll make our presents seem very ordinary by comparison, won't it, Zach?'

'Don't be silly.' Abby was quick to reassure her eldest sister, and slightly relieved to discover that Claire's gift was a small white envelope similar to the one she'd given her. Clearly her big sister was a gift voucher aficionado too!

Claire was still talking. 'Now, it's nowhere near as fancy as a Tiffany bracelet, but Zach and I figured it might be something you'd enjoy,' she reiterated as Abby tore open the envelope to find what looked to be a pair of tickets – tickets for a concert to be held back home in Dublin late the following year.

Caroline looked over Abby's shoulder. 'George Michael tickets – fantastic! Don't know why I didn't think of that,' she said, smiling as Abby turned the tickets over in her hand, examining them further.

'Oh, good one,' Teresa said happily. 'Somebody will be very happy with those.'

'So what do you think?' Claire asked, when Abby still hadn't reacted. 'Look, I know it's probably a bit boring, but as you know yourself, that concert sold out in minutes and Zach stayed up all night on the web to get them for you, didn't you?' she added, turning to her husband, who smiled proudly. 'Now, personally, *I* can't figure out why they sold out so quickly' – she laughed wryly and Caroline laughed too – 'but then again, each to her own.'

For a few moments Abby couldn't speak. 'They're wonderful . . . thank you,' she replied, trying to inject the right amount of enthusiasm into her voice, but as Claire's face fell almost immediately, it obviously wasn't quite the right amount.

'You *do* still have a thing for George, don't you?' she asked, frowning. 'I mean, I just assumed that—'

'No, of course I do, of *course* I do!' Abby interjected, reaching across and hugging her sister, all the while trying her utmost to figure out who the hell this George Michael person was, and why her entire family seemed to think she adored him.

When all the presents were opened, Zach gathered the family around the Christmas tree for some photographs.

'I'll email you all copies, if you'd like,' he said, as he took a selection of family poses, as well as various photos of Caitlyn with her aunts, grandmother and mum and dad.

'Sorry, honey,' he said, when his newborn eventually began to tire of her dad's continuous demands and started to get cranky, 'but someday you'll thank me for this when you watch them all back on your memory chest.'

'What's that?' Abby asked, intrigued.

'What, you've never heard of one?'

'You wouldn't have, Abby,' Claire said, before adding wryly, 'It's yet another one of those sentimental American inventions.'

'Hey, don't diss sentimentality,' Zach scolded his wife jokingly. 'Honestly, I don't know where I got my wife. I thought you Irish loved all that kind of stuff.'

'What*ever*!' Claire teased, sweeping out of the room, baby Caitlyn in her arms.

'So what is it?' Abby asked again.

'Aw, it's a kind of interactive program I set up for Caitlyn when she was born. Come into the study and I'll show you. I'll upload these now.'

Abby followed him through to his computer, where he tapped a few keys and brought up a program that was simply headed 'Caitlyn's Memory Chest'.

On the first page was a gorgeous picture of Caitlyn and Claire that looked to have been taken in the hospital not long after she was born. Alongside it were all Caitlyn's birth statistics: weight, length, the exact time she was born . . . even the name of her midwife!

'See – this section records how her growth is progressing from week to week.' Zach pointed to the screen. 'Here we've got photographs like the ones I took today – family celebrations and things like that. It's basically preserving all the things from her first days on the planet, the little things none of us usually remember from that far back, you know?' Then, as if suddenly remembering that Abby's condition meant something very similar for her, he reddened. 'Jeez, I'm sorry, Abby. I hope you don't . . . I just didn't think.'

'Hey, it's OK,' Abby was quick to reassure him. 'I think it's a fantastic idea.'

Rather than being offended or upset by Zach's comments, his idea had intrigued her.

Gathering memories . . .

One of her major worries about losing her long-term memory

was actually very similar to what Zach was describing. Since finding out about the damage, she was terrified she might one day forget things from her past, important things like her family, their names, what they looked like, even what they meant to her. Something like this could very well be the answer to her prayers. She could set up a file on her own computer to collect photographs and maybe record diary entries, things to help her remember the things she enjoyed and loved, just in case such memories were lost to her for good.

She and Hannah had by now discussed this ad nauseum, and Dr Moroney seemed certain that some damage was absolutely inevitable, so instead of sitting around worrying about it all, like Abby had done over the last few weeks, maybe she should think instead about trying to do something to help fight against it.

Now that the idea had come to her, a delighted shiver ran up her spine. Why hadn't she thought of something like this before?

Strangely, this trip had made her view a whole lot of things differently. When she got home, she'd start keeping a diary and taking more photographs, mementos of experiences she wanted to keep. Essentially, Abby was going to take Finn's inadvertent advice and from now on start laying down memories.

'Do you think you could design something like this for me?' she asked Zach, her mind racing as the seed of an idea began to implant itself more firmly in her brain. 'Somewhere for me to store information and photos and stuff before . . .' she paused briefly, struck by her own choice of words '. . . before I forget.'

Chapter 17

In the days since their return from New York, this idea began to develop even further, and Abby got to thinking more and more about what Hannah had said about emotion and memory being so closely related. If there was a real risk of her 'dropping' small and trivial things such as learning to play the piano, then there was a very *real* chance she could end up forgetting even more things as time went by. Unless . . .

The more Abby thought about it, the more it made sense. The incredible, amazing, *unforgettable* time she'd had in New York had simply brought it all home to her. If emotion and memory were so strongly linked, then maybe, just maybe, she could beat this thing! If she spent the next few months of her life getting out there and literally *bombarding* her memory with really positive and exciting experiences, then didn't it stand to reason that they too should be simply unforgettable?

And, she reasoned, her mind racing now, if a negative experience – such as the heartbreak she'd suffered following the break-up with Kieran – could be so strongly imprinted on the brain because of the negative emotions associated with it, then why not the other way round? Abby knew that she'd already wasted too much time sitting around and moping about this; instead, she was going take control.

She decided to broach the subject at her mum's house the following Sunday. It was New Year's Day and the family were meeting up for another celebratory dinner, this time to include

Dermot and make up for his absence in New York. Surprisingly, Abby had really missed having him around during the visit – especially when she'd enjoyed her time with the rest of the family so much.

While she'd always considered him an irritating pain in the backside, she was beginning to see that her baby brother had, almost unnoticed, grown into a mature, responsible adult. He and Kieran had never really seen eye to eye, Dermot's laid-back approach translating into sheer laziness as far as her ex-boyfriend was concerned. 'There's no excuse for him to be still living with Mammy at his age,' he'd insisted, while Dermot was still resident in the family home. At the time, Abby had no argument, but now she wondered if Dermot had stayed on with Mum for that year after their dad's death not because he had nowhere else to go but to give her support. If so, then she'd been blind and very stupid not to understand that before.

Her difference in outlook now, compared to her mother's birthday dinner at the Thai restaurant a few months ago, was startling. While back then she'd been ill at ease, and couldn't help but feel like a complete outsider in her own family, now that she'd spent more time with them she was starting to see things in a brand-new light.

Having spent much of the dinner talking and reminiscing with Teresa and Caroline about the fun they'd had in New York, Dermot eventually had to tell them to stop. 'OK, OK, so I missed all the craic at Claire's,' he groaned. 'Now can you please stop going on about it and making me feel even worse?'

'Sorry, love,' Teresa said. 'We don't mean to make you feel left out, but it was such a lovely trip, and little Caitlyn was so gorgeous.'

This was the perfect opening for Abby to tentatively explain what she'd been considering. 'It really was the best time I've had in years,' she said, her heart thumping and her eyes shining with enthusiasm as she prepared to reveal her plans, 'so much so that it's given me an idea.'

'What kind of idea, love?' her mother replied, putting down her glass.

'Well . . .' Abby went on to explain about baby Caitlyn's memory chest and how she'd asked Zach to design something similar for her.

'That's a fantastic idea!' Caroline enthused, and Abby smiled gratefully at her.

But when she recounted to the family her subsequent train of thought, and her belief that she could beat the memory decline, there was a rather . . . tense silence. Once again Abby felt ill at ease. OK, so she'd expected the family to have some reservations, and perhaps warn her that she shouldn't get her hopes up, but what she hadn't expected was this patent negativity.

'I don't know, it's just I enjoyed New York so much,' she babbled, trying to explain, 'and I'm sure it's something I'll remember for a very long time.' Out of the corner of her eye, she thought she saw her mother and Caroline exchange a glance. 'So I thought that if I actively sought out some other things—'

'Well, what kind of things did you have in mind?' Teresa asked then, putting a forkful of broccoli in her mouth. By her tone Abby knew immediately that her mother didn't share her optimism.

'Well, that's the thing, I'm not entirely sure yet. I was kind of hoping you might be able to give me some suggestions. As I said, I want to get out there and experience some other really . . . memorable things, but now that I've come up with the idea I'm not sure where to start.' While the notion of bombarding her brain with experiences equal to the one in New York seemed fine in theory, discussing it out loud was quite different.

'Memorable things . . .' Dermot mused, scraping his plate. 'Like what?'

Abby shifted in her seat, mortified now. This *was* stupid and maybe she should have thought about it some more before getting carried away like this. Clearly the others thought she was crazy. 'I don't know,' she shrugged, 'interesting things, I suppose.'

Caroline seemed to be thinking it over. 'Tell you what – you should make a list!' she declared suddenly. 'That's what I do whenever I start a project.'

The entire family stared at her, each no doubt trying to remember when Caroline had last completed a sentence, let alone a project.

'When I'm organising my wardrobe, for one!' she supplied exasperated. 'I make a list of the clothes I have, and then the things I need. Then I tick off each item one by one until I have them all, don't I, Tom?' She turned to her husband, who, true to form, nodded in silent agreement.

'A list?' Abby was turning the idea over in her head. It *was* a good idea and it also meant that she'd have a definite plan of action, something to work towards instead of just randomly trying things out. And seeing as the doctors seemed determined to keep her out of work for the best part of a year, it would mercifully give her something to fill her days with other than moping around the flat, depressing herself even further. In Caroline's words, this could be her project.

Teresa began clearing the empty dinner plates. 'Everyone for dessert?' she asked, in what appeared – much to Abby's disappointment – to be a complete avoidance of the subject.

'Yes, and it's New Year's Day too – the perfect time for lists and resolutions!' Caroline insisted, getting carried away by the idea too. 'Oh, it'll be so much fun – let's do it now.' She whipped out her handbag and, with typical enthusiasm, took out a tiny notepad and pen. 'Right,' she said, scribbling down something on the pad. 'What'll be the first thing on the list?'

Dermot nudged his sister's elbow. 'Erm, for one thing it's Abby's list, so don't you think *she* should be the one making it?' he pointed out.

Caroline nodded her head. 'Oh, sure, of course. Silly me. Here you go.'

As her sister passed the notepad across the table and Abby came face to face with the heading, 'Things to Do (unforgettable)', she faltered a little. The idea sounded great in theory, but again when faced with a blank page and such a daunting task, she wasn't really sure where to start.

The others, including her mother, were looking at her expectantly.

'Well, what's the first thing?' Caroline demanded. 'Surely there's one major thing you've always wanted to do? We all have one, don't we? I certainly know what mine is, anyway . . . What?' she asked, when the others looked at her blankly. 'You mean you don't know?'

'We're all waiting with bated breath to find out,' Dermot drawled.

'Well, to be seated front row at Paris Fashion Week!' she announced, as if this was the most obvious thing in the world. 'And photographed there too – that would be even better.' When Dermot sniggered, she gave him a dig in the ribs. 'Laugh all you like – so *you* mightn't be bothered, but we were talking about what would be unforgettable for me. We all know what *you*'d like to do.'

'Do you now?' he challenged.

Caroline sniffed, giving him a dismissive look. 'I certainly have a pretty good idea.'

'OK, then – what?'

'Well, it would be flying one of those jet-fighter things, or something macho like that, wouldn't it?' she said, with a roll of her eyes.

From his reluctantly impressed face, Abby knew that her

sister had been spot on. 'Bloody hell, Car, I take it all back,' he said, 'you *do* know your stuff.'

Caroline beamed. 'And, Mum, for a long time yours was going to the opera, wasn't it – a real, live Italian opera.'

'Yes, love.' Teresa smiled wistfully, 'That's been a big dream of mine for ages, which was why I was so thrilled with your Christmas present.'

With a slight start, Abby realised that Caroline did seem to know her family well – probably better than they knew themselves! In fact, thinking of it now, this had always been reflected in the birthday or Christmas gifts she gave them. While all Teresa's children had known that their mum enjoyed listening to opera around the house, Abby would never in a million years have thought of sending her to a real, live Italian opera. Yet Caroline had known instinctively that their mother would love this, in the same way that she'd known Abby would appreciate that gorgeous Tiffany bracelet as a memento of the lovely time they'd all had in New York.

Now she looked at her sister. 'What about me?' she asked. 'Can you think of something I've always wanted to do, because off the top of my head I really can't think of anything.'

Caroline bit her lip. 'To be honest, no – I'd have to think a bit more about that,' she said, leaving Abby feeling faintly disappointed. Was she that much of an oddball that her sister couldn't immediately pinpoint something she'd like, in the way she had with the others? 'Anyway, we're trying to make a *list* of things for you do, not just one and—' She stopped short and her eyes widened. 'That's it!' she shrieked, excitedly waving both hands in the air.

'What's it?' Abby asked uncertainly.

'Oh, it'll be absolutely *perfect*! Tell you what,' she said, turning to Abby, 'why don't you spend the next few days coming up with some things on your own. They don't have to be mind-blowing, amazing things; sometimes the simplest things can be just as nice, can't they, Tom?' Plainly unsure as to what his wife was getting at, Tom reddened a little before nodding. 'But in addition to the things you come up with, why don't you let *us* think of some to add to the list? Even better, we could do it with you!' her sister proclaimed, clearly on a roll.

Abby looked at the others, who seemed equally unmoved. 'I don't know . . .'

Caroline sighed. 'Abby, you're my sister and I love you lots, but even you have to admit that for the last few years you've been an awful bore.'

'Caroline!' Teresa scolded.

'No, it's OK, Mum.' Abby actually wasn't as insulted as she might have been, and deep down she knew all too well what her sister was talking about. She had indeed been a bore this last while, never wanting to take part in anything, go anywhere or see anyone. 'I think I know what you mean. I *have* been a pain in the arse recently, which is partly the reason I want to do this.'

'So let me get this straight,' Dermot said. 'Car, you want each one of us to come up with something memorable for Abby, something we think she'll like?'

Caroline nodded vigorously. 'And preferably something she hasn't done before,' she added. When Abby opened her mouth to say something, she cut her off. 'Some of the best experiences are the most unexpected ones, so if we're going to do this, you *have* to trust us. Just remember how I so easily cured your so-called fear of flying,' she added with a flourish, and Abby grudgingly had to admit she was right. 'So,' her sister finished, looking around imperiously, 'is everyone game?'

'Should be fun,' Dermot said with a wicked grin that immediately sent Abby's neurotic side into overdrive.

God, was she crazy getting her family so involved in all of this and essentially throwing herself at their mercy?

Then again, why the hell not? she thought, deciding for

once in her life to throw caution to the wind. OK, this could be a complete disaster and she might very well end up *seriously* regretting it, but so what? She *wanted* to shake up her life, so this was as good a way as any to start.

Caroline rubbed her hands together, a gleeful smile on her face. 'Honey, if you're looking for memorable experiences, then, by God, you'll get them!'

Chapter 18

Things to Do (unforgettable)

1. *Take at least one photograph every single day.*
2. *Visit the Grand Canyon.*
3. *See penguins in their own environment (South Pole?).*
4. *Have an adventure.*
5. *Drive a convertible.*
6. *Share a kiss with a stranger.*
7. *Watch all my favourite movies in one sitting.*
8. *Dance in public like no one's watching.*
9. *Face my fears.*
10. *Be more spontaneous.*

Hannah read through the list, an enigmatic smile on her face.

'What?' Abby asked, feeling silly all of a sudden. Making a list of the things she really wanted to do had been a lot harder than she'd anticipated, and showing it to other people was even worse.

'I like the idea,' the psychologist said, 'and I particularly like the notion of your going along with what other people think you should try.'

Abby *still* wasn't sure about that one, which went under item number ten, 'be more spontaneous', but she'd agreed to go along with it, so she couldn't back out now. Since then, Erin too had insisted on coming on board, and had reacted with gusto when Abby had outlined the idea to her in the meantime.' 'I know *exactly* what we'll do,' her friend had said without hesitation, causing Abby to wonder yet again what on earth she was letting herself in for.

'But do you think it could work?' Abby urged now, sinking further into the comfy and familiar purple armchair in Hannah's office.

The other woman paused, and to her immense disappointment, Abby suspected that she was trying to choose her next words carefully. 'I certainly don't think it can hurt. Sensory stimulation of the positive kind is always good for brain activity and function. As to how and if it will impact on your memory, it's difficult to say.'

Abby felt more than a little deflated, and hated the way Hannah could never give her a straight answer. But at the same time, she couldn't be too annoyed. She shouldn't expect her to understand really, or expect her doctor to be as enthusiastic about the project as the people close to her.

'And I really love the idea of taking a photograph every single day, but I suppose you've already realised that that one is more to do with memory *preservation* than creation, don't you?'

Abby did. She'd included that one on the list shortly after getting copies of the photographs Zach had taken of them all in New York. Looking through them, and seeing from everyone's happy expressions, how well they captured the good things about the visit, she realised that while she used to take reels and reels of photographs in her teenage years, she'd pretty much stopped over the last while. Kieran hated having his photograph taken, and when he did, always managed to look sulky and irritated, so Abby had eventually stopped bothering.

One of the first things Abby had done in the New Year was to go out and buy herself a digital camera, and had already started taking one picture – at least – every single day. More than anything, it was getting her memory chest off to a great start, with snapshots of family, friends, even objects and places that just caught her attention.

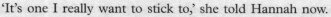

'It's one I really want to stick to,' she told Hannah now.

'Good idea, and I'm glad you've started keeping a diary too. As well as helping you, it may be a good way of spotting anything out of the ordinary.'

Abby didn't really want to think of it like that; it was just that as her days were about to get a *lot* more interesting, she might as well keep an account of them.

'So when is all of this happening, then?' Hannah asked. 'The travel-related stuff will take some planning, I'd imagine.'

'Yes.' Abby knew she'd have to wait for the insurance money to come through, so at least she'd have the means to pay for another trip to the States, although she wasn't sure how she'd get to the South Pole. 'I'll check out some dates with a travel agent soon, but the rest of the list I'm going to try and complete as I go.'

Hannah looked through it again. '"Face my fears"?' she read, arching an inquisitive eyebrow.

Abby nodded vigorously. 'Definitely. I've already done part of that one by getting over my fear of flying.' But had this been a genuine fear, she wondered again, or was it more a manifestation of *Kieran*'s anxiety about flying?

'Oh? So what's the other part?'

'The other part?'

'You said that by facing your fear of flying you'd completed *part* of that task. What's the other part?'

Abby hesitated a little. 'Well, I kind of have this thing about dogs,' she admitted. 'I don't know why, but for some reason I've always been terrified of them. It's hard to explain, really. We never had one at home or anything, so I don't know where it came from, but . . .'

'I see. Well, I think that's certainly a good idea. Dogs are wonderful animals. I have two King Charles spaniels and I wouldn't be without them.'

Abby was struck by the fact that in all the time she'd been

seeing Hannah, this was the first piece of information the doctor had offered about herself and her own life. But then she worried that this might actually be Hannah's roundabout way of introducing Abby to her dogs, something she wasn't entirely comfortable with. She wanted to get through the fun things on the list first, only then would she think about the scary things!

Thankfully, Hannah moved on to ask Abby about the other items on the list and what she intended to do in the short term. Abby was pleased to tell her that she already had something planned. This coming weekend Erin was calling over, and the two were planning to sit in and watch all of Abby's favourite movies back to back.

'While I don't relish the idea of watching three whole hours of bloody *Gladiator*, I certainly have no problem with *Forrest Gump* and *There's Something About Mary*,' Erin had said, when reading through Abby's recently composed list of all-time top-ten movie favourites. 'Oh, my God, *Con Air*?' she said, wrinkling her nose in disgust, while Abby just smiled. She had to include at least one of those cool Nicolas Cage exploding-helicopter movies in there somewhere. Erin continued reading. 'Hey, why isn't *Dirty Dancing* on here?' she asked accusingly.

Abby cringed. 'Because that cheesy mush holds the number-one spot on my all-time *least* favourite movies.'

'That's such a *great* movie – I can't believe you're putting Baby in the corner!' Erin gasped theatrically. Then she smiled. 'However, by including both *Dodgeball* and *Pretty Woman*, I think you've just about redeemed yourself.'

Abby was really looking forward to this, as she hadn't seen most of the movies on her list in years. Kieran absolutely loathed mainstream Hollywood blockbusters, and much preferred moodier and more 'arty' films like *Three Colours: Red* or anything by Ingmar Bergman. So it would be nice to just sit back and howl at side-splitting and just plain silly films like *Zoolander* without being made to feel like a halfwit.

She didn't confess this to Hannah, though: instead she merely told her about Erin coming over and how she was also going to spring on Abby *her* version of a memorable experience.

'Well, that should be interesting, certainly,' Hannah said. 'Any idea what the others have planned for you?'

She grimaced. 'Only Mum so far: as for the rest, I haven't got a clue. I'm pretty sure Dermot's will be something typically laddish, and as for Caroline, who knows? But Mum's asked me to go with her to Verona in June.' A trip to the opera with her worrywart mother wasn't something Abby was particularly looking forward to, even if it did mean a few days in Italy. She suspected it was the only thing Teresa could think of and so was happy enough to go along with it. More disappointingly, Abby could also tell that her mother believed that this entire exercise was a complete waste of time. In Teresa's eyes and much to Abby's frustration, since that incident with the piano, her memory was well and truly doomed.

Hannah obviously sensed Abby was less than enthusiastic. 'I defy anyone not to fall in love with opera in Verona – it'll be amazing. It's really good of your family to get on board and help like this, isn't it?' Hannah said.

'Oh, absolutely, yes,' Abby replied with feeling, not wanting Hannah to think she was ungrateful, as she really wasn't. She was merely wondering what was to come over the next few weeks and what on earth she was letting herself in for.

But next weekend – when Erin revealed the first of her 'surprise' memorable experiences – Abby would find out.

Chapter 19

15 January, Dublin

This back-to-back movie-watching idea was an absolute brain-wave, and I honestly can't remember the last time Erin and I had such a good time together! We spent the weekend laughing, crying and cheering our way through my favourite pics, and although Erin didn't really 'get' Russell Crowe in a skirt and sandals or Ben Stiller's hilarious antics, she was still willing to sit through each and every one of my choices, even though she'd seen most of them before – except can you believe she'd never seen *Thelma and Louise*?!

'Oh, my God, we have got to do that!' she squealed, as the credits rolled.

Well, I nearly spat out my popcorn. 'I know I said I wanted to be more spontaneous, but there's no way I'm driving a car off a—'

'No, no, I don't mean that,' she drawled, rolling her eyes. 'I mean the road trip – just the two of us. Just taking off and seeing where the road takes us.'

A road trip? Why hadn't I thought of that? It would be fun, the two of us driving around like Susan Sarandon and Geena Davis. Still, I was thinking I wouldn't fancy coming across any of those sleazy rig drivers, although we don't tend to get them here. But it seemed Erin had a much grander idea.

'Well, seeing as driving a convertible and the Grand Canyon are two of the things on your list, why not do them both at the same time?' she suggested. 'We could fly to LA, pick up the convertible and drive to the canyon from there. And even better,' she said, her eyes shining excitedly, and I could see a plan beginning to take shape in her mind, 'we could stop off in Vegas on the way.'

Las Vegas? Sin City – one of the biggest, brashest and, second to New York, possibly the most exciting city in the world! God, anyone with a snatch of imagination would probably have put this first on any list – why the hell didn't I think of it?

Actually, thinking back on the list now, my own suggestions look very dull and boring compared to Erin's. Even when I'd put driving a convertible on there, I'd been thinking about maybe hiring one for a day here in Ireland. But what better place to do it than America!

It's a fantastic idea, and I can't wait to get cracking on the plans. It being the weekend, though, we weren't able to call any travel agents just yet, so we got down to the altogether more pressing business of choosing the next film.

'I can't believe you think this is better than *Dirty Dancing*!' Erin groaned as I loaded *Footloose* into the DVD player. 'It's so cringey.'

'Rubbish, it's a classic,' I said, settling myself back on the couch and opening a fresh tube of Sour Cream and Onion Pringles. At that stage, we'd munched through two bags of popcorn, a tub of Ben and Jerry's Caramel Chew Chew and close to a gallon of Coke!

But thank goodness for *Footloose* and its crackin' sound-track, especially in that final scene where the dancing ban is lifted and all the kids get to go crazy dancing for the first time in years. The music was so infectious that by the end of it both of us got up off the couch and started boogeying like mad to Kenny Loggins (and hopefully working off some of the junk food).

You should have seen the two of us, laughing and shaking our stuff as if we too had been banned from dancing for years. And do you know something? I don't mind admitting that it felt a teeny bit like that for me. Kieran would never have danced around the sofa like this; in fairness, Kieran would never have danced anywhere full stop . . .

Lately, I find I'm beginning to distance myself from him, and am starting to think that maybe him leaving wasn't the end of the world. OK, so I'm not exactly over him or anything, but I'm coming round to the notion that yes, maybe there is life without him. And now that I know there's lots of things I want to see, and a whole lot of living to do, I'm really determined to throw myself right into it. No more hiding and no more excuses.

As Susan Sarandon says in that movie, 'You get what you settle for.'

Abby had assumed that the road-trip idea would count as Erin's suggestion for her list, but to her surprise and, she had to confess, delight, her friend had other plans. Which was why, the Saturday night after their movie-watching weekend, she was happy to put her trust in Erin for the evening. They'd had such a craic together watching the movies that Abby was willing to go along with whatever her best friend had in mind. As she had no clue what Erin had planned other than it would be happening tonight, Abby wasn't sure what to expect, though Erin had told her to dress up.

'OK,' Erin announced, when she called in at Abby's flat at around seven, 'you're probably not going to like this, but—'

Disappointed, she looked at Erin. 'What do you mean, I'm not going to like this? The whole point is to pick something I *will* like, something I won't forget in a hurry, isn't it?' she reminded her.

Erin smiled cryptically. 'Yes, well, that's the intention,

certainly. But I think that sometimes the most memorable experiences can stem from stepping out of your comfort zone and taking chances, don't you think?'

Abby squirmed, not liking the sound of this at all. 'What *kind* of chances?'

But Erin refused to elaborate. 'You'll see . . . hopefully,' she added in an aside, as Abby put on her coat and they left the flat.

'So where are we off to?' she asked as they continued walking down the street towards the city centre.

'Dame Street direction,' her friend replied, again refusing to be drawn any further.

'OK.' If they were staying in town, they were obviously going out somewhere, Abby mused, faintly disappointed. A Saturday night out in Dublin wasn't exactly an earth-shattering experience, was it?

Erin was still chatting away as they walked along, evidently oblivious to Abby's worries. 'So did you talk to the travel agent about our trip?'

Since she'd last seen Erin, Abby had spent time doing some more research on the Californian road trip, which they'd decided to book for April to give Erin enough notice to organise time off from work.

'Yep. I think I've pretty much got everything sorted. The travel agent will be sending out a full itinerary next week and then all we'll have to do is book it.'

Erin grinned. 'Fantastic. I really can't wait!'

Some fifteen minutes later, they reached the centre of town, Abby still in the dark as to what they were doing, until finally Erin stopped outside a popular pizza chain.

'We're going for pizza?' Abby asked, puzzled.

Erin was all innocence. 'What, you don't fancy it?'

'Well, not particularly.' While pizza was one of the few 'foreign' foods Abby liked, she'd thought tonight was supposed to be something *exciting*, something enjoyable. Sharing a margherita pizza over a cheap plastic table wasn't exactly ground-breaking, she thought, slightly deflated.

'Hoping for something more exciting, were you?'

'Well, yes – why did you tell me to dress up if all we were doing was going here?'

Now Erin was grinning like the cat that got the cream. 'OK, then, great. Let's go somewhere else, somewhere a bit more interesting.'

'Hold on.' *Now* Abby was starting to get it. She stood rooted to the spot, refusing to go any further until she had some answers. 'What's all this about?'

'*This* is what it's like for me and everyone else who agrees to eat out with you, Abby. We get our hopes up but instead end up having to eat bland, tasteless, mass-produced rubbish. Hey, I'm not saying this to get at you,' Erin said quickly, noticing Abby's wounded expression. 'I'm just trying to make a point. But,' she added with a wicked grin, 'now I think it's time to show you *exactly* what you're missing.'

Some ten minutes later, Abby was reluctantly pushed in the door of a small but charming-looking restaurant. The décor was all warm oranges and terracottas, and apart from the tea-light candles dotted around the wooden tables, the place was barely lit, which added to the cosy atmosphere. She and Erin were led to a small table for two at the back of the room, and the waitress was warm and courteous as she asked for their drinks order.

'What *is* this place?' Abby asked, skimming the four-page menu and finding hardly anything on it that she recognised.

'It's where you're finally going to rid yourself of that self-imposed pickiness of yours.'

'Erin, I—'

'Abby, just hear me out. When we were younger, you were absolutely fine about food. OK, so we weren't eating out

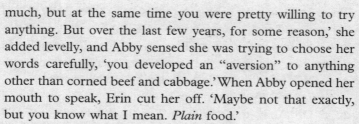

much, but at the same time you were pretty willing to try anything. But over the last few years, for some reason,' she added levelly, and Abby sensed she was trying to choose her words carefully, 'you developed an "aversion" to anything other than corned beef and cabbage.' When Abby opened her mouth to speak, Erin cut her off. 'Maybe not that exactly, but you know what I mean. *Plain* food.'

'But I just don't like—'

'How do you know you don't like things if you've never even tried them?' Erin argued. 'So here's the thing – I brought you here tonight because it's a great place to ease you into trying something new. Don't worry, I'm not going to force you to eat anything you don't like the look of,' she added quickly. 'What's going to happen is that we're going to order eight different dishes from this menu – four each – but you must promise me that you will at least taste – even the teeniest, tiniest piece – of every single one.'

'Eight dishes? But that's an awful waste!' Abby was struck by how much like Kieran she sounded now.

'It's not like that – this is a tapas restaurant; the portions are smaller and you're meant to order a load!'

'Tapas?' Abby had heard of such places but (naturally enough) had never been in one, even on that ill-fated trip to Spain. But she had to admit she'd always thought they sounded kind of cool.

'Yes. Remember that thing on your list about facing your fears?' Erin reminded her. 'Well, this is as good a way as any to start.'

The waitress returned with their drinks and Abby used this break in the conversation to think about it. A boring old margherita pizza was starting to sound like heaven compared to the scary things she might have to face now!

But as Erin pointed out, what harm could it do her? She picked up the menu and tentatively read through the list.

There really was no hiding from this, was there? Abby closed her eyes and took a deep breath. 'OK,' she said, deciding to throw caution to the wind. There was nothing here that could poison her, was there? 'Just make sure there's nothing with eyes, OK? I really couldn't eat anything with eyes.'

'Seriously?' Erin could barely contain her delight. 'You'll do it? Oh, Abby, that's brilliant. I'm absolutely positive we'll find something you like here, honestly we will! I'm going to pick some really great things, things I'm sure you'll love, and you're right, yes, nothing with eyes. And when you *do* try this . . . well, I promise you you'll never go back to boring old—' She stopped mid-sentence, a bashful expression on her face. 'Oh, look, I'll just shut up about it now and let us get on with it. I'm starving!'

It was kind of funny to think that her agreeing just to *try* new things could have such an effect on Erin. Had she *really* been that much of stick-in-the-mud in the past? And if so, how had anyone – friends or family – ever put up with her?

As per Erin's instructions, they both ordered four dishes, Abby failing miserably to pronounce the names of her choices. When some ten minutes later, the waitress returned with the first of their tapas, Abby gulped.

Erin immediately began pointing out each dish by name, but Abby's gaze became fixated on a small plate of something that looked like . . . well, there was no denying that it looked the very same as baby puke. She took a deep breath and tried to stop her stomach from churning. This couldn't be a self-induced neurosis like Erin said, could it? Not when her insides were reacting so strongly to even the *smell* of this stuff! Then, deciding not to think any more about it, Abby suddenly picked up her fork and popped some of the puke-like stuff in her mouth. She let it sit on her tongue for a few moments, almost afraid to let herself taste it until, finally, she let her jaws move. And when she did, she had an overwhelming urge to . . . *die*.

'Ugh!' she spluttered, having swooped on her drink and swallowed it down in the hope of quenching the fire on her tongue. 'What the hell was *that*?'

Erin's eyes were wide. 'Erm, the plan was for you to *ease* yourself into this, not start off with the spiciest dish on the menu!' Her friend was still laughing as she explained that what Abby had chosen was in fact some vegetable and chilli conconction, though she insisted it was actually quite mild . . .

After the fire on Abby's tongue had been extinguished by another mouthful of wine, and Erin had stopped laughing, she tried a forkful of potatoes in a creamy, garlicky sauce and some chicken with olives. She had never even tried olives before, and she even surprised herself by discovering she liked chorizo.

While Abby couldn't see herself becoming a regular at the tapas restaurant, she was really enjoying the atmosphere and the fun she and Erin were having.

'See, I told you – eating out isn't just about the food,' her friend reiterated, taking another sip of her wine. 'It's only the half of it, actually. And now that you've broken through that psychological barrier of yours, and actually started trying new things, you never know what you might find.'

Abby smiled. 'Now you're starting to sound like Hannah! But you know what they say,' she said, feeling heady and more than a little reckless now. She reached out and picked up a forkful of some other weird-looking and unpronouncable food. 'What doesn't kill you only makes you stronger!'

Chapter 20

OK, so a day's shopping wasn't something I would have chosen for myself as a particularly memorable experience, but Caroline was so excited about her 'big idea', and determined I enjoy it, that I just didn't have the heart to say no. Once again someone's decided that forcing me to endure something I normally don't enjoy is the best way to go about things!

But I couldn't say a word as right from the very beginning my big sister was determined to have me fall straight into line.

'Be ready, 'cause we're starting early,' she'd ordered over the phone beforehand, and true to her word, Caroline and her Merc pulled up outside my place first thing Saturday morning.

'There was hardly any need to collect me – we could have met up somewhere in town,' I told her, climbing into the passenger seat of her groovy coupé.

'We aren't going to town,' she replied with a conspiratorial wink that sent nervous shivers up my spine.

As usual, big sis looked effortlessly stylish in a black T-shirt and cropped cream-coloured swing jacket over a pair of skinny jeans. This city-chic look was completed with a pair of oversized sunglasses perched on her head, and of course the obligatory funky designer handbag. As usual, I felt (and probably looked) about ten years older in my ancient but comfy jeans and trusty black V-neck sweater.

'What?' I asked her, puzzled. 'Then where are we going?'

I know Caroline isn't the type to shop in the large shopping centres on the outskirts of the city, where her beloved designer labels are generally few and far between, so I'd naturally assumed our shopping spree would be concentrated between her second home, Brown Thomas, and the bijou boutiques she frequents. But perhaps for one day only, and out of respect for my, ahem . . . rather limited budget (and possibly even more limited taste!), big sis was deigning to visit the more affordable high-street chain stores.

I was wrong.

'I promised I'd take you on the shopping spree of a lifetime, didn't I?' Caroline said, lowering her Prada sunglasses. (At least, I think they were Prada, but I'm not very up on these things.) 'So in order to do that, we have to get out of boring old Dublin and go somewhere we can really go crazy. So, little sister,' she announced in one of her typically dramatic flourishes, 'I'm taking you to London.'

'London? You mean England, London?'

'Well, London, England, is how it usually goes, but yes! Our plane leaves in an hour, and I've arranged to have a car waiting at Heathrow to take us straight to the hotel, so—'

I couldn't believe what I was hearing. 'Hotel? You mean we're staying over?'

'Of course. You didn't think we'd go over and back in one day, did you?'

'But why didn't you tell me?' I cried in panic. 'I don't have anything with me – no overnight bag, change of clothes . . . nothing.'

'And you won't need one, because we're going shopping, Abby,' Caroline replied blithely. 'Claridges will have everything you need cosmetics-wise, and as for the rest . . . well, our shopping spree will take care of that.'

I stared open-mouthed at her, wondering what planet she

was on. This sounded crazy! 'Caroline, don't get me wrong, an overnight stay in London sounds great, but what I can't understand is why go all the way over there when we have virtually the same shops here.'

'Honey,' Caroline purred, driving towards the Port Tunnel, 'you've obviously never shopped in London.'

Well, there wasn't much I could say to that, was there?

So we reached Central London around midday, and having checked into the hotel, the two of us hopped in a taxi and hit the shops. First up was Selfridges on Oxford Street. I'd heard of it of course, but had never actually been inside the place.

'Right, first things first,' Caroline said, leading the way, a scarily determined look on her face.

I dutifully followed in her wake as she negotiated a multitude of shoppers, and weaved her way through the crowds with practised ease. But when I looked up ahead, I realised that we were heading in the direction of what looked to be some kind of . . .

'A cocktail bar? What's going on?' I asked, totally bewildered, as Caroline climbed the spiral staircase towards a place called the Moët Bar.

My big sister grinned wickedly. 'What's going on is that today will be a long day, so we might as well kick it off in style.' She picked up a cocktail menu from the bar. 'So what do you fancy?' she asked me airily. 'Something by Julien Macdonald, or maybe an Alice Temperley?'

I was stupefied. Trust Caroline to pick a place that even sold designer cocktails!

'Of course,' she replied when I said this. 'But if you don't fancy a cocktail, we could just go for a plain old glass of pink champagne.'

'Plain old . . .' At this, I had to laugh. Apart from that time on the flight to New York 'to calm my nerves', I really can't remember the last time I'd had a regular glass of the stuff, let alone a pink one! But seeing as this was supposed to be a girlie day out, what the hell?

'Pink champagne it is, then,' I told her, feeling slightly giddy at the flamboyancy of all this.

The two of us clinked champagne glasses, and took a seat at the funky and stylish bar. I felt a gorgeous thrill when the bubbles hit my tongue for the first time. OK, so drinking champagne at midday wasn't exactly sensible, but hadn't I spent long enough being bloody sensible? And as Caroline had clearly gone to lots of trouble to make this day special, I figured I might as well get into the spirit of things.

'Look at all that amazing stuff,' my sister sighed, turning in her seat to look out over the accessories department. 'Chloé bags, Marni belts, Chanel sunglasses . . . Ooh, sends a shiver down my spine just looking at it.'

As little old me didn't know my Chloé from my Chanel, I didn't really get what all the fuss was about, but if Caroline had her way, no doubt I would soon find out!

'So where do you want to start?' she asked me, deciding to get right down to business. 'Shoes, dresses, handbags . . . ?'

I had a little think before telling her that there was nothing I really needed.

At this, the poor thing looked horrified. 'Need! Who said anything about need! Abby, shopping for something you need is no fun at all. Is that what you've been doing all these years?' She seemed to shudder at the very idea. 'God, no wonder you haven't been bothered about it up to now.'

I could do nothing but shrug, and eventually Caroline stood up and drained the contents of her glass. Again I was struck by how much energy she always seems to have. 'Come on, enough time-wasting. Drink that down,' she chided me. 'It's time you and I went and did some serious shopping – and what better way to start than by finding you a truly fabulous dress!'

I finished my drink and followed her upstairs to the next floor, where a bewildering collection of women's clothes in various shapes, colours and sizes awaited us. While I hadn't a clue where to begin, Caroline was already zooming in on the different rails and displays, picking up and discarding dresses, skirts and tops with military precision.

'OK, daytime stuff first, I think,' she muttered. 'Diane von Furstenberg, Viktor and Rolf, Gharani Strok . . . What size are you – a ten, twelve at the most?'

'A fourteen by the looks of some of these things,' I said mournfully, fingering a multicoloured diaphanous-looking dress that would make any normal-sized woman look like Ten-Ton Tessie!

'Nonsense, that one would look fab on you,' Caroline assured me, swooping in on the dress and throwing it on the alarmingly large pile she was now holding over one arm. She peered at the label above the rail. 'Issa, good choice – hmm, maybe you do have some taste after all.'

'Cheers,' I mumbled, wondering who the hell Issa was and how he or she got away with charging an arm and a leg for something that had so little fabric in it.

But ten minutes later I was eating my words. The dress, made of silk jersey, which I had been certain would cling in all the wrong places, somehow managed to accentuate all the right ones and, with its purple and green butterfly-print pattern, instantly transformed me from a dumpy thirty-year-old to a curvy and vivacious-looking girl about town. I couldn't believe it.

'Well?' Caroline poked her head round the fitting-room door, eager to take a look at me. 'Hmm, just give me one second,' she said, her doubtful expression deflating my happy mood, until she returned and handed me a funky pair of Anna Sui brown satin boots.

Staring at my reflection in the mirror, I have to say I was

entranced. In this outfit, I was no longer my normal dull and dowdy self; instead I looked glam and fashionable and, dare I say it . . . cool!

'I love it!' I cried, doing a twirl in front of the mirror. 'It's just so . . . not me that I love it.'

'Finally, she gets the point,' my sister deadpanned with a wicked smile. 'OK, now try the Pucci one – prints really are you, actually. I don't know why you don't wear them more often.'

'Um, maybe because I don't have a rich husband and limitless amounts of cash like you do,' I couldn't help but retort, as I tried on the colourful pink and orange silk tunic. It was quite unusual-looking, what with its jewelled mandarin-style collar and self-tie belt, and speaking of cash . . . I glanced down briefly at the garment's price tag and did a double take. Oh . . . my . . . God. Seven hundred and fifty pounds!

'No excuse – the high street do some great replicas these days,' Caroline lectured, reading my thoughts. 'You just don't bother looking.'

Well, maybe that was true. After Kieran had left, I not only lost interest in enjoying life, but I suppose I also lost interest in the excitement of finding clothes that looked great, irrespective of cost. But then again, I've never been any good at that kind of stuff, never had much of an eye for it – certainly not like Caroline has, anyway.

'Not bad, not bad. Although, Abby,' my sister said, and the grimace on her face made me wonder what piece of excess flesh she was going to pinpoint, 'you should really think about getting those legs waxed once in a while.'

Waxed? I've never considered the idea in my life. I usually only bother shaving my legs when they're likely to be exposed, like in the summer or that time Kieran and I went to Spain. But when Caroline made such a point of it, I couldn't help wondering if his new wife always kept her legs smooth and hair-free, and if so, had that made the difference?

Caroline was still talking to me. 'You've got really great legs, although you definitely need a killer pair of heels to go with a dress like that. Manolos would work, I think.'

'OK.' As most of the brands and names were going right over my head, I simply nodded in agreement, and thought about maybe booking a leg wax when I got home.

'Now try this.' Caroline again sifted through the pile she was holding and held up a mid-length purple, red and white creation. 'Diane von Furstenberg – if the size-twelve Issa dress fits that well, then this should be absolutely perfect on you.'

And while I hate to boast, yes, the dress did indeed look perfect on me, as did the petrol-blue jersey Stella McCartney mini-dress, the gorgeous Zandra Rhodes pink and purple chiffon maxi-dress and the floaty cotton Anna Sui vest top over Rock and Republic jeans. And by the time I got to the Whistles vintage-style flapper skirt (which Caroline insisted I team with silver-foil and black suede Jimmy Choo sling-backs), I don't mind admitting that I was well on my way towards becoming a fashion convert!

To be honest, up until now I'd been perplexed by my big sister's thing for designer clothes, thinking it was all a bit silly, but there was absolutely no denying that these clothes really transformed me, and at the same time wasn't there also a guilty thrill to be had about wearing these designer names and their lavish prices? So while of course I wasn't planning on actually buying any of these clothes, it sure was fun trying them on!

'Right, enough of that. I think we now need to seriously up the glam stakes.' Caroline's eyes sparkled and she seemed to be enjoying her stylist's role enormously. 'Wait there for a couple of minutes. I spotted something on the way in that I think would be the absolute business on you, but we need the bag and shoes to complete the entire look. Gimme a sec.'

'OK,' I giggled, wondering what was coming next. What could be more glam than the glittery skirt I had on now, and as for those heels . . . ! Now I was beginning to understand what all the fuss was about. One of these days, I thought to myself, I'm going to treat myself to a pair of Jimmy Choos – they were just so pretty and delicate and – 'Oh . . . my . . . God!' I stepped back in awe as the most stunningly beautiful dress I had ever seen suddenly materialised in the doorway of the cubicle.

'You like?' Caroline's voice was muffled, and I could barely see her behind the ball gown's layers of voluminous fabric.

'I love!' I gasped.

I really don't know if I can describe how amazing this dress looked, but I'll try. It was a deep-plum colour, with a strapless ruched tulle corset-style bodice. At the waist there was a thick satin sash and floral corsage, which fastened at the back in a bow. But it was the full skirt and its layers and layers of plum-coloured tulle that made the gown magnificent.

'Oscar de la Renta – isn't it amazing?' Caroline's head eventually peeped over the bodice.

I was almost too stunned to reply. 'Amazing,' I eventually managed.

'Um, is there any chance you could take it off my hands here? All these layers weigh a bloody ton!'

'Oh, of course.' I lifted up the dress and immediately hung it on one of the cubicle hooks, almost afraid to touch it, it was so beautiful.

'I think these will work well. What do you think?' Caroline had also procured a pair of dusky-pink satin Karen Millen heels and a gold beaded Chloé evening bag to accompany the dress. She looked at me, frowning. 'Well, are you going to try it on or what?'

I wanted to try it on, of course I did, but it was just so

incredible I was terrified that I wouldn't be able to do it justice.

But within a few seconds of stepping into those acres of soft material and zipping up the bodice, I discovered I'd been worrying for nothing. The dress fitted like an absolute dream, and when I slipped into the three-inch heels and slowly turned to face my reflection in the mirror, honestly I felt a lump in my throat. Oh, my . . .

For once even Caroline seemed lost for words. 'Wow . . .' she said eventually, looking me up and down. 'You look . . . stunning. It's weird, really, but I feel kind of emotional looking at you, almost as if you're trying on your wedding dress or something.'

I turned to her, tears in my eyes. It was strange but just then Caroline had managed to pinpoint my own feelings exactly. I really can't be sure why I felt so overwhelmed at that very moment. It was just a dress, after all. But what a dress. And despite myself, I still couldn't help but wish that Kieran could see me in it.

'Thank you, Car,' I whispered then. 'I don't know how you managed it, but this is just perfect. This whole idea is just perfect. I'll . . . I'll never forget it.'

Caroline nodded solemnly – I think realising that this was about something more than just the dress. 'Wait a minute,' she said, rummaging through her handbag before eventually producing some lipstick and a hairbrush. 'Here, put some of this on and then use this to give your hair a quick going-over.'

I laughed, confused. 'Why?'

'Because we're going to make sure you do remember it, that's why. Where's your camera?' she asked, before fishing it out of my bag. Then, me still wearing that fabulous dress, she made me step out of the cubicle and pose in front of one of the store's nearby floral arrangements. I had to laugh, not just at the silliness of it all, but at the faces of the store assistants once they realised what was happening!

'Can I help you, madam?' one of them said imperiously, coming up behind Caroline, who was busy snapping away with my camera.

'You can, actually.' Without warning Caroline thrust the camera into the assistant's hands and ordered her to take some photos of the two of us together, all the while directing proceedings with typical aplomb.

As we both grinned at the camera, me in my 'you shall go to the ball' Oscar de la Renta dress, I hugged my big sister tightly, and decided that this had been one of the nicest days out I'd had in ages.

Later, Abby and Caroline decamped to a nearby restaurant for a late lunch, whereupon Caroline immediately ordered more champagne and the two toasted their Selfridges exploits and their fun day out. Abby was still slightly dazed by the whole experience, not just by the complete exhilaration she'd felt upon trying on that amazing dress, but also by what had happened afterwards.

While she was in the cubicle changing out of the ball gown, Caroline was outside getting ready to put back the other clothes she'd tried on. Or at least that's what Abby had thought she was doing.

'OK, so definitely that lovely Issa, the Diane V, that Whistles skirt and those jeans, then?' Caroline called out. 'And the silver Choos of course. But I'm not entirely sure about the Pucci. Would you get any wear out of it?'

'What?' Still half-dressed, Abby shot her head round the door. 'Car, you know I've no intention of actually buying anything, don't you? I mean, these clothes are gorgeous, but I couldn't possibly afford—'

'Oh, for goodness' sake, who said anything about *you* buying them?' her sister said breezily. 'This is my treat.'

Abby blanched. 'Caroline, no, no way. There must be at

least two or three grands' worth there. I couldn't *possibly* let you spend that much on—'

'You can and you will. This is supposed to be a memorable experience, isn't it?' she reminded Abby. 'Something you'll remember for a long time to come. So how on earth will you remember it if you don't take home the bloody clothes?'

'Caroline, no.'

'Abby, listen, please let me do this. It's what I had planned from the very beginning when I suggested we go on a shopping day out. In fact, after seeing your face when you tried on the Oscar dress, I'd really love to get you that too, but my credit card would probably explode and Tom would surely leave me.' She grimaced. 'But the other stuff is my gift to you, so every time you wear those clothes you'll remember how much you enjoyed this and how *great* you felt in that dress.'

'Caroline—'

'Look, I don't want to hear any more about it. I'm getting them and that's it. Don't worry,' she reassured her, 'I'm going to pick out a few bits and bobs for myself too.'

Those 'few bits and bobs' turned out to be a bewildering amount of items, including a black and white zebra Jimmy Choo handbag, a Grecian-style Vera Wang rust-coloured silk dress with gold sequin straps ('For the Marbella ball,' Caroline informed Abby airily), a truly stunning pair of leopard-print Manolo Blahnik Mary Janes with a three-and-a-half-inch stacked heel that made Abby dizzy just looking at them, as well as a pair of black patent Christian Louboutin high-heels sporting the designer's signature red sole. Finally, a squishy Lulu Guinness baby-pink suede hobo bag and a pair of Pucci-print Birkenstock sandals completed Caroline's collection, which when added to the clothes she'd chosen for Abby amounted to a sum that probably equalled the national debt of a small country.

Now, as they sat in the lovely, chic restaurant Caroline

had booked in advance, both practically *buried* in shopping bags, Abby couldn't quite get over the life her sister led. The restaurant they were in boasted a Michelin-starred chef, with the resultant menu prices enough to make your eyes water, yet Caroline seemed totally at ease in such sumptuous surroundings.

With all this drinking champagne, designer clobber and fine dining, Abby felt like a celebrity for a day, and when she confessed this to Caroline, her sister laughed. 'That was the idea,' she said. 'Believe me, I don't normally go this mad. I've only eaten here a couple of times before, but I wanted to make today particularly special.'

'Well, you've certainly done that.' Abby gave a passing waiter an appreciative glance. She giggled, the champagne obviously going to her head. 'Did you hire male models to work here for the day too?'

Caroline grinned, following her gaze. 'Nope, luckily for us that's all part of the service.' Then her expression quickly turned serious as the waiter in question approached to take their order.

'Ready to order, madame?' he asked Caroline in a heavy French accent that made Abby swoon.

'Sure. I'll start with the lobster bisque, and the lamb and walnuts, thanks. And we'll also have a bottle of your Montrachet.'

'Certainly. And for you, mademoiselle?'

Abby was still staring at the menu, unable to make up her mind and choose from the amazingly enticing selection of dishes. Thanks to Erin, she was starting to get over her hang-up about food, and as this was her first (and probably *only* time) eating in a place like this, she didn't want to go for something staid and boring. No, with all that was happening today, and in the true spirit of item number ten on the list, she decided to once again 'be more spontaneous'.

'I will try the . . . artichoke risotto, and the Cornish brill, please,' she told the waiter, only to see Caroline glance up in surprise. 'I know,' she said sheepishly, when the waiter had left the table, 'I'm as surprised as you are, but I just feel like going a bit mad these days.'

Caroline reached over and squeezed her hand. 'Good for you.' Then she topped up their champagne flutes. 'It's about time you started enjoying the finer things in life, Abby – perhaps more than anyone you deserve it.'

Abby looked at Caroline, her perfectly coiffed blonde curls, her expensive designer outfit and extravagant jewellery, and instead of seeing the pretentious, self-centred and spoilt person Kieran had convinced them both she was, finally saw her sister through her own eyes. Up until recently, Abby had always felt alienated and slightly intimidated by Caroline's wealth and lifestyle, and so had distanced herself from her, convincing herself that they had little in common. But Abby had to admit that *she* had been the one to erect the barrier, and as a result they'd grown apart.

Since the accident and subsequent diagnosis, Caroline had been magnificent, and had tried to boost Abby's spirits at every opportunity, arranging the trip to New York for the whole family in order to lift her out of her misery, and coming up with the idea of making the list. And then to top it all off, she'd arranged this wonderful weekend away, buying her all those gorgeous clothes, a posh lunch, a stay at Claridges . . . How could Abby and Kieran have ever believed her to be self-centred?

Suddenly she felt tears prickle her eyes. 'Thank you,' she said, her voice hoarse.

Caroline went to wave her away. 'It's nothing—'

'No, I mean it,' Abby interjected. 'This is truly incredible. I'm enjoying myself so much I can't even explain it. But I'm not just talking about today, I'm talking about all the things you've done for me over the last few months, all the times you've been there. I don't know how to thank you.'

'You're my sister,' Caroline said with a smile. 'And you've been through the mill lately. Why wouldn't I be there for you?'

Shortly afterwards, the waiter arrived bearing plates of food that could only be described as works of art.

'Wow,' Abby gasped, almost afraid to touch her beautifully presented risotto. 'Do you think it's embarrassing if we get the camera out again? I know I said one photo a day, but I think I'll want to remember this too.'

Her sister rolled her eyes in that casually dismissive way that used to really get up Kieran's nose, but which Abby now understood wasn't pretentious – it was just Caroline. 'Honey, you really *haven't* lived, have you?'

'Evidently not,' Abby giggled, grabbing the camera and, much to the dismay of some stuffy-looking diners, snapping all around her. 'I can't wait to see what they do for dessert.'

'Didn't I tell you? I have something else planned for dessert.' Caroline grinned wickedly. 'The day isn't over yet, you know.'

Despite Abby's pleading, her sister refused to fill her in on this plan, and when they left the restaurant a while later, Abby having eaten easily the best meal of her life, she wondered what on earth was coming next.

So, after dropping their shopping bags back at the hotel, when their cab eventually pulled up outside an innocuous-looking four-storey building on a side street, she was well and truly puzzled. When they entered the building, Abby was alarmed to discover that rather than the cake shop she was expecting, this was in fact some kind of beauty spa. The idea of immaculately groomed and mostly beautiful strangers prodding and poking her lumps and bumps wasn't the best confidence boost. Which of course was one of the reasons she'd never had so much as a leg wax. So whatever Caroline had planned for them, chances were she wasn't going to enjoy it very much.

Her sister seemed to read her mind. 'Don't worry – you're going to love this,' she said, before announcing, 'Two for Chocolate Heaven at six,' to the receptionist.

Abby's interest was piqued. 'Chocolate?' she queried, as they took a seat in the waiting area.

'And plenty of it,' Caroline said, refusing to elaborate further.

She hadn't been joking. Their two-hour Chocolate Heaven experience began with a silky-smooth skin-conditioning body wrap. The two relaxed side by side in the treatment room, both covered from head to toe in luxurious warm chocolate, and surrounded by chocolate-scented candles, their delicious aroma filling the air.

'Mmm ... talk about living up to the name,' Abby said lazily. 'I really do feel like I've died and gone to chocolate heaven.'

'Guilt-free chocolate – what could be more perfect?' Caroline said in a dreamy voice. 'And I told you you'd love it.'

Suddenly, Abby started to feel a bit guilty, and not just because of the chocolate. How much must all of this be costing? Never mind the flight, clothes and fancy hotel; the lunch alone had been eye-wateringly expensive, and then on top of all that, this!

When she again tried to thank her sister for her unspeakable generosity, Caroline simply shook her head. 'Don't be silly – it's nothing, really. You know Tom is loaded. Now don't get me wrong; every year we donate at least ten per cent of our earnings to charity, so my conscience is squeaky clean when it comes to spending "frivolously".' She laughed, putting additional emphasis on the last word. 'But we have the house we want and the cars and all that, and seeing as we have only ourselves to spend it on . . .'

Abby ears pricked up at the slight catch in her voice as she said this. She'd always assumed that Caroline wasn't a bit maternal and was way too busy enjoying life to bother with children.

'Do you think you'll ever decide to have any?' she asked hesitantly.

Caroline laughed lightly. 'We decided to have them from day one – unfortunately, things just didn't turn out that way.'

Abby sat up and looked across at her. 'What? You mean you can't . . . ?'

'Can't have children? No,' Caroline said easily, her eyes still closed. 'I'm sorry, I thought you knew that, that maybe Mum had . . . Anyway, don't worry and *please* don't start spluttering with embarrassment about it, like everyone else seems to do. It's a pity, but we're fine with it.'

Abby's thoughts raced, a million questions running through her mind. 'But are you absolutely sure that—'

'Oh, yes, we're absolutely sure, believe me, and we have all the results to prove it. No one is to blame. Medically, we can't have them and that's the long and the short of it as far as we're concerned.'

'Caroline, I'm sorry. I had no idea . . .'

'Hey, don't sweat. We really are OK with it.' Caroline opened her eyes and turned to look at Abby. 'Yes, it was a blow and a shock to the system for both of us at first, but we've got lots of other great things in our lives, so why worry? I never buy into that negative bullshit, Abby, and I'm delighted that in your situation you're not doing it either. So Tom and I can't have kids, but we've got a great life, piles of money, and we love one another to bits. Why ruin all that by driving ourselves crazy over what we *don't* have?'

'I suppose.' Abby had to admire her sister's philosophy. It was no wonder she'd never picked up any strange vibes about her sister's child-free state, because Caroline refused to allow any.

And she felt childishly gratified that her sister seemed to admire the way she was dealing with the hand life had recently dealt her. It merely reinforced that by thinking positive and doing what she was doing, she – like Caroline – wouldn't allow this setback to beat her.

She was tempted to ask more but just then their therapists returned to the treatment room to carry out the next part of their Chocolate Heaven experience. This turned out to be a luxurious exfoliating chocolate-mint body scrub, then a pampering manicure during which the girls' hands were dipped in a chocolate-milkshake soap, massaged in chocolate whipped cream, and then sealed with heated chocolate paraffin. Afterwards was the pedicure – a warm milk footbath and vanilla and brown-sugar scrub, which left Abby's toes tingling. Finally, she and Caroline each had a full body massage with warmed cocoa-butter oils, making their skin feel silky smooth and smelling out-of-this-world gorgeous.

The experience was topped off with a mouth-watering glass of hot chocolate and biscotti, and as the girls relaxed in white robes with their treats, Abby allowed herself to stop feeling guilty about how much it was all costing, and concentrated on making the most of the huge amount of trouble and effort her sister had gone to in order to make this weekend special.

'I have never, ever experienced anything like that before,' she said, when they had finally returned to the hotel.

Both shattered from the day's adventures, they had decided to stay in and order a light snack from room service rather than head out again. Abby was now lazing around on one of the room's comfy beds, watching Caroline try on her new clothes.

'Well, maybe you should treat yourself now and again,' her sister replied, before muttering quietly, 'God knows nobody else did.'

'What?' Abby asked, sitting up. 'What's that supposed to mean?'

Turning away from the full-length mirror, Caroline bit her lip. 'Look, I'm sorry. I promised myself I wouldn't say anything; after all, it's in the past now and this weekend is about spoiling you.'

'Caroline,' Abby said, 'just spit it out, will you? I won't be annoyed, I promise you.' Or at least Abby *hoped* she wouldn't be annoyed.

'Well . . .' Her sister sighed. 'I just felt that when you started going out with Kieran that you lost some of your . . . I don't know, your spark or something.'

'When I *started* going out with him?' Abby repeated, confused. She knew she'd turned into some kind of dreary hermit by retreating into herself *after* she and Kieran had finished, she realised that now, but what was all this about beforehand?

'I'm sorry, and I know it's not really my place to say it, but, Abby, I never really felt that you two were suited. None of us did, the family I mean.'

'Well, evidently you were right.' Even though it had been a while since the break-up, it still hurt to hear this now.

'I'm not trying to make you feel bad or anything, and please don't take this the wrong way, but long before you two broke up I felt that he'd taken away a lot of your oomph and zest for life.' Caroline paused before adding quietly, 'He was quite controlling, wasn't he?'

Controlling? Abby supposed that yes that might have been one way of describing him. But not controlling in a bad sense; Kieran was just more of a . . . perfectionist, really. Which was why he'd left Abby for the prettier and much more together Jessica.

'Look, I'm sorry I brought it up,' Caroline said again, when Abby didn't answer. 'Now really isn't the moment for this, not when we're having such a lovely time. But to be honest, Abby, since the accident I've begun seeing a side of you I thought was lost, the more fun-loving, optimistic, game-for-anything side. And there's a side of me – an awful side, mind you – that can't help thinking that maybe that bump on the head did you some good as well as harm.'

Abby looked at her big sister and smiled. 'Funnily enough, I'm beginning to think the very same thing.'

Chapter 21

'So a good day all round, then?' Hannah said, when Abby had finished telling her about her recent exploits.

'It was great,' she said, beaming at the memory.

'Well, your sister certainly sounds like a very generous person, all those clothes and of course your lovely Tiffany bracelet.'

Abby dangled it from her wrist. 'Yes, and I feel so awful now for misjudging her all this time.'

'It happens in families. Don't beat yourself up about it too much. But apart from this recent excitement,' Hannah said, sitting forward in her chair, 'how are you otherwise? Have you had any more headaches or noticed any more changes from day to day?'

'Nope.' There was a tiny incident recently when she had discovered she'd put her hairbrush in the fridge (of all places!), but Abby wasn't going to mention that because she honestly didn't think that doing such a thing was anything other than a case of simple absentmindedness. Everyone did those kinds of things now and again, didn't they? Things like searching for car keys when they're already in your hand, or sunglasses when they're on your head. So it was nothing, and if she mentioned the incident to Hannah, the psychologist would probably only jump on it as more proof that her brain was indeed going mushy.

'Nothing at all?' She sounded sceptical, almost as if she knew Abby was trying to hide something.

'No, absolutely nothing. Yes, the headaches come and go, and I still get tired when reading, but other than that nothing. And I was thinking,' she began, deciding this was as good a time as any to broach the subject, 'I was thinking that seeing as I am OK, we don't really need to keep doing this, do we? You know, having these meetings.'

'You want to give up our sessions?'

'Pretty much, yes.' Abby couldn't help but feel a little sad. Hannah was lovely and it was nice to be able to talk to someone about all this, but at the same time she wanted to move on with her life and put the injury and, more importantly, talk of the injury behind her. Coming in every week to see Hannah and have the psychologist monitor her behaviour made that very difficult to do.

'Abby, it's only been a few months since your—' She seemed to be about to say something but caught herself. 'Since you left the hospital. Medically, it's still very early days yet. While I'm pleased that you don't seem to be experiencing any problems, at least none that you can identify—'

'What's that supposed to mean?'

'It means that you seem so determined that there's nothing wrong with you that you may very well be ignoring the signs. Don't worry, this is perfectly normal behaviour. Nobody likes to admit to problems where their mental capacities or brain function are concerned, which is understandable, but at the same time can be very dangerous.' Then her voice softened. 'Abby, I'm not implying that this is deliberate on your part; I'm just concerned that the situation is still very fragile. We don't want to run ahead of ourselves until we know exactly what we're dealing with.'

Abby said nothing, and tried hard to fight back her frustration.

'I know this is disappointing for you, and I'm sorry, but as your neuropsychologist it would be irresponsible of me to agree to your discontinuing our sessions. On the other hand, I can't force you to attend them, but you should be aware that in order for us to grant the necessary approval for your return to work, we need to be a hundred per cent confident of your capacities.'

This was all said in the kind, friendly tone the psychologist always used, but Abby recognised the covert warning in there. Like her mother, the doctors were convinced that memory problems were inevitable. They simply didn't share Abby's faith and utter determination to overcome this and fight it every step of the way.

A few days later, she was sitting at home trying to find something more interesting to do than cleaning the flat (again!) or watching depressingly boring daytime TV when she got a phone call.

'Hi, Ms Ryan. It's Tina from the American Holidays Travel Centre.'

'Hi, Tina, how are you?'

'Good, thanks. I'm just calling in relation to the payment for your trip to California.'

The insurance money had finally come through and Abby had wasted no time in booking the flights, hotels and of course the all-important convertible for her and Erin's trip.

'Yes, I sent you a cheque at the end of last week,' Abby told her. 'Didn't you get it?'

'Well, yes, we did get it, and that's why I'm calling you, actually. We got the cheque sent back from the bank this morning saying that it's out of date. I had a look at it and it has last year's date on it instead of this year's. Easy mistake – I'm always doing that kind of thing myself – but you know how fussy the banks are.'

'Oh.' Abby felt a prickle of anxiety run down her spine.

'So I'm putting it back in the post to you today, and if you could just cross out the "2007" and put in "2008" and then initial the change, it should be fine. I've made a note on the file so there won't be any issue with late payment or anything. Is that all right?'

'Sure, that'll be fine. Sorry about that.'

'No problem.' Tina was all chat. 'As I said, I'm always doing the same thing myself. I never know where my mind is sometimes!'

Having promised to send back the amended cheque as soon as possible, Abby hung up the phone, unsure what to think.

Like the hairbrush, this was probably just another case of absentmindedness, wasn't it? Or could it be, as Hannah had suggested only recently, a symptom of something more? No, Abby thought, pushing the idea firmly out of her brain, of *course* it was just absentmindedness. Everyone did things like that at one time or another, especially when writing the first cheque of a new year. But wasn't this year . . . Abby's heart hammered with fear as a horrible sense of disorientation suddenly overcame her. No, that had to be it, she convinced herself, refusing to entertain any other explanation, it was actually the first cheque of *2008* she'd written and she just hadn't been thinking straight.

End of story.

Chapter 22

So today was Dermot's turn, and to be honest, my baby
brother's idea of what might be a memorable experience
wasn't something I was particularly looking forward to. But
when I found myself zooming round a racetrack doing over a
hundred miles an hour in a bright-red Ferrari – and loving it –
I was completely taken by surprise!

'I know what you're thinking,' Dermot said, when we arrived
at the track and he saw my cynical expression, 'and, yes,
maybe this is as much for me as it is for you. But trust me, it'll
be great.'

Dermot had kept today's destination a surprise, and as
arranged, I'd called to the apartment he shared with his mates
earlier this morning, almost dreading what he'd planned, as
like most twenty-something guys my brother's interests mostly
consist of football, rugby and probably lots and lots of beer.

Caroline had been teasing me about it for weeks. 'I think
you're very brave, putting yourself in his hands,' she kept
saying every time we tried to envision what Dermot had in
store for me.

Initially, I admit I was a bit disappointed by Dermot's kind of
predictable and laddish choice of memorable experience, but
when I saw the impressive selection of high-powered cars lined
up in front of us, I began to think that this wasn't such a bad
idea after all!

While I'm not exactly banned from driving at the moment, the doctors recommended I stay off the road other than when absolutely necessary. Apparently I might become disorientated, or make what Hannah calls 'an ill-advised manoeuvre'. Biggest surprise of the day was that Dermot had had the wherewithal to consult Hannah about his plans and she had given his idea the all-clear.

While my trusty Ford Focus couldn't hold a candle to the racecars I've always enjoyed that sense of freedom you get when you're bombing along a clear bit of road, and I couldn't help feeling a thrill of excitement at what it would feel like to really let loose on a racetrack.

I soon found out!

Firstly, me and Dermot each had a trial run doing three laps of the track in a lowly Subaru. While my little brother, of course, couldn't wait to tear round pushing speeds of up to a hundred miles an hour, I was a bit more wimpy, preferring to just get my bearings on the track before the main event.

Then the famous Ferrari 360 was wheeled out. When I lowered myself into the driving seat, I couldn't help but feel a little overawed, not to mention very cool (although this effect was slightly spoilt by Dermot grinning maniacally at me from the sidelines). I mean this kind of thing is normally reserved for Formula One racers or the rich and famous, and here was little old me getting ready to roll!

When I was all belted in, and the instructor directed me to rev the engine, I heard (and felt) the famous Ferrari howl, and I have to say I felt this incredible thrill. This was so cool!

Barely a brush with the accelerator sent the car zooming straight down the track, and trying to control the speed on the tight corners was bloody terrifying, but still heart-thumpingly fantastic! I was sure the instructor in the passenger seat could hear me laughing like a mad thing through the safety helmet

as the car zoomed along the tarmac, but I didn't care. This –
this hair-raising but at the same time amazingly liberating
feeling of almost complete and utter abandon – was incredible.
My heart was still thumping madly when I hauled myself out
of the driver's seat, and I just couldn't wait to see the pictures
Dermot had taken of me zipping along in the Ferrari.

Yet again a member of my family gets it right. I can't help
but wonder if they truly know me better than I know myself.

On the way back to Dublin, Abby and Dermot stopped for
lunch in a service station off the motorway.

'God, that was brilliant!' Dermot was almost dumbstruck
from his own experience with the racecar, which took him
to the car's maximum speed of a hundred and eighty miles
an hour. 'And I told you you'd enjoy it.'

'Well, I wasn't sure about it when you first told me, but,
yes, it was really, really great,' Abby enthused. 'And I'm
delighted you got photos, although I don't know how I'm
going to make out myself from an out-of-focus red blur!
But don't worry, I'll be transferring the whole experience
to my computer files later.'

Dermot was silent for a moment, and when he spoke again,
his tone was gentle. 'It must be strange to think that you'll
forget everything that's happening now.'

Abby shook her head. '*Not* going to happen,' she said determinedly. 'Think about what we did just now. How could *anyone*
forget that?' She grinned. 'As far as I'm concerned, this is
working – I'm really fighting it. I had a brilliant day out with
Caroline, I've got the road trip with Erin coming up soon,
and then I'm off to Italy with Mum.' She chuckled, thinking
about her list, which had now lengthened considerably!

God, it had been such a great idea. This whole exercise
had been such a great idea! She was only a little way through
the list and already her attitude and spirits had improved

no end. And to think it had all started when she'd finally cast aside *one* of her neuroses and got on a plane to New York.

The trip was still so fresh in her mind she could almost picture it. All the family together and having a laugh around the dinner table on Christmas Eve, Claire's beautiful Christmas tree, little Caitlyn's gummy smile . . . it had been brilliant. A full account of that visit, as well as her adventures with Caroline in London and a multitude of a photographs had been transferred and saved to her computer in a memory chest Zach had made for her.

Abby kept telling herself she was doing this because it was a great idea no matter what, but despite her protests that it was working, she realised that she was saving and storing up all these great experiences and memories because somewhere deep down she was afraid that they might, in the end, be lost to her. It wasn't something she would admit out loud to Hannah, or indeed to anyone else, but there was no denying that she still felt better, *safer*, doing this instead of just leaving things to chance.

'It just seems so weird,' Dermot was saying. 'I don't know what I'd do if something like that happened to me. And I really think you're right to do what you're doing, dive-bombing your head with all this great stuff. And don't tell her I said this, but it was a brainwave of Caroline's to have us arrange things for you too. I had such a good time trying to come up with something cool for you that I'm half thinking of making my own list, a sort of "things to do before I'm thirty".'

Abby smiled. 'You should, and, yeah, I have to admit I *am* really enjoying it.'

'Good. It's given you a new lease of life! Everyone was so worried when you . . .' Then he reddened and trailed off.

'I know, I know,' Abby said easily. 'I guess you must have

all been worried about me when Kieran dumped me, although from what Caroline said, it sounds as though you were a bit relieved too.'

Dermot seemed to relax a little. 'Well, no – it wasn't that we *hated* him or anything; it's just that he . . . well, he was a bit square, wasn't he? And you guys never seemed to do anything except sit in and watch TV.'

When Abby just smiled and said nothing, he seemed to sense it was time to change the subject. 'Fancy a coffee?' he asked, getting up from the table.

'Sure.' She was enjoying their chat and was in no rush to get back to Dublin.

'So, tell me more about this road trip you and Erin are planning,' he asked then, coming back with a couple of coffees. 'I can't believe you're going to do Vegas, you lucky cow – I'd *kill* to go there,' he went on. Then he gave her a sideways look. 'To be honest, you're the last person I thought would go somewhere like that.'

Abby looked at him. 'Why?'

'Well, don't hate me, but I always thought you felt all that stuff was a bit . . . beneath you.'

'*Beneath* me?'

'Yeah, you and . . .' He faltered as he realised he was back on difficult ground.

'Me and Kieran?' Abby finished for him.

'Yeah. I'm sorry, but I guess me and him never really gelled. I probably just didn't know him very well, and I'm sure he was a great guy once you got to know him and all that, but I always felt he was a bit . . . stuck-up.'

Abby sighed, realising she was hearing this kind of thing a lot lately. 'I'm sorry, Dermot, I honestly had no idea you felt that way. As for me thinking that certain things were beneath me . . . well, I really don't know where you got that from as it couldn't be further from the truth.'

'Yeah, well, I suppose Kieran reckoned that a lowly grease monkey isn't the same as a high-flying taxman.'

'How many times do I have to tell you? He wasn't a taxman, he was a tax *inspector* – and I'm sure he still is,' she added wryly.

'Anyway, I don't mean to upset you or anything, and this might sound stupid, but I just wanted to tell you that I think you're much better off without the guy. And what he did was way wrong and—'

'Yes, well' – Abby didn't really want to get into that just now – 'what about you? Anyone interesting in your life?'

When Dermot reddened slightly at this, her eyes widened. 'What? You mean there *is*! Well, come on, tell me more. Who is she, and why haven't we heard anything about her?'

'Well, it's nothing really,' her brother said gruffly, but Abby could see that inwardly he was squirming at having to discuss his love life with his sister. 'I've known her for a while, so . . . as I said, it's nothing really.'

'Nothing my ass. You should see your face!' Abby couldn't resist milking this for all it was worth. It was obvious her baby brother was smitten with this girl, whoever she was. 'What's her name, and when do we meet her?'

'Oh, for Christ's sake, it's nothing like that. As I said, it's just a casual thing and that's all there is to it. But, look, whatever you do, don't go blabbing to Mam about it. She'd have me driven demented going on about it like you are, and I don't want that.'

'OK.' Abby nodded. She was actually hugely gratified that he'd confided in her in the first place, and she wasn't going to risk losing that trust. 'But if it becomes more than just a casual thing, then I want to meet her.'

'I'll think about it.' Dermot grinned before again deftly changing the subject.

He'd really grown up in the last while, Abby mused. While

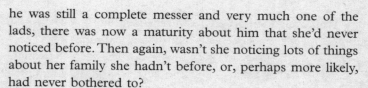

he was still a complete messer and very much one of the lads, there was now a maturity about him that she'd never noticed before. Then again, wasn't she noticing lots of things about her family she hadn't before, or, perhaps more likely, had never bothered to?

She picked up her coffee mug and drank from it. 'I'll tell you, it's a good thing the insurance money has come through now, otherwise I'd be broke by the time all this travelling is finished and— Ugh!'

'What's the matter?' Dermot asked, seeing her grimace.

'This coffee is like poison!' It was so bad Abby's first instinct had almost been to spit it out.

'Sugar might help,' her brother said, waving an unopened packet in front of her. 'You forgot to put it in. Here, two is your usual, isn't it?'

At this, Abby felt a bead of trepidation. But she didn't take sugar, did she? Seeing Dermot's suspicious frown, she quickly opened a couple of packets and stirred them in, before raising the mug to her lips once more. She'd *never* taken sugar in her coffee, she was sure of that . . . But as the liquid hit her tongue and she discovered it tasted absolutely fine, her skin broke out in a cold sweat. This was weird . . .

'Better?' Dermot asked, and Abby simply nodded, almost afraid to say another word.

Chapter 23

Finn knocked sharply on the door of his old home, but getting no immediate reply, eventually let himself in with his own key. Although he'd grown up in this house, he still didn't believe in just barging in on his father whenever he felt like it – despite Pat's repeated protests. 'Sure 'tis your house too!'

Still, since the discovery of Pat's health problems, and his yo-yoing PSA count, Finn had this irrational fear of his father collapsing in the house on his own. He knew it was highly unlikely with such a non-life-threatening condition, but now that the prospect of illness and old age had raised its head, Finn couldn't help worrying about his father and had started checking in on him at least every other day.

Other than his regular hospital visits, Pat was the same easygoing, happy-go-lucky man he'd always been, and seemed to find Finn's over-concerned behaviour amusing. 'Will you ever go away and stop treating me like an oul' fella?' he'd joked shortly after the first hospital visit, when Finn had kept finding excuses to drop by the house.

Today, though, Finn wasn't just checking in on Pat; he was going to a DIY shop in Blanchardstown and had called by to see if his father needed anything. The two of them had recently installed some decking at the rear of the house, which was probably exactly where Pat was right now, Finn thought, and why he hadn't heard the door. His father loved having breakfast out on the decking, and seeing as it was such a fresh spring day . . .

Heading in the direction of the kitchen, Finn thought he heard voices. Ah, Nora must be here too, he thought. Their neighbour and long-time friend was great for fussing over Pat and often popped in for a visit, especially since her own husband passed away a few years back. A heavy smoker all her life, Nora had an unusually deep and coarse voice, so Finn could tell it was her a mile away. The back door was ajar, so Finn bypassed the kitchen, planning to go straight out to them, but just as he was about to call out and announce his presence, something Nora said made him pause.

'I really think you should tell Finn, Pat.'

Finn stood rooted to the spot and frowned. *Tell him what?*

'Ah, I don't know, Nora. You wouldn't know how that sort of thing would affect him. He's bad enough as it is, fussing over me left, right and centre.'

'Reason enough for him to know, then.'

An icy fear crept down Finn's spine. What the hell were they talking about? What was he supposed to know, and more importantly why didn't he know it already? Then his stomach dropped as the realisation hit him and he closed his eyes. Evidently, Pat was a lot sicker than he was letting on.

'No, the timing isn't right,' his father was saying now, as Finn remained standing in the hallway, immobile.

'When will it ever be right, though?' Nora replied. 'Pat, he's a grown man, well able to handle anything that comes his way.'

'Ah, he is and he isn't,' his father said, which made Finn wonder what the hell he meant. He soon found out. 'I know he's still a bit cut up over your woman Danielle.'

Finn's eyes widened. Well, that might be true, but he didn't think he'd ever given his dad that impression.

'But that was ages ago, surely? What makes you think that?'

'You don't think it's strange that a fella his age isn't out on the town enjoying himself?'

Nora chuckled. 'And surrounding himself with good-looking women instead of dogs, you mean?'

Cheers, Nora, Finn thought. I don't see them lining up at your door either. But as he knew well she wasn't being cruel, he couldn't resist a smile. That made him sound fairly pathetic, really!

'I don't know, but I'd like to see him settled all the same. There was a bit of a spring in his step when he came back from America that time, which made me wonder, but obviously it came to nothing.'

Finn was amazed that his father could read him so well. Well, yes, he had enjoyed meeting that girl in New York at Christmas, but with the jet lag and everything, he hadn't thought it showed *that* much!

'Well, I wouldn't be using that as an excuse not to tell him,' Nora went on. 'As I said, he's a grown man and he deserves to know. But that's just my opinion. Anyway, will we go in? I know you like it out here, but it's still only March and the wind is going through me!'

At this, Finn stepped back, unsure what to do. He wanted to go right out, let them know he'd overheard, and demand that Pat confess whatever it was he was keeping from him, but at the same time he was almost afraid of hearing it. What if his dad was seriously ill? How would he handle that? As he heard the two of them start to make their way inside, Finn sneaked back up the hallway and out through the front door.

Chapter 24

Viva Las Vegas!

Really surreal to drive through the desert at night and watch this huge neon metropolis appear as if out of nowhere. I've seen the Vegas skyline so many times on films and TV that somehow it didn't feel real.

Erin and I are loving, *loving* the convertible! There's nothing quite like driving along, feeling the wind in your face and looking up and being able to see a blanket of blue sky above, although the major downside is that the wind is playing *havoc* with our hair. So much for getting my beloved curls back; at the moment, it's just a ball of frizz! Late last night, after a very long flight, we arrived in LA, but only spent the night at an airport hotel before picking up the car this morning. Then it was straight out of the city (very scary sixteen-lane highways, which, unbelievably, Erin just breezed through) and straight on to Vegas!

Having stopped off a couple of times along the route, we arrived in Vegas late evening, and driving on to the South Strip, we immediately spotted our hotel. The Luxor is a huge pyramid, and on top of this is a laser so bright it can be seen from space, apparently. Nearby are the colourfully lit skyscrapers of New York-New York, which (much to my relief!) immediately triggered memories of Manhattan. Another sign that all of this must actually be working!

Anyway, difficult to describe accurately how big, brash and utterly *mad* this place is – I suppose you could say it's like visiting a different planet. For example, when we pulled over to fill up on petrol on the outskirts of the city, we were instantly greeted by the sight (and sound) of slot machines – at a petrol station! I couldn't help but wonder why anyone would drive all the way out into the desert to spend their time gambling in a service station outside Vegas, but as there were people doing just that, what do I know?

'Well, it is Vegas,' Erin keeps saying over and over, as if either of us could forget. (Then again, I suppose in my case, this could well be possible!)

The hotel, though, is simply jaw-dropping – a humongous thirty-storey black glass pyramid with a huge sphinx guarding the entrance, and inside are huge statues of various Egyptian pharoahs. In keeping with the theme, the entire hotel staff are wearing Egyptian-themed clothing! Just as we'd expected, it is big, bold and so unbelievably tacky that I fell in love with it on sight. The lift to our room travels along an incline up the pyramid, which felt strange at first but soon had us both in fits of giggles.

We dropped off our bags and freshened up a little, and were just getting ready to head straight back down to the casino when Erin looked at her watch and said she needed to make a phone call.

'Sure,' I said easily, plonking myself on the bed.

Which was when things got a teeny bit weird.

'Um, actually,' she said, blushing, 'it's kind of private.'

Well! At first, I didn't know what to make of that, but then I thought about how bubbly and happy she's been over the last while and I started to wonder if maybe she's started seeing someone. And she doesn't want to admit this to me yet in case I get upset over not having Kieran.

After all, not so long ago *I* was the one in a relationship, while she was single, so maybe she's worried I'll get upset if the tables are turned. If so, she really shouldn't worry about that. I'm becoming more and more removed from Kieran as time goes on, but because I turned into such a boring weirdo after we broke up, then maybe I can't blame Erin for thinking that her meeting someone might set me back!

I don't know, either way she seemed so uncomfortable that I didn't want to push it, so I told her I'd head off and meet her downstairs when she was ready. Hopefully, whatever it is – or more likely whoever it is – I'm sure she'll tell me in her own good time.

So, the casino – wow. It's an absolutely massive area that seems to me to be about the size of a football pitch, all bursting with slot machines, roulette tables and poker rooms. To be honest, at first I felt a bit intimidated and disorientated by all the flashing lights, dinging bells and brightly patterned carpets.

Before we left, Dermot told us that the hideous carpets are part of a psychological tactic used by the casino owners to ensure that your eye is drawn away from the carpet and upwards to the slots, which I suppose makes sense. Also, there are no windows or clocks in the casinos, so gamblers have no idea what time it is – day or night – which is another trick to keep them spending money.

When Erin came down, the two of us decided that we'd spend most of our money on the slots, as the gaming tables looked too intimidating and complicated, whereas the slots seemed a no-brainer. Unfortunately, they turned out exactly that – brainless – and I felt like a bit of a drone sitting there pressing buttons and hoping for the right combination to come up and the machine to ring.

So when this didn't happen, I got bored and left Erin to it. Instead, I wandered across to the gaming tables where roulette was in full swing. Judging by the 'ooh's and 'aah's coming from the players and onlookers, this seemed way more exciting.

Coming up to the table, I spotted players piling their chips high on red and black numbers, and was trying to figure out how the game was played when some guy elbowed his way past me and casually placed a hundred-dollar bill on the table. A hundred-dollar bill!

Well, I was hugely impressed at this display of recklessness – it seemed a real 'Vegas' thing to do – so, eager to get right into the swing of things, I decided to do the very same thing myself, and casually dropped a hundred on the black panel right beside his red. I was so cool you'd swear I'd been doing this kind of thing all my life, although my heart was thumping like mad.

Imagine my delight (and relief!) when the ball landed on the black number seventeen and the croupier calmly placed two hundred dollars worth of chips in front of me! Just like that, I'd doubled my money! Erin's eyes nearly popped out of her head when she came up alongside me and saw what had happened. Needless to say, it wasn't long before she joined me at the table and the two of us were casually laying chips and bets like a couple of high-rollers.

The croupier, who was obviously well used to gobshites like ourselves, eventually decided to give us a crash course on how to play the game; she was no doubt sick to the teeth of warning us over and over again not to start eagerly laying fresh bets before the previous spin's winnings had been paid out – a terrible habit of Erin's. Because of my great beginner's luck with black seventeen, I then went gung-ho placing huge bets on it in almost every round, but for some reason my so-called lucky number refused to come up again, and much to my annoyance, seemed to only reappear at nearby tables. Typical!

Still, I kept telling myself that gambling in Vegas is less

about the money and more about the experience, although I can't deny the thrill I felt every time the little white ball fell on one of my numbers, or the disappointment when the croupier took back every cent of my hard-earned winnings. The house always wins.

On the first night, I slept like a baby, the combination of jet lag and the euphoria at having an early run of luck in Sin City proving a great sleeping pill, not to mention the never-ending glasses of complimentary alcohol the waitress kept serving us at the table. Now I understand why people love this place so much!

And from then on, the slots haven't had a look-in. For the last two days, we've gone from hotel to hotel trying our luck at the roulette tables in the different casinos and marvelling at how each place seems even bigger and even more extravagant than the last.

At the MGM Grand, real, live *lions* watched us from their huge glass-fronted habitat area right on the casino floor (a bit cruel, I thought, especially amidst all those flashing lights), but they seemed to really enjoy the attention and it all looked pretty spectacular nonetheless. At New York-New York, we took a ride through 'downtown Manhattan' on the hotel's huge rollercoaster, before blowing another couple of hundred in the casino. I lost particularly badly in both places, was convinced that my luck lay only in the Luxor, and for a while flatly refused to gamble anywhere else.

But it's so difficult to restrict yourself to one place in Vegas, particularly when there's so much to see and do, and so I eventually allowed myself to be dragged along the Strip to see some of the other hotels' attractions, such as Paris's Eiffel Tower (a half-sized replica of the real thing) and Siegfried and Roy's Secret Garden at the Mirage, a strange oasis in the middle of the desert filled with lush tropical plants. We also took in a trip to the observatory deck of the Stratosphere, which stands at one hundred and fifteen storeys, where we got a magnificent view of the Strip at dusk.

Then, last night, we went for a walk along the Strip. At the Mirage, scores of people gathered outside on the street waiting for the hotel's famous volcano to erupt. After a few moments of foreboding silence, cascading water began to churn and a low rumble emerged from the heart of the volcano. Then, to the crowd's delight, an eruption kicked into high gear as bright-orange flames dramatically leapt about a hundred feet above the water, illuminating the night sky. Again, tacky but brilliant!

But for me, the highlight of our trip to Vegas (apart from my brilliant first-night, never-to-be-repeated winning streak!) was the fountain display at the Bellagio. We took our places among the hordes of people gathered in front of the quarter-mile-long lake outside the gorgeous Italian-themed hotel. The first bars of Sinatra's 'Fly Me to the Moon' began and time seemed to stand still as the fountains came to life and water shot high into the air in time to the music. Some of the movement was continuous as the fountains responded to the notes, while other water jets pulsed high into the night sky, drawing gasps of awe and delight from us all.

'Wow,' Erin said, squeezing my arm. 'It's beautiful, isn't it?'

It was truly stunning, and will surely be one of the highlights of my quest for unforgettable experiences.

Next up, later today, is our visit to the Grand Canyon. I really can't wait for this. It should be absolutely amazing, and I truly think that if my brain can allow fantastic memories like these to just fade away and die, then there really is no hope for me at all! But I pray this will not be the case.

Watch this space . . .

Chapter 25

Abby returned from the America trip brimming with enthusiasm, adrenaline and pages upon pages of diary entries. She'd also taken tons of photographs throughout the holiday – her and Erin in Vegas, the two of them at the Grand Canyon and in LA – as well as lots of video, and had transferred all of the information into the memory chest Zach had created for her. Abby didn't know what she'd have done without it. It was so easy to collect and store the information, and he'd set it up in such a way that all her diary recordings of a particular time or event could be saved electronically alongside the corresponding photographs and video clips. It made it simple, and also went a long way towards ensuring that everything stayed fresh and vivid in her mind.

Both the road trip and the obvious success of keeping a record of her experiences had got Abby thinking again about going back to work. It was now seven months since her accident, and in that time she'd done some amazing things – some she'd always wanted to do, and others that she hadn't, but one way or another they'd all played a part in enriching her life in ways she could never have anticipated.

Her list had helped her formulate some fantastic experiences and memories, and there was not doubt that in the process she had become much, much closer to her family. She was grateful for the huge effort they and Erin had gone to in helping her through the worst of it, and realised just how important they were to her and how lucky she was to have them in her life.

But perhaps best of all she'd finally begun to *really* start getting over Kieran and put the hurt of his betrayal behind her, and although she couldn't say she'd completely forgotten him or everything he'd done, she now knew that she was capable of moving on without him.

And seeing as she hadn't had any major lapses or memory blips, or indeed any sign of memory deterioration recently, it also looked to Abby as though her plan to fight the damage was working, despite what the doctors seemed to think.

'We'll have to wait and see,' Hannah trotted out her usual mantra at their most recent session. 'With these things, you just never know.'

But the idea of going back to work at Duffy Masterson, back to some form of normality, was especially heartening. There was of course the thorny question of whether or not Frank Duffy would have her back. A detailed report from Hannah about how the nature of her injury should not affect the part of her brain responsible for mathematics and logic should sufficiently allay any worries he might have, although Abby knew that if he *did* let her come back, her perform-ance would no doubt be under the spotlight for a while.

That was the way things were going to be from now on, Abby realised. Everything she said and did would be assessed and examined closely for signs of anything out of the ordin-ary. She should be used to it at this stage!

So, on a sunny morning in May, Abby called in to the accountancy firm to meet with her boss, discuss with him the idea of returning to work, and, she hoped, take the next logical step in reclaiming her life.

The meeting went reasonably well, and all her old colleagues greeted her enthusiastically upon her arrival at the office, but Frank seemed reluctant about having her back. 'I'm just not sure, Abby,' he said. 'This business can be very stressful, as you are well aware.'

'I know, but instead of being reassigned to my usual clients, maybe I could start by working on some of the smaller stuff . . .'

By this she meant the easier, more straightforward accounts, clients that were usually pawned off on newer staff or trainees, and which under normal circumstances an experienced accountant like Abby could do in her sleep. She supposed she couldn't blame Frank for being wary – until she'd proved herself up to the task, she herself couldn't be sure how she would perform, so a test of her brain's ability would be welcome in more ways than one.

'Abby, love, I'm sure you'd be fine with the numbers and all that, but it's been under eight months and the doctors recommended at least a year, didn't they?'

'I know, but, Frank, I'll end up going out of my mind at home with nothing to do all day.' Granted, with having to complete the list, she had plenty to keep her occupied for a while, but once she came back down to earth, Abby knew she'd be bored.

'Look, why don't you have another chat with the doctors, then, see what they think?' he said, and Abby knew her boss was giving her the brush-off. Blast Hannah for insisting on the full year off. Surely she knew that keeping her mind occupied could only be good for her brain?

'OK,' Abby replied, her disappointment almost palpable.

Frank looked guilty. 'I'm sorry,' he said. 'Believe me, we're so busy at the moment I'd like nothing better than to have you back, but at the same time I don't want to be responsible for . . . well, you know . . . for anything going wrong.'

'Fair enough.' She supposed she could appreciate his position; after all, if anything *did* happen, he'd never be able to forgive himself, or perhaps more importantly his solicitor would never be able to forgive him! Still, it was disheartening to think that people were still suspicious of her capabilities, even though she'd proved time and time again, both to herself and everyone else, that she was fine.

'But if you don't mind my saying so, I think that old bump on the head might have done you a bit of good all the same,' Frank joked, when Abby had eventually agreed with his reasoning. 'You seem a lot more relaxed and certainly much smilier these days!'

'Yes, I suppose you're right,' Abby said, blushing a little.

It was true, she thought, while she'd always worked diligently, following the break-up she had been quiet and reserved, and had tended not to mix with her work colleagues all that much.

'Ah, don't mind me,' Frank back-pedalled, obviously worried he'd overstepped the mark. 'I was only joking. I know you've had a terrible hard time of it altogether.'

Abby shook her head. 'In all honesty, you're not the first person to think that, and there's probably a bit of truth in it. I know I can't have been the most fun person to have in the office.' She smiled. 'If anything, the accident taught me that I shouldn't take life so seriously, so, yeah, maybe it has done me some good.'

'Still, I hear there could still be some . . . some more side effects,' he ventured, his tone gentle.

'Yes, but you know what these doctors are like – always concentrating on the negative.'

'I surely do,' her boss agreed vehemently. 'Sure, I remember one time they brought me into hospital to get a verucca removed, put me under the anaesthetic and everything, and when I woke up, they told me that they couldn't find it! Can you believe it? With all their fancy diplomas they didn't think to check if the bloody thing had gone away by itself before carting me off to theatre. And I was falling down with hunger from fasting the night before! What kind of a health service do we have? I wonder. Sure, for all they know that bump could have done you no harm at all.' He grinned. 'I certainly can't see too much wrong with you, anyway.'

Exactly! Abby thought, pleased that someone else was finally coming round to her way of thinking.

'So come back to me in a few months' time and we'll see how you are then. How does that sound?' Frank said, giving her the elbow once and for all.

'OK, then,' Abby agreed with a sigh, wishing that everyone would just try and have a little more faith.

The day had started reasonably well for Finn. The weather was warm, the skies clear and bright, and as today was his day off, he'd decided to head into town for a while, taking Lucy along for company.

The two of them had taken the bus right into the centre of the city, and had disembarked at O'Connell Street. Despite the crowds on one of the busiest thoroughfares in the country, Lucy weaved through the throng of tourists and shoppers, negotiating their route with practised ease. Finn was gratified that she hadn't forgotten that part of her training. Then again, once a guide dog always a guide dog, he supposed, and thinking of which . . .

Finn reached into the rucksack he carried with him and strapped a visibility vest on to Lucy's back, a cheeky little trick of his that ensured the two of them got access to every public amenity and retail premises in the city. OK, so he knew he was being incredibly brazen and more than a little dishonest, but it was almost lunchtime, and it wasn't fair to leave poor Lucy tied up outside alone while he ate – particularly not when she was used to going into these places, and knew exactly how to behave. So while the easygoing bus driver hadn't batted an eyelid when he'd boarded with a dog in Balbriggan, Finn knew that the owners and managers of most city-centre establishments wouldn't be too pleased to allow him access unless Lucy looked to be a working dog.

Having enjoyed a hearty fry-up in one of his favourite cafés, he and Lucy eventually continued walking across O'Connell Bridge and onwards to Grafton Street, which with its multitude of determined shoppers and noisy buskers could test the patience of most humans, never mind retired guide dogs! But yet again Lucy was totally at ease with it all.

'Good girl!' Finn praised, proffering a treat when they reached the gates of St Stephen's Green.

The dog wagged and munched enthusiastically on her snack before almost instinctively standing to attention and awaiting her next instruction. Poor old Lucy was still a long way off getting used to retirement, if ever.

'OK, let's go and see if we can find a bench,' he said, thinking it might be nice to sit for a while and just watch the world go by.

As it was a gorgeous, sunny day and unusually warm, after saying goodbye to Frank Abby decided to take the short walk downtown for lunch. She grabbed a takeaway coffee and bagel on the way, thinking she would go into the green and have her lunch there – her and about a hundred others, she thought ruefully upon arrival. Office workers, young mothers and various weirdly dressed student types were sitting on benches, on the edge of the fountains and strewn out over the grass, all trying to make the most of the rare sunshine.

She was just choosing a suitable patch of grass to sit on when she spotted an elderly couple vacating a nearby wooden bench. Glad of the opportunity to eat her lunch in comfort, Abby quickened her pace and was heading towards the seat when a blind man and his guide dog got there first. Hesitating at the sight of the dog, she allowed him to claim the seat instead.

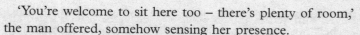

'You're welcome to sit here too – there's plenty of room,' the man offered, somehow sensing her presence.

Slightly thrown, Abby wasn't sure what to do. 'No, it's fine,' she began protesting, not at all comfortable with the dog's proximity. 'I can always sit on the . . .' Then her voice trailed off when she realised the man was looking at her strangely. And, yes, he was definitely looking right at her, not just in her direction or straining to make her out; he was looking at her and he was smiling.

'Well, hello again,' he said with a broad grin. 'Fancy bumping into you here!'

He seemed so convinced he recognised her that Abby wasn't sure how to break it to the poor man that she'd never seen him in her entire life. It was obvious he'd mistaken her for someone else, what with him being blind and all, she reasoned uncomfortably. God, this was awful. How could she tell the guy that he'd made a mistake? The last thing she wanted was to embarrass him in public, especially when the couple alongside them on the bench were very obviously earwigging!

'Um, I'm really sorry,' Abby began, mortified to have to say this, 'but I think you've mistaken me for someone else. It's understandable of course . . . I mean . . . it's not your fault and . . .' she babbled on, wishing the ground would open up and swallow her.

But at this, the man started to laugh. 'Oh, God, sorry. No wonder . . . This isn't a . . . I'm not actually *blind*,' he said, indicating the Labrador, who looked up and dutifully wagged its tail.

Abby frowned, confused. 'You're not?'

'No, not at all. This isn't my guide dog. Well, she *is* mine, but—' He broke off, shaking his head. 'Sorry – I can see why you're confused. There's nothing wrong with my eyesight and' – his voice dropped to a whisper and he looked sideways at the neighbouring couple, who were now getting up to leave – 'she's not actually a guide dog.' He grinned mischievously and again Abby was struck by the familiar way in which he spoke to her, clearly convinced they had somehow met before.

But had they? Abby didn't think so. He was very good-looking, with his dark-brown hair and even darker eyes, and she was certain she would have remembered if . . . Then all of a sudden, her heart skipped a beat, and a trickle of fear began to make its way up along her spine.

'I'm sorry, where did you say you knew me from?' she asked, somehow managing to find her voice.

'Well, New York of course,' he replied, as if this was a stupid question. 'On Christmas Eve? We met in Central Park when the squirrels made away with your sandwich . . .'

At this, something niggled in the corner of Abby's mind, something she couldn't quite get a handle on.

When there was no immediate recognition on her part, the man went on, 'I spent the afternoon showing you around the city. We did the whispering thing in Grand Central Station and went up to the Rockefeller Center, the Top of the Rock. Don't tell me you can't remember?'

Heart hammering, Abby racked her brain, trying furiously to figure out where all of this was coming from. She remembered being in New York of course – remembered staying with Claire and Zach and baby Caitlyn in their apartment. And she remembered the family having a really nice Christmas together and going to St Patrick's Cathedral for midnight mass, but that was about it. She certainly had *no* recollection of meeting some strange guy anytime during her visit, let alone spending an afternoon with him on Christmas Eve. So clearly he *must* be mistaking her for someone else and—

'Abby?' he said then, and at the mention of her name, suddenly her entire world began to spin, as she realised without a shadow of doubt that this guy really *did* in fact know her, and hadn't just mistaken her for someone else. Which could only mean . . .

'Abby? Are you all right? Bloody hell, you've gone as white as a sheet!'

Those were the last words Abby heard before her head filled up with stars, and the world suddenly went black.

Chapter 26

Abby opened her eyes, feeling something wet and cold on her face. She sat up quickly, wondering how on earth she'd ended up on the ground, and why a huge, scary-looking dog was resting alongside her, watching her intently. Then she noticed a man standing over her holding a bottle of water, and in an instant remembered what had happened. Oh, God, she'd fainted, she realised, mortified. Fainted in front of some guy who was convinced he knew her, and whom she had never seen before in her life!

'Are you OK?' the man asked, his dark eyes full of concern. 'I tried to catch you, but you slid off the bench and on to the ground before I even realised what was happening.'

'Sorry,' she said, trying to stand up and put herself a million miles away from the terrifying mutt.

'Here.' He held out his hand, and still keeping a wary eye on the dog, Abby took it, glad of the assistance. 'Now, just sit there and take it easy for a while,' he said, helping her on to the bench. 'Do you want a drink of water or anything? I used a few drops on your face to try and wake you up – didn't have any smelling salts on me today, I'm afraid,' he added with a slight smile in his voice. 'Or if you want to wait there for a minute, I can always nip across the road and get you some hot chocolate.' He smiled. 'I know it won't be half as good as that stuff we had in New York, but . . .' He shrugged easily.

Abby was petrified. This was all so . . . so surreal, having a complete stranger come up to her in the park and start chatting to her as if he knew her well, talking about things they'd done together a few months before, things about which she had absolutely no recollection! Could it be some kind of joke? Or worse, she realised now, her stomach plummeting, was it simply proof that the doctors had been right all along, and her memory really was beginning to fail?

The thought of this was way too much for her to bear, and then, without warning, Abby put her hands over her eyes and began to sob. As she did, the dog moved closer and rested its large head on her lap. Abby jumped back quickly, terrified.

'Don't be afraid – Lucy's only trying to comfort you.'

Abby was frozen to the spot. 'I'm sorry, I'm just not . . . I'm kind of scared of dogs, actually.'

'Oh, OK.' He instructed it to move away, and to Abby's relief, the animal did. But even so, she couldn't stop sniffling. 'It's OK, she won't go near you, I promise,' he went on, now looking completely at a loss.

Brushing away tears, she eventually found her voice. 'I'm sorry,' she said, with a shake of her head. 'You must think I'm some kind of psycho, fainting and crying for no apparent reason, but the thing is, I really *don't* remember any of what you're telling me. I don't remember you, or meeting you in New York. To be honest, now I'm not entirely sure if I actually remember *being* in New York.' With that, the tears started again.

He frowned, perplexed. 'I don't understand . . .'

'I'm not sure if I really understand myself,' Abby went on. 'I mean, I *think* I do, but . . .' She bit her lip and shook her head, refusing to let more tears come. The realisation that she really was losing her memory was hard enough, let alone having to deal with it in front of a complete stranger!

Although, as far as he was concerned, he wasn't a stranger

at all, was he? God almighty, Abby thought, temporarily putting her own worries aside and wondering what on earth *he* was making of all this. Imagine someone you'd met and spent time with, bawling and crying about how they couldn't remember a single thing about any of it, including meeting you. How weird was that? Abby took a deep breath, supposing that she could maybe try and explain, but then again, chances were he'd run a mile if she even tried. Who *wouldn't*?

But the guy seemed to have little intention of running anywhere, and to Abby's great relief, wasn't looking at her as if she belonged in a mental home. Instead, he seemed genuinely sympathetic, if not completely bewildered by her carry-on.

'Look, you've obviously had a bit of shock,' he said kindly. 'Why don't I go and get us a couple of coffees, and when you've calmed down a little, maybe you can tell me all about it?'

Which was how, in the middle of Stephen's Green with a strange but gentle Labrador at her feet, Abby spent the rest of the afternoon spilling her heart out to a man she was absolutely sure she'd only just met, but who was so understanding about her situation it felt as though she'd known him for years.

Finn's head was spinning with all that she was telling him. It was a crazy story, and while it certainly didn't seem as though Abby was lying about her injury, it was incredible and, in fairness, a bit disheartening that she could have forgotten him completely. Disheartening because in direct contrast, since that time in New York he'd hardly been able to forget *her*.

He'd been there attending a three-day training seminar in Brooklyn held by the Guide Dogs of America and recalled how pissed off he'd been about his early-morning flight to

Dublin being cancelled. Initially, he'd been so busy on the phone explaining to his dad about the delay that he hadn't even noticed the girl sitting alongside him on the bench. It was really only when the squirrel had made away with her sandwich and they'd struck up a conversation that he'd realised she was Irish and (there was no denying it) a bit of a looker.

Then when they'd bumped into one another again at the Boathouse, and Abby had confessed that it was her first visit to New York, he'd decided that showing her around the city was as good a way as any to spend an afternoon.

And Finn had really enjoyed wandering around showing her the city at Christmas through his eyes. There was something almost childlike in the way she marvelled and enthused at the things he showed her and the stories he told, and he found himself enjoying her company in a way he hadn't done in years with *anyone*, let alone another woman. He'd eventually ended up walking her back to her sister's place, and they'd shared a *very* nice moment outside before going their separate ways. He'd been attracted to her then, there was no denying it. Even if she had kept calling him Phil for some reason! At the time, it hadn't felt right to take it further. Almost as if they were meant to have just that one perfect day, and trying for anything else would risk spoiling it.

Back then, he'd taken that afternoon exactly for what it was – two complete strangers brought together unexpectedly amid the charm of a New York Christmas Eve, a sort of very short-lived holiday romance, if you like. But since his return, he had to admit that his thoughts had more than once strayed to the girl he'd bumped into that day, the one who'd laughed at his jokes and had been so impressed by everything he'd shown her.

There had definitely been a connection between them, no doubt about that, but Finn had never expected their paths to cross again, and often regretted that he hadn't asked for her number. So when today they'd run into each other in St Stephen's Green, it had seemed like the best piece of luck, until the girl who'd occupied his thoughts so much hadn't the faintest clue who he was.

And however crazy her explanation was sounding, it was a lot better to believe than thinking she'd deliberately put him out of her mind. She'd obviously spent the last few months convincing herself that her memory was fine, and that the great lengths she'd gone to in the hope of 'fixing' it were working beautifully. Finn had been fascinated by her notion that cramming in all these great experiences could somehow halt her memory decline.

'Anyway, none of it matters now – the doctors were right in the end,' Abby said finally. The defeated look on her face and utter hopelessness in her tone made him want to hold her. 'I was an idiot to think I could have prevented this.'

'Look, you don't know that for certain,' Finn replied, not entirely sure how to handle this but wanting to try. 'You've remembered everything else that's happened since then, haven't you?'

Abby crumpled up her empty coffee cup and shook her head sadly. 'I don't know . . . I *think* I have, but maybe that's because I've been keeping diary records of everything and saving photos . . . so now I can't tell if it's my own memory or the computer's memory that's storing it all for me.'

Finn sat forward on the bench. 'Well, does it really matter?'

'What do you mean?'

'I'm not trying to be flippant, but at the end of the day does it really matter how or where these memories are stored as long as they're kept somewhere? If your own memory is fading but you're backing up everything anyway, then you'll still be able to recall things whenever you like, won't you? You can hold on to them for as long as you want.' He shrugged his shoulders. 'To be honest, I wish I'd thought of doing something like that, keeping a diary of my experiences as they happened. I've travelled all over the world, but I can only really recall a collection of things now – things that for whatever reason stand out from the others, like those monkeys in Thailand.'

When Abby looked blank, he quickly realised that as she couldn't remember meeting him, she'd hardly remember his thieving-monkeys story. 'Anyway, what I'm trying to say is that by keeping an account of all these things, you do get to hold on to them for ever.'

To his great satisfaction, Abby seemed a bit heartened by this. 'I suppose I've never thought of it that way,' she sighed. 'But maybe that's exactly why these experiences still feel so vivid in my mind. It's also why I got such a shock when I met you. As far as I was concerned, New York was *also* still fresh in my mind, but now it seems it's only the bits I put in my diary.' She looked away, trying to blink back tears.

'You didn't think enough of *me* at the time to put in your diary?' Finn teased, and to his immense relief, Abby raised a smile.

'Well, I'm thinking now that maybe that might have been a mistake!' she said, chuckling. 'From what you've told me, it sounds like we had a great time.'

'We did,' he said, smiling wryly, 'but here's me thinking I'm a memorable sort of guy when clearly I made no impression whatsoever!' Then he stopped short, realising that flirting with a girl who'd just discovered that she was suffering major memory decline probably wasn't the cleverest idea. His tone grew serious. 'Look, Abby, you've had a big shock today, and I'm sure you have a lot to think about, but try not to be too hard on yourself or get too upset about all this. So what if you don't happen to remember me? Big deal. It was only something small, something trivial even, and certainly nothing compared to all the amazing things you've seen and done over the last while. So why worry?' He breathed out deeply. 'I suppose what I'm trying to say is, don't abandon all hope. There's a very good chance that your memory could be working fine, and there are no guarantees that this means anything. It could just be a tiny blip like those others you described, nothing major. So go home, take it easy, and have another chat with your doctor. But whatever you do, don't let this set you back. From what you've told me, you've been having a whale of a time and really enjoying life – what's to stop that continuing?'

Abby smiled. 'Thanks, but maybe I knew deep down that something like this was going to happen. There were a couple of other things . . . little things, but I ignored them: I wanted to ignore them.'

'Maybe, but it doesn't really change anything, does it?'

'What do you mean?'

'Well, forgetting about me hasn't really affected your life at all, has it?' His eyes twinkled. 'My mates reckon I'm a complete pain in the backside anyway, so think of it as a lucky escape.'

'I doubt that,' Abby said, trying to raise a smile, but he could see the worry in her eyes. Then she looked at her watch. 'Listen, I really should be thinking about heading home,' she said distractedly. 'I've already taken up enough of your time.'

'Not at all. I'm only sorry that meeting me was what brought all of this on.' As much as he'd wanted to bump into her again, Finn now had mixed feelings about doing so.

'Please don't be. I'm glad I met you. You've been great, and probably the only person who hasn't looked at me like I'm crazy for even thinking I could beat this.'

'Crazy is the last word I'd use to describe you,' he replied softly. 'To be honest, I think you're very brave.'

'Thanks.'

The two were silent for a moment before Abby spoke again.

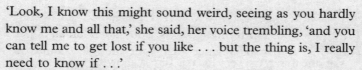

'Look, I know this might sound weird, seeing as you hardly know me and all that,' she said, her voice trembling, 'and you can tell me to get lost if you like . . . but the thing is, I really need to know if . . .'

Finn understood immediately. 'You want to find out if you can remember me again after today?' he finished.

'Yes.' She looked at him with guilty eyes. 'I'm sorry. I know I have no right to ask . . .'

'Don't be stupid. Of course you do, and for my part, I'm very glad.'

'Are you sure? I don't want you to feel as though you're part of some weird experiment or something.'

'It's not like that. Anyway, it cuts both ways because I'm really interested in finding out if I've made a lasting impression *this* time round!' he joked, and she laughed.

'OK, then, so how do you want to work it?' he asked, his tone growing serious again. This was important to Abby and he wasn't going to make light of it. Hell, it was important to *him*, and he hadn't been lying when he'd said he was eager to find out if he'd made an impression. Having been single for so long and then finally meeting a woman who'd roused his interest, wasn't it just his luck that the next time they met, she might not know him from Adam?

Despite Finn's suggestion, Abby decided in the end not to tell Hannah or anyone else. She wanted to wait until she was a hundred per cent sure that there really *was* a problem with her memory. Like he'd said, there was still a chance that this was something isolated, maybe some temporary lapse she'd experienced while in Manhattan. The strangest thing about it all was that she was sure she could recall pretty much everything else about the New York trip – she simply had no recollection whatsoever of going out on her own and meeting him. As far as she was concerned she'd spent the majority of her visit at her sister's, and since her return had been kicking herself for not seeing more of the city other than St Patrick's.

For one thing, the very idea of Teresa allowing her to wander around in a strange city on her own so soon after the accident was unimaginable, particularly as back then her mother had been watching her like a hawk. But as much as she desperately wanted to contact a member of her family and ask them if this was true, she couldn't risk them knowing that she'd drawn a blank. All hell would break loose.

It was taking every ounce of willpower she had not to diarise the events of that day, particularly when she'd really warmed to Finn – despite the shock to the system of learning that they'd already spent a considerable amount of time together.

But perhaps that was exactly *why* she'd warmed to him, because how on earth could she have absolutely no recollection of someone so gentle and lovely? Not to mention extremely good-looking, she thought with a smile, having no problem at all recalling from earlier those intense brown eyes and his handsome face.

For the umpteenth time, she cast her mind back to New York and tried desperately to remember something, anything at all that might jog her memory into action. But much to her dismay, there was nothing – nothing in the slightest resembling a jaunt around Manhattan, let alone with a good-looking Irishman. She recalled what Hannah and the doctors had said about how certain memories might very well be stored in her long-term memory, but due to the damage caused could begin to fade away much faster than was usual.

While the shock of knowing that her memory was actually failing had been horrifying and completely overwhelming, her subsequent chat with Finn had made her feel a little bit better. For one thing, his suggestion that it didn't matter what way her memories were stored as long as they were *indeed* stored made sense, and gave her back the one thing she needed in all of this: control. What he'd said about her having coped well up to now made sense too. She *had* coped well, and until today hadn't noticed anything out of the ordinary. Or at least she'd convinced herself she hadn't, Abby admitted guiltily, remembering how she had conveniently explained away any unusual incidents as regular absentmindedness.

Ultimately, though, Abby told herself, her resolve strengthening, the only way she could know for sure whether or not her memory was failing was by carrying out the experiment with Finn. That way, like it or not, she'd know once and for all.

Chapter 27

Abby knew that her mum would be keeping a close eye on her throughout their trip to Verona, constantly looking for signs of any problems. In order to combat this, she had decided from the outset to be on her best behaviour, and not give her mother any grounds for suspicion, otherwise her life wouldn't be worth living! In fairness, Teresa seemed willing to get into the spirit of the occasion and on the flight to Italy had been relaxed and chatty, and to Abby's great relief, had managed to stay away from talk or discussion about her 'condition'.

Of course, this particular jaunt wasn't about providing a good time for Abby; it was much more about ensuring a good time for Teresa, and Caroline had reminded Abby of this when dropping them off at the airport.

'Make sure Mum enjoys herself, won't you? This trip is a big deal for her.'

'Of course.' Abby didn't quite know what Caroline meant, but supposed she was in a roundabout way asking her to go easy on Teresa and try and be more relaxed about her fusspot nature.

Abby had confessed to her in London that she was finding her mother's scepticism and lack of enthusiasm for her 'project' hard to take, so no doubt Caroline was hoping that it wouldn't result in a tense situation all round. But Abby had no intention of letting such a thing happen. They were in Verona because Teresa had always wanted to see a real, live opera, and despite the fact that it wasn't exactly Abby's cup of tea, she was going to make sure they both enjoyed their time here.

She'd known that Italy was famous the world over for its stunning architecture and cultural attractions, but nothing could have prepared her for the picture-postcard beauty of Verona. Second only to Rome in terms of well-preserved monuments and ruins, the place was steeped in history, from the immense Porta Borsari, an archway that once made up part of the original city wall, to the mind-blowingly pictur-esque Piazza delle Erbe, one of the most charming and beau-tiful town squares Abby had ever seen. A busy tourist and bustling commercial area, the piazza was teeming with old Roman monuments and beautiful sculptures. The hotel that Caroline had booked for them was just a short walk away, and when they'd settled themselves in the small and equally charming boutique hotel, they decided to wander around the piazza and find somewhere nice for dinner.

'Isn't it gorgeous, Abby?' Teresa seemed just as taken with the place as she was. 'God, your dad would have loved this.'

Abby smiled. 'I'm sure he would.'

Who couldn't love Verona? It was romantic, historic, not to mention that it was also the setting for Shakespeare's *Romeo and Juliet*. On the way in from the airport, their taxi driver (who by his hair-raising driving reminded Abby of her own antics on the racetrack) advised Teresa and Abby to pay a visit to Juliet's balcony and the actual thirteenth-century home of the Capuleti family, which they agreed to do the following day.

They had an unhurried and enjoyable dinner in one of the many trattorias dotted around the piazza (although it took them both a while to get to grips with the multitude of different courses that made up a proper Italian menu), and afterwards relaxed over the delicious lemon and *bergamotto* sorbets their waiter had recommended.

Abby noticed her mother seemed quiet over the meal that evening, and suspecting that Teresa was tired after the journey, she suggested they head back to the hotel after dinner and delay their exploring until tomorrow.

'Do you mind, love?' Teresa seemed relieved.

'Not at all. An early night will do us both good – set us up for the big day tomorrow.'

Although in truth she'd love the opportunity to look around further, daylight was fading and she knew her mother wouldn't be comfortable with her wandering around a strange place on her own. Still, there would be lots of time to see everything tomorrow before the performance later in the evening.

Back at the hotel, she again noticed how tired and uncommunicative her mother was.

'Are you feeling OK, Mum?' she asked, getting into bed.

'I'm grand, love, a bit tired, but excited about tomorrow.'

Abby nodded. 'I have to admit that now that I've seen the place I'm quite looking forward to it.'

'Well, I know it's probably not really your thing, but seeing as I had a spare ticket, I thought it might be nice for you. I'm sorry I couldn't think of anything more exciting.'

Now Abby felt terrible. 'Don't be silly – of course this is exciting! I've never been to Italy before, and,' she added with a grin, 'we've never been away anywhere on our own before either, have we? No, it'll be great,' she assured Teresa. 'And I think we should make the most of our few days here by starting early tomorrow.'

'We will,' her mum said, smiling. 'Sleep well.'

The following day, they went on a walking tour around the city and took a closer look at some of the ancient and remarkably well-preserved Roman buildings. Abby had never really had any great interest in history – in her schooldays she had loathed it – but it was impossible to be in a place like this and not feel the weight of history bearing down upon you, or the power and grandeur of the Roman Empire.

Wandering along the tree-lined Via Alfredo Oriani, they eventually arrived at the main drag, a wide boulevard called Corso Porta Nova. From there, they headed for Piazza Brà, which they'd been told was where the Verona Arena was located. Entering the square beneath an impressive double arch, Abby's attention was immediately drawn to an immense Roman amphitheatre right in the centre of the square.

'That's where we're going tonight?' she gasped.

'Yes, I thought you knew that,' Teresa replied.

While she was of course aware that the opera performance they were going to attend would be held in some outdoor venue, she had absolutely no idea of the sheer scale and magnificence of the amphitheatre. For some reason, she'd been expecting something small and quaint, rather along the lines of the indoor movie theatres they had back home. So when they came across a place that looked like it was off the set of *Gladiator*, she was completely blown away. The arena was, in a word, massive, the third largest in Italy apparently, according to Teresa's guidebook.

'My God, can you imagine what it'll be like tonight?' Abby said, moving towards the outer walls.

But Teresa didn't reply, and when Abby looked round, she saw her mother still standing there in the middle of the square, gazing at the magnificent structure as if lost in a world of her own.

'Mum?' she prompted, concerned. Considering that this was supposedly something her mother had always wanted to do, she'd been strangely off form since they arrived here.

Teresa smiled tightly. 'Your father would have loved this.'

Abby frowned, realising that this was the second time her mother had said this. 'I'm sure he would,' she replied, puzzled, and went to move off again, before all of a sudden a thought struck her. 'Mum,' she said, her heart melting as she gently laid a hand on Teresa's arm. 'Was this something that you and Dad . . . something you planned to do together?'

Teresa nodded quickly, trying to hold back tears.

'Oh, Mum . . .' Now Abby understood why she'd been so quiet and uncommunicative lately. Putting an arm round her, she gently led Teresa away from the crowds towards a quieter spot on the edge of the square.

'We always said we'd go somewhere special on our fortieth, somewhere romantic. It was your dad who suggested here, and the opera because he knew how much I loved it. We had it booked and everything when . . .' She looked away, biting back tears.

Abby felt a huge lump in her throat. While she knew that her parents were due to celebrate their fortieth anniversary the same year that her dad, Jim died, she had actually forgotten this amid all the grief. But of course her mother wouldn't have forgotten something like that, and trying to get through today knowing that she and Jim should have been here together must have broken her poor mum's heart.

Knowing what she did now, Abby felt ashamed. To think that she had initially treated the invitation so casually, when this trip meant so much to her mother . . . And thinking back on it, this must have been what Caroline was referring to at the airport, when she'd asked Abby to ensure her mother enjoyed herself. Her sister had evidently known the significance of her gift to Teresa, and apparently had assumed Abby did too. Again she was taken aback by how much she'd estranged herself from her family in the last few years, and how little she truly knew them.

'Why didn't you tell me?' she asked her mother then.

'Ah, I didn't want you to feel obliged, or think that you had to hold my hand or anything,' Teresa said. 'Caroline suggested bringing one of my friends, but it just didn't seem right. If I was going to come here, I wanted someone I loved with me, someone who would understand.'

'Well, I'm glad— No,' Abby corrected herself quickly, 'I'm *honoured* you chose me, and I'm really pleased I'm here.'

Teresa smiled and squeezed her daughter's hand. 'So am I.'

★　　★　　★

Melissa Hill

6 June, Verona, Italy

Having toured around all day and seen the majority of Verona's wonderful sights – including Juliet's alleged balcony – later in the evening Mum and I put on our swankiest clothes and made our way to the Verona Arena for the performance of Verdi's *Aïda*.

While I'd been impressed by the amphitheatre from the outside, inside it was absolutely mind-blowing! The pit was surrounded by tiers of steps, which soared high above the stage. The theatre held up to twenty-five thousand spectators, most of whom were taking their places on the stalls at ground level in the pit, on numbered seats along the steps or, in our own case, on the bare steps themselves. I was pleased we weren't sitting on seats: for me, there was something about the steps that made the whole experience much more authentic and out of the ordinary. It was a wonderfully warm, balmy evening, and the fading light, coupled with the beautifully lit ancient Arena and the air of excitement surrounding the performance to come, really made for an electric atmosphere.

All too soon, the first act was announced, and almost immediately the hum and activity died down and there was complete and utter silence. Waiting for the music to begin, I found myself holding my breath, and then when the orchestra finally played the very first note, I felt a shiver run down my spine. Thinking back, I really can't believe I was so offhand about going to see *Aïda* – already it felt like a once-in-lifetime experience!

I smiled at Mum, who was also held rapt by the atmosphere and the sheer magic of the whole performance. And as the first act began in earnest, the two of us sat back and settled in to enjoy the show.

By the end of the third act, I can honestly say I had become an opera devotee. This was nothing, nothing like I'd ever seen, heard or experienced! The way the performance was capable of arousing and enrapturing the audience was little short of astonishing, and even though I didn't understand a word of what was being sung, I could feel every ounce of emotion coming through the performers' voices.

At one stage, in the darkness, I looked across and saw tears running down Mum's cheeks and I could completely understand why. This was hair-standing-on-the-back-of-the-neck stuff, an intensely emotional experience, and as the singers' incredible voices built to a stunning crescendo, I really could feel the anguish in every note.

I felt a lump in my throat knowing that Mum was undoubtedly thinking of Dad and how he should have been here with her, so I reached across and took her hand in mine, squeezing it hard. It sounds weird, but right then, I couldn't remember ever feeling so close to her; I saw a glimpse of the strong, yet sometimes fragile woman she truly is, instead of just my mum.

It's hard to imagine your parents as a couple in love with the same hopes and dreams of any other, I suppose. But mine were really devoted to each other, and now, almost three years later, Mum is still grieving heavily for the loss of the man with whom she spent almost forty years of her life, and whom she still loves with all her heart. Sitting there in the Arena, it was heartbreaking to behold Mum's grief, but at the same time very moving, and right then I couldn't help wishing that someday I would experience a love like that.

Why was I so sure after the break-up that nobody would understand and no one would appreciate what I was going through, when having experienced similar, but much stronger heartbreak, my own mother would understand only too well? Mum had lost the love of her life too, although the love she'd shared with Dad had been very different to what I had with Kieran.

I understand now that it wasn't the same for me; in fact, I know that it was nothing like it. Things were completely one-sided in our relationship, with me deeply in love and blissfully unaware that the man of my dreams was just hanging around, waiting until he found someone more suitable. His rejection still hurt of course – hurt massively – and as much as I tried to convince myself that he'd made a mistake and would eventually realise the error of his ways, now I don't really want him to.

Why did I always blame myself for his leaving? I drove myself crazy thinking that if I were that bit more glamorous, lost some weight or made more of an effort in bed, then maybe he wouldn't have left. Yet now I see that much of our time together was all about trying to please Kieran and keep him happy, which was simply impossible, as he could never be pleased. The moods and sulks, not to mention the unpredictable temper . . . it hadn't been right, had it?

But what I do know now is that as much as Mum is hurting, as much as she might be grieving, she's grieving for a love that was mutual, honest and enduring.

And I've never experienced a love like that.

Chapter 28

Exactly three weeks after his encounter with Abby in the park, Finn rang the doorbell of the address he'd been given.

'Hello?' A friendly voice that definitely wasn't Abby's drifted out of the intercom.

'Um, hi,' he said, speaking nervously into it. 'My name is Finn Maguire and I'm here to see Abby.'

'Oh. OK, just a sec, I'll buzz you in,' the girl replied in a breezy tone that buoyed his confidence somewhat. Whoever this person was, she'd hardly allow him into the apartment without checking Abby knew him, would she? Which meant that she *must* have mentioned him, he thought, heartily taking the stairs up to her floor. But if that was the case, then why—

Abby opened the door, and seeing the completely blank look on her face, Finn's heart sank. 'Hi. Can I help you?'

They'd discussed this of course. Discussed what would happen if their experiment failed and Abby didn't appear at their meeting point outside St Stephen's Green Shopping Centre. He'd waited there for a full hour past four o'clock, their agreed meeting time, all the while stupidly trying to convince himself that there might be a perfectly normal explanation for her no-show. But when five o'clock came and went and Abby still hadn't appeared he began to suspect that his (and even more so *her*) worst fear had been realised: she'd forgotten the meeting, which meant that she'd forgotten him, all in the space of three weeks. Even worse, and much harder for Finn, it also meant that as far as Abby was concerned, their conversation in the park had never happened, so in effect she still believed her memory was absolutely fine. This was the bit that had worried Finn from the outset and had almost stopped him from following through with the second part of their plan.

'How stressful will it be for you to have a complete stranger call to your flat and tell you the truth? Especially when we both saw how finding out all this affected you today,' he had added gently, referring to her fainting. 'I really don't want to be responsible for upsetting you like that again.'

Yet like it or not, they had both known that this was the only way it could work, which was why Finn had reluctantly called to her apartment to break the news that would once again shatter Abby's world.

She looked at him now, her expression so untroubled and innocent of what was to come that Finn almost turned and ran. But deep down he knew he couldn't do that; he'd made this girl a promise, and whether she knew it or not, she was depending on him. And unfortunately for Finn, this vulnerability was something that drew him to her even more.

'You were looking for me?' Abby said now, evidently wondering what the hell he wanted.

He supposed he'd better say something before she got nervous and mistook him for some kind of nutter. 'Abby, hi. My name is Finn Maguire, and I'm here because I have something very important to tell you.' They'd rehearsed what he'd say if things didn't work out, and while it had sounded reasonable enough at the time, now Finn worried it came across a touch overdramatic.

As expected, Abby was a bit taken aback. 'What? Who are you, and what's all this—'

'Abby, is everything all right?' The other girl appeared in the doorway. 'What's taking you so— Oh, hello,' she said, smiling at Finn.

He swallowed, suddenly at a loss as to how to approach this. When they'd arranged this, there had been no mention of someone else being around, and he didn't really want to break such awful news while . . . Then something struck him. Maybe this was Abby's way of ensuring that if their plan went awry, she wasn't on her own when he broke the bad news.

It certainly made him feel a whole lot more comfortable to know somebody she trusted was around, although he was a bit worried that the friend might deck him if he upset Abby. She certainly looked formidable. Then he suddenly remembered Abby mentioning her best friend when she'd spoken fondly of the experiences she'd had over the past few months.

'You're Erin?' he asked.

'That's me,' she said, and there was a brief silence as she looked from him to Abby, evidently seeking an introduction.

As there obviously wasn't a hope in hell of Abby introducing him, Finn obliged. 'I'm Finn,' he told her. 'Um, this is a difficult situation to explain, but I'm sort of a friend of Abby's . . .' His voice trailed off when he saw her staring at him in bewilderment. 'If you could just let me explain—'

'For God's sake, come in, then, and stop loitering out there in the hallway,' Erin ordered, much to Abby's chagrin, judging by the look on her face.

'Um, I'd better not, thanks all the same.' Knowing that Abby viewed him as a complete stranger, Finn decided against going inside, hoping to at least try and gain her trust before dropping his bombshell.

'OK, then, I'll leave you to it,' the friend said, going back inside, despite the daggers look she got from Abby.

'I'm sorry, but what exactly is it you want?' Abby asked, her tone suspicious now. 'What makes you think we know each other? And while we're at it, how do you know Erin?'

Finn cleared his throat yet again. God, this was a hell of a lot harder than he'd thought. 'Abby, this is going to sound very strange, and I know you think you don't know me, but I'd like you to just hear me out for a few minutes.' He took a deep breath, trying to remember it all word for word, just as they'd planned. 'I know about your accident and that you've spent the last few months trying to create the memories of a lifetime, hoping to try and undo the damage to your brain.' The fear in her eyes was enough to stop any man in his tracks, but Finn refused to break his stride. 'I know you've just come back from seeing *Aïda* in Verona with your mother. I know you lost over a grand on roulette in Las Vegas, most of it on black seventeen. I know that you really wish you'd had the guts to hit one hundred and eighty in the Ferrari. I know that when you tried on that ball gown in London, you wished that' – he looked down at his notes – 'that Kieran could have seen you in it, just so you could prove him wrong.' Finn gulped, as all at once he saw her expression change from wariness to bewilderment to outright panic. 'Yes, I know that all of these things are personal to you, things you believe nobody else knows, but I only know because you told me about them in great detail last time we met,' he blurted, eager to get it all out now. 'You told me to help gain your trust in telling you something else you already know, but because of the damage to your memory have since forgotten,' he added sadly. 'And there has been damage, Abby, that's what I'm here to tell you.'

'Who are you, and why are you doing this?' Abby gasped, her eyes filling with tears. 'Get out of here, out of my sight now!'

'I'm sorry, but I had no choice . . .' Finn went on, troubled by the depth of her despair. 'We both agreed that this was the only way to make you understand.'

'How dare you!' she cried. 'How dare you come here and say all these things to me! Who on earth do you think you are?'

At the sound of raised voices, Erin reappeared at the door, her friendliness of earlier quickly replaced with suspicion. 'What the hell is going on here?' she demanded.

Abby, by now unable to speak, turned on her heel and raced back inside.

'I'm so sorry – I didn't meant to upset her,' Finn said with a despondent shake of his head. 'Well, I knew all of this would upset her of course, but . . .' He tried to explain it all to Erin in a rush – how he'd originally met Abby in New York a few months back, and had bumped into her again three weeks before, but she hadn't remembered him, how she'd realised that parts of her memory had been fading, and that they'd agreed to carry out this experiment.

'I'd hoped that all this wouldn't be necessary, and that she'd remember meeting me of her own accord and know exactly who I was, but when she didn't turn up . . .' He trailed off, realising how outrageous all of it sounded, fully expecting Erin to tell him to get lost.

'Hold on, you're telling me Abby *knew* there was a problem with her memory three weeks ago?' She looked away, puzzled. 'But she never said a word.'

'She didn't want to in case it was just a one-off, a freak occurrence. And she asked me to help her find out.'

Erin was shaking her head in bewilderment. 'Which was how you knew my name.'

'Yes, she told me all about your road trip in America, told me lots of personal things, things no one else knew, in the hope that it would be easier for her to trust a supposed stranger. We thought it would help her believe me when I told her the truth.'

Erin was silent for a moment, and seemed to be considering this. 'So you two met on Christmas Eve and she didn't remember a thing?'

'Yes . . . Wait, how did you know it was Christmas Eve?'

Melissa Hill

She sighed and Finn couldn't decide if it was one of resignation or relief. 'Because we've all known for a long time that things weren't right, but none of us had the heart to break it to her.'

★   ★   ★

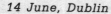

14 June, Dublin

After breaking the awful news about my memory to me, Erin asked Finn to come inside. The poor guy tried everything to make me feel better, insisting that as I'd clearly been able to live a normal life up to now, there was really no need to panic or let this revelation devastate me.

While he seems a nice enough person, emotionally I wasn't able to handle having him around just then, or listen to his sweet but pointless attempts at lifting my spirits. He must have got the message because he stayed for only a little while before leaving me and Erin alone.

'Is it all right if I call back in a few days' time, just to see how you are?' he asked, and I nodded, willing to agree to anything if only he would leave.

'Don't get too upset if I don't realise who you are,' I couldn't resist saying, but regretted it almost immediately, as I could tell by his face that the words had stung. When I started to say sorry, he just waved my attempts away.

'Hey, no need to apologise,' he interjected. Looking at him properly, I realised that he's actually got quite nice eyes. 'I completely understand. But maybe if you're up to it, I think it might make things easier if I were able to go through everything that's happened with you, maybe help you fill in some of the blanks, as it were.' Then he gave me this strange smile. 'I'm so sorry, Abby. I was in two minds about having to be the one to break this to you, because even though we don't really know one another, I wouldn't have hurt you for anything.'

Right then, I couldn't do anything but nod dumbly. I mean, I suppose I should have said thanks, but it just doesn't seem the right word given the circumstances, does it?

Chapter 29

'An interesting development,' Hannah said, which Abby thought was putting it mildly.

She'd spent the entire weekend holed up in the flat with Erin, devastated. She couldn't believe that after everything she'd done, and how hard she'd tried to fight it, her memory really was failing. She hadn't done anything to make it better, hadn't wanted to believe that it was pointless even trying. To make things worse, it seemed everyone else had known the truth all along.

Now, sitting in Hannah's purple armchair, her arms wrapped tightly round her body, she looked at the psychologist and said croakily, 'I can't believe that this is really happening.'

'It was always going to, Abby, and I know you don't want to hear it, but this was what I was trying to tell you all along.'

Hannah was right, she *didn't* want to hear it, and just then she wondered why she bothered coming here at all only to have her say, 'I told you so.'

'But there are also some major positives here. As this guy pointed out, you *have* lived a normal life up to this stage, better than normal, really. OK, so now you know you can't always rely on your memory for everything, but as it's only episodic memories you're losing, it's not the end of the world.'

'Not the end of the world? Hannah, I have absolutely no recollection of ever meeting him before Friday! And not only that but I *do* remember everything about New York except the part about meeting him!'

Hannah allowed her to calm down before speaking again. 'Well, let's use that to try and make sense of what's happening here. You remember being in New York with your family because you've all spoken about it and shared the experience many times since. But what you actually remember is the semantic version of events, not the episodic one. And through talking and reminiscing with your family about that time, you reinforced the experience.'

'You're saying that my memories of New York aren't real?'

'Of course they're real, Abby; it's just your recollection of them that's the important thing. Tell me, can you cast your mind back now to Claire's apartment and tell me what colour her front door is, or precisely how the dining table was decorated for Christmas dinner?'

Abby attempted to do so, but to her dismay, she realised that no matter how hard she tried, she couldn't – she couldn't actually put herself back in Claire's apartment. She knew she'd been there of course, but at the same time she just couldn't remember any of the specifics, except the dinner, the Christmas presents and all the other things that the family had done together. It was weird and very scary, but at least it gave her some idea of what Hannah was talking about.

Then, before she knew it, she started to sob, and for a while Hannah let her. She let her get it all out – all the disappointment, worry and fear of what the future held.

'Abby, I know it's hard, but try to take some positives out of this. OK, perhaps some of it has faded, but you did in fact retain a lot of that visit to New York, which tells us that your memory can cope through continuity. And as I said, reinforcement is obviously hugely important too.'

Abby sniffed. 'I don't know what that means.'

'Well, by "reinforcement" I mean that because your family remembered and made reference to the event, their own recollections of it reinforced your memory. Your memory of it is essentially anchored by theirs. On the other hand, you appear to have no recollection of wandering around by yourself, because this memory hasn't been reinforced by anyone else – you were on your own for most of it. The only person that could have reinforced it was that guy you met – Finn is it? Yet by the time you bumped into him, the memory had already faded to nothing and was lost.' She paused, trying to make things as simple as possible. 'I suppose it's a bit like studying for exams. We take in a huge amount of information just for the exam, but unless this information is reinforced, our recollection of it tends to fade over time. It's not quite the same thing as what's happening here, because in your case this process obviously occurs much faster, but it's a reasonable comparison.'

'OK.' Abby nodded but she still didn't feel any better. 'I don't see how knowing this is supposed to help me.'

'Well, for one thing we now know that the quality of your memories are dependent on continuity and reinforcement. And you've already come up with the means to give your memory both those things.'

'I have?'

'Yes,' Hannah said, as if it was the most obvious thing in the world. 'With your diaries and photographs and all the mementos you saved over the last few months. Abby, by deciding to make a record of your day-to-day life and the major events as they happen, you've actually given yourself the means to hold on to all the important memories and experiences – and ensure that they're never really lost for good. While everyone does this to a certain extent, you've actually taken it to another level.'

'I'm still not sure . . .'

'Take for example photographs – we all tend to take snaps of important events and celebrations so we won't forget them, when really there is no rational reason for us to do so. But

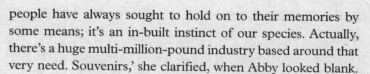

people have always sought to hold on to their memories by some means; it's an in-built instinct of our species. Actually, there's a huge multi-million-pound industry based around that very need. Souvenirs,' she clarified, when Abby looked blank.

'So you're saying that it's OK if some of my memories fade away because I've saved them somewhere else anyway?'

'I'm just saying that's one way to look at it. While your memory will inevitably end up losing some things, you also have the means to hold on to the more important ones.'

While thinking about it like that made Abby feel a little bit better, it still raised some other, perhaps more troubling questions. For one, was this the worst it was going to get, in that she'd be able to retain information about an event or experience for a week or two, but unless she kept an account of it, it could very well fade away for ever? And if so, did this mean she'd have to spend the rest of her life living vicariously through her diaries?

★   ★   ★

17 June, Dublin

So how do I feel now that I know my memory is really banjaxed? Terrified mostly, but as Hannah keeps saying, at least I've established some plausible way around it. It is a bit surreal having to take time out every day to keep a really thorough record of ordinary things like I'm doing now.

When I was doing it for Vegas and Italy and everything, it didn't seem so necessary – more like something you'd do anyway for those kind of amazing holidays. But if this is what I have to do to lead a normal life, then I suppose it really isn't too much to ask, is it?

And despite what Mum thinks, I *know* I can live a normal life. She, Caroline and the others have admitted to me that they have had their suspicions over the last few months, but how was I to know that George Michael is an international superstar and that I've had a crush on him since I was ten? Something I still can't figure out, because when I Googled him recently, I thought he looked like an ultra-tanned Greek waiter! But who knows? Maybe he sings better than he looks. I'll find out when I go to the concert later in the year. I have to go now, seeing as Claire and Zach went to so much trouble to get the tickets. Anyway, Erin is a big fan too, apparently, so no doubt she'll be happy to go along with me.

'I noticed a few things in Vegas myself, smaller things, like a blank look you'd sometimes have in conversation,' Erin's admitted. 'To us, all these things pointed to the truth, but because you were so doggedly determined not to admit there was anything wrong, we just didn't have the heart to shatter the illusion.'

I suppose I can see where they were coming from, but it's a bit of a shock to the system hearing these things now.

Still, as far as I can figure out, apart from forgetting Finn, my only blips were not remembering learning how to play the piano, forgetting my crush on an eighties singer and other silly little things like not remembering to put sugar in my coffee – stuff that isn't exactly worthy of major panic, is it?

24 June, Dublin

A little bit more to report about Finn. After that first (or should I say third!) time we met, he's called over on a few occasions to help me, as he described it, 'fill in the blanks'.

I'm so sad I can't remember our day in New York – it sounds wonderful, especially the Christmas tree and the lunch in Central Park. It all comes across like such a fairy tale that if I didn't know better, or feel I can trust him so completely, I don't think I would believe it. Still, I think he's probably embellished a few things here and there – just to make himself sound better.

Not that he has to try too hard.

But then he called again today, and this time he gave me (another!) terrible shock. I opened the door to find him and a huge dog at my front door! Naturally, I nearly had a heart attack when I saw it, but then a very weird thing happened. Catching sight of the dog – which in fairness didn't move a muscle and, instead of barging in and jumping on top of me, sat patiently on its hindquarters – I felt an unbelievably strong sense of déjà vu.

'This is Lucy,' Finn said. 'You two have met before and I know she's anxious to make sure you're OK.'

'We have?' Some instinct deep down told me that there was no need to be afraid of this particular dog, which meant that he must have been telling the truth, and because we'd met before, I knew I could trust this one.

This was weird and more than a little scary. Like everyone, I've experienced déjà vu many times over the years, but this was the first time there might actually be a real explanation behind it. So while I've certainly never been as near to any other dog without seizing up in fear, in this one's company I felt almost relaxed.

Finn kept going on about how the dog 'knew' that I was scared of her, which was why she seemed extra gentle around me, and because she was there when I fainted in St Stephen's Green, she was a little overprotective of me. I still can't believe I fainted in public like that . . . How embarrassing!

But Lucy the dog is kind of cute, especially the way she so obviously dotes on Finn, and I have to admit I was touched by the way she seems to want to help me get over my fear. All through the visit she kept coming over to where I was sitting and leaning against me.

'I think she wants you to pet her,' Finn informed me.

While I wasn't too keen, I kept thinking about item nine on my list – 'face my fears' – and how it had served me well up to now. So sure enough, I moved my hand down to rest on the back of the dog's head and gave it a little rub. And as I did, I was amazed (and actually quite pleased) to see her huge tail begin moving from side to side. So I think yes, Lucy could definitely grow on me.

And her owner isn't half bad either . . .

Chapter 30

Finn and I met up again this evening, but this time in town instead of just my place. We went to Butler's Chocolate Café off Grafton Street for a hot chocolate (seeing as I couldn't remember the supposedly delicious one we had in New York. We were having a laugh and getting on really well, but after a little while his face grew serious.

'Can I ask you something?' he said.

'Sure, go ahead,' I told him, wondering what was up. He's normally so joky and easygoing that this was a bit odd.

'Well, be sure and tell me if I'm being nosy, but remember when I came to tell you about . . . everything?'

It is kind of sweet that he's still embarrassed about having to put me through all that, when the truth is, I'm now actually very grateful. 'Of course. What about it?'

'Well, beforehand you gave me a list of things to tell you, personal stuff that would help prove that I'd met you before and that I knew what I was talking about. Well,' he said, and I had to smile at his gentle, almost hesitant tone, 'one of the things was that you wished some guy had seen you in a dress you tried on in London.'

I'm still squirming with embarrassment at the mention of this, something so private and personal that I'm almost sorry I shared it with him, even though at the time it had been for a very good reason. 'That's right.'

'Do you mind my asking who this Kieran guy is?'

I really didn't want to get into it, but figured that telling him wouldn't hurt; after all, he didn't know Kieran or how broken-hearted I'd been after him, did he? 'Kieran is my ex,' I said as offhandedly as I could, and Finn nodded as if he'd guessed as much. 'But if you don't mind, I'd really rather not get into it now.'

'Hey, no problem,' he said quickly. 'And I'm sorry for being nosy, but it was just something that stuck in my mind and I wanted to ask you about it.'

So, having successfully negotiated the conversation away from that thorny subject, we went on to talk about much more interesting things, like our favourite books and music. And for such a supposedly intelligent guy, let me just say that Finn's got some, well, rather weird taste in music!

'I really like eighties rock, Def Leppard, Guns N' Roses, that kind of thing,' he told me, while I struggled to hold in the laughter and not spit out my hot chocolate. How cheesy is that?

But aside from his taste in music, he's really interesting to talk to and fun to be with, and there's no denying that he's making me feel a hell of a lot better about everything . . .

Abby found it hard to believe how close she and Finn had become in the space of just a few weeks. While however hard she tried she couldn't remember meeting him in New York, it was starting to feel like she'd known him for ever. It was now over a month since she'd discovered the truth about her condition and since then Finn had spent almost every moment he wasn't at work by her side.

Now, she was making coffee for them both at her flat. Opening the freezer, she took out a bar of her beloved frozen chocolate. The first time he'd seen her do this, she'd had to explain it wasn't another symptom of her condition – like putting her hairbrush in the fridge – but just the way she liked it.

'Did you remember to put sugar in your coffee?' he asked, and maddeningly Abby realised that she hadn't. Oops . . .

'Thanks for reminding me,' she said, handing him a cup before joining him on the sofa. She'd noticed that he seemed a little bit tense this evening, almost as if there was something on his mind. Maybe she'd taken up too much of his time lately and he was waiting for the right moment to tell her he wouldn't be around so much. Despite herself, Abby felt disheartened by this. Perhaps he felt he'd done his duty by being around for her in the aftermath of finding about her injury, but enough was enough.

'Are you all right?' she asked him. 'You seem a bit . . . distracted.'

Finn looked at her and smiled. 'I'm fine. It's just . . .' He sighed. 'Look, something's been bugging me, and I know you said before you didn't like to talk about it, but . . .'

'But what? Tell me.' Abby didn't know what was coming.

'I just can't help wondering about that guy Kieran and what you wanted to prove him wrong about. I'm sorry – I know it's none of my business and—'

'Hey, it's OK.' Abby supposed she might as well get this over and done with, especially as Finn seemed to be giving it much more importance than it deserved. 'Look, the reason I don't particularly want to talk about it is because, well . . . things ended pretty badly between us. Well, bad for me, anyway,' she added with a nervous laugh. 'We were together for five years, and within six months of our break-up, he ended up marrying someone else.'

Finn sucked air through his teeth. 'That's tough. I'm sorry. Shit, I feel awful for bringing it up again now. I'm an idiot.'

Abby smiled. 'That's OK, and, yes, it was tough, but not as tough as finding out that while I'd always assumed we were heading for happily ever after, he was just filling in time waiting for something better to come along.'

'Oh, come on,' Finn began to protest. 'I sincerely doubt that and—'

'I'm not just surmising here,' she interjected firmly, a knot in her stomach as she thought about it. 'I know this for a fact because he told me.'

'What?'

She nodded, struggling to retain her composure. Then she took a deep breath. 'One day, he came home from work and out of the blue told me that he wanted to finish things, that he'd found someone else. But out of respect for me, she said, rolling her eyes, 'he wasn't going to take up with her until it was over between us. Now, I know what you're thinking,' she said, when Finn went to say something. 'It sounded lame to me too, but Kieran has always been straight up like that, too straight sometimes,' she added, almost as an afterthought.

Apparently, he'd been biding his time for ages, waiting for the right moment to tell her that he was ending it. And while she couldn't be sure, Abby had since suspected that the so-called 'surprise' weekend away at Dromoland Castle had been intended as a celebration of Kieran's freedom, a new beginning for him and Jessica.

'It's funny, but before then a visit to Dromoland Castle would once have been the very *first* thing on a list of memorable things to do,' she explained to Finn sadly, 'but now I don't think I could ever set foot in the place.'

'I'm so sorry,' he said, his tone gentle.

'So, anyway, after I'd picked myself up off the floor, I tried to find out where all of this had come from, why he found it so easy to cast aside a five-year relationship just like that.' Abby looked down and began to study a piece of carpet. 'And he said, "But surely we both knew you were never the kind of woman I'd marry?"' She gave a watery smile and swallowed hard before continuing. 'So, as you can imagine, my next question was exactly what kind of woman did he *think* he was going to marry.'

Evidently realising how difficult this was for her, Finn said nothing and waited for her to go on.

'"Well, someone with class and style, I suppose," he told me, as if this was the most obvious thing in the world. Kieran could be very brutal sometimes,' she added, almost to herself. Then she gave a carefree shrug, as if all this was water under the bridge now, but the truth was that this expression had been imprinted in her brain ever since. 'Someone with class and style.'

Which, naturally enough, could only mean that she had neither.

'And from what I've seen of his new wife, yes, she is indeed beautiful and classy – nothing at all like me,' she said wryly.

Finn seemed appalled. 'What an arsehole!' he spat.

'Well, I suppose I realise that now, but to be honest, it took me a very long time to get to grips with it. I've never told anyone that, you know – what he said to me that day. It was too embarrassing and, worse, all too easy for someone like me to believe. I've never been good at the whole fashion and dressing-up thing,' she told him. 'So then in London, when I tried on that gown . . .'

'For God's sake, Abby, he was an idiot,' Finn muttered. 'Any fool alive could tell you that you don't need some posh dress to prove him wrong.'

The fact that he was so genuinely annoyed with what Kieran had said was incredibly endearing, and made Abby feel a whole lot better, but it was what he said next that really made her smile.

'You'd look great in a bloody bin bag!'

She knew he didn't really mean this, and was only saying it to make her feel better, but the time that he'd made for her and the kindness he'd displayed over the last few weeks touched Abby to the core.

And then, quite spontaneously, she threw her arms round Finn and gave him a huge hug. 'Thank you,' she said, holding him tightly. 'You don't know how much better that's made me feel.'

Finn hugged her back at first, but then he gently broke away. There was a brief tension-filled moment as their eyes met and then, before Abby knew what was happening, their lips brushed and they were kissing.

He tasted of fresh coffee, and his skin smelt of soap, and she felt the prickle of his stubble at the corner of her mouth. Her hands ventured away from his shoulders, under his arms and down to the small of his back. She didn't stop to think about whether this really was a good idea. All she knew was that she was kissing Finn, someone she'd only known for a few weeks, practically a stranger . . . !

As she melted deeper into his embrace, Abby had a sudden flash of the sixth item on her list – 'share a kiss with a stranger'. And she very quickly decided that seeing as she *had* only known Finn a few weeks, then technically he really *was* a stranger. So, she persuaded herself, smiling inwardly, by doing this she was merely carrying out her obligations and getting through another thing on her list.

And once again enjoying herself immensely in the process.

Chapter 31

1 August, Dublin

Mum met Finn for the first time today. She invited the two of us and the rest of the family for Sunday dinner. To say it was a tense affair would be an understatement! When we first arrived at Mum's, Caroline and Dermot did their best to make him feel comfortable – Dermot chatted to him about football, and Caroline asked him all about work – whereas Mum just flitted around the place looking stressed. Despite Caroline's approval, Mum thinks I'm mad for even thinking about a relationship, considering.

'I don't want to upset you, love, but how can something like this possibly work?' she said to me when I first told her that Finn and I were spending a lot of time together. 'What with everything that's going on . . .'

As usual, she couldn't bring herself to mention my 'condition', which I find kind of funny in a way.

Honestly, though, I think that's part of the reason I've become so close to Finn so quickly; he never tries to pretend that I don't have this problem, which strangely enough has helped me come to terms with it a lot more easily.

He knows how to handle it, and more importantly knows how to handle me, and doesn't treat me like Mum does – tiptoeing around the subject as if a mere mention of it might shatter me into a thousand pieces. Caroline and Erin are much more upbeat, although I can sense that they both worry about my ability to handle it all long term, as does Claire, judging from the conversations we've had on the phone. Surprisingly, Dermot has been great, a bit like Finn in that he tends to crack jokes about it now, much to Mum's horror.

But at the same time, Finn doesn't treat any of this lightly. He seems to know instinctively when I'm down, and just lets me have my little black days, instead of trying to make me feel better. It's like he knows that these phases I go through now and again of feeling sorry for myself are a perfectly normal part of accepting what's happening to me, and doesn't come out with stupid platitudes to try and bring me out of it. I love that. Then there are other times when we have a good laugh and poke fun at my absentmindedness, if you can call it that.

To sum it up, it's like he understands me, and what I'm going through much better than anyone else. I don't know, maybe it's because he's a guide-dog trainer and is used to people coping with all kinds of difficulties. Either way, having him around is a gift.

And speaking of gifts, I think I've fallen in love with Lucy! She's so calm and gentle, and despite her size, follows me around like a lost puppy. Finn still thinks that after my 'episode' in the park she reckons I'm a bit delicate and need looking after, which, after all, is what she is trained to do. Strangely, I don't mind in the slightest, and because she's so lovely, I'm not in the least afraid of her. I love the way she wags her floppy tail and nuzzles against my legs every time she sees me.

'I'm beginning to feel a little jealous here,' Finn said the last time they called over to my place and Lucy spent the entire evening with her big furry head on my lap, gazing up at me.

Thinking of it now, it's hard to believe that I ever had such a fear of dogs, but then again, lots of things have changed over the last few months, haven't they? It's also hard for me to believe that I could feel this close to someone I met only a few weeks ago (OK, I know it was really a few months ago, but I'm still drawing a blank on that!), and that after all this time, I think I've finally managed to forget about Kieran. Ha! Forget him? Ironic, isn't it?

But Finn is so different from Kieran it's incredible. To be honest, I can't understand how someone hasn't snapped him up well before now. Not only is he gorgeous in that very strong, masculine way, but he also has such a sweet and generous nature that he has to be irresistible to most women!

'Boy, you've certainly landed on your feet this time,' Erin said when I told her about The Kiss. 'I'd take a blow to the head any day if it meant someone like that would come knocking on my door!'

She hasn't mentioned a new guy in her life get, although I still suspect there's something she's not telling me. Maybe it's just early days for them so she doesn't want to jinx it. Again, I'm sure she'll open up when she's ready.

In all honesty, I can't help but wonder if Finn is holding back something too. At times, there's a slight melancholy about him that I can't quite pinpoint, which makes me wonder if, like me, he's been hurt in the past. If that's the case, then we make a very good pair!

Anyway, Finn and I arrived at Mum's at around one o'clock. Funnily enough, he seemed nervous, although perhaps, thinking about it now, this was understandable, given the way I complain about her fussiness all the time.

As I said, Mum was being Mum, making a huge hoo-ha about dinner and who should sit where, so much so that she barely managed a quick hello to Finn when we first arrived. She calmed down a bit when dinner was served, and when we all took our seats around the table, she eventually started asking Finn about his work, which of course he was only too happy to talk about. At times, I reckon he seems more comfortable around dogs than people, and seeing him visibly relax when telling my mother about the guide-dog centre makes me certain I'm right. Which makes you wonder why he's spending so much time around me!

For some reason, all the talk about dogs seemed to soften my mother up a bit too, and for a while it looked as though Finn had charmed her in the same way he had the others, so for the rest of the meal we were all quite relaxed and at ease with one another and chatted away.

But after dessert, poor Finn put the kibosh on it. I don't know, I think he must have either been too relaxed or too nervous, because it really wasn't like him to say something out of turn. And like I said before, we joke like this among ourselves all the time now, so I'm sure it just slipped out, and it certainly didn't bother me.

Anyway, just as we finished eating, I sat back in my chair and said to Mum, 'That was fab, Mum. Definitely the nicest meal I've had in ages.'

'I don't know if that's a compliment, Mrs Ryan,' Finn piped up then, grinning at me. 'Most of the time poor Abby can't remember what she's had for breakfast, can you?'

And just like that, there was complete silence around the table. Nobody knew where to look. Even Caroline seemed shocked.

'Very funny,' I shot back, trying to keep my tone as light as possible, although I knew the damage had already been done.

Mum looked as though she wanted to murder him, and I suppose, looking at it from her point of view, you could hardly blame her. As Finn admitted himself afterwards (poor thing, he was kicking himself!), not only did it look like he was insulting her daughter, but in a roundabout way it also seemed like he was insulting her food!

'I don't know what came over me,' he said later, cringing. 'It was such a stupid thing to say – especially in front of your mother – but I really only meant it as a joke.'

I knew that of course, and I suppose he doesn't really understand how hard my mother finds all of this. I only wish she could be as light-hearted about it as Finn is, at least for my sake.

For the rest of the day you could cut the atmosphere with a knife, and despite all the support Finn's given me over the last while, I think he got a serious thumbs-down from Mum!

Oh, well, I suppose things can only improve . . .

Chapter 32

Finn couldn't believe his father's attitude. He'd been so sure Pat would be thrilled that he'd finally found someone he liked.

Abby had spent the day in Balbriggan yesterday, and when Pat had popped over in the afternoon for an unannounced visit, they'd been introduced. Then today his father had returned, not to congratulate him as Finn had hoped, but to give him an earful.

'I just don't think that getting involved with a girl like that is the best idea,' Pat said, when Finn mentioned that he and Abby were more than 'just good friends'.

'A girl like what?' he asked incredulously.

'Lookit, she seems very nice, but who knows what could happen with her in the long run? It's bad enough that she drew a blank on meeting you in America, let alone back here. I know you were only trying to help the poor girl, son, but really you should have run a mile.'

'What? What are you talking about, Dad? Abby's fine now. OK, well, not *fine*, obviously, but she's learning to come to terms with all this, and I'm helping her do that.'

'Bloody hell, Finn, thirty-five years of age and you're still rescuing lost puppies and making them your responsibility!'

Finn's head snapped up. 'I can't believe you just said that.'

'I said it because there's more than a grain of truth in it, and you know it.'

He understood the point his father was trying to make, but this time Pat was wrong. While yes, of course he'd wanted to help Abby and would do anything to make things better for her, it wasn't just about that. He'd felt something for her in New York – and again at the Green – back when he'd known nothing at all about her head injury. And while the look on her face when he had to break the news to her about her memory loss had been enough to break his heart, it wasn't the reason he was with her now.

Mindful that starting a relationship or getting involved with someone in the fragile state Abby was in would be a difficult and indeed selfish proposition, Finn hadn't intended to do or be anything other than a shoulder to cry on. And as an outsider, someone who hadn't been there from the very beginning, and one of the few people close to Abby who didn't doubt her abilities or mental faculties, it seemed easier for her to let him into her life and share her trust. While he was fully aware that whatever kind of relationship they had would never be completely normal, when they'd shared their first kiss that time, he knew that this was someone he really wanted in his life.

'It's not about rescuing Abby or feeling responsible for her,' he told his father now. 'I care about her.'

'Like you cared about that Danielle one? And look what happened there.'

From day one Pat had never accepted Danielle, but in fairness to him, he'd kept his mouth shut and his oar out, until the day Dani packed her bags and left. Now Finn suspected he was trying to prevent the same thing happening again by having his say well in advance.

'There are plenty of nice, normal women out there, Finn. Why go for the one that's damaged?'

'For God's sake, Dad, that's a terrible thing to say!' Finn said, raising his voice. 'So Abby has some problems – big deal. She can get around them; *we* can get around them.'

Pat gave a deep sigh. 'That's what *I* thought, son,' he said eventually, looking him directly in the eye, and Finn realised he was referring in some way to his long-absent mother. Something Pat never did if he could avoid it.

'What are you talking about?' he asked, his voice tentative.

Pat sat down on the sofa. 'I suppose you know I'm talking about your poor old mother.'

Poor old mother? That wasn't quite the way Finn would have put it, seeing as she was the one who'd deserted them all those years ago.

After a brief pause, Pat went on. 'When I married her, she had a problem too. One that I, like yourself, thought we would be able to overcome together.'

'What kind of problem?'

His father sighed. 'The same one that stalks the length and breadth of this country and always has. The demon drink, Finn.'

'What?' This was the first he knew of this. 'Mam was an alcoholic?'

'In the end a chronic one,' Pat said, nodding. 'Oh, she wasn't too bad at the beginning, at least not that I knew of. I was aware she liked a drink, sure we all did, but usually on a Saturday night when we were out with the rest of them and not a half-bottle of whiskey in the middle of the day with a baby crying in the other room.'

Suddenly the significance of what his father was saying hit home. 'Mam drank when I was a baby?'

Pat nodded, his eyes weary. 'And every day when you were growing up. You don't remember any of it at all, Finn? Her being fast asleep on the kitchen table in the middle of the day, or not being there sometimes when you came in from school?'

Finn now cast his mind back to the day he found out his mother had left, and the pieces of broken glass on the floor. He remembered thinking that Rex, their dog, must have bumped into the table or something, causing havoc like he usually did. But now, he also recalled noticing a funny smell, the bitter and not necessarily nice smell that he'd always associated with his mother. One that he now realised had probably been whiskey.

He'd been seven years old when she left. He couldn't remember much before that day, couldn't really remember all that much about *her*, or what it was like having a mother in his life. Perhaps the memories just weren't all that strong, or perhaps he'd blocked them out intentionally, Finn couldn't be sure. All he remembered was arriving home from school one day to find his father sitting at the big oak kitchen table, his head in his immense, callused workman's hands. Finn had never before (or since) seen his father cry.

The family dog, Rex, who upon Finn's arrival had been lying at Pat's feet, jumped up to greet him.

'What's wrong?' Finn asked, setting his schoolbag down on the floor in order to pet the sheepdog behind the ears. 'Dad, are you OK?'

Seemingly caught unawares, his father looked at the boy as if he'd never seen him before; as Finn recalled, he seemed to stare right through him.

'Dad?' he repeated, continuing to run his fingers through Rex's silky coat. 'What's wrong? Why are you crying?'

'Me – crying? Would you get away out of that!' his father said, attempting a half-hearted laugh. 'Haven't I gone and got something in my eye – a chip of wood, I think.' Pat made a great show of rubbing one eye as if trying to dislodge something from it. 'I was doing a bit of sawing in the workshop, so I had to come inside and splash some water on it.'

'Oh.' With some relief, Finn returned the smile. He picked his schoolbag off the floor and hung it on the back of one of the chairs. 'So when's dinner? And where's Mam?'

Pat stood up from the table and walked to the window

above the sink, turning his back to his son. 'She had to go away for a while.'

'Where did she go?'

His father was silent for a long moment, and his shoulders heaved a little before he spoke again. 'Just away.'

Finn frowned. This was odd. His mother was always here when he came home from school . . . OK, so maybe not always, but *nearly* always. Where could she have gone? Why would she leave without saying goodbye? And who would make his dinner?

Once more uneasy, Finn called Rex over, and again began softly caressing the dog's head. 'But where did she go? And when will she be home?'

'Soon,' Pat replied flatly, but Finn realised that throughout the entire exchange his father had never once turned to look at him. 'She'll be home very soon.'

But of course his mother never did come home, and to this day Finn could still recall the sound of his father crying softly to himself at night, when he thought seven-year-old Finn was asleep and wouldn't hear. He remembered lying wide awake, Rex sprawled at the bottom of his bed, and keeping him warm, listening to the muffled sobs coming from his parents' room. And despite his nightly tears, Pat behaved for all the world as though there was nothing unusual in Imelda, his wife of nine years, taking off and leaving him and their young son to fend for themselves. In hindsight, Finn understood that this was simply his father's way of trying to make things easier for him, that by carrying on as normal, maybe Finn wouldn't notice his mother's absence.

'So what happened?' Finally it felt like the right moment for Finn to ask his father to explain. He'd wanted to know all his life, but had never been able to get Pat to talk about that day, much less explain it. 'What happened that day to

238

make her leave? Clearly, it had something to do with the drink, so what was it?'

Pat sighed. 'I came home earlier that day to find her passed out on the kitchen table – again. Although I loved the woman dearly, by that stage I was sick to the teeth of what was she doing, to us and our marriage, but more importantly to you. So many times I'd come home from work and find her holed up in our bedroom drinking away while you were downstairs on your own with nothing to eat and no company but poor old Rex. I'll tell you, you got more encouragement and attention from that bloody sheepdog than you ever did from your mother. Sure, you didn't start talking until you were gone two.' Pat looked pained. 'Imelda might have abandoned me and our marriage long before, but I wasn't going to let her do the same to you. So a few months before that I'd given her an ultimatum, either she stopped drinking or I would insist she leave.'

Finn was horrified. 'What? How could you do that? Alcoholism is a disease, surely you know that much? You can't just kick someone out and abandon them! She needed help.'

'She got help and plenty of it many times through the years,' Pat told him in a flat voice. 'You don't remember her being in and out of hospital a lot when you were a boy? Then again, I suppose you couldn't have been more than five or six at the time, so perhaps not. Anyway, as I said, she got plenty of help. But this time it was her last chance. I told her she had to choose between us – you and me, her family – or the bottle.' Now he looked at Finn. 'Son, don't think for a second that it was easy for me or that I was some kind of callous husband, only too happy to get rid of her. I loved that woman with all my heart – still do. But she had love for one thing and one thing only. So as I said, I told her that this was her last chance, that if she touched another drop, she'd have to leave. I had to, Finn – there was no other way.

239

So when I came home that day and I saw the half-empty bottle of whiskey on the table . . .'

Finn said nothing, and waited for him to continue.

'I sat down in front of her, poured out my heart and soul to the woman, told her what she was doing to our family, and what she would end up doing to her life, but I knew she wasn't taking any of it in. She never did. While she'd promise you the moon and the stars and you'd believe her, the next day she'd be off somewhere with another bottle or two. So finally, I put both the whiskey bottle and the picture of the three of us on your Communion day down on the table. And I made her choose.' His voice broke then, and he looked away. Finn could guess what had happened next.

'I'm sorry, son, I know it hurts you to hear this now, and it hurts me to have to talk about what I did back then, let alone *do* it. But it was the only way I could ensure you had the best possible chance in life. She was making life hell for both of us with her carry-on. She was no good to you as a mother. She couldn't handle responsibility like that. So, in the end, as you probably realise, she chose the bottle and in effect chose to leave.'

Finn ran a hand through his hair, unable to believe what he was hearing. 'But where did she go?'

'She has relations in England, a brother, so I presume she went there first, but to be honest, I'm not really sure. I thought the fact that I'd followed through with my threat and shown her how serious I was by packing her bags and asking her to leave might be enough to make her realise the significance of it all. But no, she just walked out the door and I haven't heard a word from her since. I thought maybe a birthday or a Christmas card, but nothing.'

Finn didn't know how to feel.

'And in case you're wondering, yes of course I tried to track her down, many times over the years. I loved the woman,

Finn, even with everything she'd done. I got in contact with the brother, but to be frank, he wasn't terribly forthcoming and I got the impression he'd washed his hands of it a long time before. Back when you were a teenager, you used to talk about wanting to try and find her, and if you're thinking about doing that now, just keep in mind that what you find might not necessarily be what you're looking for.'

Naturally enough, Finn *had* been thinking of looking for her, seeking his mother out and seeing for himself what kind of person she was. But first, he had to get his around the fact that she – his own mother – had chosen a bottle of whiskey over him. While he'd always felt her rejection very keenly, this was rejection of an altogether different kind. And Finn knew it would take him a long time to come to terms with that, never mind thinking about coming face to face with her after all this time.

'But why didn't you tell me this before? Why tell me now?'

'Because I knew you'd probably go off on some mad search for her and try to rescue her, that's just your way. You'd feel responsible for her, but like me, it wouldn't matter because you still wouldn't be able to save her – nobody can. As I'm sure you've heard said many times before, no one can cure an addict who doesn't want to be cured. If anything, she could very well end up dragging you down with her. And if that happened, then what I did all those years ago would have been for nothing. So no, I didn't tell you and I still stand by my decision.'

Finn cast his mind back to the conversation with Nora he'd overheard. Was this what she'd been trying to convince his father to tell him? 'Nora . . . did she know anything about this?'

'She's been living alongside us for as long as we've been here, Finn. Of course she knew. Why do you ask?'

Finn explained about what he'd heard and how he'd worried it had been something to do with Pat's health.

'Ah, go away out of that, sure you know I'm fine,' his father said, waving an arm in protest. 'Anyway,' he continued, after a brief pause, 'so now you know.'

Finn wasn't sure what to think. So he'd been right all along about his mother abandoning him, and now he knew the reasons behind it.

His mother was an alcoholic.

But then he remembered the reasons this discussion had come about in the first place, and while he appreciated what his father was trying to say and the comparisons he was trying to make, there was no doubt in his mind that the situation he was in now was completely different.

'It's not like that,' he told his father, when Pat again tried to point out the comparisons. 'Abby doesn't have an uncontrollable addiction, something that could ruin her or my life. OK, so there might be challenges ahead, but we can get through them, I know we can.'

His father didn't seem convinced, and Finn didn't need to read his mind to know what Pat was thinking: *I thought the very same thing.*

But the opportunity to discuss it any further was lost, as just then, the telephone rang. Finn answered it.

'Hey there, buddy – still good to go for the hanging on Saturday?'

Finn smiled. It was his good mate Chris, whose wedding he was due to attend the following weekend. He'd asked Abby to accompany him and she'd agreed – another step in their relationship and an outward sign to Pat, and indeed to everyone else, that what they had was built on something real and not just on sympathy.

'Of course I'll be there. I'm looking forward to it. How are you? Not getting cold feet, I hope?'

'Nah, nah, nothing like that. Listen, just a quick call, really,' Chris said, his voice growing more serious. 'I wasn't sure whether or not you know this, but I thought I should let you know that Dani's invited too, and as far as I know, she's coming.'

Finn exhaled deeply, not sure how to feel about this. Talk about strange timing! He hadn't seen his ex in two years; since the break-up, they hadn't crossed paths once, and now, just when he'd finally started to get over her and found someone else—

'And not only that,' Chris continued, interrupting his train of thought, 'but there's something else I think you should know . . .'

Chapter 33

Abby stared once again at her reflection in the mirror, more nervous about this wedding than she cared to admit. Not only would she be meeting the majority of Finn's friends for the very first time, but she'd also be coming face to face with the famous Danielle.

As would Finn.

Well, maybe I have nothing to worry about, she thought, sitting on the edge of the bed and fastening the straps of her shoes. Maybe Danielle was small, cross-eyed, overweight and bushy-haired. And seeing as Abby herself was small, slightly overweight and had, well, maybe not bushy, but certainly *frizzy* hair, they'd get on like a house on fire. The cross-eyed bit would be the only difference between them and should give Abby a clear advantage over the girl who'd broken her beloved Finn's heart.

Abby groaned. As if. From what she could gather from Finn, who really didn't go into too much detail about his ex other than the fact that the relationship had ended two years ago, Danielle liked the more glamorous side of life, which was one of the reasons they'd broken up in the first place.

'Scrambling through fields with a load of excitable puppies just wasn't her scene,' he'd told Abby during a recent (and rare) discussion about his previous relationship. 'She much preferred big city life, going out on the town and socialising till all hours.'

Abby could tell by his tone that despite their very obvious

differences in personality, he had nonetheless cared a great deal for his ex. Unfortunately for him, this alone hadn't been enough for Danielle. Well, perhaps Abby more than anyone else could understand that feeling, given her own experiences with Kieran.

'Ready?' Finn asked, popping his head round the bedroom door. She'd stayed over the night before at his house so it would make it easier for them to drop off Lucy at Pat's before heading straight to the wedding.

'As I'll ever be,' she replied, exhaling deeply. Thanks to Caroline and their shopping spree, Abby – dressed in her Whistles sequinned skirt, satin bodice top and her beloved Jimmy Choos – looked considerably better than she felt.

'This should be fun,' Finn said, as Abby climbed into the Jeep. Was it her imagination or did he sound somewhat nervous too?

They arrived at the church just before one, and as they pulled into the car park, Abby was vividly reminded of the last time she'd attended a wedding. She grimaced. Ironically, Kieran's wedding was one memory she didn't think she'd ever forget. Finn parked the Jeep, and the two of them headed towards the front of the church, where some guests were standing outside chatting. They were about to go inside when they heard a male voice shout from nearby, 'Finn Maguire – talk about a blast from the past!'

Finn's expression broke into a smile, and catching Abby's hand, he approached a group of men and women standing to the right of the doorway. 'How are you doing, Gerry?' Finn said, shaking a tall, fair-haired guy's hand as everyone else looked on, smiling. 'Long time no see.'

'Where have you been hiding?' said another woman, greeting Finn with a hug.

When they'd finished saying their hellos, he turned and introduced them to Abby. To her immense relief, Danielle didn't seem to be among this particular group of friends, and while they all seemed very friendly, she could sense that the women in particular seemed a bit taken aback that Finn had brought someone to the wedding. God, had he been *that* heartbroken over his ex?

When Finn and his friends had finished catching up and it was time for everyone to go inside, Abby and Finn entered one of the pews on the groom's side of the church. As they took their seats, she got the distinct impression that he seemed a bit self-conscious, almost on the alert for something. Danielle, obviously.

Abby was almost sorry she'd agreed to come here. If Finn were this on edge now, what would he be like when his ex was actually in the same room?

She could think of little else throughout the ceremony, and while she'd thought her outfit looked fine leaving the house this morning, she now felt dowdy and dated compared to a lot of the other guests. Evidently, despite Caroline's best efforts, she was still pretty green when it came to fashion, and there were so many designer labels on show here that the wedding could easily have been mistaken for a high-profile footballer's.

'Are you OK?' Finn asked, when the service was over and everyone began to pile out of the church and back into the sunshine. 'You seem very quiet and—'

'Hello, Finn,' said a throaty female voice from beside them.

It was as if every single one of Abby's nightmares had come true. Far from the pudgy, cross-eyed munchkin she'd hoped Danielle would be, she turned to see a tall, tanned Helena Christensen lookalike with stunning aquamarine eyes, perfect skin and an even more perfect body, dressed in a wispy chiffon dress whose designer Caroline would be able to pinpoint instantly. Abby didn't know and didn't need to; Danielle was the kind of woman most designers had in mind for their creations – elegant, classy, sexy – and certainly not short, pale, spare-tyre-carrying women like Abby.

Naturally enough, Finn seemed dazed by her appearance, almost as if over time he'd forgotten how truly stunning she was.

'Dani, hi. How are you?' he said, leaning over to kiss the former love of his life on the cheek, and as he did, Abby thought about just slipping away, grabbing a cab home and forgetting all about him. It wasn't as though it would be that difficult given the circumstances . . .

But then he surprised her by turning away from the gorgeous Danielle and reaching for Abby's hand. 'This is Abby,' he said.

Despite his efforts, she still couldn't help but feel like a spare part in the middle of the two, so palpable was the history between them.

'Hi,' she said, feigning what she hoped was a friendly and confident smile.

'Abby, hello. Really nice to meet you,' Danielle said, smiling back, and to Abby's great surprise, there was no glance of disdain, or any looking her up and down with a contemptuous gaze. Instead, Danielle seemed . . . well, she gave the impression of being quite nice, actually. 'Wow, I love your shoes. They're great with that skirt.'

'Thanks.' For a second, Abby felt oddly proud, but then instantly berated herself for being so gullible as to let a simple compliment about her shoes make her feel better when she should be terrified of this woman for clearly holding some kind of spell over her boyfriend!

And thinking of it now, Finn hadn't said she was his girlfriend either, had he? Nope, he'd simply introduced her by name.

'Well, I guess I'll see you back at the hotel later?' Danielle was saying, and Finn nodded.

'Sure, looking forward to it.'

I'm sure you are, Abby thought, her heart freezing as she saw the look on his face as he watched Danielle walk away. She'd been wrong to come to this wedding today, and Finn had been wrong to ask her.

Particularly as any fool alive could tell that he was still in love with the woman who'd broken his heart.

Finn's stomach gave a little flip as he watched Danielle walk away. He'd been wrong to come here today, and doubly wrong to have brought Abby. It wasn't fair on her to have to see this, to witness his coming face to face with Dani for the first time in the two years since she'd left.

She was still as stunning as ever, no doubt about that. Still as graceful and elegant. Then again, why wouldn't she be? Looks were everything to Danielle, always had been, which was another reason why she'd found living in the country so difficult and so 'pointless', as she used to put it herself.

What was the purpose of going to all that effort to look amazing when in the country there was no one to admire her, no one to appreciate her fabulous clothes and perfectly styled hair? No one except Finn, and evidently, he didn't matter. He'd tried his best, tried to make her feel loved and secure, but Danielle was the kind of woman who could only feel secure if everyone's eyes were on her.

And right now, she was definitely getting her wish. Notwithstanding the bride, who by rights should have all the attention, Danielle was still the best-looking woman at this wedding by a very long shot.

'She seems nice,' he heard Abby say from alongside him, quickly bringing his mind back to the present and his gaze away from Danielle.

He tried to think of something light-hearted and casual to say, something to try and conceal the mixture of emotions he was feeling, but nothing came to hand. 'She is,' he said simply, as he and Abby followed the rest of the wedding party out of the church grounds.

'I suppose it must have been a bit of a shock seeing her again like that,' Abby continued, and again Finn couldn't do anything other than agree.

'It was. I mean . . . I knew she'd be here of course, but . . .' Preferring not to talk about it just now, Finn let the remainder of his sentence trail off.

As they drove to the hotel, Abby grew silent, much to Finn's relief. Evidently, she understood that he wasn't inter-ested in making idle conversation, and he really appreciated that.

In truth, chit-chat was the last thing Finn wanted just then. He was too busy thinking about his reaction to Danielle, and how he was going to get through the rest of the day with her in the same room.

Chapter 34

The day was turning into a nightmare for Abby. Finn had barely said two words on the way to the hotel, and she sensed he was completely preoccupied with Danielle. She was too. When they arrived at the old country hotel where the reception was to be held, she couldn't really relax until she'd studied the seating plan and discovered that Finn's ex was mercifully seated at a different table.

Even then, it was hard to enjoy herself. She really didn't know any of Finn's old friends, and it was very difficult to get to know them when it was obvious they saw her as something of a curiosity.

'So you might not remember any new things at all unless you make a record of them?' Jayne, one of the wives, probed. All the women were left seated together around a table in the lounge while the men were up at the bar.

Abby shifted self-consciously in her seat. Her situation wasn't easy to explain at the best of times, let alone to a group of strangers. 'Well, I can remember most new things, actually,' she replied lightly, 'but certain things fade away very quickly.' She gave a rueful smile. 'It's a bit strange, I know, but I've just had to learn to live with it.' She didn't elaborate any further, hoping that they'd understand she was kind of uncomfortable talking about it.

'So you might not remember meeting *any* of us here today, unless you decide to write about us?' another woman, called Frances, said, with a hefty dose of scepticism in her tone.

Abby patiently explained that she'd now got into the habit of sitting down and recording all the events of the day in her diary as a kind of back-up for her memory. 'I know it sounds strange,' she said, shrugging awkwardly, 'but it works for me, and that's the important thing.' She went on to explain Hannah's 'reinforcement' theory, but could sense that most of it was going right over their heads.

She didn't mind. Chances were, these people weren't going to play an important part in her life, anyway, so there was little point in trying to make them understand. It had been years since Finn had seen some of these couples, and according to him, it was likely to stay that way.

'I've got nothing in common with them any more,' he'd explained to Abby beforehand. 'We used to have a bit of a laugh when we were younger, but now they've all got their own lives and I've got mine. I'm only going to this wedding at all because it's Chris's, and he's my best mate.'

While all the old gang had moved on to marriage and kids, since he broke up with Dani Finn had remained the eternal bachelor. At least until now.

'It must be really tough for Finn, though,' Frances persisted. Abby tensed, wishing they could change the subject, and because such a comment had understandably touched a nerve. 'To think that you could easily forget all about him just like that.'

'Finn's not *that* easy to forget!' joked another girl, whose name Abby couldn't recall. Lyndsay was it? 'Abby, I think it's great that you guys are managing to work it out,' she said, evidently sensing her discomfort. 'Finn's a great guy, and we're all thrilled to see him happy, aren't we?'

One of the other girls, Jayne, nodded. 'Yes, to be honest, after Dani we were all worried he might never . . . well, you know.' She looked away awkwardly, as if suddenly realising that this might not be the best time to discuss it.

Abby just smiled, unwilling to betray her insecurities.

'Doesn't she look amazing today, though?' Frances sighed. 'I couldn't get over how well she looked at the church earlier.'

'Stunning,' Jayne agreed, nodding vigorously. 'I don't know how she does it myself. Every time I see her she looks younger.'

'That dress really suits her too, although I have to say I thought the plunging neckline was a bit much.'

'So soon after the surgery, you mean?' Jayne enquired, and at this, Abby's ears pricked up. Hmm . . . evidently, the paragon's beauty wasn't completely natural after all! 'Yes, but you know Danielle – she always likes to make a statement.'

As the other women continued to sing Danielle's praises, Abby was surprised they could be so insensitive. Didn't they understand how uncomfortable all of this would make her feel? It was bad enough having Finn going all gooey-eyed over his ex, let alone his friends rubbing it in about how amazing she looked!

Still, if nothing else, she was glad that she'd managed to move the conversation away from her memory problems. She was also relieved that today would be the first and hopefully last time she'd have anything to do with this shower of gossips. The witches of *Macbeth* had nothing on these three!

'Well, it's about time!' Lyndsay chided, as the girls' husbands eventually pulled up seats at the table, Finn having been waylaid by another guest. 'I thought you lot had abandoned us for the day.'

Well who could blame them? Abby thought to herself, rather uncharitably.

'Abby, I was just telling Finn I think he really landed on his feet with you,' Frances's husband, Ray, piped up.

She smiled, relieved that at least *one* of Finn's friends didn't seem to think he'd made the mistake of his life by walking away from the wonderful Danielle. 'Really, why's that?'

'Because if you two have an argument, unlike the rest of

us, he doesn't have to put up with all the sulking and pouting for days afterwards, does he?'

'Why not?' his wife asked.

Ray chuckled and winked at Abby, clearly delighted by his own wit. 'Sure, won't the whole thing be forgotten about in the morning?'

The rest of the evening passed quickly and without notable incident. After Ray's cheesy joke (although Abby way preferred this to the incessant questions from his wife), Finn's friends seemed to shy away from mentioning anything more about her situation, and when the group retired to the banqueting room, she discovered to her relief that she and Finn were seated away from the dreaded Frances, and at the opposite end of the room from Danielle.

She spent much of the day engaged in superficial chit-chat with Lyndsay, who was by far the nicest of Finn's female friends, and unlike Frances, wasn't in the least bit inquisitive about her memory troubles, or indeed about her relationship with Finn.

Finn was still incredibly distant, which really worried her. While he'd chatted away throughout dinner and had joked with the others about the length of the speeches, she couldn't help but notice his gaze occasionally gravitate towards Danielle's table. Abby tried to tell herself that she was just being silly, that it was only natural that Finn would be a little thrown by his ex-girlfriend's presence after such a long time. And as the night wore on and the glasses of wine she'd consumed started to take effect, she gradually began to relax and enjoy herself.

She and Lyndsay were quickly on the dance floor when the happy couple finished their first dance and the band ramped up the tempo. What will be will be, Abby decided, bravely boogieing as though she hadn't a care in the world, although inwardly she couldn't help but be very concerned indeed.

Finn, muttering that he'd be back soon, had disappeared somewhere shortly after the meal and hadn't returned. Abby tried to convince herself that there was nothing strange about this; it was his best friend's wedding after all, and there were plenty of people he hadn't seen in a while.

At around midnight, needing a break from the dance floor, she agreed to accompany Lyndsay outside to the terrace for a cigarette.

'I can't help it – I've been off the bloody things for months now, but the drink is wearing me down,' the other girl persuaded. 'Roger would kill me if he catches me. Come on, you can keep a lookout for him.'

'All right, then,' Abby agreed. This was Lyndsay's third request and she could do with a bit of fresh air, although achieving this among a crowd of smokers would be difficult, she thought giddily.

But had Abby *not* done this – had she not gone outside and on to the smoking terrace – she would never have glanced idly around the hotel grounds, and spotted Danielle and Finn sitting together on a bench nearby. Engaged in deep conversation, the two seemed oblivious to anyone else, almost as if immersed in their own private cocoon. She would never have spotted the way Finn looked at his beautiful ex, the way his head inclined closely towards hers to hear something she was saying, the way he shook his head and smiled at whatever it was she had said.

Lyndsay, who was facing in the other direction and busily lighting up her cigarette, was completely oblivious to Abby's horror. 'Yep, Roger would *murder* me if he found out I'd taken it up again,' she babbled. 'He can be a complete nag sometimes. Is Finn like that with you?'

'No.' Abby could barely get the word out.

Now, their gazes seemed locked together, and Danielle was tracing a finger along Finn's cheek, while her other hand was clasped in his. Oh, God . . .

Suddenly, the ground began to move beneath her, and Lyndsay's voice seemed very far away as Abby stared wordlessly at Finn, hardly unable to believe what she was seeing. Why would he do that? And in front of all these people.

'I have to go,' she gasped, racing inside before Lyndsay could react. What did it matter? After this, it wasn't as though she and Lyndsay were ever going to see one another again, was it? Abby hurried back to the table to retrieve her things, barely registering the enquiring looks on the others' faces, before going outside to reception to call a cab.

She'd been such a fool to think that someone like Finn would choose someone like her over Danielle, someone like her over *anyone* else, she realised, pacing out front as she waited for her cab. She'd been a fool to think that he might love her, that *anyone* might love her when there was a very real chance that someday she wouldn't be able to remember something as simple as what she'd had for breakfast. How could any relationship be expected to cope with that?

So why had Finn insisted that theirs could, that the two of them could get through it, no matter what? Why had he gone to so much trouble to help her come to terms with what was happening to her, in helping her to admit that there really was something wrong? And why had he told her he cared about her when all the time he was longing for someone else?

God, the irony, she thought, realising that history was repeating itself. However, she mused, her thoughts racing, in this case her situation could very well be a blessing in disguise, because Abby had a sure-fire way of ensuring that Finn's betrayal wouldn't be the same as Kieran's. That she wouldn't think about it and be hurt by it every waking moment. That the image of Finn and Danielle together wouldn't keep replaying itself over and over in her mind like the image of Kieran marrying Jessica had.

No, this time, Abby realised grimly, this time she had a foolproof way of ensuring she'd never have to experience that kind of pain again.

The cab had finally arrived, and Abby had been back at her flat for about an hour when Finn appeared at her front door.

'What the hell is going on?' he demanded, running a hand through his hair. 'Why did you just leave like that? Jesus Christ, I thought something had happened, that you might have had some kind of . . . episode or something.'

'As if you'd care,' Abby shot back, slightly overwhelmed by the intensity of her feelings. It wasn't as though they'd been together as long as she and Kieran had, but Finn had been there for her during a difficult period of her life. It almost felt like he'd been around for ever. She'd shared everything with him, all her fears and worries, and the happier, optimistic feelings too. He knew pretty much all there was to know about her; she'd trusted him, and he'd let her down. She'd fallen heavily for him and he'd thrown it back in her face.

So what else was new?

'Why wouldn't I care?' he asked, frowning. 'Why are you being like this, Abby? What the hell happened?'

'What the hell happened?' Abby couldn't believe he was even asking her that. 'You and Danielle sitting and cuddling in a corner happened. You not being able to take your eyes off her all day happened. Why did you do it? Why bring me to that wedding when all you wanted was an excuse to get back with Danielle?'

'Abby, calm down – you've got it all wrong.'

'Finn, I might have a head injury but I'm not stupid! Don't patronise me by trying to tell me I've got it wrong. I saw the way the two of you looked at one another. I saw the way she was stroking your cheek, and the two of you holding hands. The only thing I am thankful for is that I managed to get out of there before you got down to the serious business!'

'The serious business . . .' Finn breathed out heavily. 'Abby, look, you really have got it wrong. Yes, Danielle and I were sitting together, and yes, it felt a bit strange seeing each other again after all this time. I told you before that things didn't end well with us and—'

'End? End? To me, it looked like nothing at all had ended; in fact, it looked like everything was about to begin all over again! What I can't understand is why you thought you felt it was OK to string me along when you are clearly still in love with your ex,' she said, her voice breaking. 'Or were you just planning to carry on regardless, because even if I did find out you were sneaking around behind my back, chances are I wouldn't be able to remember anyway, would I?'

'Abby, for God's sake, please calm down.'

'Actually, I'm perfectly calm, but to be honest, I'd be even calmer if you'd just leave now and stop trying to explain all of this away. You can say what you like, it doesn't matter to me because I have absolutely no plans to make a record of today. In fact, I have no plans to keep a record of anything concerning you at all!' Folding her arms across her chest, she looked away, and tried to blink back tears.

'What? What are you talking about?'

'Look, we made a mistake in trying to think we could make a go of this, and luckily, there's no need for you to feel guilty. Just give it a bit of time and soon I'll have forgotten you and everything about you. So then you can go on back to your precious Danielle. I certainly won't stop you.'

'I still don't understand,' Finn said, frowning. 'What are you saying?'

Her jaw tightened. 'It means that I've got rid of it all, Finn, everything from the last couple of months . . . it's all gone.'

He looked horrified. 'You deleted the records, the ones of us?'

'Yep.' Abby's mouth was set in a firm line.

The blood began to drain away from his face, and Abby wondered why he appeared to be so worried. At least this way it would all be over and done with quickly, wouldn't it? He wouldn't have to worry about leaving her in the lurch, and the two of them could move on with the rest of their lives without looking back.

He could have the gorgeous Danielle, and Abby would have . . . well, Abby would have all the other memories apart from the ones featuring him. It was quite liberating in a way; it meant that instead of spending months trying to get over a broken heart and mourning his absence, she could now do it as easily as the flick of a switch. What broken-hearted woman in the world *hadn't* wished for that at some stage or another? Wished there was some way she could magic away all the hurt and pain a broken relationship had caused?

For once, this whole thing had proved a blessing in disguise. She wasn't ready for a relationship, probably never would be, so it was better to find this out now, before she and Finn wasted any more of each other's time.

'I don't believe you,' he was saying. 'I don't believe that you would throw away everything we have just because you think you saw something between me and an ex.'

'I *know* what I saw.'

'No, you don't. What you saw was two people who hadn't spoken in a very long time catching up.'

She stared at him. 'Do you normally catch up with people by crawling all over them?'

'I wasn't crawling all over her! It was emotional, yes, I'll admit that, but—'

'Well, if it was so emotional, why don't you go back with her, then? Why make a fool of me in front of your friends,

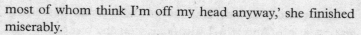

most of whom think I'm off my head anyway,' she finished miserably.

'What? That's rubbish,' Finn said, exasperated. 'Abby, you really don't know what you're talking about.'

'Clearly I don't. But I know what I saw, and to me, it looked far from innocent. In all honesty, I don't know why I didn't realise it sooner. Goodness knows all your friends kept going on about how well she looked and how affected you were by her.'

His head snapped up. 'What? Who said that?'

'Well . . . Frances and Jayne. They couldn't stop going on about how wonderful she looked. It's obvious they think you're still in love with her, so I know it's not just me being paranoid.'

'Abby—'

'Well, isn't it true? Did you think I wouldn't notice that you went all quiet and unresponsive after bumping into her outside the church, or that you couldn't relax for most of the day, at least not until you'd managed to get near her again?' She closed her eyes. 'Then you looked very relaxed.'

'Abby, stop it, please!' Finn said, his voice rising in frustration.

'Finn, you were holding her hand. The two of you were close enough you were practically entwined, and—'

'Danielle's sick, Abby,' he cut in flatly.

'What?' She frowned, looking up. 'What are you talking about?'

Finn sighed wearily. 'She's got breast cancer. I only found out from Chris last weekend. He thought he should say something before I bumped into her at the wedding.'

Breast cancer . . . Instantly, Abby's mind flashed back to Frances and Jayne's comments about Danielle's low neckline and the mention of surgery. She'd assumed they were talking about a breast enlargement or something; she certainly hadn't considered for a *second* that it could be anything else . . .

'That's why I was quiet after meeting her outside the church,' Finn went on. 'And why I was fidgety for the rest of the day. I just didn't know how to react. I knew I'd have to say something, let her know that I knew about the treatment and the operation . . .' He shook his head. 'Abby, I spent three years of my life with Danielle and I cared about her a lot – I still do – but not in the way you think,' he added quickly. 'At the moment, she's going through something huge and I wanted to talk to her about it, let her know that if she needed anything . . .' His voice trailed off, and Abby knew for certain that this wasn't a front; he was genuinely upset and worried for his ex.

She thought back to the two of them on the bench, how intimate they'd looked. Straight away she'd assumed they were being flirtatious, but thinking about it now, the whole thing had been . . . well, quite *tender*. Finn wasn't trying to come on to Danielle; he was sympathising with her about her illness. This was why Frances and the others had kept going on about how well she looked. Abby had stupidly assumed that they were alluding to the obvious differences between herself and Finn's ex, but they were merely alluding to how well she was looking, considering.

Abby felt like a heel. 'I'm sorry . . . I had no idea. I couldn't have imagined . . .' She shook her head, ashamed. 'When I saw you two together, I just assumed . . . She's so beautiful, and you'd been acting so strangely . . .'

'Abby, what Danielle and I had is long gone. I still care about her in the same way I'd care about any friend who's going through what she is now, and yes, I'll admit that hearing about it from Chris and then seeing her today knocked me for six. But that's all there is to it. It took a lot for her to appear at the wedding knowing that everyone's heard, and she was nervous about how her old friends would react. I wanted to let her know that we're all rooting for her, that we're hoping she comes through it OK.'

'And how is she?'

He shrugged. 'She's devastated naturally, same as anyone would be. It's difficult to explain, but for a woman like Danielle . . .' He shook his head. 'Granted, no woman is keen on the prospect of losing a breast, but for Dani the notion is even harder to take. She's always been very insecure about her looks, and something like this is a massive blow for her.'

A woman like that insecure? Abby couldn't comprehend it.

'I know what you're thinking, but believe me, it's one of the reasons we eventually split up. Danielle needs to be constantly reassured of how wonderful she is and how well she looks. That's why she hated moving to Balbriggan. It was a world away from the bright lights and glamour of Dublin. Here in the city, she got all the reassurance she needed, but way out there . . .'

'But surely she got all this from you?' Abby couldn't help but be reminded of how she too had yearned for Kieran to say something nice about her appearance or pay her a compliment. But she knew now that this was because her own self-confidence was at an all-time low, and her relationship with Kieran was on the rocks. She just couldn't imagine how a woman as beautiful as Danielle could *ever* feel that way.

'It wasn't enough. Nothing was ever enough for Dani.' He looked away, and Abby could see how much this had hurt him. 'She was like one of those rare exotic flowers that needed constant care and attention in order to thrive. I just couldn't provide that for her.'

'But you really loved her. Wasn't that enough?'

He shook his head. 'Not for Dani. I don't know, I've tried to get my head around it, but I could never figure out why she felt so insecure. Her parents split up when she was younger and I think she may have been a casualty of that, got left behind in the upheaval, but to be honest, I'm not entirely sure. All I know is that in all the years I've known her I don't think she's ever been comfortable in her own skin. And now, her body's let her down in the worst possible way.'

'So Chris told you about all this beforehand? About Danielle's illness, I mean.' Abby really wished she'd known.

'Yes. And before you ask, I don't know why I didn't tell you about it too. I suppose I just wanted to come to terms with it first. I got such a shock, and then to think that I'd be seeing her again after all this time and in those circumstances . . . To be honest, I didn't know how to feel. But if I'd known you'd mistake my actions today for something else entirely, well, then of course I'd have said something. I just wasn't thinking straight. I'm sorry.'

Abby moved across the room, and put her arms round him. 'No, *I'm* sorry. I shouldn't have been so paranoid, and I shouldn't have doubted you. But from my own point of view, it was always going to be hard for me to come face to face with your ex, especially one who looks like her.' Finn hugged her back. Standing in his embrace, she looked away guiltily. 'I feel so awful for her now, knowing what she has to go through, and doubly awful for causing you even more grief by running off like that.' She hung her head in shame. 'But when I saw you two sitting together like that, and you holding her hand . . .'

Finn kissed the top of her head. 'I'm sorry – I wasn't thinking about that. I really thought you and me were fine, and that you'd know I'd never dream of hurting you. But Danielle was so emotional and so scared, and I knew she'd really appreciate my saying something. My heart went out to her, you know, although not in the way you thought.'

'I know, and again I'm so sorry.'

'And the girls kept talking about how she looked?' He rolled his eyes. 'No wonder women are so paranoid! And I didn't see any of them go near her all day either, did you? Obviously she was right for worrying about how everyone would treat her. Silly cows.'

Abby bit her lip. 'To be honest, I didn't really take to them much. Lyndsay is quite nice, but—'

'Lyndsay has her moments too.' Finn scowled. 'As I told you before, we all used to get on in our younger days, but I've got nothing in common with them any more. The lads only want to talk about business and property, and boast about how much money they're making, while the wives just bitch and backstab one another. I can't be bothered with all that stuff any more.' He looked at her and smiled. 'There are more important things in my life now.'

Abby smiled back, and they went to sit together on the sofa.

'Were you really that mad at me that you got rid of everything?' he asked then. 'The diaries, letters and photographs, the entire file?'

Abby nodded, a lump in her throat.

'You were willing to just wipe me out of your life without giving me a chance to explain? Abby, I love you. Surely you know that?'

Abby's heart leapt. He *loved* her?

'I was angry and hurt, and oh, I'm sorry,' she gasped now, tears in her eyes. *Oh, God, what had she done?* 'I've made such a mess of everything.'

'Not necessarily,' Finn said. Going to her computer, he pulled out a chair and sat in front of it while Abby bit her lip, waiting for him to bawl her out for doing something so stupid.

But instead, Finn smiled. 'You deleted the file from the desktop?' he asked.

'I know. I'm sorry – I should have thought more about it first, but I was so angry and I just wanted to—'

'No, no, it's fine,' he said, cutting her off. 'Don't worry, you didn't delete it all completely; it's still in the recycle bin.'

'What?' Abby stared in amazement as he clicked on the desktop's recycle bin icon, inside which the file named 'Finn' was still intact. Then, within the click of a few keys, it was right back in its original location. 'The recycle bin . . . I never even knew it existed!' Abby said, now feeling like she'd won the lottery. She *hadn't* deleted the archive; it was still there, every last bit of it!

Finn grinned, and put an arm round her waist. 'Honey, you ain't getting rid of me that easily.'

Chapter 35

There was no room for mistakes. This had to be perfect – *better* than perfect if it was to work at all. Finn had gone over the plan so many times he was now seeing it unfold in his sleep. It would be perfect, and with any luck, it would work. It had to work, didn't it?

Abby's reaction to what had happened at the wedding a few weeks back had really galvanised him into action. He loved her and needed her to believe that. But with everything else that was happening, she was hesitant and insecure about his feelings towards her, which merely made Finn even more determined to prove to her and everyone else that they could have a relationship – a normal relationship – just like any other couple.

He'd arranged a weekend in Paris, just the two of them, and they were due to leave this Friday.

'Are you absolutely sure about what you're doing?' Pat had said, questioning him yet again. 'Because this is something you need to be in for the long haul.'

'I know that, Dad, and it holds no fear for me.' Finn didn't intend to make this sound as though he was getting at his father for not being in it for the long haul with his mother, but he couldn't help it if his father decided to take it that way.

No, Finn's intentions now were to remove any uncertainty or insecurity where Abby was concerned and for them to make life a whole lot simpler.

And with any luck, perhaps someway memorable too.

* * *

8 September, Paris

Guess where I'm writing this now – Paris!

I can hardly believe we're here. Finn sprang a huge surprise on me the day before yesterday by telling me we were going away for the weekend. But I really didn't expect Paris!

We flew over yesterday (aren't I doing well these days flying here, there and everywhere?) and arrived at our hotel late in the evening. It's a gorgeously romantic baroque building central to all the sights, and we had a nice quiet dinner there before heading out to visit the Eiffel Tower – something I just couldn't wait to do. We managed to take some great photos, but decided not to take the lift up to the observatory as the queues were a mile long. Still, the majestic-looking tower, which was beautifully lit, looked just as good to me from ground level, and I'm sure we'll get to go up sometime before we leave.

This morning after breakfast, Finn suggested we pay a visit to Montmartre. He's been here before, and told me it was very pretty and Parisian, what with its authentic cobblestone streets and maze of narrow alleyways. It is, and I adored it on sight!

We spent some time exploring the magnificent Sacré-Coeur Basilica and its surroundings, wandering hand in hand for a while before eventually strolling over to an area called the Place du Tertre. It was very touristy, but at the same time so uniquely French that I couldn't help but fall in love! The square was full of painters and artists dressed in authentic Parisian garb, with their striped T-shirts, neckerchiefs and black berets. As Finn and I ambled along enjoying the buzz and atmosphere, one of the painters approached us.

'Monsieur, madamoiselle, I paint your portrait?' he said to me in a gorgeous French accent that made me blush.

Certain that Finn wouldn't be at all into that kind of thing, I was taken aback when he enquired about the price.

'Ten euros, monsieur,' the artist told him.

'Sounds good. Why don't you go for it?' Finn said, eyeing me.

'Me?'

'Hey, you're the photogenic one around here!' Finn joked. 'Anyway, you know how I can't sit still for long, whereas you can, and we can use this as one of your mementos.'

I must admit that I loved the idea of such an unusual keepsake, so the artist – who told us his name was Pierre (what else?) – set me up on a tiny stool before sitting down in front of his easel and getting to work.

'I hope this isn't one of those caricature-type things,' I joked to Finn out of the side of my mouth, 'otherwise I can easily guess what feature will be the most prominent!' I had visions of a picture of myself with a large protruding nose, but as the rest of Pierre's portraits seemed standard drawings, I reckoned I'd be OK.

Pierre worked diligently for about ten minutes, and throughout this time Finn loitered alongside him, keeping a close eye on proceedings. Sitting there on my own, I really wished he'd posed for the portrait too – it would have been nice to have a picture of the two of us together – but I knew this kind of thing wasn't really his style.

Eventually, Pierre stood back from his easel, and as Finn looked pretty impressed, I was hoping for the best.

'Looking good,' he said, winking at me.

When Pierre turned the easel round to show me the drawing, I was completely taken aback – and in a good way. The likeness really was amazing! Although my first thought was disappointment that the drawing was in charcoal and I really would have preferred it to be in colour, just as quickly I realised that some of it was.

'What's this?' I asked, pointing out a necklace that he'd included in his drawing of me, even though I wasn't wearing one.

A key-shaped gold-coloured pendant, it was the only detail that was in full colour, which was why I couldn't help but notice it in the first place.

'Ah, zees,' Pierre explained with a smile, 'zees is zee key to 'appiness.'

'Oh, OK.' Inwardly I rolled my eyes at this, thinking, Here we go . . . It was obviously some kind of tourist ploy, but seeing as my likeness was good, I wasn't going to complain.

'Merci, thank you very much indeed,' Finn said, taking out his wallet to pay Pierre, who rolled up the portrait and tied it with a piece of red ribbon.

Then the artist kissed me on both cheeks and wished me well. Again I had to smile. Touristy or not, I was loving this!

Having left Pierre to his work, Finn and I continued through the Place du Tertre and down another street before heading into a quieter, more peaceful street called the Rue des Saules. The atmosphere was wonderful and so intrinsically French with all its little shops and cafés that I was completely trans-fixed. A little way down the street, a brightly dressed woman selling jewellery smiled at us and waved.

'Let's go take a look,' said Finn, leading us towards her, again to my surprise. He really was getting into the swing of things! Paris must have been working its magic on him too, I reckoned.

'Something you like, mademoiselle?' the woman asked, still smiling at us both.

'No, thanks,' I said quickly, not exactly blown away by any of the stuff the woman was selling. But then I stopped short, unable to believe what I seeing. There, on the display, was a chain almost identical to the one Pierre had sketched me wearing! Attached to the chain was a small gold pendant in the shape of a key! What was going on?

'Ah, you have good taste, mademoiselle,' the vendor told me. 'All my jewellery holds extraordinary powers, the promise of beauty, good fortune and especially,' she added with a smile, 'everlasting love.'

Yeah, right, I said to myself sceptically, deducing that there was definitely some tourist scam being carried out between the vendors. Mysterious pendants and everlasting love, my foot! Did I have the word 'sucker' written on my forehead or something?

But Finn was also smiling. 'That's incredible,' he said to the woman, before unfolding the portrait and pointing out the self-same pendant. 'What an amazing coincidence.'

I stared at him, wondering what the hell he was at, but then I reckoned he was deciding to play along for the fun of it.

'Amazing indeed!' replied the woman, looking from the portrait back to me. 'Well, then, this has to be a sign.' With that, she picked up the pendant and went to clasp it round my neck. 'Here, mademoiselle, take it. Clearly it is destined to be yours.'

'Um, no, thanks,' I said, stepping back.

At this stage, I was feeling more than a little wrong-footed by these intimidating sales tactics. It wasn't at all what I'd expected in the supposedly cultured and sophisticated Paris. But then again, you get that kind of thing in touristy spots everywhere nowadays, don't you? I shot a nervous glance at Finn, who, to my great surprise, seemed to be finding all of this very amusing indeed!

'No, no, you misunderstand,' the Frenchwoman protested, continuing to hold the chain out to me. 'There is no charge. This is a gift – it is yours.'

'What?' By now I was completely baffled, and when I looked again at Finn, he just shrugged.

'She said no charge.'

'Yes, but I don't really want it,' I murmured, as the French-woman finally succeeded in clasping the chain round my neck.

He was openly laughing at me then. 'But she says it has magical powers!'

'Mademoiselle, it is yours. No charge.' The seller was determined that I keep the key-shaped pendant, whether I wanted the bloody thing or not, so what could I do but take it?

'OK, then,' I said, wondering yet again what the punch line was going to be. Would I now have to buy more jewellery in order for these so-called 'magical powers' to work?

But it seemed there was no punch line – at least none from this vendor – as satisfied that I'd accepted her 'gift', the woman smiled and moved on to another customer.

'What on earth was all that about?' I asked, fiddling with the necklace as Finn and I continued on down the street.

He was still laughing. 'I have no idea, but whatever it was, it was worth it simply for the look on your face. Talk about a suspicious Irish tourist!' Then he glanced sideways at me. 'I think it suits you, actually.'

'But there's obviously some kind of scam going on, isn't there?' I insisted. 'Why else would anyone just give me a free necklace? I mean, I know it's not real gold or anything, but . . .' And then all of a sudden the thought struck me. Pickpockets! I opened my bag and began frantically searching for my purse, but to my immense relief, it was still there. 'Check for your wallet, quick!' I urged Finn, who, clearly non-plussed, reached into his pocket and calmly produced it.

Weird . . . I thought. I'd been so sure I'd discovered the real root of the vendor's generosity, was certain it was some kind of elaborate diversion to keep the two of us occupied while an accomplice relieved us of our money.

'I can't believe what a paranoid little mind you have,' Finn said, putting an arm round my shoulders. 'A nice woman gives you a free gift and all you can do is jump to conclusions.'

'It just seems so strange, that's all.'

Finn laughed again before saying that all the intrigue was starting to make him hungry. 'Fancy some lunch?' he asked.

We stopped at a nearby café, and spent a lovely hour sitting outside on the pavement taking our time over delicious chocolate crêpes and a couple of fabulous French roast coffees.

I was loving the laid-back vibe. 'It's beautiful, isn't it?' I said to him. 'Now I understand why people love Paris so much. It's very romantic.'

Finn laid a hand on mine. 'I'm really glad you're enjoying it.'
'How could I not?'

'Well, you've visited so many other amazing places this year . . . it must be hard to find a favourite.'

'There's a big difference, though, isn't there?' I said, kind of embarrassed as I admitted it. 'I wasn't with you.'

Even though he's told me almost every day since his friend's wedding that he loves me, I'm still hardly able to believe it. I suppose I just keep waiting for the axe to fall and for him to realise that he has taken on too much by being with me. But so far (touch wood) this hasn't happened.

After lunch, we continued strolling along the narrow Parisian street, me still trying to figure out why the vendor had gifted that pendant to me.

Then, out of the corner of my eye, I noticed an agitated-looking man running down the street towards us. He seemed to be in a bit of a panic, and kept anxiously looking behind him as if afraid he was being followed. To my horror, I noticed the way he kept his hand beneath his jacket, almost as if he was hiding something . . . Suddenly, the man rushed up to me and Finn, and to my absolute shock, he reached into his jacket and pulled out a . . . Well, it looked like some kind of box, I realised then, relieved. I'd been so sure it was a knife or a gun or some kind of weapon!

But I was thrown completely when the guy thrust the box into my hands.

'For you, mademoiselle,' he whispered breathlessly.

'What . . . what are you doing?' I cried, confused by the fact that, unlike me, Finn didn't seem to find any of this at all

worrying, or in the least bit surprising! 'What the hell is . . . ?'
But the rest of my sentence was left hanging in the air as the
man raced off again, almost as quickly as he'd appeared.

I stared at Finn, who seemed to be having trouble meeting
my gaze, and, I spotted, keeping the bloody smile off his face!
'What is all this?' I asked him, completely at a loss. I looked
down at the box, a small wooden chest, and spotted that it
had a golden lock that looked suspiciously the same size as
the key-shaped pendant I was wearing round my neck . . .

'Finn, what's happening?' I asked, starting to feel somewhat
relieved as I realised that whatever kind of joke this was, he at
least seemed to be in on it.

'I'm sorry.' He was red-faced with suppressed laughter. 'Your
face . . . it's such a picture. Anyway, aren't you going to open
that box?'

Taking a seat outside nearby café, I sat the mini-chest in my
lap, all the while stealing surreptitious glances at Finn to try
and figure out what the hell was going on, and what part he
had to play. I removed the chain from round my neck, and
using the key, I opened the box. At first, it seemed empty, until
I noticed a piece of paper lying at the bottom.

> *Gotcha! How does dinner and a sunset cruise on the Seine*
> *tonight sound?*
> *Love, Finn xxx*

I was flabbergasted. 'This – all of this – was you?' I said,
staring at Finn. 'The portrait and the pendant and this . . .'

He smiled boyishly. 'Surprise!'

'But how did you . . . ?'

'Well, it took a bit of arranging, but don't you worry about
that now,' he told me, still grinning. 'So what do you think?'

I picked up the parchment and read it again. 'You did all
this . . . just to tell me what we're doing tonight?' I was still
completely blown away.

Finn was blushing. 'Hey, I have to do something to make it memorable, don't I?' he said with a shrug.

But hearing this, I was struck with a sudden sadness that he needed to go to such lengths because of me. Why couldn't we be just like any other couple and be able to enjoy Paris for what it was? Just enjoy being together without having to go to elaborate lengths like this. It really wasn't fair to him, was it?

'What's wrong?' Finn asked, reading my face.

When I confessed what I'd been thinking, he wasn't having any of it. 'Don't be silly. Doing something like this makes everything a lot more fun and much more enjoyable, doesn't it? And don't forget, these are my memories too, so what's wrong with making them memorable for both of us?'

I shook my head, stupefied by the lengths he'd gone to, the elaborate plan he'd constructed just to let me know about this evening's dinner arrangements. He's incredible; all of this is incredible!

So maybe, like Finn says, maybe I should try and forget about the downside of everything, and let both of us enjoy this for what it is. It's been one of the best times I've had so far, and I reckon tonight will be fun too. Will keep you posted . . .

Chapter 36

At seven o'clock that same evening, hotel reception phoned Abby and Finn's room to announce that their transport had arrived.

'What transport?' she asked him, bewildered.

'Well, to the boat, I'd imagine,' Finn replied in a tone that suggested he was up to something once again, and knew more than she did.

Going downstairs, they found a magnificent black Bentley MK VI, complete with chauffeur, waiting outside.

'Wow, I'm impressed!' Abby beamed, while once more Finn just smiled and said nothing.

When they were both comfortably settled inside the car, the driver cut across the Parisian boulevards before eventually stopping at one of the quays, where a large yacht was moored. Upon arrival, the chauffeur held open the door of the car, and as Abby and Finn stepped out, they were immediately welcomed by the captain and invited aboard the luxurious steel and mahogany boat.

'A private boat too?' Abby gasped, realising that they were the only passengers on board.

'Of course,' Finn replied casually, as if renting private boats for trips along the Seine was something he did every day.

As the boat pulled away from the port, they headed for the deck, where a waiter offered them each a glass of champagne. Then, glasses in hand, Abby and Finn took a seat and began to relax and enjoy the magnificent show put on by Paris and its riverbanks.

As darkness fell and the boat cruised along the River Seine, the city's most majestic and glorious buildings passed before their eyes: the Eiffel Tower, the Grand Palais, the Hôtel National des Invalides, the National Assembly . . . And as the last rays of sunshine disappeared behind the monuments, they sat together in each other's arms and Abby recognised a Michael Bublé number playing softly in the background.

'This is amazing,' she whispered, completely overwhelmed by the romance of the day. 'I can't *believe* you managed to organise all of this without my knowing. It's incredible.'

'You deserve it,' he said, drawing her close to him, and they shared a lingering kiss before the waiter gently interrupted to let them know that dinner was ready to be served.

They moved to sit at the beautifully set table for two, also out on deck. The meal, like everything about the evening, was superb, and Abby was once again hugely grateful to Erin for ridding her of her food phobia. For starters, they chose from scallops in champagne sauce and various delicacies like foie gras, duck and lobster. This was followed by a smooth champagne and mango sorbet, before a main course of veal medallions with truffles, crunchy pigeon dressed in poppy seeds and honeyed duck fillet with pears. Next up was an astonishing selection of delicious desserts, including crème brûlée, chocolate pâtisseries, mini apple Danish pastries and blackcurrant sorbet.

After that incredible feast, Abby and Finn sat back for a while and enjoyed the passing sights in silence. Some ten minutes later, Abby noticed the yacht suddenly reduce its speed and come to a gentle halt.

She raised an eyebrow at Finn. 'I hope we haven't run out of diesel or anything. Not that I'd complain about being marooned in a place like this!' she added with a grin.

'Non, mademoiselle,' the waiter supplied helpfully. 'We are stopping at the Pont des Arts. It is considered by Parisians as the lovers' bridge.'

'Oh, right.' Abby hadn't known this. Well, the bridge certainly was elegant and pretty, and like most bridges in Paris, had a spectacular setting, being so close to the Louvre.

The waiter was still speaking. 'Two centuries ago, this bridge was a real suspended garden adorned with small shrubs, flowers and benches, which is how it obtained its romantic association.'

'Right, thanks a million,' Finn grunted pointedly, and was Abby imagining it or did he seem annoyed by the interruption?

Evidently deducing the same thing, the waiter bowed imperiously before retreating inside the cabin.

'What's up with . . . ?' But the rest of her sentence trailed off as something else caught her attention.

To Abby's total amazement, right in front of her eyes she then saw what could only be described as a *cascade* of red roses drifting gently down from the bridge and on to the ship's deck – right in front of where they were sitting.

'Oh, my goodness!' she gasped, turning in amazement to Finn, who had a strange expression on his face and seemed unaffected by the display. It was only then that she realised he was holding something in his hand, something small and shiny, and for a second, it crossed her mind that he'd brought along that cheap pendant he'd used to spring this morning's surprise.

But this was no pendant.

'Abby Ryan,' he said, his voice thick with emotion, his dark eyes locked on to hers, 'will you marry me?'

And there, in the moonlight on the River Seine, while hundreds of red roses showered down from the bridge above, a romantic and memorable setting that she wouldn't have dreamt of in a thousand years, Abby gave her reply.

'Yes,' she said, her tears falling almost as quickly as the roses. 'Yes, Finn, I would love to marry you.'

Chapter 37

'You're what?' Abby's mother gasped, when immediately upon their return from Paris, she and Finn called to the house to announce their happy news.

'We're getting married!' she cried, joyfully thrusting out her right hand so her mum could inspect her ring, a setting of three large diamonds in platinum. It was *exactly* the type of ring Abby would have chosen for herself.

The rest of their stay in Paris had been magical. That night on the boat, after she'd said yes before practically launching herself at Finn, the waiter had arrived with a fresh bottle of champagne and a couple of glasses. The champagne cork had popped, and she and Finn had clinked glasses against the magical background of subtly lit Parisian buildings. She still hadn't been able to believe that such a wonderful thing was really happening to her. She'd picked up one of the roses, determined to keep it as a tangible memory of the entire incredible experience.

Back at port, the Bentley was once again waiting to chauffeur the two of them back to their hotel. On the way there, Abby kept going over and over everything in her mind, trying to recall every second of what had happened, terrified that this particular memory would fade away.

But as it happened, there was no real need: Finn had indeed thought of everything. Beforehand, he'd asked the company who'd arranged the cruise (along with the charade in Montmartre) to videotape what had happened at the bridge, which meant that she now had a visual record of his proposal, and her delighted reaction, for posterity.

Later that night, after they'd made love and Finn lay fast asleep beside her, Abby hadn't been able to resist committing to her diary the overwhelming emotions she'd experienced that night. She was terrified that what had easily been the happiest moment of her life could so easily be lost, and right then, if she could have made a deal to swap the memory of that night for every other before the accident, she would have. If she could hold on to just one memory for the rest of her life, it would unquestionably be that one.

Now back home in Dublin, her mother was staring at Abby's engagement ring with a mixture of awe and confusion in her eyes. 'You're really getting married,' Teresa repeated, apparently blindsided by this development.

'Yes, we are.' By his tone, Abby knew Finn was a bit stung by her mother's so far unenthusiastic response to the news, and by her ongoing uncertainty about their relationship. Abby, too, was a bit put out by her mum's reaction – couldn't she see how happy and in love they both were?

But it seemed that this time they'd both misjudged her, as without warning tears sprang to Teresa's eyes and her mouth broke into a wide smile. 'It's a beautiful ring,' her mother said, sniffling, 'and I'm so pleased for you – for both of you,' she added, looking at Finn. 'I'm sure you'll be very happy.'

'We will.' Thrilled that her mother seemed to have come round, Abby engulfed her in a huge hug. 'We couldn't *wait* to tell you!'

'Well,' she said, looking a bit embarrassed, 'I suppose you know I've had my worries about how the two of you will cope with everything, but you seem to have managed fairly well up to now.'

'Abby's the best thing that's ever happened to me, Mrs

Ryan,' Finn said, squeezing his fiancée's hand. 'And we're in this together, for better or worse.'

Abby looked at him then, suddenly realising the significance of that vow – especially for him. For better or worse? But what if . . . if things got out of hand and her memory deteriorated even more? What kind of life would they have then? Or more to the point, what kind of life would *Finn* have?

Suddenly, Abby began to get an inkling of the concerns her mother and Pat had. And she wondered if for Finn's sake she might have been too hasty in accepting his proposal.

'You're a good man,' her mother was saying to Finn, hugging them both in turn. 'So have you set a date yet?'

Abby was so overcome by the doubts she'd just experienced she couldn't think straight.

'We're thinking we'd better get it done as soon as possible before she forgets about me altogether,' he joked, winking at Abby.

This time, it wasn't Teresa who was appalled by his words.

'Are you all right?' Finn asked, when Teresa went into the kitchen to organise a plate of biscuits and put on the kettle, champagne never having been a staple in the Ryan household. 'You've gone a bit pale.'

'I'm OK,' she said, feigning a smile. The all-consuming joy she'd felt earlier had suddenly been deflated by the notion that spending the rest of his life with her might not be as straightforward as Finn thought.

'You're being silly,' he argued, when later that evening, back at her flat, Abby broached her concerns. 'The stupid brain injury doesn't matter to me at all. Why would it?'

'Why *wouldn't* it?' Abby countered. 'For goodness' sake, it's bad enough to think that by this time next month I probably won't be able to remember what's so far been the best day of my life, let alone try and plan another one!'

She'd been able to think of nothing else throughout their visit to her mum's – how she'd been rash and unfair to automatically agree to marry Finn without thinking about the consequences.

Finn seemed to misunderstand. 'So you're saying that you don't want to marry me because you might not fully remember the wedding day? OK, fine, let's do something small in the registry office, nothing too extravagant – as you say, it seems a little pointless if you can't remember it, although we will have photographs and—'

'That's not it,' she said, frustrated that she couldn't get her feelings across. 'I just don't know if we should go down this road so soon.'

He looked at her, stunned. 'You mean you've changed your mind completely and you don't want to marry me after all?'

Abby shook her head. 'No, no, that's not what I'm saying. I'm just thinking that maybe we need to be a hundred per cent sure we can cope with . . . with my situation,' she dropped her gaze to the ground, 'before committing to one another for the rest of our lives, or at least before you commit to *me* for the rest of your life.'

He strode across the room, and kneeling in front of her, took both of her hands in his.

'Abby, I love you, and as far as I'm concerned, that's all that matters. I want to spend the rest of my life with you, no matter what.'

A lump came to her throat and she sorely wished that she had the strength of his conviction. 'It doesn't bother you that without the help of stupid diaries and computer programs I *might* not remember you from day to day?' she said, ashamed to have to admit this yet again, and even more ashamed that despite this, he could still love her so unconditionally. 'It doesn't bother you that I don't fully remember all the wonderful times we've had together since we first met?

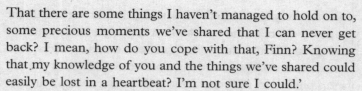

That there are some things I haven't managed to hold on to, some precious moments we've shared that I can never get back? I mean, how do you cope with that, Finn? Knowing that my knowledge of you and the things we've shared could easily be lost in a heartbeat? I'm not sure I could.'

Finn's dark eyes bored into hers. 'I cope with it because I love you. And because I know that the love you have for me isn't just because of what some computer tells you. How could it be? You have to feel it too, don't you? Something else – something separate from your memory must register, surely?'

She locked eyes with him, the realisation hitting her like a thunderbolt. 'You're right,' she said, and a tiny flutter of joy unfurled inside her as she realised it was true. That whatever she remembered in her head, surely Finn would, without doubt, always be in her heart . . .

Erin was over the moon. 'I can't believe it!' she cried down the phone when Abby broke the news to her the following afternoon.

'Will you be my bridesmaid?' Abby asked, restored to her original elation after her conversation with Finn. 'You can say no if you like, it's just—'

A high-pitched squeal from the other end immediately gave Abby her answer. 'It would be an *honour*!' her friend gasped. 'And are you having Claire and Caroline too?'

Abby was, much to Caroline's delight.

'Oh, my *God*, think of all the fun we'll have shopping for dresses! We must go back to London, or maybe even New York – see if we can get you something like that Oscar de la Renta number you liked. Wouldn't it be just *gorgeous* in white? Then again, maybe Vera Wang would be better, or even Sharon Hoey, or . . .'

Abby had listened patiently while her label-loving sister ran

Melissa Hill

through every wedding-dress designer in the book. But she supposed Caroline did have a point. If she got herself a drop-dead-gorgeous and simply unforgettable wedding dress, then afterwards it could make up part of her mementos of the day itself, couldn't it? Still, the dress and the day weren't just for her, were they? They would be for Finn too, and she owed it to him to look incredible. It was going to be a day for him to remember, just as much as her.

Chapter 38

At their next session, Abby couldn't wait to tell Hannah her news.

'And you've set a date too?' Hannah said. 'I'm so pleased for you, Abby – that's fantastic.'

Now that her family had been told, the wedding arrangements had begun in earnest and the previous weekend she and Finn had booked the church and hotel. They'd decided on a Christmas Eve wedding to mark a full year since their first meeting.

'You don't think I'm taking a huge risk?' Abby asked tentatively. 'Or should I say *Finn*'s taking a huge risk?'

'Is that what you believe?' As usual, Hannah had to answer a question with a question.

Abby shrugged. 'I don't really know. We've managed well up to now, but my problem will always be in the background, won't it?'

'You *have* managed extremely well up to now, and from what you've told me, Finn sounds like the kind of man who knows exactly what he's doing.'

Abby smiled, gratified by this.

'Anyway, all relationships and marriages face challenges of one kind or another, Abby. Yours are unusual, certainly, but they're evidently not insurmountable.' Then she sat back in the armchair and crossed her legs. 'Now, let me ask you something. Do you remember when we first met and you were recovering from not only your head injury but also a broken relationship?'

'Of course.' Unlike before, Abby wasn't at all self-conscious about the subject this time.

'Well, how do you feel about all of that now?'

'About Kieran?' she clarified, exhaling deeply. 'Looking back, I can't believe how much of an effect it all had on me. I'd let myself sink to such depths of despair I never went out, never did anything interesting, was *definitely* no fun to be around . . .' She shook her head. 'Caroline was right. I'd shied away from living my life.'

Abby chuckled softly, thinking about all the wonderful experiences she'd had over the last year, not just the travel or the time she'd spent with Finn, but also the little things, like reconnecting with her family and Erin, or something as simple as trying out new food in a restaurant.

It had been a huge journey of self-discovery, and through it all Abby had come to realise just how much the people closest to her mattered. Not to mention that she'd gained a spectacular wardrobe, a keen appreciation for opera, and was even a bit of an expert on gambling!

When she explained this to Hannah, the other woman smiled. 'And that girl – the one you just described as having shied away from life – how did she come to be like that?' she asked, her tone level and, Abby thought, a bit studied. '*Was* it just a broken heart?'

'No,' she replied firmly, having come to this realisation some time ago. 'Kieran wasn't right for me, or perhaps we weren't right for each other, I don't know. He was strict with money, so *I* was strict with money, even though I know I wasn't always like that. Then his food foibles gradually became my food foibles. We could never go out to eat anywhere because when we did his fickleness became so uncomfortable that there was no point. I can see all this now, even though this time last year I would never in a million years have admitted that he had that sort of influence on me,' she

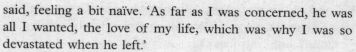

said, feeling a bit naïve. 'As far as I was concerned, he was all I wanted, the love of my life, which was why I was so devastated when he left.'

'And do you still feel that way?'

'Devastated?' Abby shook her head firmly. 'Not at all. In fact, now I know he actually did me a favour.' She grinned feebly. 'Hindsight is a wonderful thing.'

'So you now believe the relationship – ultimately – was bad for you?'

Abby was surprised by the conversation's complete change in direction. Instead of discussing her and Finn, Hannah now seemed to be unusually interested in Kieran and her feelings towards him. Since that first time, the psychologist had hardly made mention of her old boyfriend, and if she had, it was only in passing.

'I would never have said it at the time, but yes, I would have to agree that the relationship was bad for me.'

'In the sense that . . . ?'

'In the sense that we became too dependent on one another, or should I say *I* became too dependent on him and his approval. As I said before, he could be . . . difficult with money and certain other things, and I suppose I should have put my foot down more. We both earned reasonably good salaries, yet while all our friends were out enjoying life, we were sitting at home watching DVDs. At the time, I wanted to be with him no matter what. I loved him and wanted to keep him happy.'

Hannah nodded, and seemed to be pondering something. 'Difficult question, I know, but how does your relationship with Kieran compare to the one you now have with Finn?'

Abby smiled. 'There's a world of difference. I don't know . . . With Finn, he kind of . . . Well, it's difficult to pin down, but it's like he lets me be myself. I don't have to agree with his outlook or everything he says, whereas Kieran used to take offence at my not going along with what he wanted.'

'Controlling, you mean?'

Abby looked up. That was the second time someone had used that word to describe him. 'Well, that's quite a strong word, but I suppose it was something like that, yes.'

'So you ended up being the kind of person he wanted you to be, instead of being yourself?'

'Yes, sounds sad, doesn't it? Sad pathetic, I mean.'

'Not really. You two were together for a long time, so naturally some form of convergence would take place – by this I mean that couples often adopt each other's ways, sometimes even mannerisms. It's a form of consensus. I'm sure Kieran adopted some of your traits too.'

Abby shook her head. 'Nope.'

'Really? That's interesting.'

For some reason, Abby felt once again obliged to defend him. 'Look, it wasn't a fault on Kieran's part. I actually think he was just a much stronger personality than I am. He wasn't horrible about it or anything.'

'I can imagine,' Hannah said, before adding smoothly, 'But he must have been difficult to argue with.'

Now Abby felt a little defensive. Why all these questions about Kieran all of a sudden? What did he have to do with anything now? 'We didn't argue much, actually,' she said quickly, her expression closing.

'Well, that's good.' Hannah smiled, almost as if she hadn't noticed the subtle change in mood, but Abby suspected she had. 'And good that we've established that you're finally over Kieran.'

'Definitely.' Abby crossed her arms, doing her best to signify to Hannah that she didn't want to continue the conversation.

But the psychologist had another question for her. 'Abby, there's one thing about your brain injury that's always troubled us, and as it seems to be the very thing that's making your condition so unpredictable, it would be good to get to the bottom of it.'

'What's that?' Abby frowned, not sure what she was getting at. She didn't think too much about the mechanics of her brain or the injury any more. Now that she had a good handle on how things worked, it seemed rather pointless.

'Well, you remember the secondary injury, the older trauma that appears to have a bearing on the newer one?'

'Yes.' Although in truth, Abby had pretty much forgotten all about that. At this stage, it hardly seemed relevant.

'So now that some . . . time has passed and you've gained emotional distance, do you have any idea, any idea at all, where you might have got that older injury?' When she said nothing, Hannah prompted further. 'Maybe a bump on the head from a fall or possibly a—'

Abby stared at her, finally understanding what she was getting at. 'Oh, my God,' she exclaimed. 'You think that *Kieran* did something? That he could have . . .'

Hannah said nothing, and by the look on her face, Abby knew that this was exactly what she thought.

'My God! I can't believe you would say something, even *think* something like that!' she cried. 'OK, so Kieran wasn't perfect, I know that now, but he would never, *ever* do anything to hurt me in the way you're thinking. No way!' Abby was horrified by the notion and incredibly angry with Hannah.

'I'm sorry,' the doctor said now. 'And I don't need a degree in psychology to tell me that I'm obviously very much mistaken. Forgive me, but I had to ask the question.'

'Well, you've got a hell of a cheek, Hannah! I loved Kieran. And I might have been wrong about his feelings for me, but he never lifted a finger to me. Yes, he broke my heart, but it was nothing like that!'

The two of them sat in silence for the next few minutes,

Abby still appalled that Hannah could even think such a thing.

Finally, Hannah spoke again. 'Just one more question about Kieran if you don't mind. Don't worry, it's nothing like that,' she added quickly, seeing Abby's wide-eyed expression. 'I just wondered, seeing as he was obviously someone of great importance in your life, if you happened to bump into Kieran now on the street, how you think you'd react.'

Although she was annoyed that Hannah had persisted, she couldn't dispute that this question was a good one, and if Abby was being truthful, not one she'd really considered lately. What would she say, and how would she react if she happened to bump into Kieran now?

But there was only one real answer to that.

Abby smiled. 'It wouldn't affect me in the slightest,' she replied confidently.

Chapter 39

Although Finn and I have the occasional hiccup now and again, for the most part things are going great. This habit I now have of detailing everything that happens day to day has literally saved me, and I don't know what I'd do without these records. Because Finn and I see each other pretty much every day now, my memory seems to have the continuity Hannah insists is so important, so I am to all intents and purposes functioning pretty well in everyday life. Something I'm quite proud of actually!

Still, there's no doubt that my reliance on records makes me vulnerable and a teeny bit sad from time to time, especially where Finn is concerned.

Like his proposal in Paris. I've watched the DVD of it umpteen times since, and it's one memory I really wish I could recall in vivid detail, because regardless of seeing it on film or reading about it in my diary, there's just no way of capturing and reliving how I felt at the time.

Granted, I have a pretty good idea, as even just watching that unbelievably romantic night he arranged is enough to set me off blubbing! But I'd give anything to be able to relive what it was like to be there that night: the look in Finn's eyes when he asked me to marry him, the magic and wonder of it all when those hundreds of roses began cascading onto the boat.

God, it's things like this that really frustrate me about this stupid injury! At times I can't help but feel so annoyed about my situation, but how can I be that bitter when all of this inadvertently led me to Finn?

This time last year I was holed up here, hiding away from the world and from everything that life had to offer. Now I've done the most amazing things, seen the most incredible sights and fallen in love with Finn – definitely the most unforgettable experience of all! How would I have got through all this without him? He's helped me overcome the worst of it, and has made me understand that my problems don't have to be the end of the world. No doubt we still have some challenges ahead of us, but as Erin keeps telling me, don't all couples?

But what would it have been like if I'd never met him?

If I hadn't had that day with him in New York and bumped into him again back here in Dublin, who knows how long the fantasy that my memory was fine would have been upheld? Would I ever have discovered the extent of my problems without meeting him?

It's all academic now of course, but it really brings it home how important Finn is to me and how lucky I am to have him. And Lucy too, of course! Who would have thought I'd ever be comfortable with a dog in the same room, let alone be about to share the rest of my life with one! Turns out that was just another irrational fear to add to the list . . .

Since meeting Finn I've been happier than I've ever been in my life. And I know without question that my wedding day will be the happiest day of all, so really who cares if I might not be able to recall every last minute? Most people don't think to sift through the details and distill every moment down to the best and most important things like I can, so I guess I should take Finn's advice and try to look at this as a positive thing.

I just wish his dad could be as upbeat about it all though. He's obviously still so worried about us.

While he's always lovely to me, there's simply no denying he feels our engagement is a bad idea. To be honest, I'm a bit taken aback at the strength of his convictions. I know he's worried that Finn's getting himself into the kind of situation Pat was in in his own marriage, but I'm nothing like an alcoholic! I'm well in control of my own moods and feelings, and while of course having to keep a diary of every little thing just in case I forget it isn't exactly normal, I'm doing my best . . . But unfortunately that doesn't seem to be enough for Pat; he's still making no secret of his belief that Finn is taking on too much of a burden in marrying me. And the worst of it is that I can see his point.

Because I wonder the very same thing every single day.

Things to remember:

1. *Put your rubbish out on Sunday night.*
2. *Your next appointment with Hannah is on Monday at ten.*
3. *My flight's back around lunchtime on Monday.*
4. *Put two sugars in your coffee!*
5. *I love you.*

Finn xxx

Abby smiled as she read the list that Finn had left for her on the fridge. It was Sunday morning and he had left for a work trip to Manchester the night before. Although they weren't yet living together, lately he'd taken to leaving little notes and reminders like that around her flat, some tongue in cheek, but others a genuine effort to help her remember small but important pieces of information when he wasn't around – like when to put the rubbish out or put sugar in her coffee, which, try as she might, she just kept on forgetting to do.

But there was no fear of her forgetting her appointment with Hannah on Monday, as all Abby's appointments and meetings were recorded in her electronic diary, as of course was the time and date of Finn's return. This would be the first time they'd spent a couple of days apart from one another and Abby was slightly nervous about it and worried that something might happen while he was away. Judging by the note on the fridge, evidently Finn was worried too.

After a lovely lazy morning, she eventually got up at twelve and threw on a pair of comfy tracksuit bottoms and grey zip-up top. Today she was going to enjoy just slobbing about and taking it easy. Not that she'd done much else these last few months, she thought wryly. She'd really have to think again about going back to work soon, definitely after the wedding anyway.

While recently she'd had the wedding plans to occupy her, now pretty much everything was done and Abby was starting to get bored. The church and hotel were booked, the flowers and dresses were ordered, so really all she and Finn had to do was turn up on the day. And book their honeymoon of course. Abby smiled. There was one thing on her list that she hadn't yet managed to do, one major destination she desperately wanted to visit, and perhaps the best part would be that for this one, Finn would be joining her.

'All the way down there just to see a couple of dopey penguins?' he'd laughed, when she'd told him she wanted to go to the South Pole on their honeymoon.

Smiling at the memory, Abby picked up her keys and headed out to buy the Sunday papers and a litre of milk from the corner shop. Only when she got there, she didn't have enough money on her.

Which meant that a trip to the cash point was in order.

It was a lovely, clear October day and Abby had a spring

in her step as she walked to the end of the road and to the nearest ATM. There was a small queue ahead of her, and as she waited obediently in line, she began daydreaming yet again about her and Finn's upcoming honeymoon to Antarctica. It would be fantastic and such a great start to their life together, she mused, a smile on her face.

She was so caught up in these pleasant thoughts that she barely noticed that the queue had very quickly dispersed and it was now her turn to use the machine. A tap on her shoulder quickly brought her out of her reverie.

'Excuse me, are you waiting to use this?' a man asked.

At the sound of the voice, every single nerve ending stood to attention and Abby stood rooted to the spot, almost afraid to move. It couldn't be . . . could it?

Time seemed to stand still, and so did Abby, as she tried to get her head around what was happening. Numbly, she finally turned round and came face to face with . . .

'Kieran?'

'Oh!' her ex replied, evidently just as taken aback as she was. 'Erm, hello Abby,' he mumbled. 'I . . . erm . . . didn't recognise you.'

Contrary to what she'd assured Hannah, and indeed what she'd believed herself, all the old insecurities came flooding back at once. Her hair was unwashed and greasy, she had no make-up on and was wearing her hideous grey zip-up top, the first thing that had come to hand that morning.

But her embarrassment about her appearance wasn't just brought on by Kieran's presence; it had, in fact, much more to do with his companion. Or should that be *companions*?

Kieran's wife, Jessica, was watching her with undisguised interest. The two women had never come face to face before, and Jessica was undoubtedly wondering why on earth Kieran had taken so long to break it off with a girl who was clearly no competition.

Abby, however, barely noticed this; she was too busy staring at the buggy sitting between them.

'You have a child?' she gasped, stepping backwards in horror as she looked from the child to Kieran, an avalanche of emotions crashing over her, followed just as quickly by a rush of questions.

It was October, just over a year since her accident, so Kieran and Jessica could only have been married just over a year too, but this child . . . this child was—

'Yes, his name is Alan and he's almost one,' Jessica supplied, confirming Abby's horrified suspicions, and the faint smugness in her tone validating them even further.

Her mind reeling, Abby scrambled to get her bearings. Almost a year old . . . But he and Jessica had only got married and Abby and Kieran had been together still only six months before that, which had to mean . . . it *must* mean . . .

'I'm sorry – I have to go,' she cried, suddenly desperate to get away from them.

'But don't you want to . . . ?'

Abby was moving so fast she barely heard Kieran call out something about the ATM, and she knew he and Jessica were probably a bit taken aback by her sudden haste to get away.

No, scratch that, why *would* they be taken aback? It was much more likely that they were now laughing at her, laughing their heads off over what she was too stupid to realise at the time. Kieran and Jessica had a one-year-old son . . .

She'd been right all along: Kieran *had* betrayed her, despite all his bullshit about doing the right thing, the honourable thing, by saying he was breaking up with her before he and Jessica got together. Honourable, my foot! And to think that she'd given him that, had respected him for it even, despite the fact that he was breaking her heart in two. How could he be so callous and deceitful?

Abby felt like she had lead in her veins as she tried to put enough distance between her and the man she'd spent so long trying to forget. But now, having discovered the full extent of his betrayal, all the old grief came rushing back. A one-year-old son . . . It meant that the child *must* have been conceived before they split up . . . because that had been only eighteen months ago. Abby tried to remember back that far, tried to recall what Kieran's behaviour had been like at the time and—

'Abby, wait!' she heard a voice call out behind her. Kieran.

At this, and despite the fact that she didn't want to speak to him, didn't want to even look at him, her legs began to slow, almost as if by their own accord.

Seconds later, he appeared in front of her. 'Are you OK?' he asked, and the fake sincerity in his voice was the final straw.

'How can you ask me that?' Abby gasped wretchedly. 'How dare you ask me if I'm OK?'

Kieran looked perplexed and uncomfortable. 'I'm sorry . . . look, I know it must have been awkward back there, but I thought we were over that and . . .' He shrugged. 'I know it's been a while, but it's good to see you, Abby.'

Now she felt as though she'd passed into some kind of parallel universe. What on earth was wrong with him? Why did he expect her to be happy to see him out of the blue, especially with what she'd discovered? Or was he so caught up in his own life that he didn't even realise the significance of what had just occurred? Was he really that stupid, that heartless?

'Kieran, you have a one-year-old child,' she began, willing him to do the maths and make the connection. 'I know it mightn't matter much to you now, but it certainly matters to me!'

'What does?' Again he seemed genuinely confused. 'So I have a child – big deal. What's Alan got to do with anything?

You know I'm happily married now and what happened between us was a long time ago.' He wrinkled his brow. 'As far as I'm concerned, back then I tried to do the best by everyone. Now, I don't think for a second that it was easy for you, but—'

'Don't you have any idea why I'm so upset?' He seemed so clueless that briefly Abby wondered if *he* was the one with the memory problem! 'Any idea at all? Kieran, your son is a *year* old! Which means he must have been conceived while you and I were still together – in other words, behind my back! Yet you swore that you and Jessica weren't getting together until it was over between you and me.'

Kieran frowned, and was it her imagination or was he starting to back away a little?

'Abby, I really don't know what is wrong with you, but somewhere along the line you must have lost the ability to add and subtract. Yes, Alan is one, but believe me, I know exactly when and where he was conceived and it certainly wasn't behind your back.'

Abby really couldn't believe she was hearing this. What did he think she was – stupid? 'Why are you doing this?' she demanded. 'Why are you still trying to pull the wool over my eyes? I'm not an imbecile, despite what you seem to think. The child is almost one, add in another nine months and you have almost two, whereas it's barely a year since you two got married, so—' She stopped in her tracks when she realised Kieran was looking at her very strangely, as if she'd lost her mind or something.

'Abby,' he said then, his voice slow and firm, almost as if he were speaking to a particularly slow child. 'I married Jessica in September 2006. Alan was conceived at Christmas.'

'What . . . ?'

Then suddenly, just like that, it hit her. In that moment Abby realised that while she hadn't exactly lost her mind, she'd almost certainly lost something else. Her world began to spin on its axis as she finally understood why dates – particularly the current *year* – had kept confusing her lately. That time with the cheque, she hadn't been absentminded in writing it at all; instead, something else had been at play.

'You two got married in *2006*?' she repeated in a whisper.

'Yes. So you must realise that our son couldn't possibly have been—'

Her mind reeling, Abby reached out and held on to a wall for support.

Although she'd questioned this privately a few times, it was indeed 2008, although Abby had initially believed it was 2007. Unwilling to admit to herself or anyone else that this had confused her, she'd eventually put it down to a possible side effect of her injury, one that didn't really matter much in the scheme of things. No big deal. But one thing she could be *absolutely* sure about was the year of her accident, which had occurred shortly after Kieran's wedding, and which he'd just confirmed had taken place in 2006. So if the injury had happened in 2006 and it was now 2008 . . .

It could mean only one thing, Abby deduced, flabbergasted. A full year had passed, a year about which she had no recollection.

A lost year.

But in order for this to have happened, she realised grimly, it wasn't just her memory that had been playing tricks on her.

Everyone else had too.

Chapter 40

'How long has this been going on?' White-faced with shock, and her cheeks wet with tears, Abby appeared at her mother's door. 'How long have you been lying to me?'

Teresa visibly paled. 'Love, what are you talking—'

'Don't lie to me!' Abby cried, brushing hastily past her. 'You've been doing that long enough – you, Caroline, Erin and whoever else is involved!'

After discovering through Kieran that she'd lost a year of her life and the significance of it, Abby had immediately called Finn, who she feared could be involved in this. But she couldn't get him on the line and had no choice but to leave a tearful, rambling message on his voicemail. 'I really need to talk to you,' she sobbed. 'I've just bumped into Kieran and he . . . I found out that . . . I found out something, and I don't know what to do or what to think . . . I really need to speak to you. Please call me as soon as you get this.'

She didn't know what she'd do if she discovered that Finn was in on this, if he too had deceived her in such an awful way.

Now, Teresa stared at her daughter, her expression panicked. 'Involved in what? Abby, I . . .' But just as quickly her face crumpled, and now she looked resigned and fearful. 'Love, why don't we both sit down and talk this over, OK?'

'How could you do this to me?' Abby insisted, fraught with terror, distrust – a million and one things were going through her mind. They'd deceived her and she wanted to find out how, where and, most importantly, *why*?

'Love, we were only doing what we thought was right.'

'You thought lying and pretending and making a fool of me was right? How did you work that one out, Mum?'

'Abby, please sit down there and I'll make you a cup of tea, OK?'

'I don't want a cup of tea, and I don't want you to patron-ise me!' Suddenly weary, she sank on to the sofa, her eyes filling with tears. 'What's happening to me, Mum? I don't know what's real any more.'

'Honey . . .' Moved by her distress, Teresa sat down next to her daughter and gathered in her arms, and for a brief moment, Abby relaxed in her embrace. However, just as quickly, she remembered the reason she was here.

'Mum, please tell me what's going on.'

Teresa exhaled deeply and shook her head. 'What happened? How did you—'

'How did I find out that everyone's been messing with my head? I bumped into Kieran today – Kieran and his one-year-old son!'

'Oh.'

'Is that all you can say? Somehow I lose a year of my life and all you can say is "Oh"?'

'We never expected . . . We were going to tell you eventu-ally,' Teresa struggled, not sure what to say.

'You were going to tell me when? When another two or maybe three years had passed?'

'Dr O'Neill said—'

'What?' Abby's head snapped up. 'What's Hannah got to do with this?' Then it hit her. 'Of course, she has to be in on it too . . . God, I don't believe this.'

This was a blow too many. Hannah, to whom she'd confided so much of her thoughts and feelings, and whom she'd trusted no end . . . Now Abby realised that this too was all another charade, another betrayal. Wasn't there *anyone* she could trust any more?

'Love, maybe it would be better if you spoke to her about it; she'll be able to explain it all much better than I can.'

'For goodness' sake, you're my mother! Why can't you explain why everyone's been lying to me all this time!' Now the tears had started to flow, despite Abby's best intentions.

Again, Teresa floundered. 'They advised us to wait until after the wedding because of the stress of it all, you see . . .'

Abby shook her head vigorously. 'Mum, you're not making sense! What's the wedding got to do with it? And what do you mean; "they advised you to wait"? Who's "they"? Please,' she implored, when she saw her mother hesitate, 'I really need to know.'

'This won't be easy for you to hear, and I wish you'd let me phone Dr O'Neill – she really would be much better able to explain—'

'Forget Dr O'Neill,' Abby interjected. 'Whatever it is, I want to hear it from you.'

Teresa waited a couple of seconds before speaking, as if trying to decide the best place to start. Then she sighed. 'Love, when you woke after your head injury a year ago . . . it wasn't the first time you'd woken up,' she continued, her gaze falling to the floor. 'It was the fourth.'

'What?' Abby gasped. 'What do you mean?'

'Abby, as you know, your accident didn't happen last year like you think it did – it happened the year before.'

Abby couldn't speak. Even though she'd figured out that much, it still stunned her to hear her suspicions confirmed. A whole year of her life really had been lost.

'But how . . . *Why?* Was I in a coma or something?'

'No, no, nothing like that. As I said, that last time was the fourth time you came to.'

'Came to from what?'

Teresa took a deep breath. 'From another blackout.'

'Blackout . . .'

'Love, I can only imagine how confused you must be. So maybe I should just start from the very beginning, and then you might be able to understand.' Her mother sighed again. 'Abby, as you know well, that blow to the head you got caused terrible damage, especially to your brain.'

She nodded, unable to speak.

'But when you woke up in the hospital the first time, the extent of that damage was plain for all to see. There was a major gash on the side of your head, and the doctors had to shave off most of your hair.'

Abby's hand instinctively went to her head. 'Shave it off?'

'Yes. It was completely gone. It's grown back fairly well now, although I know it seemed so much shorter when you woke up the last time.'

'But Hannah said—'

'I know they told you they had to cut it to examine the wound, but that was so you'd think it was the . . . first time. And of course the wound has also healed well.'

Hearing all this, and the extent of their lies, Abby was gobsmacked. 'Go on.'

'Well, as I said, you woke up with a fairly severe head wound. But everything pretty much happened the same as it did the way you remember: the doctors sent you for an MRI and a CAT scan to try and determine the extent of the damage, and they came up with the same diagnosis – the damage to your hippocampus and how it would affect your memory.' Teresa paused and looked pained. 'But, love, you took it very badly,' she told her. 'You were distraught about the prospect of losing your memory, none of us could comfort you, and you wouldn't go outside for weeks on end because of your hair and the way you looked – not to mention that you were still broken-hearted about Kieran. The doctors suggested that you see a psychologist to help you deal with your emotions, but you wouldn't have any of it.'

Abby stared at her – unable to believe that all this had happened without her remembering it. It was as though she'd stepped into some weird parallel universe.

'Hang on a second,' she interrupted then. 'You're saying that the doctors explained the damage to me and I couldn't deal with it?'

'Pretty much, yes. It's hard to explain, love, but as soon as you realised that you were indeed forgetting little things here and there, emotionally you just couldn't cope. And you wouldn't let any of us help you. I wanted you to move in here with me but you refused and . . . well, we were all very worried – the doctors included – about how you were going to manage in the long term. As it happened, we soon found out.'

'What? What happened?'

'It was a couple of months after the accident. You were found unconscious on the street near your flat. The doctors told us you'd had some kind of epileptic fit, which apparently is often a side effect of traumatic brain injury.'

Abby was stunned. 'Epilepsy?'

'Yes.' Teresa shook her head, and Abby could only imagine how terrifying it must have been for her mother to learn of this, to say nothing of how she herself felt hearing about it now. *Epilepsy.* 'The attack was very severe and caused a blackout of some sort . . . I don't really know.' Teresa's hands were clasped tightly in her lap, and Abby could see it on her mother's face that the burden of explaining all this was taking a lot out of her.

But hearing it was taking a lot out of her too.

'How long . . . how long was I out for?' she asked then.

'Maybe a couple of hours or so between the time you blacked

out and when you woke up, the doctors said. But, love, the crucial thing is that when you woke up that second time, all you could remember was leaving your flat that morning. It took us all a while to figure out that you weren't talking about leaving it *that* morning – the morning of your blackout – but the morning of the accident, the day you first got hit by the tile. It was as if the previous few months had never happened.'

'I don't believe you,' Abby cried. 'My entire memory wiped clean, just like that?'

'The doctors said it must have been all the pressure you were under. You were under such an incredible amount of stress trying to cope with all this on your own, which must have been so overwhelming for you . . .' Her mother's guilt was plain to see. 'But you wouldn't let any of us help you: you just insisted on locking yourself away from us all, like you had after Kieran, and eventually I suppose it just became too much . . . But then when we found out that the seizure had caused your memory to . . . reset itself almost, we knew that the doctors' fears were realised and the damage was real.

'Again the doctors went through the process of explaining the memory loss to you, except this time they could tell you for sure that there were no maybes about it – your blackout had proved that. At first, you didn't believe that so much time had passed, until you discovered the date and admitted to yourself that you couldn't account for the months that had gone before. So this time, after lots of convincing, you agreed to take their suggestions on board, and meet with Dr O'Neill to talk things through and try and ensure that the same thing didn't happen again.'

That explained why Hannah was in on it too, Abby realised now.

Abby was still struggling to comprehend. 'So what about the third time?' she urged. 'You said that the last time I woke up was the fourth time, so what happened in between?'

'Unfortunately, barely a month later you had another attack, this time before my own eyes here at the house. We were having a family dinner and you and Caroline had a bit of a run-in about something . . . I don't know . . .' she added, looking pained. 'Anyway, you got so upset you had another seizure – you were out for four or five hours.' She bit her lip and tears came to her eyes. 'It was an awful time. Caroline was inconsolable: she was convinced it was all her fault.'

Abby realised now that her sister's recent closeness may have had much to do with this.

'And again, when you woke up for the third time, all you could remember was leaving your flat that morning, same as last time, despite the fact that by then several months had passed since you first got hit. And again, the doctors went through the same procedure, explaining your injuries and taking scans, except now they needed to find out what might be triggering these seizures, and if they were causing any more damage to your brain.' She paused then, as if to give Abby time to let it sink in.

'And I remembered nothing at all again, not a single thing?'

Teresa shook her head. 'No, we were right back where we started, and had to explain everything to you all over again. Again, you reacted very badly but once more agreed to see Dr O'Neill.'

'So what happened to cause the latest seizure? The one I woke up from . . . a year ago.'

'We're not sure, love, as this time it happened again when you were out and about. The doctors seem to think that stress brings the seizures on, but because you can't remember what happens beforehand, we've no way of knowing what brought this last attack on. This time, you were at the DART station, but we don't know what you were doing there or where you were going.'

Abby thought hard, but try as she might, she couldn't recall a single thing about being at a DART station, or indeed any of the other events her mother was describing. The neurologists had been right all along, she admitted to herself, terrified. Her long-term memory was in fact useless, which meant that all the time and effort she'd spent trying to cope with this had been completely pointless.

To think she'd spent all this time believing she *was* coping, that she could get through it . . . The thought of this terrified her beyond belief.

'But why did you decide to keep me in the dark this time?' she asked then. 'Why trick me into thinking the accident had happened last year, instead of the year before? What was the point of that?' Then, to her horror, she started to sob. 'Why give me all that false hope, and let me think that I could actually get through this, when you knew that there was no chance, and I was only kidding myself? Why did you do that, Mum? Why give me false hope when you knew – you *knew* – it was all hopeless?'

'It wasn't my decision—'

'But you're my mother!' Abby was in full flight now, the realisation that all was lost well and truly hitting her. 'Surely you couldn't agree to such a horrible and *hurtful* deception, no matter whose decision it was! How stupid do you think I feel now?' Tears were racing down her cheeks. 'I don't know what to believe, don't know who to trust . . . You're my mother – how could you possibly agree to do something like this to me?'

'Love, of course I didn't agree with it, but in the end I had no choice. The decision was made, and although I didn't like it one bit, everyone else said it might be for the best and—'

'But what gave Hannah or the doctors or whoever,' she said, deciding that this was the most likely scenario, 'what gave them the right to mess with my head? And for Christ's sake, *why*?'

Teresa's hands were shaking. 'I don't know . . . I—'

'What do you mean you don't know? Surely you *must* know when you were involved in this as much as any of them. Mum, why can't you just tell me why you did this, why you decided to turn my life upside down by lying to me like this? Why?'

Teresa looked at her, a world of hurt and regret in her eyes. 'Love, only you can answer that,' she said in a small voice, 'because the decision to do it was all yours.'

Abby stared at her, stunned. 'What? What are you talking about? Why would *I* . . . *How* would I—'

'This is why I wanted you to speak to Dr O'Neill first,' Teresa went on quietly. 'She knows more about that side of it than I do. You broached the idea and discussed it with her before you came to us.'

'*I* asked you to pretend that the accident had just happened, to pretend that a whole year hadn't gone past without my noticing it? Why would I do something like that? And did you really think I wouldn't notice?' Abby was flummoxed. But of course she *hadn't* noticed, had she? And whenever she had felt slightly wrong-footed or confused about the date, she had naturally put it down to simple side effects and refused to contemplate otherwise. She'd never even entertained the notion that she might have been right!

'As I said, Dr O'Neill is the one to ask. All I know is that you came to me and begged me to go along with it. You told me you had your reasons, so how could I say no? I would have done anything to take away the worry and stress you were under.' She paused. 'And, love, you have to admit it worked. Instead of being upset about it, you came out fighting, and making that list seemed to give you a new lease of life. You were a different girl, a positive, optimistic and deter- mined girl. I hadn't seen you so vibrant and so . . . happy for a long time. Instead of being depressed and defeated by what had happened, you picked yourself up and went out and grabbed life with both hands. So whatever the reasons, it was working. You haven't had another attack, and you seemed happy and worry-free, so we weren't going to risk your progress by telling you and stressing you out all over again. But of course we could never have anticipated your meeting Finn.'

'Was he in on this too?' she asked carefully, although she was pretty sure she knew the answer.

'No, of course not. Sure, you bumped into him that time in New York and none of us knew anything about him. God, no,' Teresa went on, seemingly upset by the very notion. 'He had nothing to do with it, and wasn't he the one who helped you realise that there was actually something wrong?'

Abby was so caught up in the explanations that she'd almost forgotten that Finn had been the one to tell her the truth about her memory loss.

Heartened by the fact that there was still at least one person she could count on, Abby went on, 'But when I found out from Finn that I was in fact losing memories, why didn't you tell me, then? Why continue with the charade?'

Teresa shook her head. 'We talked to Hannah about it, and she felt that it was all still too fragile, and that if anything, it might set you back. As it was, you were so taken with Finn and he with you that we didn't want to risk ruining the relationship. The two of you were so determined you could make this work . . . and the thing is, you have. I'll admit I was very worried at the start, and I really wanted to tell you the truth, but what if you turned against us and didn't believe that we were acting on your own wishes? In a way, I'm glad it's all out in the open now.'

But Abby couldn't share her mother's feelings as just then, the actual significance of everything she'd told her hit her square in the solar plexus, and all her worries and insecurities about marrying Finn came rushing back. How could they have a future if she could black out at any stage and not remember a single thing about him or their relationship? No marriage could ever survive that, surely? And in spite of Finn's faith in their strength to fight it together, she now knew for certain that she couldn't beat the memory loss, had never beaten it, despite them both foolishly believing otherwise.

How could she expect him to live with that, to run the risk of knowing that at any stage in the future he could realistically be lost from her memory? What kind of life could they possibly have? Not a normal one, that was for sure. And Abby knew deep down that Finn was banking on her being able to fight this, that he'd convinced himself that the diaries and archives they were keeping and the photographs they'd taken would be enough. He hadn't even considered the possibility that it might not work.

Now that Abby knew the truth, that the two of them had been fooling themselves, she knew in her heart that she couldn't keep the reality from him. And, she realised now, she was terrified of how he was going to feel about it.

Chapter 41

Later that day, Abby entered Hannah's cosy and familiar office, understanding now why she'd felt that very strong sense of déjà vu the first time she'd come here (or what she'd *believed* was the first time).

From behind the desk, Hannah studied her carefully. 'So now you know,' she said evenly.

Having learnt from her mother only some of the background surrounding the deceit, Abby had immediately phoned Hannah and asked to see her. And despite the fact that it was a Sunday and out of normal hours, her psychologist had agreed immediately.

'Now I know,' Abby said, her mouth set in a hard line, 'and I want answers.'

Hannah got up and perched on the front of her desk. 'What kind of answers?'

'Well, for one thing, how did this come about? *Why* did it come about? Why did you and everyone else agree to lie to me and let a whole year disappear from my life without my knowing? What was the point?'

'What do *you* think was the point?'

'For goodness' sake, Hannah, just answer the question for once – please!' Abby collapsed into her usual armchair, except this time its warmth and softness didn't give her any comfort. Her eyes shone with tears. 'I'm going out of my mind here.'

At this, the psychologist looked genuinely remorseful.

'I'm sorry,' she said. 'Believe me, the last thing I wanted was for this to happen.'

'Then what *did* you want? What were you trying to achieve? Was it some kind of psychological experiment? Was I the lab rat?'

'Of course not – that wasn't it at all.' Hannah looked horrified at the notion. She took her usual seat directly across from Abby. 'You said your mother explained about the previous bouts of epilepsy?'

'In a way. She said that every time I had a seizure, my memory would lose everything that had happened since the accident.'

Hannah nodded. 'We couldn't figure it out at first, although the doctors knew it related to the damage to your hippocampus. It was only when they sent the scans to the States last year that we became aware of the other injury, that older one I tried to get to the bottom of before,' she added, eyeing Abby steadily, 'and the Americans concluded that this had to be having some effect on or interaction with the later one.'

Something that they'd been trying to tell her all along, Abby thought.

'After the accident, Dr Moroney had mentioned the case to me in passing. He was understandably concerned about the damage such an injury was having on your emotional state, and then after the first seizure, he insisted you see me.' Hannah met her eyes. 'Abby, you wouldn't believe how angry and resistant to the idea you were back then. You were suspicious of the doctors, of me, your family – everyone. It's such a horrible, scary thing to happen to someone, losing chunks of your memory like that, and naturally enough, you were finding it difficult to cope. But eventually you started trusting and confiding in me.'

Again, Abby found it difficult to get her head around the fact that she remembered absolutely nothing at all about any of this. It was a terrifying sensation.

'I don't mind admitting that your condition intrigued me from the very beginning, and eventually, it got to the stage where I almost looked forward to our sessions. The damage to your brain was – *is*' she clarified, meeting Abby's gaze, 'so unique that none of us knew what you might fail to remember from one day to the next.'

'So I *was* a lab rat, then?' Abby said stubbornly.

'No, that's not what I meant. I'm trying to explain how I eventually became almost as wrapped up in your condition as you. We became very close, you and I, as close as a doctor and patient can be. In a word, I'd say we became friends. I worried when you worried. I tried to be there for you and give you as much emotional assistance as you needed, but then, when you had the second seizure, we had to go through the same process all over again.

'Once more, you were distressed and distrustful when you learnt from the doctors and your family what had happened, and that you'd lost all memory since the accident, not once, but twice. You were of course wary around me too – I had to regain your trust to the point that you were comfortable discussing your feelings and condition with me.

'But then, when you had the second seizure, and discovered that it *was* the third time you'd woken up and lost your memory, you started to lose hope altogether. Up until then, you'd started talking about maybe fighting it, trying to find a way to beat it somehow. But the second seizure took every ounce of fight out of you. As far as you were concerned, any effort in this regard was futile, because you were going to lose your memory again anyway. What was the point in trying to overcome it? What was the point in doing *anything*? You became depressed, and eventually stopped coming to me altogether. As your psychologist, I was concerned, but as your friend, I was worried and all I wanted to do was help.'

'So you decided to lie to me the next time I blacked out?

And when I woke up, pretend that it was the first time it had happened? How did that help anything?'

'No, we decided that together.'

'But why, Hannah?' Abby said, shaking her head in bewilderment. 'That's the bit I really can't understand, the bit that I've been trying to get my head around since I first found out about all this. What was the thinking behind it?'

The psychologist took a deep breath. 'Abby, how did you feel up to this morning – *before* you discovered the truth? Be honest, what would be your assessment of the last year?'

When Abby said nothing, Hannah decided to answer the question herself. 'Wouldn't you say that it's been wonderful? The best year of your life, possibly? You did so many amazing things, saw so many wonderful sights, reconnected with Erin and your family. Unlike the aftermath of the break-up with Kieran, you let them in, allowed them to help you get through this. But most significant of all—'

'I met Finn,' Abby added quietly.

'Yes, but furthermore you really believed there was a chance you could beat this,' Hannah went on. 'You were *sure* you could beat it.'

'Yes, but that's because I didn't know the damage was permanent!' Abby argued, feeling really stupid now.

'But wasn't this something to cling on to, the thought that you might just be able to live a normal life, that you could learn to live with it?'

Abby shook her head. 'I'd *fooled* myself into believing there was hope, you mean.' But then, almost as soon as those words were out of her mouth, the realisation hit her and she understood. She looked up and saw that Hannah was wearing a satisfied expression on her face. 'That was it?' she asked, things finally beginning to make sense. 'That was why it came about? To give me back a sense of hope?'

The psychologist nodded. 'How else can anyone deal with

the dark times in life? There has to be some light at the end of the tunnel. You might call it fooling yourself, Abby, but didn't it give you back that all-important optimism? The belief that you might be able to beat this thing fuelled everything you did this year, and gave you additional benefits that you and I could never have imagined.'

Well, yes, that was true, Abby admitted, but now she was right back to square one, wasn't she?

'Are you?' Hannah replied when she put this to her. 'Are you really? It's been a year since your last seizure, you've started living your life with unquestionable gusto, and at the same time, you've even managed to find a fail-safe way of holding on to your memories. Abby, whether you admit it or not, hope *has* given you a way to beat this thing, and not only that but through meeting Finn, you've also managed to move on with the rest of your life.'

At this, Abby looked away guiltily.

'What?' Hannah queried, seeing her expression.

'Not any more.' Although her tone was hard, her eyes filled with tears and her voice was croaky.

'What do you mean?'

'I'm going to end things, Hannah. I have to, when he finds out that all of this has been a big lie.'

Hannah's eyes widened. 'But you haven't lied to anyone, Abby! OK, so yes, to a certain degree you've lied to yourself, but—'

'I can't expect him to live with this, to live with the knowledge that I could black out at any time, and end up losing all memory of our time together. It isn't fair.'

'But he loves you, and if he knew—'

'It doesn't matter,' Abby interjected. 'I've made my decision. I'm not going to be a burden on him – I can't be.'

'Well, as your fiancé, don't you think he should have some say in this decision?' Hannah pointed out.

'But *I* would never know!' Abby cried, the truth coming out now. 'I would never know if he was staying with me out of pity, knowing that I'm a ticking timebomb and that the tiniest bit of stress might set me off. What kind of marriage could anyone have in a situation like that? Hannah, please don't make this any harder than it already is.'

'Well, I'm sorry but I really think you're making a big mistake. Finn's partly the reason you're doing so well, Abby, probably the *main* reason you're doing so well and—'

'Exactly! So how is it fair of me to expect him to live with the obligation of being entirely responsible for my well-being? If the situation was reversed, I know I wouldn't be entirely comfortable with it. So I've decided to put an end to it now, before this thing ends up destroying both of us.'

'I can't believe you would be so willing to throw it all away.'

'I'm not willing, Hannah; as far as I'm concerned, I have no choice! It's because I love him so much that I have to end it.' Abby bit back tears. 'There's no future for us, knowing what I do now.'

Hannah still seemed unconvinced. 'And are you going to tell him the truth? When he comes back from Manchester, are you going to tell him what you've learnt?'

'I don't know,' Abby lied. 'I haven't decided yet.'

When she returned to the flat that evening, she switched on her mobile and listened to her voicemail.

'Abs, hi, it's me,' Finn said. 'What's happened? Are you OK? I'm sorry I missed you earlier – I was in a meeting, but I have the phone on now, so ring me when you get this, OK? I'm worried about you.'

The mere sound of his voice sent daggers through her heart, and she knew there and then that this would have to be done as quickly and remotely as possible. She would never be able to do it otherwise. She would not allow herself to see him in person or she would never be able to go through with it. How could she look into those kind, gentle and seemingly fathomless brown eyes and not falter? Playing the message once more, Abby sunk to the floor on her knees. Was she crazy doing this, like Hannah and Erin both clearly thought she was?

'Abby, no,' Erin had pleaded, when following her meeting with Hannah, Abby had called over to her friend's house to let her know that she now knew the truth.

Having had a long heart-to-heart about it all, Erin was worried but at the same time greatly relieved that everything was now all out in the open.

Then Abby had confessed to her friend what she'd planned.

'There must be another way,' Erin had argued. 'There's always another way. He loves you and you love him. You're getting married.'

'But how can I expect him to live with this, knowing what I do about his mother and what he went through as a child? All Finn wants is a secure and loving family, that's all he's ever wanted, and now I know he can never have that with me.'

'It's not up to you to make that decision, though. Finn loves you and he knows what he's getting into.'

'No, he doesn't,' she insisted. 'He believes it's only a possibility. Who knows what he'll think when he finds out that it's a certainty and has been all along? Erin, I can't put him through that, and I can't face the thought that he'll stay with me out of pity.'

'Well, if he's the guy I think he is, I suspect he'd do no such thing.'

'Erin, his father put up with his mother out of duty for a long time, and I know from Finn the damage it caused to the family. I can't do the same thing to him. I just can't. Think about it. With the way I am, we could never have kids, never have the kind of normal life that other people do.'

Erin considered this, and to Abby's relief, seemed to understand her reasoning. 'But you can't just break it off and say nothing. Surely he'll wonder why it came out of the blue just like that. He won't accept that you want to end things for no apparent reason.'

'It won't be for no reason,' Abby said determinedly, having already considered this. 'As far as he's concerned, it'll be for a different reason entirely.'

After spending the last few hours persuading Erin (and indeed herself) that this was realistically the only course of action she could take, Abby now found herself alone in the flat, surrounded by ironically tangible memories of the happiest time of her life. Was Erin right? she wondered, staring at a recent photograph of her and Finn together. Should she risk throwing it all away in the belief that he wouldn't want her once he found out the truth?

She was sure he loved her, there was no question about that, but didn't he in turn deserve someone who could love him completely, and who wasn't the equivalent of a ticking time-bomb, ready to explode at any time? They couldn't go through the same charade over and over again; it was crazy and pointless and completely unfair to both of them, but mostly to Finn.

How would *she* feel if he woke up one day and had absolutely no memory of knowing her and loving her or of the experiences they'd shared, normal everyday things that *normal* couples shared. She'd put up with it, certainly, but how long could it realistically last? Could she see herself in ten years' time doing the same thing and going through the same scenario every time something happened? No, it wasn't fair to expect that of someone, no matter how much they might love you now. Things changed and marriage was hard at the best of times, never mind with something like this.

In her research about her condition, when she had been so afraid it meant she had Alzheimer's, Abby had read first-hand how devastated and hurt the families of sufferers were when a loved one failed to recognise and remember them. She couldn't expect Finn to go through that every time she lost her memory; it would feel every time as if a little piece of him had been worn down, and eventually he would grow to resent her.

And conversely, how would Abby react each time she woke up from an episode knowing that she was married to someone who, as far as she was concerned, was a complete stranger? Who knew what kind of reaction she would have, or the stress she'd put them both under by having to relearn everything about their marriage? It wasn't right and it wasn't normal, and Abby knew she couldn't put Finn through it. Besides, that was only the start of it, as she'd tried to explain to Erin, what if by some stupid reasoning, they decided to have kids? Would Abby have to get to know them all over again every time too? No, it was crazy; she couldn't do this to herself or to Finn. What was happening to her wasn't normal, and while she now had to try and figure out what to do with the rest of her life, she couldn't drag Finn down with her. He deserved so much better.

Realising that she didn't have the courage (or indeed the energy) to speak to him that night, she decided to send him a quick text and then think about it some more overnight.

Hi. Sorry about earlier. Don't mind me – I'm fine now. Was over at Erin's and only back now. Will talk tomorrow, OK? x

As much as she wanted to, Abby couldn't bring herself to end the text in their usual way by telling him she loved him. And, she realised miserably, if she went ahead with her plan, it was unlikely she'd ever have the opportunity to do so again.

He phoned first thing the following morning.

'Hey it's me. What's going on?'

Abby's heart plummeted at the sound of his voice. She hadn't slept a wink the previous night; instead, she'd tossed and turned and fretted until daybreak. While last night she'd convinced herself beyond doubt that she was doing the right thing, hearing him on the other end of the line was now seriously testing her convictions.

'Hi,' she said quietly. 'Nothing much.'

'Well, what about that message you left me yesterday? You sounded really upset.'

Abby swallowed hard. 'I was, but I'm OK now.'

'You're sure?'

'Yes, it was nothing, honestly.'

'Well, I'm not sure if I heard right, 'cos you were speaking so fast, but did you mention something about bumping into Kieran?'

'That's right, yes.' Abby tried to keep her tone even, and there was a brief pause before he spoke again.

'So how did that go, then?'

'It was . . . strange,' she said, hesitating a little. She'd thought about doing it over the phone, but it wasn't fair, and in any case, she knew he wouldn't accept it. Much better to just wait until she saw him in person. Still, would she able to do it if he was standing right in front of her? It would be agonising, but still she would have to do it.

'"Strange",' he repeated, and Abby knew he was waiting to hear more.

'Yes, look, can we talk about this when you get back?' she said, again trying to keep her voice as normal as possible, although in reality her hands were shaking and her legs felt like jelly.

'OK, well, I'll see you this afternoon, then. All going well, I should be home around three. I'll pop over to Dad's to collect Lucy and then we'll both come over to you—'

'Maybe better not to bring Lucy this time,' Abby interjected, trying to think of some excuse not to have her around for what she was about to do. No doubt it would make it even harder. 'It's just, um . . . well, I've cleaned the carpet and I don't want her hairs getting all over it.'

Finn hesitated a beat before replying. 'OK, well, then, I'll leave her at Dad's for a little while longer.'

'If you wouldn't mind.'

'Fine.' Now it was obvious that he knew something wasn't right. 'See you later, then.'

'Bye.' Abby replaced the receiver, and putting her head in her hands, slumped heavily on to the sofa.

Chapter 42

Finn arrived at her flat that afternoon, and one look at him told Abby that this was going to be even harder than she'd thought. There was a dark covering of stubble on his jaw, which made him look even more attractive than usual, and those probing liquid brown eyes she was so worried about now bored heavily into hers.

'Hey,' he said, coming inside, and as he didn't make any attempt to hug or kiss her, Abby knew that their conversation must have successfully laid some groundwork. She was grateful for the fact that he *hadn't* made physical contact – if he had, she could very well have faltered.

'Hi,' she said levelly. 'How was the trip?'

'It was fine. Look, Abby, what's going on?' Finn asked, leaning on the back of the armchair. 'You sounded really strange on the phone yesterday. What's happened? And why didn't you want me to bring Lucy?'

She looked away, unable to meet his gaze.

'Something's happened,' she told him in a broken voice.

'Well, I kind of guessed that much.' Finn gave a short, humourless laugh. 'So what's up?'

'Maybe we should sit down . . .'

'OK.'

With that, he came round and sat down on the armchair, but instead of relaxing into it like he normally would, he perched on the edge, his pose tense and rigid.

Again, Abby was struck by how much she really loved this

man, how she adored every inch of him. But strangely enough, rather than make things even harder, it actually brought home to her how necessary this was and, in a way, gave her the strength to see it through. This was no longer about her feelings; it was *entirely* about his.

Summoning every ounce of courage she had, Abby swallowed hard and began. 'Finn, I bumped into Kieran yesterday.'

'I know – you said.'

'And . . . well, it was a bit surreal.'

He said nothing, waiting for her to elaborate.

Oh, God, I can't do this, Abby thought, a momentous battle raging inside her. 'Finn, I don't know how to say this, but . . .'

Now he frowned, and his expression became guarded. 'Say what?'

'We've had a wonderful time together, and you've helped me through so much, but . . .'

'But what?' he asked, his eyes widening.

'I'm really sorry' – Abby fought back tears – 'but straight away I realised I'm still in love with him.' The lie came out a lot easier than she'd anticipated.

'With Kieran?' Finn was staring at her with a mixture of horror and confusion. 'What? But he's married.'

Abby shook her head. 'Not for much longer – the marriage failed, he doesn't love her, they're getting divorced, he made a big mistake.' Somehow lie after lie gushed out of her mouth, but she couldn't help it. She had no choice.

'"He made a big mistake".' Finn repeated sarcastically. 'And when did he discover this? Was it before or after he'd dumped you for someone else after five years of a relationship just because you weren't classy enough?' She knew he was trying to hit her where it hurt, and she tried not to let it get to her. 'Or was it when he realised his new wife wasn't as easy to control, or didn't bow to his every need like you did?'

His words were cruel, but Abby knew she deserved them. Anyway, they also proved that Finn didn't suspect anything untoward, and believed every word of what she was saying.

'It wasn't like that,' she protested. 'We had a very long chat and I understand exactly where he is coming from. Apparently, the marriage was over before it had even begun. Anyway, that part of it doesn't really matter. What matters is that I found out that the feelings Kieran and I had – *have* – for one another are still very strong. And I can't just ignore that.'

'Oh, I see. But you seem fully prepared to ignore *my* feelings, and what *we* have, not to mention everything we've been through over the last few months!' he said, and she knew that this wounded him more than anything. 'But then again, that's nothing new with you, is it? With the ways things are, I'm lucky if you remember from one day to the next who I actually am!' Each word felt like a dagger through her heart, but it merely brought it home to Abby how difficult their situation already was, let alone what it would be like if they carried on. No, this might be agony now, but at the end of the day, it was the best possible thing for both of them.

'I'm sorry,' she said mutely.

'You're *sorry*? Is that all you can say? You're telling me you're dumping me for some guy, who as far as I'm concerned sounds like a controlling, penny-pinching arsehole who couldn't be more wrong for you, and certainly doesn't deserve you! Does he know about you? About your head injury?' he asked. 'What does he make of that, then?'

'He knows what to expect.'

'You're seriously prepared to throw away everything we have for some guy who treated you like dirt?' Finn gasped, shaking his head in amazement.

'It wasn't like that; we were both at fault and—'

'Oh, don't give me that crap, Abby. If you honestly believe that, then you have even bigger problems with your memory

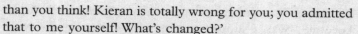

than you think! Kieran is totally wrong for you; you admitted that to me yourself! What's changed?'

'I don't know, it's difficult to explain. Please don't make this any harder than it is, Finn,' she cried, and now the tears were genuine. She couldn't keep this up much longer; it was bad enough that she had to lie to him at all, let alone have to hear home truths about her relationship with Kieran. 'I can't help how I feel.'

'So you're breaking up with me, is that it? Now that the wonderful Kieran is back, you've decided to just cast me aside like some old plaything?'

'It's not like that. I care a lot about you, but when I met Kieran, I—'

'I don't fucking believe this!' Finn ran a hand through his hair. 'You're actually considering going back to him?'

'I'm not considering it,' she said, landing what she hoped would be the final blow. 'I've already decided. I love Kieran, have always loved him, and I just can't help how I feel. Look, we had a fantastic time together, and I'll always care for you—'

'Is this some kind of joke, Abby? We're engaged, for God's sake!' He looked at her finger and seemed to realise only then that she was no longer wearing her ring.

'I'm sorry, Finn, but you have to understand that I can't marry you now, not knowing what I know. It wouldn't be fair.' It was the only piece of truth she'd uttered since he had arrived.

'Abby, come on, you can't be serious.' Those intense brown eyes seemed to penetrate her very soul and again she had to look away. 'After all we've been through?'

She nodded, her face impassive. 'I'm sorry. Please don't try and change my mind,' she added, trying to make her tone hard and devoid of emotion. 'It's no use.'

At this, Finn's bewilderment finally turned to anger. 'So now that lover boy's back, you want me to just turn tail so you can get on with your life as if I never even existed?' he bellowed. 'Well, I suppose *that* much will be easy for you – God knows you might not have a clue who I am if it weren't for those bloody records!'

Abby had never seen him so hurt and upset, and was forced to remind herself yet again that she was doing this – *had* to do it – for his benefit.

'OK, then, if that's what you want, fine – let's do that,' Finn fumed. 'Let's end it all here and now. And while we're at it, why don't I do the job for you?' Following that, he got up and stormed into her bedroom.

'What . . . what are you doing?' she asked, shocked and more than a little scared by the ferocity of his anger. She went after him into the bedroom to find him standing in front of her computer, furiously tapping the keyboard. 'Finn, what are you doing?' she asked again.

'What am I doing?' He turned to look at her, and Abby didn't think she'd ever forget the look of pain and betrayal in his eyes right then. 'Can't you figure it out?'

She looked at the screen and realised that he was opening up all the files – all the diaries, pictures and video clips, all the memories – she'd kept of him and their relationship over the last few months. Wonderful, happy memories, like pictures of the two of them on their own and with Lucy, with her family and his dad just after their engagement, the video of his amazing proposal . . .

'I'm taking myself out of the picture, out of your life, just like you want,' Finn went on. 'Hey, you tried to do all this yourself before, remember?'

Abby could do nothing but stand and watch as his fingers moved over the keys with alarming speed and he deleted each and every item, every memory. And unlike the time when she'd tried to do it, Finn didn't forget to move them out of the recycle bin.

Delete selected items permanently? the computer prompted when he'd deleted them all individually.

'Hell, yeah!' Finn grunted, stabbing the 'Yes' button with added determination.

Finally, he stood back and turned to meet her gaze for what Abby now knew for sure would be the very last time. As he did, she saw that his eyes were red-rimmed.

'There you go,' he said angrily. 'The slate's wiped clean. Have a nice life.'

Then, without another word, Finn marched out of the flat and out of Abby's life.

Chapter 43

One month later

'My God, it's been so long since I was here I'd almost forgotten how *huge* this place is!' Claire gasped, marvelling at her sister's luxurious home.

It was late November and she, Zach and baby Caitlyn were home for a visit. That particular afternoon, Tom and Zach had gone out for a game of golf, and as Teresa had insisted on spending some quality time with her only grandchild, the three sisters had decided to get together for a catch-up at Caroline's Dalkey home.

Abby's sister had had the kitchen redesigned for what must have been the third or fourth time in as many years, and now she marvelled at Caroline's bravery in going for bright-red kitchen units along with a stark white tiled floor. It wasn't something she would have chosen for herself, if she ever had a house of her own, that was, but in this huge open-plan room it really worked.

And it was great to have Claire home; she hadn't seen her since Christmas, and having her here helped take her mind off her own situation – at least temporarily.

For some reason, Abby felt a dull ache in the pit of her stomach at the thought of Christmas. She wasn't sure why – after all, she'd had a lovely time at Claire's the year before – but maybe that was it, she decided, an ordinary Christmas at home this time wouldn't hold a candle to the novelty of last year.

Now, as the three of them shared a bottle of wine beneath the patio heater on Caroline's decking, she listened distract-edly to her sisters discussing the merits of red kitchen units over wooden shaker ones, and wished she could summon up the enthusiasm to do the same.

She didn't know what was going on with her, but lately she had been carrying around this numb feeling that she just couldn't rid herself of. She supposed it was inevitable, given what she'd discovered recently, that she wouldn't exactly be full of the joys, but at the same time, she knew she had to at least try and come to terms with the truth about her condition.

'You haven't had a seizure in ages, so there's no reason to believe they'll continue,' Hannah had tried to tell her the last time she'd seen her, but Abby could no longer bring herself to care.

Having found out the horrifying truth about her memory, she'd decided that it was best to end her sessions with Hannah completely. The psychologist had tried her utmost to convince her not to, but there seemed little point in carrying on. She knew the truth, and now she had to move on and try and learn to cope with it on her own. While she believed Hannah that it was she herself who'd *insisted* upon the idea of the deception in the first place (and the psychologist had shown her a signed release testifying the same), Abby no longer felt able to trust her.

In truth, it was hard to trust anyone now, and in the mean-time, she'd pleaded with her family and Erin to stop hiding things from her. 'No more secrets, please,' she'd told them, and it was only then that she'd understood that maintaining such an elaborate deception had had a considerable effect on them too.

'Well, trying to break the news of Claire's pregnancy was very tricky,' her mum confessed, 'particularly as she was so far gone when you had the last blackout. So we had to pretend that she wanted to keep it under wraps for as long as possible, whereas the truth was that all of us – including you – had known for months.'

'And we couldn't celebrate Tom's fortieth either,' Caroline had chipped in. 'As you know, he was thirty-eight at the time of your accident, and when you woke up that last time, we couldn't run the risk of you noticing how much time had passed.'

But the hardest thing of all (and the one Abby felt most guilty about) was the fact that Erin had indeed started seeing someone.

Dermot.

'We couldn't admit that we'd got together while you were ill,' her best friend had informed her sheepishly, and Abby immediately thought back to how Dermot had almost let it slip that day in the service station, and how strangely reluctant Erin had been to confide in her. 'I don't know, I'd never really taken much notice of him before,' her friend had confessed, pink-cheeked. 'But we got chatting at the hospital and I suppose things just went from there.'

Abby was thrilled for them, but felt awful that they'd had to keep their relationship under wraps like that.

And of course, there were some other things Erin had had to keep hidden too. 'I nearly had a heart attack when we met up that time after you got out of the hospital, and you commented that I didn't have much of a tan,' she had said. 'I'd completely forgotten that you'd naturally assume I was just back from Dubai.'

So many secrets, so many lies . . . Although the truth had been devastating, Abby was in a way glad that they'd all stopped hiding things from her and treating her like a special case.

Much better to have things back to normal – although she didn't think that the word 'normal' could ever be applied to her situation . . .

Just then there was a loud rustling from the bottom of the garden, and the girls looked up in the direction of the noise. All three sisters jumped in fright when, from behind thick bamboo, a small Jack Russell terrier emerged. The little dog, evidently oblivious to his surprised audience, squatted down and started to poop right on Caroline's perfectly manicured lawn.

'Bloody neighbour's dog again. Why don't you poop in your own garden, you little bugger?' Caroline jumped up and went to shoo him away, and as she did, Abby was struck by how mild her own reaction to the animal was. Normally, she'd run for cover at the mere *sight* of a dog, but for some reason, this time it didn't bother her in the slightest.

'Well, I never thought I'd see the day,' Claire said, surprised. 'After that St Bernard, I was sure you were ruined for life!'

Abby looked at her. 'St Bernard?'

'The one that knocked you over when we lived in Wood-brook?' she said, referring to a housing estate the family had lived in when they were kids. 'I always thought he was the reason you were terrified of dogs. And to be honest, I wouldn't blame you; you went down like a ton of bricks that day. Hit yourself with a hell of a whack on the kerb.'

Having chased the cheeky dog back through the hedge, Caroline sat down. 'Got a hell of whack where?' she said.

'Right here,' Claire said, pointing to the left-hand side of her head. 'It was so bad I'm surprised it didn't knock you out altogether. Luckily, it didn't bleed, so I got away with not saying anything to Mum about it. You were only six, and I was supposed to be looking after you, and . . . What?' she asked, frowning, as Abby and Caroline stared open-mouthed at one another.

But Abby knew exactly what Caroline was thinking.

In one fell swoop, Claire had not only told Abby the cause of her long-held doggy phobia, but had also solved the mystery of her first, so-far-unidentified brain injury.

Later that evening, when Claire and Zach had returned to Teresa's house, where they were staying, Abby and Caroline chatted some more.

'I still think you should tell Hannah about that accident with the dog,' her sister said, referring to the cause of the first injury.

'What's the point? It doesn't matter now, does it?'

'Well, for what it's worth, I think you made a mistake giving up seeing her.'

Abby tensed. 'Well, I don't,' she replied. 'I don't need her any more, do I?'

'Look, she was only doing what she thought was right – we all were. And you have to admit that keeping you in the dark did you nothing but good in the end.'

'If it did me nothing but good, then why I am so down all the time?' Abby sighed. 'Why do I feel so . . . I don't know . . . so miserable?'

Caroline seemed to want to say something, but then decided against it.

'I don't know, lately I just feel sort of . . . numb.' Once again, Abby struggled to accurately describe this particular feeling.

'Well, you've been through a lot emotionally,' Caroline soothed. 'And it must be difficult for you to get your head round it. But, Abs, try and not let it get to you too much, OK? It was stress that triggered off those seizures in the first place, remember?'

'I know, I know.' Abby was worn out from hearing this now. 'Maybe I'm just feeling down because I'm no longer working through that list. There are still a few things I didn't do – I never danced in public like no one's watching, and I never went to the South Pole. I can't think why I didn't finish it off.'

Caroline again looked like she wanted to say something, then stopped herself.

'Abby, while the list was a wonderful idea at the time, I think it's probably served its purpose,' her sister said gently. 'It was great that you managed to do most of those things and you know we enjoyed doing them with you, but now the truth is out it's probably best for you to try and get back to some form of reality.' She looked sideways at her. 'So, how *is* your memory these days? You're still keeping your diaries, I presume?'

Abby was, but not with the same level of detail. It was hard to see the point – not when she could very well end up blacking out and going right back to square one. Anyway, the significance of her discovery had sent her into such a tailspin that she didn't particularly *want* to remember what she was feeling these days. While she'd written in great detail about bumping into Kieran, and having it all out with Hannah and her mother, after that she'd been so upset and confused that she hadn't diarised much of her feelings at all. It just seemed easier not to.

'I'm doing my best, but I find it all a bit pointless, to be honest,' she said, in answer to her sister's question.

'Well, I don't. If you do happen to black out again, all those records will help keep you up to speed and get you back to where you are now, won't they?'

'I suppose so.' But the truth was, Abby wasn't sure what to think. *Everything* seemed hopeless at the moment.

And she just couldn't figure out why.

A week later, Caroline was in Dundrum Shopping Centre immersed in her favourite pastime. She'd just dropped a *fortune* in Mamas and Papas on baby gear for a good friend who'd recently given birth, and she decided to stop off for a quick bite to eat before heading into Harvey Nics to do even more damage to her credit card.

All the Christmas party stuff was in the shops now, and as well as updating her own wardrobe, she was planning on buying Abby a brand-new handbag, or perhaps a killer pair of heels – something that might help cheer up her little sister somehow.

She really felt for Abby, perhaps now more than ever. While the situation with her injury had always been horrible, and the family had hated having to keep the true extent of it a secret, she had thought that it had been all for the best, given that this time round Abby had improved in leaps and bounds.

She remembered how, over a year ago, Abby had come to them and practically begged that if she relapsed again to pretend that they had no idea of the true nature of her injury and were as much in the dark as she was. While their mother had been horrified and had at first been completely against the deception, Caroline had to admit that the idea had some merit, and couldn't be completely sure she wouldn't do the same thing herself. After all, what was the point in explaining the reality to Abby and destroying any optimism she might have had about getting through it?

But it was still a relief in a way that all this deception was finally over. Well, nearly all the deception. Because although Caroline could appreciate why Abby had felt she needed to let Finn go, she believed very strongly that her sister should have at least given him a say in the matter, rather than let him believe something completely different.

It was now very difficult to watch Abby struggle with her unexplained misery following the break-up, without being able to tell her what had caused it. To think that after all the couple had been through and how much they'd shared, without the necessary continuity it was still possible for Abby to forget all about him. That by not seeing or speaking to him for a while he could be so easily lost from her memory. But having promised Abby that she wouldn't try and refresh her memory if she succeeded in forgetting about Finn, Caroline couldn't do a thing about it.

It merely highlighted to everyone yet again the fragility of Abby's situation, and of course exactly the reason her sister had to let him go in the first place, Caroline mused, as she waited patiently in line at the food court. It was all very sad.

'I don't bloody believe this!'

Caroline turned round sharply at the sound of commotion coming from the deli queue, a little way across. Two men were squaring up to one another over what seemed to be a spilt bottle of Coke, and speak of the devil . . . one of them was Finn! Although he had his back to her, Caroline would recognise that voice anywhere, not to mention that the worried-looking Lab by his side was very definitely Lucy!

'Aren't you even going to apologise?' Finn snarled at the customer, who'd evidently been trying to balance two bottles of Coke on a tray with one hand. Both bottles had fallen to the floor and exploded all over Finn, who happened to be ahead of him in the queue.

'It was an accident – what's your problem?' the man replied, not looking or sounding in the least bit apologetic either to Finn or indeed the hapless employee who was now trying to clean up the mess.

'My problem is that I'm covered in fucking Coke!' Finn retorted angrily. 'Accident or not, you could at least fucking apologise!'

Caroline didn't think she'd ever seen him so worked up, and she'd certainly never heard him use bad language! Poor Lucy, who was now looking very sheepish alongside him, gently nudged the side of his leg, hoping to calm him down.

'Piss off, arsehole – people like you shouldn't be out on your own, anyway,' the man said derisively, much to Caroline's and indeed everyone else's horror.

'People like me . . . ?' Finn seemed momentarily confused, but just as quickly he understood that Lucy's presence had given the man the wrong impression.

As both men continued to stare each other down, Caroline could see Finn's jaw working furiously, and realising that the situation was about to explode, she hurried over to his side.

'Finn, hi, long time no see!' she exclaimed, quickly putting herself between the two men. At the sight of this diversion, Lucy looked up and gratefully wagged her tail.

'Caroline . . .' Finn said, glancing at her. 'What are you doing here?'

'Tosser,' the other man grunted, moving away, and when Finn went to go after him, Caroline held him back.

'Don't,' she soothed. 'I saw what happened. He's not worth it.'

'Can you believe the bloody ignorance of it, though?' Finn gasped, and to her discomfort Caroline saw that his eyes were red-rimmed and bloodshot. 'I should have put him through the wall for saying something like that – never mind drowning me in Coke.'

'Look, I was just getting something to eat – why don't you and Lucy take a seat and I'll bring some paper towels over, help you dry off a bit? And something to drink too?'

Finn looked at her warily before nodding. 'All right,' he sighed eventually. 'Just a coffee, thanks.'

As he trundled away from the waiting area, Caroline couldn't believe how dishevelled and . . . despondent he looked.

And she knew well that this wasn't all to do with the recent fracas; with his bloodshot eyes and irritable behaviour, Finn

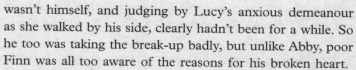

wasn't himself, and judging by Lucy's anxious demeanour as she walked by his side, clearly hadn't been for a while. So he too was taking the break-up badly, but unlike Abby, poor Finn was all too aware of the reasons for his broken heart.

Right, Caroline thought, as she watched a clearly defeated Finn slump heavily into a seat nearby (rather reminiscent of the way Abby had looked the week before at her house), enough of this nonsense – maybe it was time to put some things to rights.

Two fresh coffees in hand, she eventually joined him at the table. 'So, how have you been?' she asked, reaching down to pat Lucy on the head. The Labrador gave her a look that seemed to convey immense gratitude for stopping her master from getting into even more trouble. Remembering how close Abby and Lucy had become, Caroline suspected that Lucy too might be feeling Abby's absence.

'How have I been?' Finn drawled, clearly not bothering to put a brave face on things. 'Just fine, considering your sister dumped me to go back to the same idiot who messed her around before. Then again,' he added nastily, 'she's probably forgotten that already.'

Caroline took a deep breath. 'Finn,' she began, knowing that she shouldn't be doing this, that she shouldn't be betraying her little sister's wishes, but at the same time she was fully convinced that it was right, 'I'm very sorry to have to tell you this, but you've been misinformed.'

Chapter 44

The heavy, leaden feeling still wouldn't go away, no matter what Abby did to rid herself of it.

Today, she'd arranged to meet Erin for lunch in the Italian quarter of the city, her friend apparently eager to try out one of the new restaurants there, although Abby suspected that this was more than likely another ruse of hers to get her out of the flat, and stop her dwelling on her circumstances.

It was like a dark fog had enveloped every inch of her being, and no matter what she did she just couldn't work through it. It felt a lot like those early days after her break-up from Kieran, when she had felt that everything in the world had turned bleak and horrible. And deep down, Abby also got the sense that she was missing something, something important.

She put on a coat and left the flat thinking it was a strange feeling to know that you couldn't even trust yourself, let alone other people. In all honesty, Abby had expected to feel much more upset and considerably more paranoid, but the truth was, she just didn't have the strength. It was almost as if the entire life force had been sucked out of her over the last few weeks, and these days, she just didn't care what happened to her. It was probably understandable, given the blow she'd received – maybe comparable to someone running a marathon only to discover that the race had finished the day before. Spent, drained and numb that such an immense effort had gone to waste. One more seizure and she'd be right back where she started. This must be a little bit what purgatory is like, she mused, with a humour-less laugh.

The cold winter weather was really starting to bite now, she thought, wrapping her coat tightly round her. Christmas was well and truly on the way, and she supposed she'd better pull her finger out and start picking up a few presents for the family.

As she walked down the street, a large handwritten sign on a nearby lamp-post briefly caught her attention.

Your favourite colour is purple.

Must be some new marketing thing, Abby mused, as she spied similar sign further along the path.

You take two sugars in your coffee.

O-K.

By the time she passed the third sign, she'd pretty much put aside her own musings and her curiosity had been piqued.

Your favourite book is To Kill a Mockingbird.

By the fourth it was very *definitely* piqued.

Your favourite song is 'The Long and Winding Road'.

Abby looked further down the street and saw that every single lamp-post along the way was covered in these odd posters.

Your favourite film is Gladiator!

And strangely, she thought, shaking her head at her own gullibility, it was almost as if they had something to do with her, as every statement she'd read so far was true for her. Well, it just went to show how unimaginative and common-place her own tastes were, didn't it? she mused, moving on.

Your favourite food is chocolate,. but only fresh out of the freezer.

Another read, while the following sign announced,

*Your favourite number is seventeen, even though it lost you
$1,000 in Vegas.*

Hold on . . . Now Abby was feeling more than a little
spooked. What the hell was going on here? Every single one
of these signs meant something to her; in fact, they seemed
to be referring *precisely* to her and her life! Surely there
weren't that many other people who ate chocolate out of the
freezer, loved the movie *Gladiator* or bet on seventeen in
Vegas? Abby moved on, agog with confusion, while passers-
by seemed to be moving past the signs without interest – or
indeed concern.

Your hardest memory is your father's death.

Now Abby was feeling very exposed indeed. What *was* all
this? OK, so she was feeling paranoid these days in any case,
but all this really had to be about her, didn't it? She moved
on to the next sign.

*Despite what you might think now, your best memories are
yet to come . . .*

Then tears came to her eyes. Looking up ahead to the final
sign, Abby realised that there was someone standing alongside it, someone who was watching her closely as she
approached, and had been all along. To her trepidation, she
realised this was a face she recognised, although how she
knew it, or even *who* the person was, she couldn't say.

All Abby knew was that when she'd first laid eyes on him,
her heart had immediately skipped a beat, and she had the
clearest sense of déjà vu she'd ever felt in her life.

Then Abby read the final sign:

And I plan to be there for every last one of them.

Chapter 45

'I don't know where to begin,' the man said, regarding her uncertainly as they faced each other. 'I suppose you've probably guessed by now that we kind of . . . know one another.'

Abby nodded wordlessly. He had amazing brown eyes, dark brown, almost mahogany, but more than that, she decided, her heart hammering with the realisation that they seemed unquestionably *familiar*.

'I suppose I might as well start from the beginning—'

'There's no need,' Abby interjected, her voice a whisper. 'I know.'

Those remarkably dark eyes widened as he picked up her hands and held them in his. 'You mean you remember?'

'No, I just know.' She gulped, feeling more sure than she'd ever been in her life. 'It's the reason I've been carrying around this weird feeling over the last while – you're the reason.'

'Abby, why did you do it?' he asked softly. 'Why didn't you tell me the truth? Why push me away like that? When Caroline told me, I—'

'I pushed you away because it isn't fair,' she said, not needing to know the details, not when it was so obvious that this man's absence was what had caused her so much pain. Why *wouldn't* she have pushed him away, when it was patently clear that she was in love with him?

'We can deal with this,' he said, speaking quickly. 'We've dealt with it up to now. And even without all that stuff I erased, we'll start again.'

'Ah.' Now Abby understood why she had no memories of him (at least not any tangible ones) and nothing to recall the time they'd spent together.

'I'm sorry . . . I was so angry, I just couldn't help it. But we can build it all up again, get more photographs, make more memories. I meant what I said, Abby – the best is yet to come.'

Her heart melted, but still she was unsure. 'I want to believe you, but you don't know that.'

'Yes, I *do*,' he argued. 'And I know that I don't give a damn if every morning you wake up beside me and don't recognise me – just as long as you *do* wake up beside me, Abby.'

Tears fell down her cheeks. 'You don't really mean that.'

'I do. Look, I love you and I want to spend the rest of my life with you. Don't push me away again. For better or worse, remember?'

At this choice of words, she couldn't help but laugh. 'Surely you know by now that word is meaningless when it comes to me?' she said, with a loud sniff.

'Don't I just?' he replied, laughing too.

Abby looked deep into his eyes, and studied every contour of his face, all the while furiously trying to recall some memory, some recollection of this man who clearly was of such immense importance to her, but still there was nothing.

But, she realised suddenly, neither of them seemed to care.

'You know what you're getting into, then?' she asked, and tentatively lifted a hand to his cheek.

'You'd better believe it,' he replied, drawing her close and into his arms.

The two of them stood there for a very long time, wrapped in each other's arms, locked in one another's gaze, each willing the memories to come back. But Abby didn't need memories to tell her that she was deeply in love with this man and would trust him with her life. Finally, and without breaking eye contact, he inclined his head towards hers.

'Oh, and by the way,' he murmured so softly Abby could barely hear him over the pounding of her heart, 'just in case you're wondering . . .' he went on, managing to get the rest of the words out just before his lips met hers '. . . my name is Finn.'

melissa hill
wishful thinking

Louise wishes she could be slim, pretty, and popular.
So she can't believe it when it seems her wish is coming
true. If only it didn't all cost so much . . .

Dara wishes she could go back in time, and change
everything. But she's married now, and nothing can
change that. Can it?

Rosie wishes she knew how to make her children happy.
Even though they're both grown up with their own lives,
they seem to need her more than ever.

Three very different women, about to make a journey
that will change their lives forever.
You should be careful what you wish for . . .

Available in Hodder paperback

HODDER

melissa hill
the last to know

Eve knows what she wants.
After nine good years and two lovely children together,
it's about time Liam made an honest woman of her.
After all, they're as good as married anyway.

Eve's sister Sam knows more than she should.
Sam has always thought that Eve's too good for Liam.
And she can't help but be suspicious about the
long business trips to Australia that take him
away from his family all too often.

Meanwhile, on the other side of the world,
Brooke knows nothing.
Then a mysterious delivery arrives and promises
to change her life forever. It seems someone doesn't
want Brooke to be the last to know . . .

Available in Hodder paperback

H
HODDER